Also by Stephen Swartz

After Ilium

A Beautiful Chill

A Dry Patch of Skin

The Dream Land
I. Long Distance Voyager
II. Dreams of Future's Past
III. Diaspora

AIKO

愛
子

A I K O

a novel

Stephen Swartz

MYRDDIN PUBLISHING GROUP

UNITED STATES · UNITED KINGDOM · AUSTRALIA

ISBN-13: 978-1-68063-020-6

ISBN-10: 1-68063-020-2

www.myrddinpublishing.com

Cover Design by Stephen Swartz

("The Great Wave of Kanagawa" by Katsushika Hokusai)

見るところ花にあらずと云ふことなし、
思ふところ月にあらずと云ふことなし。

Miru tokoro hana ni arazu to iu koto nashi,
Omou tokoro tsuki ni arazu to iu koto nashi

There is nothing you can see that is not a flower;
There is nothing you can think that is not the moon.

—Matsuo Bashō

1

BEFORE THE LETTER ARRIVED that would turn his entire world around, Benjamin had always tried to do the right thing. He certainly was no pervert; he had never considered himself one of those guys.

When he entered the room and the door swung shut, the first thing he did was to listen for anyone else who might be there, hiding in the stalls. Satisfied he was alone, he started toward the last stall but halted as he caught sight of himself in the huge mirror. He laughed, surprised at the man he saw there, a man who was not quite the one he expected. He saw a man who could still play football with the guys, who could take his lady out dancing at the end of a sixty-hour week in the office and then golf all weekend with his boss. He was fit enough.

He washed his hands carefully, deliberately, using plenty of soap and hot water, wiped them dry with paper towels, then tried a jump shot at the gray plastic barrel in the corner, hit it and pumped air.

Going on to the last stall, the one against the wall, he entered and quickly closed the door. He pulled off his coat and the rolled up magazine bobbing in the side pocket fell to the floor. He hung the coat on the door hook, then retrieved the magazine and rolled it up and placed it in the pocket again. From the other coat pocket, he retrieved the paraphernalia he needed. With a deep breath, he vowed he would succeed this time.

I, Benjamin F. Pinkerton, do solemnly swear I'll get it right this time.

As he released the buckle and unzipped, he had an odd feeling. He dropped his trousers to his ankles, making sure nothing touched the floor, then lowered himself on the seat, found a comfortable position, and took another breath. He needed to relax but he found his body was not quite ready. He was still worked up, angry over an encounter in the parking lot when he and his wife arrived.

He thought of the two men in the parking lot: the young guy dressed for the gym who had shouted at the man in the business suit getting out of a luxury sedan. The car was parked in a handicapped place and the businessman seemed to walk just fine over to the doors of the office building. However, the younger man complained, saying the businessman was "about as handicapped as a professional athlete." Ben had laughed, then calmly said to the younger man, "That's not really fair. We can't know what condition he may have by looking at him. Just because we don't see him using crutches doesn't mean—"

The younger man, despite the cool, rainy weather dressed in a tanktop that showed off his muscles, cut him off with a colorful string of swear words before rushing on into the building.

Benjamin was stunned. He was a reasonable man, a rational-thinking individual who tried to live his life with compassion and dignity. Then some jerk comes along and ruins the day! Why can't more people do the right thing? He was trying to do the right thing. Even now.

It was not really so weird, but he could not avoid the sensations of guilt that lingered. After all, it was not so different from what he'd done as a teenage boy—what most teenage boys did . . . well, on occasion, or so he presumed. Even those young men who had steady girlfriends still indulged in a bit of self-indulgence. But being in a restroom stall, in a public building, made it more perverse.

He stared down at the crumple of pants and resumed his activity. The doctor had told him to switch from briefs to boxers, better for keeping the family jewels at the right temperature. He didn't like the way the boxers bunched up, however, and frequently went without either choice while at home — much to the annoyance of his wife. Today he opted for comfort and wore the briefs. He figured he wouldn't be wearing them long enough to make a difference anyway.

Only then did he realize he had left the pamphlet on the counter. He was not about to go out and get it now. Too much trouble to hitch up everything and return to the stall to start over again. He knew what to do; he had always known what to do.

He had not forgotten the magazine rolled up in his coat pocket. It was awkward even carrying it around, afraid it might fall out of his pocket and there it would be, flopped open for the world to see: one standard issue *Playboy*. February 1990. Already a year old, he thought, wondering how many other men had carried it around.

He took it from the coat pocket and unrolled it, flipped through the pages as though searching for stock market data. He was alone but he still did not want to let himself become aroused in a public place. He was not one of those perverts —

There was Miss Pamela Anderson, Playmate of the Month: blonde and busty, far too blonde, far too busty for Benjamin. She posed so seductively at five-foot seven, measuring 38-22-36 — *apparently*. Not his type. What did other men see in her, in her type? If he were standing at the foot of the bed where she was spread out naked, he'd probably ask her if she wanted to play a game of chess. He was not amused — nor aroused.

Hah, he snorted, thinking of the times he had tried to hide such magazines from his parents. Now a woman had given the magazine to him, and done so with a straight face. He was supposed to use it — use the images — to stimulate his fantasies. He was not really a fantasizing kind of guy.

He thought of his wife, Addy, and visualized the last time they had made love. How long ago was that? More than a month, he calculated. But he thought of her anyway, remembering how sexy she had looked in the red negligée, lacey and delicate, perfect match for her auburn hair, her breasts perfectly sized for his cupped hands — 34, he guessed, comparing them in his mind to Miss Anderson's—

He was becoming aroused, though he hesitated admitting it.

Their first time together was in a house she was showing him, there on the floor in an upstairs bedroom devoid of furniture. He bought the house and five months later, happily married, she moved in, too. They thought it would be a good room, a lucky room. With his eyes closed, he held her image in his mind, saw her crawling across the bed to him, the two of them kissing. He directed his mind to call upon his dream hands to peel off that red negligée and begin caressing her, then slowly—

The door slamming next to him broke him from his fantasy. Someone had plopped down and was making a concert of gas and grunts.

Benjamin shook his head, willing away the distraction.

"Jesus H. Christ," the man in the next stall muttered. He groaned as a stench filled the room. "Well, there's a load off my mind." The man cleared his throat. "Sorry about that." He tapped the wall. "You doin' awright over there?"

Ben paused, wondering if the man meant him. "Fine," he replied, "doing just fine."

"Glad to hear it," said the neighbor, followed by a flush.

In a minute the man was gone. Benjamin held his hand over his nose and tried to conjure his wife's sexy nakedness in his mind once more. Then another man came in and she evaporated. The man talked his young son through the ritual at the urinals, helped him wash, and they exited.

Benjamin started again. From scratch. He looked through the magazine again, stopped at some ads where the girls were more his type. But not close enough. He went to the last pictorial, studied it as an art lover might a room full of paintings, silently critiquing them. Big breasted—skinny—blonde hair poofed up—fake grin on her face, like she'd been caught coming out of the shower and *Oh, my! What are you looking at, Mister?* He closed the magazine.

Married life was not what he had expected. Sure, he loved Addy. She was everything he desired. Besides, they were both professionals, had busy lives, career ambition. Being with her made a lot of sense. They were supposed to be a power couple. Addy was an independent woman who still let him be the man. Most of the time. They were partners, equals in the maintenance of their home and their careers. The income they each brought home were similar and their schedules were close enough to be similar. Being a realtor, Addy's schedule had more flexibility yet she always seemed to arrive home within fifteen minutes of Ben's return from the office. Some days, dinner was delayed by late afternoon trysts in the lucky bedroom. The bedroom was their friend—had been until recently.

That was counterproductive, he realized. Thinking of their careers and how he had met Addy was not going to help. He checked his watch. They were probably wondering what was taking him so long. Usually—*or, let's say, back in my youth*—he'd be up and done in a few minutes. When he was with Addy, of course, she would draw it out, make it last, make a game of it so that love making was fun. He remembered the fun times in bed with her.

Oh, yes . . . .

Yes, he remembered having fun making love . . . .

Back from three tough years living in Hawaii, he was ready to search for a suitable house in the Seattle area, something a bachelor could live in—but with hopes for a family in the future. His boss had introduced him to Addy, his sister's business partner, the realtor who had set up several of his friends with homes. Addy showed Benjamin many homes and condos, and through the weeks they developed a playful relationship. They enjoyed flirting with each other as they went from house to house. A few times when they went late, he invited her to dinner. He knew he was taking too long choosing a residence, but he wanted it to be right. She did not seem impatient; in fact, they often lapsed into conversations full of double entendres and bad jokes and lost track of the time.

That day Adeline Robinson wore a crisp Navy business suit with cream blouse, her auburn hair put up, looking very professional, her green eyes bright and smile slightly askew like she had a big secret she wanted to tell. He was backing out of the walk-in closet of the master bedroom and bumped into her. Turning, their eyes met. He was about to speak, standing inches from her, close enough he could smell mint on her breath. Suddenly they kissed. Just for an instant — then a longer kiss followed by a flurry of kissing and groping. Falling to the carpet, they continued kissing as his fingers unbuttoned her blouse and her fingers released his zipper; her skirt pushed up, his trousers pushed down, then — *yes, that's it!* — flesh to flesh, making love on the carpet, lost in the heat of love, churning in a kind of frenetic passion he had almost forgotten —

"Well," he had said afterwards, "that was unexpected."

"But nice," she added, then: "I think I got a rug burn on my butt."

She apologized for not acting professional, then took an hour convincing him she was not that kind of woman. He took nearly as much time insisting he was not that kind of guy, not a playboy.

"This house feels lucky for me," he said. "I'll take it."

Addy kissed him. "Now we've messed up the carpet, you have to buy it."

For a moment he forgot where he was and why he was sitting in the restroom stall of a medical office building. He listened for other people, so sure that any other guys using the facilities would snicker at him for his wanton display of manliness and the crude vocal utterances that gave him away: hiding like a pervert in the corner stall. Thankfully, the room was silent.

Glancing down, he saw that he had hit the mark, gotten it all into the clear plastic cup without spilling a drop. He snapped on the lid, pinched it tightly around the rim, afraid he'd drop it — like last time. A childish grin spread across his face, one part embarrassment, one part physical satisfaction — and a smaller part just thankful he did not need to continue the spectacle. He was done before anyone caught him. Addy would be proud, happy for his sacrifice. She should care about what he was having to go through, all the consternation he was experiencing in order to provide a good sample for the procedure.

He pulled up his trousers. When he exited the stall, he went straight to the counter to retrieve the pamphlet.

"Artificial Insemination," he muttered, reading. He read silently down the page, pursing his lips as he reached the bottom. "The latest technique for making babies. Perfect for couples whose parts aren't quite compatible, whose materials don't quite match." He folded the pamphlet roughly and stuffed it into the trash barrel. "When regular sex for two years is just not enough."

He held the cup carefully in his left hand and laid his coat over his hand and arm.

At the elevator, a family with three young girls gathered around him. They squeezed into the elevator together, his cup-filled hand bumping hard the side wall. Ben stepped off at the third floor.

He made his way through the back door of the doctor's suite, the same door he had exited earlier. The nurse was surprised, wondering where he had gone after he had refused the empty examination room next door. She took the cup from him and disappeared. He knew Addy would be ready. She was always ready.

He knocked on the door of her exam room, was invited in, and waited patiently beside the table while the ob/gyn did her medical magic. If everything went well, and his boys could get a free ride past the deadly gatekeepers, Benjamin and Addy would in nine months welcome into the world a beautiful little baby.

That was the plan, at least.

2

AS THE LETTER WAS BEING DELIVERED, Benjamin and Addy were exiting the medical building's parking lot and heading home. A late winter rain began spotting the windshield. Traffic was light on this Saturday so they were able to drive through the streets of Seattle practically in a daze, the route becoming habit now. Three months of making the trip: introductions, testing, the first trial. The second trial. It was not a fun experience, Benjamin understood.

He glanced at Addy as he drove, hoping to see anything like a smile, some sign of the joy that must be building within her. She would make such a beautiful mother. Instead, her face remained expressionless. She seemed tired.

"Are you all right?" Benjamin asked as their car swept down onto the floating bridge over Lake Washington. "I said I'm sorry."

"You know, you could've let me know," said Addy, crossing her legs. "I was laying on that table with my legs open for god knows how long. Waiting. Worst sex ever."

Benjamin pinched his lips, unwilling to say anything. He did not wish to discuss his reasons for leaving the doctor's suite for what he thought would be a more private venue. It was done now, no matter.

"I don't know what you were thinking," she said after a minute.

"What was so bad about being in the room next door? Then you go . . . . The restroom? Hardly a sterile environment. I don't know what I've got in me now."

They rose from the lake through forested hillsides packed with houses, suddenly a new world to him.

"Sweetheart, you're supposed to stay calm," he said. "Relax and let nature take its course. That's what the doctor said. The main thing is we got it done."

"We got it done. Nice expression."

She zipped up her parka and he took the cue to turn up the heat even though he was already sweating. This was her day. He would accommodate her every wish, just to help her relax. That was more important than explaining anything.

He turned on the wipers to clear the drizzle.

Uncomfortable with the silence, Benjamin turned on the radio and Madonna was finishing "Justify My Love." Ignoring the commercials that followed, he tried to think of something to say, but then "All the Man that I Need" came on. He listened to Whitney Houston's sexy voice, then decided it was not the right song for the moment and turned it off.

The drizzle grew into rain, and a few flurries drifted in the air. He adjusted the wipers as they exited the highway and arrived at the stoplight. They waited for the green light, no other cars anywhere around.

He cleared his throat. "You don't know what I go through—"

"You don't know what I go through," she said. "The shots, the meds. Letting the whole world see—"

"It's different for a guy. A lot of pressure."

He wanted to go on, running down the list of social customs and irrational habits that might serve to excuse his flaws, but he knew it would not be helpful. *Must relax.*

The light finally turned green and he could concentrate on driving again. They drove a few blocks farther.

Benjamin wanted to apologize and encourage her at the same time. He wanted to assure himself that everything would be all right.

"Can you swing over to Burrstone," she said suddenly, flinging her hand to the right. "I want to have another look at the house."

"Everything is fine, I'm sure," said Ben.

"I just want to have one last look before the showing. It won't take any time."

He sighed, refusing to fight. He turned the car and went over to the street where her latest house showing was being staged. Her assistant, Julie, had prepared it, he knew, yet he also knew how much Addy worried about everything little detail, needing everything to be perfect.

"I'll call her when we get home. She can be forgetful. Need to make sure she bakes some cookies," said Addy. She peered out the window as they rolled slowly past the yard. The welcome sign was in place. "It's good to have the house smelling like cookies."

Ben chuckled. "Have we ever baked cookies at our house?"

She finally smiled. "When I took you to see our house, no, I did not bake cookies."

"And I bought it anyway."

"All right," she said with a soft *hmpft*. She gave the house a long look. "We can go now."

Turning into their cedar-lined neighborhood, they rounded the curves of winding streets as Benjamin imagined neighbors' children bounding in front of the car. Soon their child would be playing with those children. He pulled into the driveway of the cedar-free home, an expanded, glorified New England cottage: blue-gray with darker gray trim, dormant flower boxes across the front and a cute little porch connected to the driveway by a stone walk. So different from the rather plain house he had bought more than two years ago, Ben thought. Addy had certainly added her touches to it.

He pushed the clicker and the garage door rose.

"Please just relax, sweetheart. That's what's important now."

He drove into the garage, shut off the engine, and pressed the button again to close the door. They sat there a moment, neither willing to get out first. It had to be settled.

"Forget about today. Just think about our cute little baby that will be giggling in your arms," said Ben. "That's what everything we do is all about now. The baby."

"You're right." Her voice was softer, which surprised him. She took a deep breath, acting as though she didn't need it. Calming herself, he guessed. "I know you're right. For once."

He laughed, something forced but expected. Perhaps he should have repressed it, he thought. She seemed to not appreciate his attempt at humor.

She placed her hand on his knee. "I know it's the stress, Ben. The stress of the entire process. It's not the way I expected to have a baby. My sisters got pregnant, no problem. Ally . . . Wendy . . . practically the first try. And Sandy didn't even wait to get married. But me? I'm the oldest. The last to get pregnant. And now I'm thirty five. Thirty-six when this one is born—if it worked. Not much more time before I'll be over the hill."

He couldn't see clearly in the darkness but he knew tears wetted her face when she raised her hand and wiped her cheek.

"Hey, hey now, sweetheart," he said, leaning over and trying to wrap his arm around her shoulders. He settled for patting the back of her shoulders. "Forget about your sisters. They've got their lives and you have yours. There's no rules to follow. There's no law that says you—"

"Thirty-five is the cut-off age if you want a healthy baby."

"That's what they say but . . . you see celebrities who have healthy babies even at forty. Medical advances continue to, umm, you know, advance."

"I know." She wiped away more tears, sniffled.

"Besides, today is the beginning of a beautiful friendship: you and the baby. And me. Me and the baby."

"Not for forty-eight hours. Then we'll know if it worked."

"So we should relax the next two days. Get you de-stressed."

"Tomorrow, yes, but not Monday. I have way too much to do. I'm showing four houses."

"You need to cancel. You need to stay in bed . . . relaxing, staying away from stress. Let nature take its course. Let the baby grow and *pop*! There it is, attached to you."

The rain rattled against the garage door and they listened for a moment.

"Thank you," she said. She took his face in her hands. "But I'm fine. Baby or not, I need to make a living."

"Got to relax, though," said Ben. She released her hands. "Take the day off. All you need to do for the next two days is stay relaxed."

He started to open the car door, but her hand moved up his thigh.

"You know a good way to relax?" she asked.

"Sure, I'll give you a massage."

He could see her smiling, even in the dark.

"That would be good," she said, "but I had in mind making love."

He turned to her, their eyes meeting. "But we just did that — sorta. With help."

"That was business," she said, pulling him closer by the collar of his coat. "This is pleasure. No need to worry if it works or not. It's for us. Let's just have some fun. To help us relax. Like you said."

"Did the doctor say it was all right?"

"I never asked."

"I don't want to do anything to bother the, uh, baby."

"We can be gentle."

They kissed.

"Just to relax," he said, and got out of the car. He went around and opened her door. She stood and leaned against him as he closed the door.

They went inside the house arm in arm, bumping the walls as they pushed through the doorway, crashing through the kitchen and falling into the living room. Up the stairs to the master bedroom.

"Just like old times, huh?" he said.

Her lips pushed against his, parted.

"Are you sure this is the best place?" she asked. "The baby will be crawling over this carpet."

"All right, the bed," he said with a sweep of his arm.

He placed his hands on her hips and walked her backwards to the foot of the bed. Lips met, pressed, as they fell back on the quilt. As they had done on the carpet in that same room three years before, he unbuttoned her blouse as she unzipped his trousers. A little slower than that first time, thought Ben, though he did not object. They lay together, hands touching, eyes locked in a gaze of joy. He kissed her belly.

"For good luck," he said, and she pulled him up to her and kissed him.

Before they could finish, the phone on the nightstand rang.

Ben blinked, listened to the phone ring a second time, then a third. He reached for the receiver, still on top of her.

Addy glared at him. "You're going to answer it?"

"It could be important."

She pushed him off and rolled to the other side of the bed.

"Hello?" he spoke into the phone. He regarded Addy as he listened, brushing his hand down her back. *It's Mother*, he mouthed when she looked back over her shoulder.

With a frown, Addy got up from the bed and went to the bathroom, grabbing her robe from the hook on the door. After a minute he heard the shower running. They would not be resuming their lovemaking, he understood. So he sat up on the bed, pulling a corner of the quilt over his lap as he listened to his mother babble on about the latest gossip of her retired neighbors mixed with complaints about his father's sour disposition and bad habits.

"There's some mail for you," said Ben's mother as he gazed at Addy caught in the steamy mirror, stepping out of the shower. "I can drop it off on my way to Bridge Club tonight."

"Thanks, but you don't h—"

"There's a letter from Japan. Another one. I thought she stopped writing you long ago."

Ben held his breath, watched his wife wrap a towel around herself, then collect her hair in another towel.

"Yes, I think so, too." The words echoed around the bedroom. He knew his voice sounded phony. Probably Addy was paying no attention. "No hurry, Mom. I can pick it up tomorrow."

"It looks different from the other letters," his mother continued.

"Different handwriting. I like the stamps, though. All right if I keep them?"

"Sure, you can have them."

"Thanks, see you shortly."

Before Ben could remind her that he would come over tomorrow, she had hung up. He held the receiver a moment, thinking of twenty different things, half of them about Hawaii, half about Japan. With a quick sigh, he set down the receiver.

Addy stood in the bathroom doorway, rubbing the towel against her hair.

"So what's the news?"

Ben got up, turning to smooth the quilt.

"Nothing important. Junk mail. I think she's going to stop by in a little while."

"She's not staying for dinner, is she?"

"No, it's Bridge Club night."

"Thank goodness."

3

AFTER A SIMPLE BREAKFAST OF EGGS, biscuits, and fruit on that gray Sunday morning, Addy went as she usually did to her home office to study swatches of fabric and Ben went off to his den. He would use the quiet morning to catch up on some office work. Being early February, however, he was determined to knock out the taxes before the end of the month. So once again he laid out the documents he needed. The clock on his desk ticked away the morning.

The silence of the house was interrupted by the sound of Addy going down the staircase.

Ben looked up, glanced outside the windows at the soft, foggy front yard. Through the fog he saw the yard was dusted with snow. He paused, listening, expecting that he would have to get up and do something. He had more paperwork to finish before he dared take a lunch break.

"Hmm, a letter from Japan," said Addy, flipping through the mail left in the basket by the front door. "Who do you know in Japan?"

That word jumped out and slapped Ben in the next room, sitting at the desk. Aside from daily economic reports, the word *Japan* had special meaning for him. He had never visited that country and at that moment had no plans to, but hearing that word was like finding the key that fit the lock which opened his private vault of memories.

"It's got your name on it," Addy said, coming into the den and handing it to him.

He recalled his mother dropping by to give him a bundle of mail collecting at her house and, lost in conversation about his father's heart condition, the doctors' diagnosis, and upcoming tests, he had simply set the mail in the basket there. Addy called him to dinner when his mother left for her Bridge Club meeting.

They talked over dinner, then watched television, one of Addy's favorite shows. After the late news, they watched *Saturday Night Live* and she fell asleep on the sofa soon after the Weekend Update segment. When the show ended, he turned off the light and helped her stumble up to the bedroom.

There was only one person in Japan who might write a letter to him, thought Ben, but he had not heard from her in well over a year and he presumed that the relationship they once had was finally extinguished. His mother had mentioned the letter, asking about the "poor girl" when she phoned him, but he had broken off the topic. There was nothing new to be said. He had never given her the address of the house where he and Addy now lived; after Hawaii, he had not known where he would be living so he gave her his parents' address. They had planned to write to each other forever. A couple of years was close enough, it seemed.

"Who do you know in Japan?" Addy repeated. Her voice had been light, merely curious with her first questions. Now it had an edge.

"I don't know anyone in Japan." He did not look up, pretended to read tax instructions.

"Someone knows you, it seems."

He glanced up. "I made some contacts in Hawaii. I mean business contacts. Hotels and resorts. I played golf a few times with Japanese businessmen."

She held up the letter: feminine stationary. "You sure this is from some businessmen?"

He took the letter from her hand.

"Relax," Addy said with a laugh. "I know you used to be quite the playboy."

"No, I wasn't."

It was not a business letter. The small beige envelope showed handwritten addresses, both his parents' home and one in Japan. A colorful collection of stamps covered the right third of the envelope. He studied the handwriting, the crooked letters of his name, all capitals, reminding him of his grandmother's arthritic writing.

He started to tear it open, then paused and looked up at Addy, hoping his expression said everything, but she did not get it.

"Need some privacy?" she asked.

"Perhaps that might be . . . ."

"Prudent?"

He frowned, a deer caught in headlights.

"Could I have some privacy?" said Ben, fearing the worst, that like one of the old letters it might begin with *My dearest Benjamin.*

"As you like," she said with a scowl, exiting.

He thought she seemed more amused than angry.

Pulling the thin airmail paper from the envelope, he saw that he had nothing to worry about. The letter was all in Japanese. More crooked handwriting. He could not read it. So what was he to make of it? He examined the vertical lines of characters—*kanji*, the squarish pictographs, and *hiragana*, the other marks he knew to be phonetic symbols. Nothing was familiar. Despite a night class he took after moving back from Hawaii, only a few numbers were all he could understand.

Probably it was a mistake. Wrong address, wrong name . . . .

That night, while Addy slept, Benjamin awoke with an urge to look at the letter again. In the dim light of the desk lamp, the door of the den closed, he slipped the letter out from the drawer and unfolded the pages. He looked at them more carefully. Some *kanji* characters he did recognize. He started from the beginning, examining each character individually. At three separate places on the first page, he saw the same characters, and they were some of the few characters he knew. They were the characters he most feared recognizing. It was still guesswork, but he had a bad feeling.

He sat back, pondering the characters he recognized. Then he went to the bookshelves and dug out a dictionary he bought a few years earlier when he had the intention of learning that language and signed up for a night class. He blew off a thin streak of dust and cracked its cover. With some effort, flipping back and forth among the pages, the dictionary helped him decipher the two characters—rather, confirmed what he already suspected.

As he studied the characters on the page, Addy appeared.

"I thought you said you couldn't read it," she mumbled with a yawn, pulling her bathrobe around herself.

He gave her a quick smile. "I was curious, that's all."

"Awfully curious getting up in the middle of the night like this."

He tried to chuckle. "Just a mystery, that's all. I already figured out a couple of the characters."

She crossed her arms over her chest, her head tilted to one side.

"I didn't know you were so interested in Japanese."

"I had a class a few years back," he said. He watched her face and it seemed that his excuse was going to be believed. "It seemed a good idea at the time. Pick up some of the language for when I have a meeting with some businessmen. The era of Japanese business is coming, you know. Internationalization. We need to be ready to meet their commercial expansion—"

"What are you so secretive about?" she asked.

"I'm not secretive." He took a breath. "I'm just curious. I like a good mystery."

"Who would send you a letter in a language you can't read?"

"Someone who thinks I can read it."

"Or someone who doesn't know English. Someone who can only write in Japanese."

"Right."

"Like that Takakura family last fall. They bought the house on Moseby Lane, remember? The split-level, not the ranch. I had to get someone to translate for us."

"I remember them," said Ben with a sigh. What he remembered was how much Addy had complained. So much formality. So much haggling—as though they thought she could set the price herself. And the language barrier. She finally found the limit to her patience. When she closed the sale and was done with them, she took Ben out to celebrate.

"Well, if you're so determined to figure it out," said Addy, turning to leave, "why don't you go down to the university tomorrow and see if you can find somebody who knows Japanese. I'm sure there are plenty of Japanese speakers in the Seattle area. No reason to lose sleep over it."

"You're right," he replied. He put the dictionary down on the desk, the letter creased between the pages. "It's nothing important."

He went and got a drink of water, then joined her in bed.

Laying there, wide awake, he was unable to wipe from his consciousness the two distinctive symbols, the *kanji* characters he had recognized and confirmed with the dictionary. One of them meant "flower" and the other meant "child"—together forming the name *Hanako*.

"Why does she keep writing you?" Ben's mother asked over the phone a week later when another letter arrived. "Same handwriting. Same stamps—I assume I can have them. Haven't you told the poor girl you're married now?"

"Yes, I did. I told her two years ago."

"Then why does she keep writing you? I can't understand it. Desperate for an American husband, I'd say. Poor girl."

Poor girl, his mother had always called her. Ben hated that. She knew nothing about the young woman he had met in Hawaii.

"It's nineteen-ninety-one, Mom. People don't talk that way now. There is no war now and she's not after an American husband—"

"Anyways, it's here for you whenever you want to pick it up."

"Thanks," he said, feeling the car keys in his pocket. "I'll be right over."

"There's no hurry, dear."

But Ben was already setting down the receiver.

A thirty minute drive across town and he had the newest letter in his hands. As with the first letter, he closely examined the envelope: same stationary, same aged handwriting. He carefully opened it, afraid to tear it. Inside was a short note in Japanese, one page only. It was artistically folded at an angle around a slightly bent photograph. He separated them.

Setting the paper down, he gazed at the photograph. A woman stood in front of an old house, a residence in traditional Japanese style, somewhere in a forest. The woman wore a blue and white striped *yukata*—a thin summer gown. Draped around her shoulders was a rough, brown shawl. Beneath the hem of the *yukata* her bare feet were set in wooden *geta* clogs. Her stance placed her in front of the humble entrance to the house, the sliding door panel half open. Between the even, black hair crossing her forehead and framing her round, passive chin, her face possessed the strange, silent requisite for a woman of mystery. She divulged neither smile nor frown but something quite expressionless.

He knew her. But he had no idea where or when this old picture of Hanako was taken.

"Nice picture," said his mother, looking over his shoulder.

"Yes, it is," he whispered, breathless and transfixed by the half-faded picture, locked on her silent eyes.

"Is that her?"

His heart skipped a beat. "Yes, it's her."

"What's the poor girl's name?"

"Hanako." He spoke the name slowly, certain of the syllables. "Her name is Hanako."

"Not a very difficult name, I suppose. Easy to say." She stared at the photograph. "She's pretty. I can see why men'd be attracted. No smile, though."

He stared at the photo, felt an unusual coldness, as though it had just come out of the hold of the mail plane.

"What's that?" asked his mother.

Only then did Ben notice it, his attention drawn by his mother's unbiased eyes. In Hanako's *yukata* covered arms was a bundle which was barely distinguishable from the robe's fabric except for what seemed to be a tiny, pink face. In the cool autumn air of the photograph, the cheeks were rosy. The baby seemed to be sleeping a pleasant sleep.

"Ah, what a cute little child," his mother remarked. "It's hers, I suppose."

A disturbing sense of warmth spread quickly from his fingertips, pressed against the photograph, on through his arms and up to his head. His mother's glare pierced his shoulder, began to hurt, and he wanted to turn away. But there was nowhere he could turn.

Then it hit him, like a howitzer, and the answer fell quickly from his mouth.

"What did you say, Ben?"

He looked up, staring both at his mother and at his future captured in the photograph.

"It's mine. The baby is mine."

Benjamin sat through the green light near his house, absorbed in thought, knowing that the night that was about to begin would last a lot longer.

"So how's your dad doing?" Addy asked, turning down the TV.

Ben drew out his answer for a half hour. His mother's obsession with Bridge flowed easily from that. From Bridge to Bridge Club night to the mysterious letter, to its contents and its seemingly anonymous sender, took them through the evening news and into the late night talk shows. Ben dared turn off the TV, not wanting any distraction. He knew what was coming next. He had to be honest with his wife.

"Your mother got another letter?" Addy asked.

"Yes," he said with a sigh.

Addy seemed uninterested as she got up from the sofa and went to the kitchen, grabbing a can of Diet Coke from the refrigerator.

"So . . . ?" she called.

"Well . . . ."

He imagined her laughing at his consternation over receiving a letter from an old flame. Cute, she'd say. Sure, they both had previous loves. But now they were with each other. Married, in fact. Time to move on. That's what she would say when he told her. He felt more reassured. Honesty is the best policy.

"So what's the big mystery?" she asked, returning to the living room and taking a sip of the soda.

Ben tried to laugh. "Mystery?"

As she waited for an answer—apparently she wanted one—she gathered several interior decorating catalogs from around the room and placed them into a shoulder bag sitting at the end of the sofa. Her back was to him.

Ben took a deep breath, which caught Addy's attention. She turned.

"It's from a girl I used to know," he said in even tone. "Well, it's *about* her, I guess, not *from* her. Someone else wrote the letter. I don't know who. But there's a picture this time. It's definitely her." He knew the photo was safely locked in his desk. He did not want to risk Addy snatching it away and ripping it to shreds. "It must've been taken a few years back. I mean, after we parted. Somewhere in Japan, obviously. And . . . ."

He regarded Addy, not knowing how his expression sat on his face, unable to change it even if he wanted to.

"And she's holding a baby in her arms."

Addy's face tightened. "A baby . . . ?"

The long, painfully slow explanation eventually exploded into a full-blown conflagration when Ben said "And its probably, well, likely the baby is mine."

He naively thought she would be happy for him. After all, they were trying to have a child. Now he could prove he was healthy. And the relationship with the Japanese woman ended long before he ever met Addy, so he believed he was outside the statute of limitations, or whatever it was called.

"It was a relationship," he said, trying to explain, trying to give the facts some context. "It was not a frivolous fling, as you're thinking. It wasn't just an affair. It was a relationship — like what you and I have now."

"Like now? What do you mean?" Her tone was full of blood.

"I mean something that's based on compatible personalities and interests, something more than physical. We didn't even have sex for the first six months."

"Hah! But you sure caught up after that, huh?"

He frowned, trapped again. "No, I — we — we were in love. If you must know. I told you before that I was with someone in Hawaii."

She glared at him a moment. "You wanted to stay with her?"

He stood frozen in the living room.

"Didn't you?" Addy gave her words more force. "You would've stayed with her if you didn't have to come back here, right?"

"No, that's not it. She couldn't stay." He paced around the living room. "I don't know. It was a difficult situation. Both of us had to leave. We did not have very many options. It was a different time."

"Just answer the question."

He stopped, took a breath. "It was almost five years ago. I don't remember how I felt then."

"Who broke up with who?"

"That really matters?"

He glanced around the room, his eyes landing on framed pictures of her family members, his hotel properties, scenic views of the California coast, Hawaiian beaches, big rocks at Astoria — tokens of affection they had offered to themselves. They had built a home together.

"It was mutual," he said. Whose home was he thinking of? The one in Hawaii? "But not in anger or hatred. We both had to return home. That's all."

Addy crossed her arms, acting the stern school marm she had once trained to be and gave three years of her life to before taking up real estate.

"Did you know then?"

He shrugged. "What? About the baby?"

"Yes, the baby!" She threw her hands into the air.

He could be so stupid sometimes, Ben sensed her thinking. Just a boy who played around, enjoying each new game. She only accepted him because he was cute in his playful demeanor. Yet he had not changed, had not yet grown up, and she was tired of trying to direct him into the kind of husband she expected he would become after a couple years of marriage. Now she probably realized how utterly disappointing he was.

"Of course not." He remembered the day she departed, flew away, left him alone at the boarding gate. "I did not know — she probably didn't know, either. Not that day." He took a few breaths. "I only guessed it when this letter arrived." He regarded Addy across the room. The coffee table sat between them. "And the photo. Holding a baby. Then I knew. I guessed."

She stood her ground, backed against the piano and did not relax. Ben grasped the sofa. They exchanged rough, noisy breaths, eyeing each other.

"I'm sorry —"

"How can you be so sure?" asked Addy.

A fair question, but the answer would be difficult for her to accept. If he simply said to Addy that he just knew it was so, that would have confirmed that his heart was still filled with *her*, with Hanako. Instead, he offered up the biggest lie of his life. He told Addy that an official at the consulate downtown had translated the letter and that's what it said. Instead, he knew the truth more certainly than any translation could confirm.

She grabbed the edge of the piano, at the low end of the notes, a dissonant chord filling the room. She fell into the brown wingback and sank into its cushions. He hated seeing her collapse that way, looking defeated — especially when he had lied. But he had to make things right. The quicker he ended the conflict between them, the better. He sure did not feel like a victor.

"Then it's true . . . ." said Addy with a sigh.

"I'm sorry, Addy."

The ticking of the wall clock grew old. A light rain was falling outside, tapping the windows.

"I'm sorry, sweetheart," said Ben, just above a whisper.

Addy shook her head slowly. "No . . . ."

"No?"

She looked up at him. "No, I'm not your sweetheart."

4

BEN WORKED LATE—late enough that he walked over to a hotel for the night, unable to face Addy, unwilling to put up with their constant arguing. He called to tell her he was too tired to drive home, left the message on the answering machine. Without trying, he found himself staying later and later at the office. Then the weeks settled into a cold, quiet season, a truce reigning over the battlefield.

"No luck," was all Addy shared after her next appointment, acknowledging their second try did not take.

"I'm sorry," he responded sincerely. He thought his voice seemed too casual to Addy and he repeated his words, pulling a darker hue over them.

She did not respond at first and he listened to her breathing on the phone line.

"Come home," she said so softly he wanted her to repeat it. "You can sleep downstairs."

He started to say more, then heard the receiver put down. He sat on the edge of the hotel bed for a long time, thinking of the old sofa in the finished basement.

Benjamin's mother was not helpful. Of course she took his side, although she had little to say in support of his official position: 1) It was before he met Addy, 2) It was a serious, loving relationship, not a quick affair, and 3) They had split up mutually due to circumstances beyond their control. The last item also implied that they would not seek to reunite in the future. Addy interpreted it that way, but Ben's mother kept tossing in suggestions that with air tickets dropping in price it could be possible to visit each other.

But to what end? Addy had argued. Did he really want to be with that woman again? They had so little in common. Different culture, language, race. It was all the differences that had attracted them to each other, she could understand, but those same differences could never be a foundation for a long-term relationship. She had more in common with Ben than that other woman. That relationship was done. Ben seemed to accept that fact. But why the letters? And the photograph? Was she trying to re-establish their correspondence? Why had she started it again after a couple years of silence?

Ben had no answers. In one moment he acted innocently naïve but in others a deceitful cad, happy to have gotten away with some act of infidelity. And yet, in his mind, there was no infidelity. That's what he continued to assert. He met the woman, fell in love with her, and parted before he met Addy.

In fact, he and Addy had long discussions of their lives, checking out each other's suitability to enter into a new and hopefully long relationship. There had been little to disclose. She was a work-a-holic with ambition, a fair amount of drive, good connections, professional kind of beauty with an inner tigress. He was upwardly mobile, too, although he always seemed on the verge of getting fired, too often playing free and easy with his responsibilities for organizing hotel services, handling hospitality management, approving hotel and resort designs. Still, he was Rich's right-hand man.

Then this woman raises her head. No, decided Addy, the woman had held out her arms in the photograph, presenting a baby to Benjamin. She was both jealous and enraged at the woman. Someone who did not deserve him had managed to capture him with the same simple act her sister Wendy had used to get her husband. And by the time Sandy got pregnant, it was permissible in society to go it alone, even though the guy eventually did marry her a few months after the birth of their son.

Addy sighed, staring out the window of whatever house she was showing that day, wondering what the future now held for her and Ben. She doubted the other woman had planned anything, not likely she had schemed to get him back. If she had, this situation would have come to fruition a while ago, not now. It had to be a coincidence; Ben never knew he fathered a child. Yet now that he did know, what would he do? Leave her for the mother of his child? Stick with her but always think of that other woman and their child?

Had she lost him already? The thought made her choke up and the lovely young couple she was escorting through the two-story brick Georgian asked her if she was all right. She smiled, nodded.

Did *she* still want *him*? That idea made her pause and the couple became annoyed by her apparent dismissal of their house-hunting interest. No sale.

The rain dampened their mood, sending both of them into a sobering depression. They seemed to be on a life raft, riding the waves up and down, worried they might be tossed overboard at any moment.

Benjamin remarked how bad he felt and even his boss, Rich, remarked on it, gave him a couple days off to rest. He couldn't get any work done. His mind was consumed with how he might make things right with Addy and what he should do about the "Japan situation," as his mother referred to it.

His father chuckled that it was "Sayonara time" — referring, Ben guessed, to the story of the Army colonel who fell in love with a Japanese actress after the end of World War II. His father had a similar story to tell — using "this buddy of mine" when Ben could guess who the real protagonist of the story was. Ben wondered: *Do I have a half-sibling in Japan?* He shook the thought out of his head. It was the '90s now, more than forty years since that fragile period of history when there were laws preventing American servicemen from marrying their Japanese girlfriends or bringing them back to the States. But times were different now. And yet . . . . Ben never thought his Japanese girlfriend would be accepted in his family, no matter how much his father seemed to joke about his time on duty there after the war. To his father, an Asian girl represented a good time, not a good wife. The passage of time did not seem to change that idea within his family.

With the first cool, sunny day of spring, he and Addy started talking again. Addy was rested and recharged, and when Ben least expected it, she launched her attack, catching him unprepared to defend himself. She wanted the issue decided once and for all. It had been more than a month. She had lost sales. She needed to get all of it out of her head. She needed to get on with her life—whatever that meant.

"Yes, it's still there," said Ben in response to her attack. "It's not going away."

"I wish it would. Just forget the damn letters."

"I can't do that."

"I don't understand," Addy swore, again storming around the living room in full fury. "I can't understand it. How can this girl jump into our lives like this? What makes her think she can do that? Huh? And why did she wait so long to spring it on you? I just can't figure out why. She has a plan to blackmail us, I'll bet. She wants some kind of payment, I'm sure. Child support. How old is the kid now? She'll be asking for child support going back three, four years. How can she do this? I just can't accept it. I can't. How can this Jap girl barge into our life like this? What makes her think she's got any right to do that, huh?"

Ben stood his ground. "She's got the child, so she's got the right." He responded as calmly as he could manage. His sense of decorum demanded that he maintain control, even as he prepared to defend himself against her next attack.

"No, she doesn't."

They stared at each other. Ben was surprised she had brought up the issue, feeling unfairly accused. It was all in the past.

"What are you saying?" he asked cautiously.

"Look, Ben, we've got a perfect life. We've both got good careers, a wonderful house, two new cars, and we've been planning for our own family. We're making our own child. It isn't fair, Ben. It's just not fair. She can't come barging in like this."

"What about the child, then?"

"You mean, what if it's yours?"

"Yes," said Ben. "What if the child is mine?"

"I thought we were already assuming that."

He regarded her. "Were we?" He studied her face a moment. "You've been so quiet all these weeks I thought you had decided to accept that reality. Now you come back with the same anger and hatred. We're not discussing a mortgage or a new dishwashing machine. It's a child."

She pursed her lips. "I did not forget. And I did not accept the situation. I just thought that at some point you would decide what you were going to do about it. I mean, about *your* child."

"My child . . . ." He dared grin. "That sounds like you accept the situation."

"What is the situation?" She took a step back, arms crossing over her chest. "Yes, Benjamin Pinkerton, just what exactly is the situation now?"

He started to speak, then stopped, searching for the right words.

"Apparently I have a child."

"With no proof."

"With enough proof."

"So you say."

"I would like to see what the truth is."

Her breathing seemed to stop. "Why? Are you planning to contest it?"

Ben shook his head. "She's in another country. Those kind of laws can't be enforced across international borders. Don't worry."

"I'm nothing but worry!"

"I just want to be sure the child is mine before I do anything else. Whatever else comes after that, I don't know."

"And how are you going to do that?"

They faced one another and Ben sensed those final words of hers already being loaded. He sensed she was about to fire them, so he launched his own words preemptively, striking her in the heart:

"I have to go there."

Her eyes widened and she stuttered a moment, a flash of weakness running through her.

"You're going to spend our money, our hard-earned money — on a trip to Japan — to to see if if that *bitch* is telling the truth?"

"If it is my child, I want to know." He breathed deeply. "Any father would. And if he is mine, then I want to meet him. I want to know him, know about him, that he exists. I don't think I can live peacefully knowing that my child is out there somewhere in the world not knowing who his father is."

It was Addy's turn to take a breath. "That's it?"

"I've got to go."

She pouted.

"And please don't call her a bitch. You don't even know her."

Her pout melted into a grotesquely twisted grin.

"What about me? What about my feelings?" She shook her head. "You're saying this lady from the past is more important than me, your wife. Your present wife?"

He turned away, unable to think of a satisfactory response.

"I have to go and see."

"That's no answer, Ben."

"Addy —"

"All right, let's say, just for the sake of argument, that the child is yours. If you go there and see the child with your own eyes, what are you going to do? Are you going to just *see* the child? And that's all? And then come home? Or more?"

"I won't know that until I get there."

"But if you're going all the way over there because you think you want to do more, like return to that woman and have the family you always wanted with her *with her*, then then I can only guess what that what that kind of future is going to be. For you. And for me — us."

"What? Tell me."

"No, you tell *me*. What if the child is yours? Can't you leave it alone? Everything's been all right so far, so why disrupt the balance? No, you tell me what you're going to do. Oh, uh-huh—I'm beginning to see it all so clearly now. It's not the child you care about, no, not the innocent offspring. No, you want to see her. *Her*. Your *luvaaah*. You want to go see this Jap girl you played around with in Hawaii. You want another fling!"

"Addy, stop it! Why are you talking like that?"

"Like what?"

"You don't talk like that. That's not you. Besides, you're being a little unfair."

She launched into a charge around the room, her arms cutting the air.

"Me? Unfair? You just told me you're going to Japan to see your kid. Surprise, surprise! You told me you're going to see your kid. And you want me to be fair? Where's the fairness for me? You want to go see your kid. Do you want me to go looking for the son I gave up for adoption when I was sixteen? Do you? Well, I wouldn't know where to even look. It's not a part of my life anymore. Let it lie, Ben—like I did. Leave it alone, Ben. Even if you're well-meaning, you're only going to upset her life. Stay away. Let them go."

She stopped when the weight of Ben's stare landed on her.

"You had a son at sixteen?"

Addy turned away and the sound of sobbing came gradually to his ears.

"But you said your sisters got pregnant before you," said Ben.

"Yes—legitimately." She sniffled back her tears. "Only my mother and grandmother knew. I did the semester vacation thing, went to Spokane. Maybe my sisters guessed later, but . . . I . . . ."

Ben held his expression steady. "Things happen, Addy. People deal with them."

"If you loved me . . . ." She looked at him, locked her eyes on his. "You'd forget about that girl, if you loved me. And that child. But you want to let them into your life again. I feel that. I see it in your face. And in what you're saying and how you're acting. It's all so clear to me, Ben. For the first time in our marriage, the truth finally comes out. I'm not the best for you, I'm only good enough. That's it, isn't it? You really want her. You've wanted her all along."

He went to her, arms extended to take her into his embrace. She stepped away.

"You married me on the rebound, didn't you?"

"No, Addy."

"Sounds like it."

"I simply met you after I returned to Seattle."

"But you were heartbroken, weren't you? She broke your heart, didn't she?"

"I guess so."

"And you needed to fall in love again quick. You wanted to get over the pain."

"Addy, you're not being reasonable."

"No, Ben, you're not being reasonable. Hell, go if you want to. I can't stop you. You've got your own money. You've got vacation leave. You've got everything of your own. Shit, Ben. You are clever, but I know the truth now. We don't share anything, not really — the house, perhaps — but everything else is either yours or mine. Maybe you were keeping things that way so it would be easier to divide them . . . later. That must be it."

"Divide things? What are you talking about?"

Addy had backed herself against the Hummel display case in the corner and stood defiantly. She seemed ready to pounce, her eyes calm and cool but unable to hide the fire inside her. One Hummel figurine had fallen yet she ignored it this time.

"Go ahead," she grunted. "I can't stop you from going to Japan and seeing your girlfriend again. All I can do is wait."

"Wait?"

"For you to decide."

She glared at Ben, her eyes red and her cheeks wet.

"Decision? What the hell are you talking about, Addy?"

She sniffled but refused to wipe her face.

"When you get there and see that kid, and you find out the truth, and you're satisfied that you've seen it through, then you'll have to make a decision. You'll have to decide whether to let them into your life again, or come back to me. If you still want to be with me. If you choose them, then the answer's obvious. If you choose me, then . . . . Well, you've already blown that."

"Oh, come on, Addy!"

"It's over, Benjamin. We're finished. I need to move on. I have a career that can't be screwed up because of a mess like this. What am I saying? You want to know? Huh? When you get back—if you come back—I will be gone."

5

ABOUT FIVE YEARS BEFORE THE LETTERS ARRIVED, Benjamin had been leaning against the railing of the balcony, up on the fifth floor of the Hotel Akala, breathing in the salt air and regarding the sea. It was near dusk on a day when most tourists were back in their home countries. The unseasonably cool September evening made him suddenly feel homesick. Growing up in land-locked Kansas City, he had developed a fascination with the sea, seashores, seascapes, the endless horizons. After college, he had moved to the West Coast, San Jose at first for an Information Technology job, then up to Portland briefly. He was living in Seattle, had a management position with Prime Properties, when he was transferred to Hawaii. He even had a small sailboat down at the marina in Seattle that he seldom had time to sail.

The sudden transfer to the islands was like an overblown dream. There was so much sea there. From his office window he could take it all in, from his fifth floor hotel room balcony he could embrace it, and in the evenings he could hear it rushing to shore, crashing on the beach. In the daytime, everyone talked about it, longed for it. He went down to the beach nearly every day, whether it was afternoon — on a slow day of meetings or conferences — or later in the evening on long, busy days. Walking barefoot across the sand, smelling the salty air, seeing the glassy sheen spreading as far as he could see, always seemed to soothe his restless spirit. It made him feel less lonely being stuck on that fragrant, happy-go-lucky volcanic rock so lushly overgrown with palm trees, endless pineapple and sugar cane fields, temporary home to three times as many tourists as residents. Seattle never had such tension for him.

That September evening was perhaps too chilly for swimming. He had been thinking about the day he would return to Seattle. He would revel in the melancholy greenery and the drizzly skies, once again sailing around Puget Sound—once he bought it back from his colleague.

A delicate laughter had caught his attention and swept away his idle thoughts. Distracted, he had removed his eyes from the sunset-streaked horizon and turned to regard some girls who were trying to swim in the bouncing surf.

They were Japanese girls, he could see, and they were beautiful. The quartet wore brightly colored swimsuits yet their arms and legs were quite pale and their hair was jet black. Although they were hardly the first Japanese he had seen in Hawaii—there were thousands of tourists every day—these held his attention. They delighted in their play, frolicking as only summer tourists did, or like children, oblivious to social constraints.

It was a cool evening. Everyone else out on the beach wore jackets. These Japanese girls, perhaps in Hawaii for the first time and not wanting to pass up the chance to swim ignored the cool air. So he studied them. He recalled the black and white images stamped in his head. History books. TV shows. Samurai dramas or Godzilla movies. They were all stereotypes. Having always thought of Japanese girls as being something like the chubby, round-faced, almond-eyed ceramic Hakata dolls tucked away in his grandmother's world-wide doll collection, what he saw playing on the beach were very pleasant surprises.

It was the 1980s, he considered, wondering where his youth had gone, already in his thirties and fearing he had missed something.

Japan was opening up to internationalization, long past recovering from the ravages of war and hardships of reconstruction. Now Japan had stepped out as an equal among nations, pressing for leadership in the international community. Stereotypes were falling away. No longer were images of geisha and samurai what people thought of first; endless varieties of electronics and quirky pop singers with pink hair and thigh-high boots were the most noticeable imports.

Ben had to smile: he had never had any interest in Asia—not the culture, not the food, not the people, their languages, their fashions, nor their ways of doing business. He had only limited experience, anyway. In college, his girlfriend had roomed with a student from Japan. In his high school there had been a girl named Yuko, but he never considered she was only half-Japanese. She was just another American to him. Then he arrived in Hawaii.

He watched the young women with fascination. Yes, they were very different. They ran on long, slender legs like nimble gazelles. They flung their straight, black hair in the breeze with the casual sophistication of care-free American girls. They wore their Western swimsuits particularly well, too; their slight curves matched the shape of the suits. He had never bothered to notice such things before and wondering why he did now puzzled him.

Returning his eyes to the sea, their laughter stayed with him. He regarded them again, deeply impressed.

It had not taken long to decide which one was the prettiest, and his eyes focused on her. She wore a yellow one-piece suit, the sides marked with wide, black stripes from armpit to hip. She was the most attractive. Another was a little older, one was a little chunky, one was too tall and too thin. Even as he was amazed at himself for thinking of her that way, he pressed on with his ratings. The light was fading but he concentrated on the black zipper which ran downward between her breasts. Her hair flowed freely, dropping to just below her collar, a yellow ribbon matching her swimsuit held her hair to one side.

The four girls chatted casually, like birds on the first excursion out of Mother's nest. They alternately splashed in the surf and stretched out under the barely warm sunset.

She was the most cheerful of the group, calling and waving to her friends so enthusiastically. She was the most beautiful, too. And as he compared her with the women of his life, she easily ranked near the top. She was more beautiful than Cindy, the girlfriend he had left back in Seattle—and he had always thought Cindy was by far the best. However, Julie from his college days was the most beautiful. The most beautiful Caucasian, that was. Or was it Lacey back in San Jose? No, Cindy was the best—but she was having trouble deciding if it was worth the cost of calling him long-distance or not. She hated writing letters.

Cindy suggested they should break up, see other people, see what happens. See what happens when he returned to Seattle, that is. It would be her loss, he had said. *No, my loss,* he corrected himself. What did it matter if all he did was watch the Japanese girls on the beach? He was free to date anyone. But what would he say, what could he say, to *her*? He wondered if she knew English.

He got up and went downstairs to the lobby and out the back to the hotel patio, waving at the bartender who knew him well. For a while he leaned against the concrete wall dividing the patio from the beach, stretched his arms in the air like he had nothing to do. Then he stepped onto the sand.

Walking slowly past the girls, he decided to buy an Hawaiian Punch at the refreshment stand near the Kalakaua Avenue sidewalk. As he returned, walking in front of them again, he turned his head slightly to catch a glimpse of her. Her attention at that moment was on her friend, the tall/thin one, who was buoyed in the surf, struggling comically to paddle back to shore against the tide. He moved on to his original vantage point at the hotel patio, craning his head back to see her, memorizing her features, her face, wishing he had his camera with him. He did not wish to forget her beauty—there was something special in the line of her face, the shape of her body, the melody in her voice.

He wished he knew some Japanese. Other than *sayônara*—from that old movie of the same name, and *bonsai*—those miniature trees—he did not know any. And *sukiyaki*, he suddenly added, that beef stew dish — and the corny song. But if he had left then, at that moment, he probably would never see her again.

Right then, staring out at the sea, he decided that the tall/thin girl was not struggling comically but was actually in trouble, unable to return to the shore. He dropped his drink and kicked off his flip-flops and raced into the surf. A few steps in he was throwing his arms forward and kicking with his feet, driving toward the girl. When he reached her he grabbed her flailing arm and pulled her, wrapped his arm around her shoulders, buoying her, then began swimming with her toward the beach.

Her friends were in a panic as they arrived and stumbled into the surf to tend to their friend. He dropped to the sand, breathing hard.

After a few frantic moments, when the struggling swimmer was secured, the girl he'd had his eyes on turned to him and thanked him. He gazed up at her as she bowed to him. The others took the hint and also bowed to him. Then they gathered their friend and helped her back to their towels, packed up, and went away to wherever they were staying.

He returned to his room, dripping, glad that he had finished that YMCA lifesaving course when he was younger.

It had started to become a habit, ever since Benjamin first transferred to Hawaii. Like the residents, he would rush from his office early to catch the late afternoon sun for his daily dip. Others caught their designated wave. Still others just a few rays of sunshine. He never would have admitted going to the beach for girl watching. Every girl on the beach was either a suspicious tourist or a more suspicious resident. Look, but do not dare even think about touching. That was the unwritten rule. And he had to endure this until the Ala Moana condominium construction was completed?

Maybe that Japanese girl would be different, he wondered late one night before dialing the number of a phone back in Seattle. Cindy was not at home when he called but the guy who answered said he would give her the message. And who are you? I'm her roommate. Oh. Ben hung up.

He sat by the phone talking to himself. *What are you doing here? What in the world are you doing here, Benjamin Franklin Pinkerton? You're in Hawaii and you're not enjoying yourself?* He cursed all through the night, every night. *What is the matter with you? You need a hobby. Or go work in some volunteer organization. Daughters of the American Revolution keeps your mother out of trouble, doesn't it? Her devotion gave you your patriotic name, dammit. You're certainly not working too hard.* And he wasn't. Two meetings yesterday, a few phone calls, a three-hour conference this afternoon, looking over designs, writing a short report to be faxed back to Seattle, edit a legal brief for the boys in Honolulu. He had walked through the worksite every day for months now. *What's the problem? It can't be that you're lonely, can it?*

He called his boss back in Seattle, Richard Williston, and told him what he had been telling himself for a few months.

"Maybe so," Rich replied, sympathetic yet distracted.

"Why did you send *me* out here?" Ben asked.

"Because you're one heck of a project supervisor. You get things done. I can trust you."

"Heck of a supervisor or not, how did I get to be the one stuck with this? You should have sent Howie. He likes surfing. I can't even get a decent tan."

"You know the condo biz, guy. You're the most qualified. They love you out there. That's what they tell me. Really. You're doing a bang-up job there, and we all appreciate your hard work. It's a tough job but somebody's got to do it, you know."

"Rich, I'm dying here. I'm alone in a crowd. I'm out of place. I'm not a tourist. They can get away with anything. I'm not a native, either. They can relax here. Let me come home."

His boss was laughing so hard that Ben wanted to punch him.

"I've never heard anybody beg to leave Hawaii. You can stick it out another six months. And I'll sweeten it, too. When you get back, I'll give you a promotion."

"Again?" He was getting those kind of promotions about every other month.

"Sure, again," Rich answered. "I'll put you on this new project we're getting together in Alaska, if you can stand sunbathing on the beach up there."

He told Rich he worked hard, that he did not care what title was on his desk, or what the figures were on his paychecks — so long as they were high enough to beat inflation, of course. The 1980s were boom times, but they would not always be that way, he knew.

"All right, I'll give you a pay *cut*," said Rich. He asked Ben what was wrong. "Get a hold of yourself, dude. So what if you're hitting thirty-three and still unmarried. I was — two or three times, in fact. You don't need that Cindy what's her name. You're living company-paid in Waikiki. What more could you want?"

He told his boss the place was a dump. Built back in the 1920s, for chrissake. And there were all these little lizards — geckos, he thought they were called — crawling around the walls at night, and sea gulls shitting on the window sills.

"All right, so it's not the Royal Hawaiian, but it's company-paid, so lighten up," his boss in Seattle told him. "You're our ambassador of goodwill. Give the condo guys what they want, and you can come home."

Ben went on with his list of complaints until his boss cut him off.

"Try to enjoy yourself," was the last thing Rich said.

A couple weeks passed, depression settling in, as Benjamin spent more time with the project people, less time on the beach.

Then one October evening he was again strolling along the beach, welcoming the sunset after a particularly rough day of arguing with contractors, distracted with cost overruns. It was warm again on that autumn evening in the tropics, and he was watching the stars come out and the lights of ships out at sea. The long, curved beach was nearly deserted, but out of the dark waters emerged a mermaid, a gorgeous sea nymph. He had stared at the Japanese swimmer as she strode up the beach to her towel. The swimsuit had changed to a pink and blue one-piece, but the face was the same. Even in the sunset shadows he knew her, and aside from the shock of realizing the odds, he was glad to be gazing at her again.

She arrived at the beach towel, grabbed a smaller towel there and began wringing the water from her hair. In her haste, she had not noticed him standing barely two steps away from the edge of her towel, lost in the spreading darkness.

"Ah!" she cried, startled upon seeing him.

"Sorry," said Ben. "Didn't mean to scare you."

She stood before him, and he had spoken to her. He considered apologizing further, so she wouldn't think he was some kind of pervert. After all, she had caught him watching her.

And yet, she did not seem to recognize him as the same man who had helped her friend in the surf. He wondered if he should mention that, let her know he was a good guy.

"Excuse me," he said after what seemed an interminably long pause. "I was just watching the ships out there."

"Shippsu?" she asked, turning to look out at the sea.

He noticed her accent, the way she hissed the *sh* of 'ships' and the extra *u* sound she added, and decided it was cute.

He pointed to a string of blue and white lights on the horizon.

"Those two ships out there. Container ships, I guess. There was an oil tanker earlier."

"You like shippsu?" she inquired, pleasantly surprising him with her willingness to talk. All he could think of was the image of a demure woman in a colorful *kimono*, her face stark white with make-up, shyly covering her mouth with her hand. It was a photograph he found once in a trunk his father kept in the basement, a souvenir of the war. He hated when a past he had never experienced intruded on his present.

"Yes, I do."

"Why you like?" she asked, smiling.

He tried to ignore her pretty face, trying to focus on her question and his answer.

"I like the lights. Reminds me of home."

She turned fully, still wiping her arms with the towel, and gazed with him out at the distant points of light.

"*So desu ne*," she said, a sense of wonder in her voice.

"Are you Japanese?" he asked, knowing it was a stupid question as soon as it left his lips. He had waited until she had turned her back to him, gathering her belongings into a bag.

"*Hai*—yes," she replied, cheerful or proud—he could not tell which. She spun around to face him.

Words rolled through his head, stacking up. Her beauty was . . . he had to think . . . a drug which made his world go suddenly into slow-motion.

"*Nihongo o hanashimasu ka? Amerikajin desu ka?*" she asked him.

"Huh?" he responded.

"Are you American?"

"Yes, I am."

"Are you Hawaiian?"

"No." He grinned, enjoying her. "I'm from Seattle, actually."

"See-at-ull?"

"In Washington." He watched her thinking. "I mean, Washington state. North of California."

"Ah! California, yes."

"Way, way over there," he said, sweeping his arm out toward the ocean.

"Are you tourist?"

"No, I work here," he replied, and for the first time felt glad that he did. "My company is building some condos over there." He swung his arm in the direction of the worksite even though it could not be seen from where they stood on the beach. "I'm in charge of the project."

She paused a moment, as if contemplating the revelation. Or translating what he said.

"You build condo?"

"My company builds them. I watch."

She giggled and threw the towel around her shoulders.

"What's your name?" he asked, thinking his voice was too strong, too demanding.

It was so abrupt it stopped her, but she blurted the answer right out: "Nakamori *desu*."

"I meant your first name."

"It is first name."

"That's beautiful," he told her. He decided to bow, certain he did it wrong. He did not understand at that moment that Japanese put the family name first, given name second.

"I'm Benjamin." He extended his hand.

She regarded his hand, then held out her hand. He shook her hand, laying limp in his.

"Harrow, Benjamin-*san*."

"No, Benjamin is my first name."

She had given her hip a slap, as though acting out some gesture she thought appropriate.

"Ahh, *so desu ne*! I'm sorry. My name — first name — is Hanako."

"Hanako . . . ."

He had swirled her name around in his mind as though tasting wine, then he had told her that *Hanako* was also a beautiful name.

6

BENJAMIN AWOKE SUDDENLY. He batted his eyes for a couple of minutes as he realized he was strapped into a seat on an airplane. The dream lingered in his head: Hanako, a beach, a kiss, a future that evaporated as soon as he awoke.

He quickly took in the cabin of the plane, remembering where he was and why he was flying to Japan.

"Do you need anything, sir?" asked the flight attendant, a woman of Japanese descent.

"No," said Ben, sounding unsure. "I'm fine."

He straightened himself in the seat, shaking off the dream. The jiggling of the airplane in the Pacific turbulence did not help, and his stomach was rising higher and higher.

Surveying the cabin, he remembered how Rich had given him a long yawn, exaggerating it just to make Ben feel worse for getting his boss up early on a Saturday morning to drive him all the way down to Sea-Tac.

"I'm going to need you back very soon," said Rich, pulling off the highway. "We're starting work on the Forrester project. I promised them you'd be here to deliver the initial design. Do that and I won't need to send you out to Royal Gorge for a year. You hate Wyoming, as I recall."

"I don't hate it . . . ."

"And you're going to owe me for this early vacation leave, too. Drinks are on you when you get back."

"Fair enough."

They pulled up alongside the curb at the departure gates.

"Get there, take care of business, and get home," said Rich.

They shook hands. "I'm taking Carlton paperwork," Ben added. "I can finish the design by the time I arrive there."

"That's industrious of you," Rich said with a chuckle. "Be sure you get everything settled. Don't let this side trip become a lifetime diversion. I need you back here ASAP. I'm sure Addy does, too — even if she won't say it."

Ben had watched the dark clouds closing out the early morning sun, thought of his marriage and sighed. "I hope a week is enough time to sort out everything."

"She understands. In her heart, she knows you're doing the right thing. Women are that way when it comes to babies. She'll come around."

"I hope you're right."

Ben closed and opened his eyes twice. The cabin of the airplane did not change. He felt a bit paranoid, thinking everyone around him knew his story, knew his reason for a trip to Japan.

Why does any man go alone to Japan? Business, of course. Or pleasure.

His business was not going to be pleasant, he believed. As Rich had told him, he was going there to have a look, talk things out, make a tentative plan for the future, and return to Seattle ready to work on the Forrester project, a resort lodge in central Alaska. Far away from the sea and far away from anything Japanese or Hawaiian.

He had his excuse, however, and he wished everyone around him knew what it was. Then they could keep their eyes to themselves and stop wondering about him.

That man across the aisle, portly and bearded, dressed in business casual, dozing, was definitely up to no good. Probably had a mistress there he was seeing while he was supposed to be in Vancouver on business. And the young couple in front of him? He saw them when they sat down: American guy, Japanese girl. Likely going to meet the in-laws, Ben decided. Good luck. The older Japanese woman behind him had given him the evil eye when they were jostling for overhead luggage space. He decided to be kind and offered it to her; he put his bag under the seat. Still she had glared at him—as though she suspected he was going to Japan for some kind of mischief.

"So what's your business in Nipponland?" asked his seatmate, a burly cowboy in boots and a plaid shirt.

Ben was startled. He coughed and took a breath. "Me? Just seeing the sights."

"Lotta sights there. Castles, temples, shrines, old neighborhoods ain't changed in a thousand years . . . . Where're you headed?"

"Nagoya," said Ben, thinking it over a moment.

"Yep, my little girl's there. Near there, anyways. A place up in the mountains called Gifu. Nagoya's a fine city, though. My third visit."

Ben smiled. So this cowboy had fathered a child, too. It must have been a long time ago from the look of him. Ben felt slightly better.

"That's nice."

"She's been teaching English for three years now. Some gov'ment program."

"Teaching English?"

"Yessir, after she graduated college she wanted to see Japan, so she signed up. Works in a junior high school, up in the mountains. Loves it."

Ben smiled sheepishly. "I see."

That was a good excuse: seeing your grown daughter who is merely working in Japan. He wished his excuse was as simple and straightforward. He didn't know what he was doing, he suddenly realized. Where was he going? Who was he seeing? What would he do when he saw her again?

"I'm going to see someone I used to know," Ben eventually said.

"Is that so?" asked the cowboy.

"Someone I met in Hawaii. I was working there. She was a . . . a tourist. We've kept in touch. Now it's finally time for me to visit."

"That's great," said the cowboy. "So your lady friend's Japanese?"

"Yes," he replied, then as an afterthought added: "*Honto*. That means 'true' — I think."

The cowboy smiled. After a moment, he spoke. "Is your wife okay with that?"

"My wife . . . ?"

"I see you got a weddin' ring on."

Ben blinked, his fingers automatically withdrawing, curling into his palm.

"She knows." He was not sure what to say. "This is just a business trip. That's all."

Again the cowboy smiled, more of a knowing grin this time.

"It's not like she's divorcing me or . . . ."

"Sorry to hear that," said the cowboy, and he seemed genuinely sorry.

"She only said she was thinking of it." He stared down the aisle at the flight attendant preparing meal service. "If I went on this trip. I mean, if I visited her just to see what . . . ."

"I know whatcha mean," said the cowboy. "Hell, divorce can be a beautiful thing. If you don't get too burned on the way through it." He chuckled to himself. "And if you get enough in return to make it worthwhile."

"That's not what I meant."

Nobody believed him, of course, but he did not need to go on speaking to this stranger. Or perhaps he did, simply because he was a stranger. He'd never see this cowboy again.

"I have a child there." Ben cleared his throat. "At least, I want to see if the child is mine. I mean, if we're related."

"Well, then, you got a helluva good reason."

"I think so."

"Your wife, maybe not so much, huh?"

"I guess not."

Ben thought about the house he'd left, the basement sofa he had slept on and left unmade with twisted sheets. He recalled the way the house smelled from the Italian dinner Addy had made the night before and ate alone. The sound of the wall clock had ticked loudly as he waited for Rich to pick him up.

"I shouldn't be on this flight. It's too late now, of course, but . . . . I think she was ready to overlook all of this, but then I decided I just had to see for myself. I need to know if it's true. So here I am. Thirty thousand feet over my fate." He shook his head. "I don't know what will be there for me when I get back. But I've got a week of vacation time to sort it all out. If I can."

His neighbor spoke some encouraging words but Ben only heard a blurry line of nonsense. He was lost in his own thoughts. He was on an airplane to Japan to do the right thing, he wanted to declare to the world. Addy had to appreciate his sense of obligation. He needed to check out the situation. Only then could he make whatever choices needed to be made.

"We've been fighting about it for two months," Ben blurted out, "but I know this is right. So finally I just said to her: 'I'm going.' And then I said: 'I'll come back.' I have a week's vacation leave so far and I'm using it. I said I'd be back. And I will come back."

"Of course, you'll come back," the cowboy intoned.

"She can't really be planning a divorce," said Ben. "I'm doing the right thing. It has to be the right thing." He regarded the cowboy. "Isn't it?"

"Ya gotta do what ya gotta do, yessir."

"And I am."

"If it's the right thing, then everything'll work out in the end. That's what my missus always says. You gotta see it through if you wanna know if it's right or not."

Ben nodded and sat for a while. Then he stared out the window on the opposite side of the cabin. The woman eventually felt his gaze and stared back. He grinned apologetically and looked down at his carry-on bag full of old cards and letters.

"I guess you're right."

"Well, good luck with that," said the cowboy. "So what're you gonna say to her when you see her?"

Ben shook his head. "I have no idea. I'll start with *Konnichiwa*."

"*Konnichiwa* . . . . That's 'Hello'?"

"Good morning, good afternoon. *Konbanwa* for 'Good evening' —
first word I ever learned from her."

Ben sank into a trance. What would he do when he arrived? He
did not know how her house looked. He would walk up to the door
and ring the doorbell and wait. He would be dressed in a nice shirt
and trousers, make sure he was clean-shaven, hair combed. He would
smile sincerely, holding the pose until the door opened. The girl he
knew four years before would probably be dressed in modern
clothing, not the traditional *yukata* she wore in the photograph. Her
hair might be longer, perhaps clipped into a ponytail. Her face would
be like cherry blossoms, pink and rosy and pure. Her little nose and
large brown eyes the same as before. Her lips would part and he
would hear passionate words spoken in her light voice, something
like: "Oh, Benjamin, you've come for me!" And she would throw her
arms around him and hug him tightly —

"You awright?" asked the cowboy.

And he would hold her tight, too. He could smell the scent of her
skin, of her hair, as her cheek pressed against his cheek with her black
hair brushing his face. Everything would come back to him, and he
would say something romantic, pulled straight from his heart and not
sent through any filter, something that would make her melt in his
arms — again.

"Must be a good memory," said the cowboy with a chuckle.

And then Addy would appear from the side yard, a spade in her
hand, rubber gloves and kneepads, taking a break from gardening.
She would see him with this woman in his arms and the spade would
grow heavy in her hands. He would see it coming and try to twist
Hanako aside and take the glancing blow on his own body.

The letter and photograph were slipped neatly into his shirt pocket as
Benjamin arrived in Nagoya. It was clear that spring had arrived just
twenty-four hours earlier. The plum trees were in bloom, their small

purple petals littering the ground. As he walked, bags in hand, he was forced to step around splatters of berries. He could also see that the cherry trees with their delicate pale pink blossoms, the beloved *sakura*, were soon to follow. The sun was warm on his face, but the air remained cool and he felt chilled walking through the shadows cast by the tall office buildings and whenever the wind blew along the wide, tree-lined avenues of Japan's third largest city.

He had searched through the trunk of memories in his parents' basement and found the old letters and cards from Hanako, stuffed into a large, tattered envelope held together with a few rubber bands. Carefully copying the address from them, drawing the characters slowly and carefully with an uncertain hand, he remembered the promise he made to her to take a Japanese language course once he returned to Seattle. He did — barely. Work had distracted him and he had skipped many of those night classes. He studied on his own for a while, then gave up when her letters stopped arriving.

Nagoya was the place the cards and letters had come from. That was her home, he knew. It was also her home base after she was transferred back to Japan, leaving him alone in Hawaii. He tried not to think about that last day.

But it was not the last day. He would be seeing her soon, perhaps tomorrow.

A nervous fever swept through him.

Ben's travel agent suggested he contact the American consulate and inform them of his business in Japan, in case he needed their assistance. He was glad they knew what his business was; he didn't. Apparently his case was one of many such cases down through the years: the poor ol' American guy who sleeps with a Japanese woman, then wants her and the baby to come back to the States with him. The paperwork would likely be extensive but not insurmountable, he guessed.

What he didn't know was what he was searching for, what he expected to happen. Why was he even thinking of paperwork? More than once on the plane he wondered if he should simply turn around and hurry back to Addy before it was too late. He had that thought again as he boarded the shuttle bus from the airport into the city.

Why am I here?

He had spent the last ten hours on the plane and he still had not decided. Was he looking for a glorious reunion and living happily ever after? Addy would not allow that. He was not sure he wanted that, either. Or was he looking for a brief visit with an old friend and her new child, just to confirm the child's existence, then leave them in peace and forget that she did exist and continue living his life with Addy, possibly sending Christmas cards and birthday gifts to Japan? He could not allow that. There had to be something in between.

As Ben rode in from the airport, he took in all the sights. It was his first visit to Japan, after all. He had promised to visit when she left Hawaii. It was never that he didn't wish to make the trip. It was more that life pulled that idea out of his head and hid it in a lockbox down at the bank. And in his office. Work, work, work. Never time to make a trip. Then the letters stopped arriving anyway.

Although he didn't really speak Japanese, he still found himself remembering phrases Hanako had taught him while in Hawaii. The words had been relegated to his subconscious when he married Addy. But listening to other passengers on the bus poked his brain, made him remember. *Domo arigatô* ("thank you") and *sumimasen* ("excuse me") would serve him quite well. For anything more, he had the trusty Berlitz book in a jacket pocket, though he was embarrassed to use it openly in public.

After fifty minutes winding in from the rice fields around the airport, through the industrial districts to the densely-packed though elegant city, they arrived at Nagoya Station, the big transportation hub of the city and the Chubu region. There were crowds of skiers freshly back from their short weekend jaunts into the Japanese Alps, just a few bus or train hours north of the city. The station featured an endless maze of corridors, a labyrinth of shops and restaurants.

He grabbed a hamburger at a hole-in-the-wall McDonald's there, ordering it by the English name and pointing to the menu on the wall. The sandwich tasted exactly the same as back home but cost twice as much—as Ben calculated the exchange rate. The Colonel also had a franchise next door. He did not feel he was lost in a foreign land. It was strangely familiar — except for the cacophony of unrecognizable words surrounding him. There were signs marking exits, in Japanese characters and the Roman letter equivalent, but he still did not know which exit was the right one.

Finding his way up to the surface, he consulted the map on a signboard alongside the street. He compared the streets of the neighborhood around him on the signboard map to the map the travel agent had printed for him. It was a short walk to his hotel, he calculated. Fighting the high cost of a trip to an expensive country, the travel agent had arranged for him to stay in a relatively cheap 'business' hotel — cheap by Japanese standards — called the Mont Blanc. In the Japanese *katakana* set of characters used to spell foreign words phonetically, it was 'Mon Buran Hoteru.' This kind of hotel was for businessmen on short trips, travelers who needed none of the luxuries tourists demanded.

He was on a business trip, after all, so he felt at home entering the double doors and stepping into the lobby. The man at the front desk greeted him with a "Good morning" and asked how he might help him. So checking in was no problem, the desk clerk speaking English quite well and the uniformed girl taking his bag up to his room with a sharp, professional demeanor. He offered her some Yen as a tip but she waved him off.

With the door closed, he settled into the closet-sized room. The fatigue of the flight hit him and he sat on the edge of the single bed. The cabinet at the foot of the bed held a TV and across the narrow space to his left was a small desk. The bathroom was a cubicle he had to step up into, but it had a toilet and shower. He stripped down and stepped into the mini-shower, washed off the trip, then pulled on the *yukata* robe that was folded on the bed. He examined the robe: blue and white stripes, the same as what Hanako wore in the photograph, but his robe had the hotel's name and logo on it.

Feeling the start of an adventure, he threw himself on the narrow bed, bumping his head against the wall, and stretched his arms out. He closed his eyes, not sure if he was going to begin dreaming or awaken from a dream. The afternoon traffic din did not disturb him in his seventh floor 'suite' and he drifted off to sleep, forgetting the bustle, not to mention the hustle, of the airport, the rumble and exhaust fumes of the bus, the noise of the underground crowds, and the never ending foreign language around him. For this one moment in universal time, he was free. There was nothing to do this afternoon or evening. He wanted to be well-rested and in good spirits when he went to see Hanako and her child in the morning.

He awoke after his nap and was confused at first. He looked out the window of his room at the city, lights twinkling in office buildings rising like Christmas trees as far as he could see. It was a different world he had entered, but he resigned himself to press on with the reason he had come all the way to Japan. He dressed and went down to the lobby.

After a small, expensive, beautifully set but somewhat bland dinner of Western-style steak and potatoes at the coffee shop attached to the hotel, Ben returned to his tiny room.

He sat on the bed, rummaging through the bundle of old letters he had saved, snatched at the last minute as he hurriedly packed his bags. Reading them, his heart grew warm and he slipped into the past. There, a photo of Hanako on wide Kailua beach in windward Oahu. Here, a clipped ad for what became their little apartment in Aiea. There, a long love letter, adorned with a *haiku* poem, written in blue ink on a sheet of lavender paper which smelled of violets. Here, a photograph of the shy couple taken by the waitress in the Odoriko restaurant in Honolulu, where they dined Japanese style in their own little room with a private serving girl. Hanako wore a *kimono* that night and looked quite gorgeous, even across the years. She always used fancy stationary, often with English phrases imprinted on the sheets of paper, quotes which had no intelligible meaning for a native speaker. Benjamin enjoyed them, nevertheless.

He read the next letter, sent from Japan to him in Hawaii, and remembered exactly what he had been doing the moment before he pulled it from the mailbox. He regarded another photo of the two of them at Waimea Bay on Oahu, bathing in the sunshine, she in the new blue-red-yellow spotted bikini he bought for her. He knew she would look great in it. He wore the short, racing-blue trunks she got for him. He smiled, remembering her claim that he could swim faster wearing that skimpy suit. He was never concerned with swimming, however. Then, somehow, the photo of her in the *yukata* with the baby got stuck in the pile of letters and his fatigued eyes fell on it.

Regarding the photograph at leisure and with a scrutinizing eye, he caught more details of significance. There was, for example, the whale bone clip holding her hair back in a loose ponytail. He had haggled for ten minutes with a Samoan woman at the International Marketplace in the heart of Waikiki to get it. Evidently, she still thought enough of it to be wearing it a few years later.

And a closer look at her bare feet beneath the *yukata* showed the only blemish she had. He could still make out the scar where she had cut her foot while they hiked in the Hawaiian Volcanoes National Park on the Big Island. Driving out for a long day of sightseeing, they did not anticipate having the urge to hike over the jagged, broken lava rocks and so had not dressed appropriately. Wearing flat straw and bamboo sandals that were good only for sliding along the sidewalk or over the smooth sand of Hanauma Beach, she attempted hiking, breaking her sandals on the rough terrain and falling, cutting the top of her foot on the lava rocks. Benjamin picked her up and helped her back to the car, cleaned her wound, and took her to the hospital back in Hilo where they were staying. He saw that scar and remembered everything from that day.

Why do bad things always leave scars and good times leave no tracks?

His fingers came upon another picture. Hanako stood at the entrance to the waiting area in the international terminal of Honolulu Airport. He knew it was the last day he saw her. She stood stiffly in her crisp, navy blue flight attendant uniform, her cap straight on her head, her wings shiny, perched on her breast pocket. He looked closer and saw a smudge on her cheek. Longing for a magnifying glass, he pulled the photo up to the ends of his eyelashes. Staring at the paleness of her cheek he saw the line of tears. She wore that undistinguished smile, the same one she'd used as she held her baby in front of the house in the woods, neither admitting joy nor showing melancholy. That day at the Honolulu Airport was sunny with a high of 88, he remembered. Japan Pacific Air, flight 06, departing at 11:33 a.m. from Gate 21, on May 29, 1987. He was not reading it from anything written on the photo. He knew it. He would always know it. He would never forget it.

Staring at the picture for another hour, Ben finally took a deep breath, then set the photograph aside, along with the *yukata* picture. Collecting all the letters, he replaced the rubber bands holding them together, and turned off the light.

Warm in the *yukata*, he stretched out in the darkness and conjured the images he expected to see the next day: warm smiles, bright eyes, chubby cheeks, and old blue and white *yukata*s.

And *tsuru*.

She had always talked about the Snow Cranes, as if doing so were the same as praying for good luck. They were on his *yukata*, too, he realized. He regarded the pattern, and a voice rose in his head, calling to him, a tender laughter on the wind, maybe on a beach.

"Sometimes I miss *tsuru*," she would say—like one calm, breezy Sunday morning in Hawaii when it seemed that spring had finally turned into summer.

He recalled it so clearly as he lay against the pillow, as though he were reclining on a beach towel at Waimea Bay.

"I love the snow cranes," she had said.

"I love you," he responded.

She had taken his hand as they walked along the North Shore beach, the surf washing over the rocks just off shore.

"When I was little girl," she told him, "I go many times to my grandmother's house in Ishikawa. It is very old house, in the wood. It is my name, too: 'in the wood'—*Nakamori*. Do you know? She always take me to see the *tsuru* dance in meadow. I miss it now. I miss *tsuru*."

"And why is that?" he asked, dodging a sea gull.

"They are symbol of my home."

"That's all?"

"It is warm here, *ne*? I enjoy in Hawaii, yes, but I must go see *tsuru* sometimes. For me, it is a rule, something I feel inside. *Tsuru* are symbol of my land, and when I become sick of home, I think of the *tsuru*."

He smiled, repressed a chuckle, and she asked why.

"Because you said when you get sick of home you think of the snow cranes."

"It is strange?"

He hugged her.

"We call it 'homesick' but it doesn't mean 'sick of home.' It means 'wanting to go home.'"

"Ben-*san*, I am Japanese. We are one people and we must obey our rules. They are not written rules. They are silent rules. I must do things because I must do them. That is only reason. *Wakkata?* You understand?"

"As well as I can," he replied as they walked on.

"Some day I must go my home," she said suddenly. "Will you be sad for me?"

"Yes, of course. And I'll be sad for me, too."

"For you? What do you mean?"

"When you go back to your home, I'll miss you."

She thought for a moment. "Will you cry?"

He had stopped then and looked deeply into her beautiful dark eyes. "I think so."

She lowered her gaze.

"And will you cry?" he asked, the warm wind blowing harder.

"I cry now," was her answer.

"Yes, you do," he said after a pause. "You're not a very good Japanese. You cry all the time, Hanako. I thought Japanese were supposed to hide their feelings. How can you hide them if you're always crying?"

She brushed her windblown hair out of her face, gazed up at him.

"That is how I hide them."

He was puzzled, regarding her.

"Please don't explain it . . . because I don't think I'll ever be able to understand, anyway. It's a good thing I'm not a Japanese."

She broke into laughter. "You be terrible Japanese!"

He laughed, too.

"That's why it's good I have you, my dear Hanako — my 'flower child.'"

She stopped her laughter, surprised that he had managed to translate her name. She asked what his name meant and he had given her the whole history of Benjamin Franklin, elder statesman and inventor. That had impressed her.

But what would she think of him now, showing up at her door?

7

APRIL FIRST, A DAY FOR FOOLS. Bright, clear blue skies, warm sunshine, cool breeze—a day for happy reunions, a day when no new letters were delivered.

After sleeping late and having a leisurely lunch downstairs, Benjamin dressed neatly, carefully, as though he were setting out on a first date. He did not want to arrive too early, did not wish to disrupt the morning routine. He guessed she would be tending to their child's feeding and bathing, then some play time. Or shopping for child things. Doctor check-up, perhaps. He did not know what she would do but he thought it best to arrive after lunch.

He returned to Nagoya Station, a short walk from the hotel, and spent a few anxious minutes trying to decipher the ticket machine. Next he studied the route map posted on the wall. He was assisted by a couple of high school girls dressed in blue and red sailor uniforms. He knew they must be sixteen or so but in those school uniforms they looked like cute twelve-year-olds. They helped him buy the ticket. Then the three of them were pushed by the crowd through the gate and he parted from the girls, found his way to the right platform and, after a several minute wait, he boarded the Fujigaoka Line, heading out to the eastern suburbs.

His stop was the next to the last: Kamiyashiro. That turned out to be just over an hour's ride. As he sat, he stared out the windows that framed the ever-changing, ever-steady view of old traditional houses with their blue tile roofs with upturned corners, mixed with square, modern apartment blocks rising like mountains, and the perpetual power lines crisscrossing the urban landscape.

When the train rolled to a stop beside the small platform, Benjamin stepped out. A finely dressed elderly woman with a cane followed him out of the train car and continued to the end of the platform and down the steps. He held back a moment, scanning the neighborhood from the platform before descending and exiting the station.

Following the hand-drawn map given to him by the front desk attendant, carefully duplicating the printed map they had across the countertop, he made his way the few blocks from the station, turning at the corner grocery, and proceeding up a steep hill that was half slope, half steps. Once at the top he continued through the streets.

A few boys watched him, followed him, then shouted *"gaijin"* at him. Benjamin waved innocently back at them, put on a friendly face. One boy then called "Hallo."

"Have a nice day," Ben called back.

He turned at the next corner, where the street intersected three others and formed a plaza, half-filled with irregularly parked mini-trucks and a couple of white sedans.

According to the map in his hands, the house straight ahead was his destination. The higher position he had there gave him a good view of the house and its yard, separated from the neighborhood by a shoulder-high wall with even higher bushes and two trees. There was a door in the wall. He could see that the doorway led straight to a low veranda. He could see a Japanese-style garden to either side of the stone walk: raked pebbles swirling around small clumps of flowers. He had seen several similar gardens next to the houses he passed while riding on the train.

It felt strange to be looking down upon the house where his one-time lover had grown up. It was Japanese style for the most part, but some modern features had been added, such as the TV antenna, the air conditioner unit set in the second floor window, and the car port.

As Benjamin stood at the crest of the hill, regarding the house, he could see no sign that anyone was at home. The house looked lonely, and a chilly breeze stroked his cheek. He heard the voices of children and turned to see where they were but they were out of sight, their cheerful noises merely echoing through the streets. Except for the architecture, it could have been a neighborhood almost anywhere in American suburbia. It felt like his own childhood nest in Kansas City.

Is one of those voices my child?

He ignored the steady, strengthening wind and pushed himself down the sidewalk, eyes focused on the metal numbers tacked to the post in front of the small driveway. Clouds had collected across the sky, the sky now darker and gloomy.

He stood before the entrance, deciding it did not match the house in the photograph. Nevertheless, this was the right address, the one from the letters Hanako had written while he was in Hawaii.

He saw the doorbell but decided to knock on the rough, oak beam the door was set in. It barely made a sound. He pushed the doorbell button and a clanging sound echoed inside.

"*Hai!*" came a cry, a woman's voice. "*Chotto matte, kudasai.*"

The metal latch fell away and the door swung open.

"*Ara!*" the old woman cried, her voice filled with surprise and, he sensed, tinged with fear.

"*Konnichiwa,*" Benjamin spoke using a soft voice. He was sure he had pronounced it correctly. It was the first phrase he had learned: 'Good afternoon.' No doubt the woman was surprised that a foreign man was at her door.

He assumed the woman, in simple dress and white apron, was Hanako's mother, her *okâsan*. But from her cry of disdain, he gathered that she recognized him, maybe from all the photos she had seen of them. Or she merely guessed who he was. She did not seem pleased that he had come all these miles at great trouble and expense to knock on her door.

"Hanako-*san, onegaishimasu,*" Benjamin uttered, just as he had rehearsed from the phrase book. 'Hanako, please.'

"*Imasen*." The woman's face was expressionless. Rather than being surprised, she now seemed confident and gained resolve in her stern stance. Obviously, it was a problem, all these foreign men coming by, trying to sell some insurance. He understood. Grinning, he tried to appear sincere. He added a bow, hoping to put her at ease.

"*Sumimasen. Watakushi wa Nihongo wakarimasen*," he spoke slowly, remembering what he had written out earlier. He probably did not actually need to tell her that he did not understand Japanese.

"*Hai. Mo kochira ni inai no desu*." And as she continued, her voice became halting and sad. Or irritated.

"*Wakarimasen*." I don't understand.

"*Mo kochira ni inai no desu yo!*"

He had no idea what she was saying, but he could tell she was upset at his presence. Or, perhaps, he suddenly considered, he was at the wrong house. Maybe she was telling him Hanako did not live there. Needing to clarify the matter, he pulled out his phrase book and flipped through the pages, found what he wanted to say and was glad the woman was patient enough to wait for him. He knew the phrases, but in his nervousness they hid from him.

"Hanako-*san no otaku desu ka*?" Ben asked, hoping they were the right words.

"*Mae wa so deshita ga!*" she exclaimed, and turned quickly back inside her house.

"Give me a break, lady," he muttered. Then, in a polite voice to her: "Sorry. *Sumimasen*. After all, I've only studied Japanese for one semester, just a night class. And that was a few years ago."

The door was swinging shut.

"*Sumimasen*," he called. "Does Hanako Nakamori live here?"

She shook her head and closed the door, but he did not know if her shake was a negative reply or if she was just losing patience with this American fool.

"I just want to know if this is the right house," he called.

With the door closed, Benjamin stood on the doorstep for another minute, the chilly wind blowing against his back. Either she did not know who he was, thought Ben, or he had the wrong house. Or, she knew who he was, all right, but did not want him to be there, hating him for what he had done.

What does she know? What does she think I did?

Walking back to the subway station, Ben stopped a couple of high school girls, easy to spot in their uniforms, and showed them the address he had written down. One of them pointed back in the direction he had come.

"Nakamori?" he asked, making sure they were on the same page.

"*So da no,*" one replied. 'That's right.'

He motioned with an arm back towards the house a few blocks away, waved the paper with the address, and pleaded, "*Dozo, dozo.*"

He dipped his head in thanks, an attempt at a bow.

Looking at each other, the girls gradually understood what he was wanting and led him back to the house. The same house. The girls examined the address again, and again pointed at the house Ben had just visited.

"Hanako Nakamori?"

"*Hai. So deshô.*" She pointed to the *kanji* characters on the name post. "*Na-ka. Mo-ri. Nakamori desu.*"

He bowed again and they departed, talking loudly and giggling.

Staring once more at the weathered wooden house, he felt cold. From the corner of his eye, he caught sight of the window curtain sweeping open, a face looking out, and the curtain falling back just as quickly. It was the right house. It was the house that matched the address he had. And the girls had confirmed that it was the house of the Nakamori family, if not also Hanako.

Emotionally exhausted, he shook with frustration and anger. What else could he do? The anxiety he had since boarding the plane at Sea-Tac, the hours of expectation crossing the Pacific, so long suppressed had no place to go but leak out through his eyes, running down his face so unexpectedly. The wind in his face brought more moisture to his eyes and he wiped them with his finger and turned from the house.

His Japanese words had been clear enough, at least when he asked if Hanako lived there. Lived, meaning resides, occupies, is a member of the household, physically present. He was not unclear. The old woman had to have understood. What more could he do? He could not just barge in.

The train from Meito-ku became a subway before it reached the central business district. Feeling the need to think, preferably with some strong coffee, Ben decided to get off at Sakae station and find some place to sulk in the station's huge underground shopping plaza.

Endless shops. It was a strange habit of his, especially being a man, but he window shopped when he was depressed. He thought it had started long ago when he went in search of some gift to purchase for a girl who rejected him. He never found a suitable peace offering, he recalled, but he browsed the windows as a way to distract himself from any unpleasant thoughts. He imagined happier moments—like those affectionate couples strolling arm in arm along the shopping lanes he now saw. He trudged through the maze of corridors, became lost, found his way, became lost again, on and on. Finally, he came to the end—one of the dozens of ends.

Taking the escalator up, he found himself in the middle of a park.

Standing over him, partly blocking the afternoon sun was a brightly painted orange and white metal tower in the design of the one in Paris. This was not the Eiffel Tower, but they had sure made a clever copy of it, thought Ben. Five hundred yen bought him a ride up an elevator to the observation deck of Nagoya Tower, the beacon for half a dozen radio and television stations in the metropolitan area. There were souvenir kiosks and coin-operated telescopes on the observation deck.

He gazed out the finger-printed windows at the sprawling city. The mosaic of bland rooftops, unbroken by any skyscraper, stretched to the horizons in every direction, only the distant crags of the Japan Alps to the north broke the expanse. More immediately to the north was the great magnificence of Nagoya Castle, its two golden dolphins crowning the top of the *donjon*, the main tower, surrounded by its moats and trees, almost sterile in its post-war, rebuilt form. To the south was a narrow blue-green strip of water that must be the busy harbor; he knew it was there from the map but today the water was hidden by the glare of the brilliant sun.

He studied the orderly street pattern, the trees lining the avenues, green canopies like yarn balls marking the parks, the clearing sky now a royal blue. *What am I doing here?* His hands gripped the railing in front of the windows. Fathers and children were also regarding the city from the windows. They laughed and smiled. *Where is my child?* His throat tightened.

Descending in the elevator, the high-pitched, robotic voice of the elevator girl was soft and cute. It helped soothe his depressed mood. The girl was so doll-like that he wanted to take a picture of her. Setting his camera, he decided against it as they came to a halt at the ground floor. It would seem perverse, he decided.

"*Domo arigatô gozaimashita,*" she robotically intoned. Thanks a bunch.

"You're welcome," he mumbled. *But I'm not very welcome here.*

The broad boulevard of Sakura-dori was swept by a brisk wind, and as Ben's fate would have it, the breeze battered his face as he was forced by geography and his map to walk straight into it.

On the way to his hotel to contemplate his next move, Ben came upon a tall, stately, modern building with a humble English sign in front announcing it as the Nagoya International Center. Thinking at least somebody would speak English there, he entered and, checking the directory, found his way up to the English-language library. He said he had a problem and asked if someone could help him. The librarians directed him up to the information and counseling offices.

He sat in one of a dozen chairs, waiting his turn, feeling as though he was seeing a psychiatrist. He was alone, perhaps because it was late. Or, there were not many people with problems, he thought.

A blonde, blue-eyed young man called his number in Japanese, then seeing only Ben sitting in the office repeated it in English.

Ben stood and went up to the counter.

"I'm a bit lost," he began, feeling embarrassed.

"We get that a lot," said the young man with a grin. He was as opposite as anybody could be from the local folks. "That's the sort of problems we fix best."

"Good."

"Where do you want to go?"

He pulled out the address paper, showed it.

"I went to this address but the woman there was not too friendly, so I'm wondering if it was even the right place. That's the first thing. Was it the correct address? I copied it down from a letter I received a couple of years ago. So . . . maybe they moved?"

"I see." The young man took the piece of paper and studied it.

"I'm looking for this person . . . ." Ben pointed to the name written in *kanji* on the paper. "Hanako Nakamori."

The young man gave a loud sigh, spun around in his chair, and called to his partner in the back office.

A tall woman in black slacks and blue sweater, her black hair in a bun, came out to the desk, looking Japanese but somehow not. The American man showed her the address and they discussed directions. She waved Ben back behind the counter and he joined them.

She retrieved a street map, unfolded it and laid it across a long table there.

"Come take a look," she called.

Ben stepped forward, seeing her name tag: CARMEN. Her finger pressed against the map, red-painted nail marking a location. He nodded. He had always been good at geography; with a map in his hand he never got lost. Ben knew that the point marked by her finger was the right location, the place where he had just been.

"Is this the place you're looking for?" asked the woman.

"Pretty sure it is. Actually, I'm trying to find a friend of mine." He looked over her arm at the map. "She lives at this address. Or she used to. Maybe the family moved."

"That's doubtful. They don't move for generations."

"Well, then, I guess I just couldn't understand what the woman was saying to me."

"What did she say?"

"I don't remember exactly. It was all in Japanese and I don't know very much of it. What I remember her saying was '*Mo kochira inai,*' or something like that. Does that sound like anything? Maybe I heard her wrong. She wasn't too happy I knocked on her door, I guess. I thought Japanese were super-polite."

"She said '*Mo kochira ni inai no desu*'? Is that closer to what you heard?"

"Yes, that's it—I think."

"'Not here' is what it means. Or, in other words, she 'doesn't live here anymore.'"

Ben's face went pale. "What?"

"She doesn't live there anymore."

"Oh. So did she move out? Who is living there now? And if she did move, where did she move to? That's what I need to know."

"I can't help you with the answers to those questions, but it would seem that your girlfriend has indeed moved out."

"She's not my—"

He started to insist, out of momentary embarrassment, that the woman he was looking for was not his girlfriend. What difference did it make? It used to be true.

"In that case," he continued, "I was wondering if I could ask a favor of you."

She looked up from the map. "And what's that?"

8

CARMEN TSURUTA'S HAIR WAS MOSTLY BLACK, streaked with Japanese red, a shade of brown. Her cheeks were marked with deep dimples when she smiled fully and her cocoa eyes were warm beneath the straight, Japanese style bangs. She spoke fluent English and, as Ben hoped, fluent Japanese.

As Ben learned, she first came to Japan as a high school exchange student and later returned for a year of college. Finally, she returned again to work for the Japan branch of an American company but found the work stifling her pursuit of her Japanese cultural interests. Now thirty, she worked for the Nagoya International Center as a translator and interpreter, at night working on her doctorate in Asian Studies. When he asked about her name, she replied that she had been married briefly to a Japanese jazz musician. Then he became a salaryman, she explained with some disdain. Actually, she was a Latina from southern California.

"Slow day today, so don't worry about it," she said to Ben as they walked along the breezy sidewalk. "I wanted to get out of there, breathe some fresh air, you know."

They descended into the nearest subway terminal, boarded the Fujigaoka line, heading east, returning to Kamiyashiro in Meito-ku.

"Are you going to get my subway ticket?" she asked, her hands offering to work the ticket machine if he gave her some coins.

He handed over a five hundred yen coin. "Is this enough?"

"Yes, hundred-twenty yen a piece."

She dropped the coin, collected the change, and gave him a ticket, and led him through the turnstile.

"I really do appreciate you coming with me, Missus Tsuruta," said Ben over the steady rumble of the subway car.

"Sorry, but I hate being called 'Missus,'"

"'Mizz,' then?"

"How about Carmen?"

"All right, Carmen."

"And what's your name, *Mister* Pinkerton?"

"Benjamin."

"Nice to meet another *gaijin*."

"*Gaijin?*"

"That's right: a foreigner."

"I knew that, just surprised to hear you say it."

"That's what we are: 'outside people.' But the Japanese usually mean the blonde, blue-eyed kind of outsider. Like Jeff in the office. What I mean, by way of example, I'm not usually called *gaijin*. But don't take any offense. There's a handful of us here that are famous. They're on all the game shows all week—the same *gaijin*, the same shows. I get tired of seeing them. I came here to look at *Nihonjin*. Sometimes that's a mistake, though."

"Why is that?"

"Oh, nothing. Just bitching."

Studying the advertisements on the panels inside the subway car, Ben waited, then replied, "I see."

The house was the same. Maybe the woman was expecting him to return, Ben considered, seeing her standing there. The woman was waiting at the door when they stepped through the small garden and up to the entrance with Carmen in the lead.

He smiled at the woman he had spoken with before but she did not return any smile.

"*Konnichiwa*," Carmen began. "*Shitsurei desu ga. Nakamori-san desu ka?*" Good day, sorry to be rude, but are you Mrs. Nakamori?

"*Hai, so desu.*" — Yes, I am.

"*Sumimasen, Nakamori-san. Jaa, watakushi no tomodachi wa hito saga shitsureishimasu. Hanako-san toiu hito . . . .*" Sorry, but my friend is looking for someone named Hanako.

Ben regarded them as they talked, bowing to each other every sentence or two, the old woman seemingly in a better mood now. His interpreter also became remarkably Japanese in her behavior and speech. Standing silently, he was ignored except for the old woman's occasional wave of her hand toward him. There was usually a scowl on her face when she did so. If this was really Hanako's mother, he wondered, what was she thinking about him? And could this woman be his once-upon-a-time mother-in-law-to-be? It did not seem like a pleasant prospect. Perhaps she recognized him from the start but, hating *gaijin*, pretended not to know him.

He and Carmen were not invited inside and after nearly fifteen minutes of smiling, bowing, and apologizing, Carmen bowed one final time and turned to Ben with a nod of her head. She ushered him through the tiny garden and out to the street.

"Well?" asked Ben.

"Yes and no."

"What do you mean by that?"

"I didn't want to make a scene in front of her, but she . . . . Well, I couldn't just ask you in front of her about the things she said."

"Why? What did she say? Is this the right place, at least?"

"Oh, yes, it's the right house."

"Then where is she?"

"She didn't say. Not exactly. She was too upset to talk about it."

"Upset? By what? She was smiling most of the time you talked."

"That's the custom. Like Pagliacci. Never let anyone see your true feelings. But I've seen enough to know when they're feeling hurt. The eyes don't lie. You hit a nerve, Benjamin, a very raw nerve. She was crying inside."

"Why? What happened? What did she say?"

"You should know. Don't you know?"

"I don't get it."

"The same reason you came here, I guess."

He could not say anything at that moment, the secret laid out in the sun for the world to see.

"Let's go," she said.

The subway was quiet, so she told him what was said between them.

"I asked her if your friend lived there—as you heard—and she started telling me about you coming there earlier asking about her daughter. So I asked her if she would be back later. That's when she started trying to hold her smile. She said something about not having a daughter. Not anymore. Well, what she said was *'koko kara oi dasaremashita.'* That translates literally as 'she was sent away from here.' I'm not sure what she meant. Then she said *'musume wa hitori mo imasen.'*"

"What's that?"

"Literally, 'I don't have a daughter.'"

"You mean she ran away, or something?"

Carmen nodded.

"I asked her if she knew where we could find her. I said what you wanted me to say—about you being an old college friend. Yes, that was believable, hah. And she said *'kanojo no koto wa shirimasen,'* and *'tada hitotsu no wa Ishikawa e ikimashita.'* You heard her."

"She went to where?"

"You're picking it up already, I see."

"I got the *ikimashita* part. That's 'going'—right?"

"Past tense, *went*, but yes, that's right. She said she didn't know where she was, but the only thing she knew was that she had left for Ishikawa."

"Ishikawa? Where's that?"

"Up north, on the Japan Sea. Other side of the Alps."

"Why there? Isn't it cold?"

"That's where her *'haha no uchi'* is."

Ben stared at her a moment and she pursed her lips then translated: the house of Hanako's grandmother, up in Ishikawa Prefecture.

"She went there quite a while back, I suspect."

"But why there?" he asked.

They climbed from the subway station to the street near the NIC.

"Her job transfer was back to Nagoya," Ben said. "Why would she go to this Ishikawa place?"

"That's where her grandmother's house is."

"I mean, why did she go all the way up there to her grandmother's house?"

"You heard Nakamori-*san* ranting. Didn't you figure it out? The woman kicked her out of the house. She kicked her own daughter out. She must have done something bad to be treated like that. And having no where else to go, she must have hiked up to grandmother's house. You know, the grandparents will always look out for their grandchildren."

Returning to the NIC, Ben opened the door for Carmen and they proceeded up to her office.

"I want to thank you for your help."

"Sure. Want some coffee?"

"Yes, thanks."

She began pouring.

"Why was she kicked out of the house?"

It was Carmen asking instead of him. He held up the cup of coffee, staring into the brown liquid, smelling the warm aroma. The cup was hot in his hand.

"I don't know."

"You must have some idea. She was your friend — your girlfriend."

"She — was," he began, wanting to wet his throat and wash down some guilt.

"Was? Oh, I get it. Old flame."

"Well, we met in Hawaii. I guess we were pretty close while we were there. I was there for two years, working. Tough assignment, I know, but—hey, somebody's got to do it, right? And she was flying there two times a week. A stewardess. They call it flight attendant now. One day I met her, we fell in love, spent a lot of time together. Later she had to return to Japan. Then I went back to Seattle and tried to forget her. Why? Because I never expected to be able to come to Japan. Too far for a date, and . . . . Anyway, we were very good friends. Now I'm finally here and she's gone. I certainly never did expect things to turn out like this."

She held up her cup, took a sip. "Like what?"

He reached for the photo in his shirt pocket.

"Like this." He thrust forward the image of Hanako standing at the pine-framed door in her blue-and-white *yukata* with the baby in her arms.

Carmen took it gently from his hand like a fragile paper doll, a priceless gift, and stared at the Japanese girl and the *akachan*.

"Nice looking girl."

"Thanks."

"Yeah, she sure is pretty. I can't blame you for . . . for being very good friends with her, you *tomodachi* you."

"Look closer," he said.

She did.

"Ah, the plot thickens." Her eyes were fixed on the picture. "And the baby? Boy or girl?"

"I don't know."

"Yours?"

He took a sip of coffee. "I presume so."

She looked up.

"So that's why you're here. Family reunion time. Yes, it all fits now. I guess you were pretty close, after all. That must be why the old lady was so upset. Your friend did a no-no. Does she know you're coming?"

"Maybe that's why she went to grandma's house. I mean, if she didn't want to see me."

"Now you're thinking like me. But I've gotten cynical from my own experiences. What about you?"

"I'm not cynical."

She laughed, spilling her coffee.

"You'd never admit it. That's what makes people like you and me cynical." She went across the room and grabbed some paper towels.

He nodded, surrendering to the day's pace. "I suppose."

She soaked up the spilled coffee and tossed the wet paper towels in the wastebasket. "So what are you going to do now?"

"I guess I'll have to go to grandma's house for the family reunion."

"Do you know how to get to Ishikawa? Do you have an address there?"

The letter Ben received in February came to mind. The return address, although in *kanji*, was not quite the same as the earlier letters. It must have been her grandmother who wrote them.

A light bulb went on in his head.

He told Carmen.

"So maybe she doesn't know to expect you, if her grandmother wrote the letters," she suggested. "She's a kind old lady who wants to see her granddaughter together again with her *koibito* and the father of her child. Sounds like a winner, tough lady like that. I like her."

"Don't say that too loudly. I'm still wondering if I'm ready for it."

"Hey, go for it."

A sly grin spread across his face and he tried to hide it.

"What's that?" asked Carmen. "I know a cynical smirk when I see one. What are you thinking?"

"I'm sorry, I wasn't thinking anything."

"Yes, you were. Come on, now. I'm the queen of cynics. You can't fool me. Besides, we've had enough personal revelation today. A little bit more won't hurt, will it?"

He paused, willing his grin away.

"There is a slight problem that makes me hesitant about 'going for it' as you say."

"And what's that?"

The grin returned.

"I'm married."

Carmen suppressed a chuckle.

"You're married? Wow. You do have problems, don't you? Well, don't worry. It's every day stuff for me. Any kids?"

"No. I mean, not with her."

"That's tough. Does she know? Well, of course she knows. She wouldn't let you come here if she didn't know. Am I right?"

"It was difficult. I told her I just wanted to see my child, confirm whether or not it was mine. I couldn't live in peace knowing I had a child in the world."

"And she bought it?"

"Yes. Of course. Why not? That's the truth."

"*Honto ni*? Is it really? Most men wouldn't bother going across the street to take a look at their kid, much less across the world."

"Sorry. But I'm not like that."

"Good for you. Then what're you going to do? Take a look at your kid and then go home like nothing ever happened? That's no answer, either."

Sitting on the edge of the desk, he dropped his chin to his chest.

"Yes, I know. I had the same conversation with my wife. I haven't figure it out yet, but the first thing is still to find her and the baby."

Carmen hopped up from her chair.

"That's right. And that reminds me. I've got a late appointment."

"Oh? But I was going to invite you to have dinner. Any Mexican restaurants in town? Some kind of payment for your time and trouble today."

"Oh, it's my pleasure. And my job."

"Really? Shall we go? How did you say it? *Ikimashô ka*? Is that it?"

"That's it, but I've got a date tonight. Seriously."

"Japanese?"

"Of course."

"I thought you'd given up on Japanese men after your divorce."

"Oh, they're lousy husbands, but they treat you great on a date."

"Hey, Carmen," her colleague, Jeff, the blond young man, called, "before you get all excited about tonight, I got a message for you."

He handed her a slip of paper.

"I see," Ben continued. "How about a rain check, then?"

"You are persistent." She took the memo casually, starting for her jacket. "If you're in town long enough, then all right."

"Great."

She pulled on her leather jacket, paused to read the note.

"That bastard."

"What?"

"I said, 'that bastard.' He canceled again. Third time in a row. Damn overtime work. If he thinks that'll put me off this time, he's crazy—"

"Then you're free tonight."

She crumpled the note in her hand, dropped it in the wastebasket, shrugging her shoulders and nodding.

"Whatever bad traits American men have—and there's plenty—these Japanese men have them magnified by a factor of ten."

"Are you serious? I find Japanese women to be better than most American women."

"That figures," she sighed, frowning. "You're lovesick over them. That makes you a little biased, too. A lot's been written on the subject, trying to analyze why Western men are so hung up on Japanese women. Ask me again sometime and I'll let you read them. Maybe I should change my dissertation topic, I know so much about Japanese women . . . ."

He followed her out of the office. In the corridor, she turned to him.

"Well, you take care of yourself. Hope you find your girlfriend and your kid. Good luck getting up to Ishikawa. That's what they call Snow Country, you know. They probably still have some this time of year. And good luck . . . for whatever."

"Thanks, but if your date canceled, let me take you to dinner."

"Benjamin Pinkerton," said Carmen with a loud sigh, "you are a married man with a Japanese mistress, and she's got your child. And now you're coming on to me? What a guy! Don't you ever give up? You've got a big neon sigh on your forehead that's flashing 'unsafe' in red and yellow. If I go out with you, not only will I be helping you continue your sleazy ways but I may get corrupted as well. I don't think I can handle it tonight."

"I'm not coming on to you. You're just the only English-speaking person I know in this whole city."

"How about Jeff, back there?" She chuckled, thumbing at her colleague.

"I get along better with ladies, and I feel like talking. There's no reason we should both eat supper alone. Come on, you probably know a good place. Otherwise, I'll be stopping in at that pizza place near my hotel."

"Ugh! You know they put squid and corn, octopus and potatoes on pizza over here? I'll save you from that major sacrifice. I've been craving some Mexican food—which isn't too available here. But I know a place."

Benjamin carefully wiped his mouth with the wet cloth he had first used to wipe his hands when they sat down at the table. He looked across at his guest.

"I always remember the events of my life," he said, "as though I'm looking down on myself from a cloud, regarding someone who is a stranger. I know it's crazy, but that's the way it is."

Hiding a cynical smile, he sat back in the seat across from Carmen in the intimate and expensive La Mex restaurant, watching her finish the last bite of her Japanese-style burrito—something on the menu called the 'Tiwana.'

"There I am, but I'm just somebody, an acquaintance." He glanced around, wondering if anyone noticed his ranting. "I observe him— me—as someone else who can act as I did but without me—the real me, and if the present me is not the real one then I don't know which one is—without me having to take the responsibility for anything 'I' might have done. It's much too embarrassing for me to tell perfect strangers."

"I'm hardly perfect." She sipped her wine. "You're just trying to hide your past." She took a longer sip. "Or hide from your past. That's probably it." She arranged her fork and knife on the plate, signaling she was finished. "Sure, Ben, you just change from first person to third person and you're scot free. Neat trick, that. What a con artist!"

"That was four years ago," he said. "That wasn't me, that was someone else. That was *him*. That was Ben Pinkerton, third person, that's who. For better or worse."

"I know what you mean," she said followed by a long sigh, slyly regarding him over her wine glass.

"Okay," he conceded, "maybe I did tell it a bit more dramatically than it really happened, but it doesn't matter what we really said, does it?"

Actually, Ben thought, the questions and answers he and Hanako spoke to each other were of no interest or worth to any passerby or archivist, or even a lowly gossip. Nor did the words mean much to the two of them on that evening, but years later perhaps they would wish to recall them, if only for their own amusement. He ran them through his memory again that first night, laying in his bed, feeling a rush of excitement he had not felt since high school. The wonderful sensation of puppy love. He played back the conversation they'd had and he cheerfully concluded it was not mere infatuation but the real thing. The real thing, he knew, grinning.

"Puppy love lives on," Carmen said with a smirk, pushing her plate away and waiting for dessert. "I could use some of that these days. Love conquers all, doesn't it, Ben?"

"Well," he went on, "eventually, we got to learn about each other. I met her later near her hotel, and she was dressed in casual clothes — a pair of pink shorts and a knit pullover. She was even more striking than when she was in her swimming suit. We went for a late-night snack, then a drink. She had the next day off, she told me between drinks — she had orange juice, and I, in her honor, had a Pepsi instead of a beer."

"And?" Carmen pressed.

"I told her I had the day off, too. Really, I was taking the day off to spend time with her. I suggested we go see more of Oahu." He was beginning to relax a little, he recalled, but he had still tried not to stare at her. "And she said 'that would be nice.' She was wonderful. I mean, her voice was so tender, so soft and warm, it really relaxed me. See, as a flight attendant, her time in Hawaii was always brief. She never had the opportunity to explore much beyond Waikiki. I told her that's the worst part of Hawaii. It is, you know. But it's the only place where there are hotels. You have to go there if you're a tourist. I told her I'd take her to see the real Hawaii. So the next day we drove up the coast to see some other beaches. She was very thankful."

Carmen laughed.

"Benjamin, I don't believe a word of it. I mean, how old were you? Almost thirty, you said?"

"Thirty-three."

"Sounds like 'Tales of Adolescence' to me."

"It's absolutely true. I swear. Ah, you're probably jealous because it was so sweet and innocent. But what's wrong with that? Can't a tarnished thirty-year-old soldier be impressed with innocence? You want corniness, huh? Well, I even bowed—very solemnly, Japanese-style—when we finally parted, after we set a time for the next day."

"All right, Ben, I believe you. I wish you all the luck in the world finding this lovely lady of yours. She sounds too good to be true. How'd you ever let her get away, then?"

The thoughts crept back into his mind, the long, lingering dramas repeated in his long flight's nightmares. How *did* he ever let himself forget Hanako and fall into a comfortable but dull marriage with Addy that now seemed to be so fragile?

"That's another story, I'm afraid," Ben said. "A very long story."

"Then it'll have to wait until next time. But when that'll be, I don't know. You're leaving for Ishikawa in the morning, so maybe I'll never get to hear it. Too bad."

"Well, don't worry, it's not so interesting."

"It could be, depending on how you tell it," and she tilted her head to one side, her dark eyes beaming in a way he had not seen all evening, and for a lot longer than that at home in Seattle. "And you wanted to read my books, don't you? About why you guys fall in love with Japanese gals?"

"I already know the answer to that."

"Do you?"

"Yes, I do."

She gazed into his eyes a moment, then looked away as though expecting to see her boyfriend in the shadows of the restaurant.

"Thanks for the dinner, Ben." She reset her eyes on him. "I guess you're a gentleman, after all. Why don't you come back with me and finish your story? I'd love to hear it. It's been a long time since I've been with another . . . American."

Ben stared at her, wondering at first if all the Sangria had affected her or whether it was her cheating Japanese boyfriend. Either way, it felt awkward. It suddenly made him *feel* truly married. He could not go back home with her without giving thought to whether it was right or wrong.

"Do you do this often?" he asked, swirling the last swallow of wine around in the glass.

"That wasn't cool of me, was it? You said you're getting divorced. But I guess you're still too close to it. On the other hand—" She took the glass gently from his hand and finished it for him—"you could be saying 'screw the bitch back home' and be screwing me, too."

For a moment they regarded each other, the dim lighting in that corner of the restaurant helping protect them from the seriousness of each other's gaze.

Ben burst into laughter which swept away the mood.

"I'm sorry. That was not me talking. It must be the wine. I'm a bit woozy now, Ben."

"I guessed it was." Embarrassed, he still managed to maintain his composure. How silly he must have sounded to her, telling her a dumb story like some lovesick schoolboy.

"Goodnight, Ben," she said, offering her hand.

"Are we finished?"

"I need to get to bed. Got a big day tomorrow. I'm taking some businessmen from Nebraska to see some wheat fields up in Gifu. This is the worst part of the job. Thanks again for dinner. I'll get the wine tab."

They got up, each grabbing for their own bill.

"Say, what if I need a translator again?"

"Didn't you say your girlfriend spoke English?"

"Yes, but I meant on the way there."

"Sorry, but I just met you," she said with a chuckle that seemed hollow.

"Okay, okay."

"Sorry." She looked at Ben with eyes that warned she was about to give him a kiss.

"That's all right. Thanks for your help today, Carmen. Couldn't have done it without you."

She pulled out a *meishi*—business card—from her purse and handed it to him.

"You're welcome. And if you do get into trouble, here's my number at NIC. Hell, call for any reason. I like talking to you, Ben. Look me up on your way back."

She stretched up then and pecked his cheek with her moist lips.

"*O-genki de,*" she said. Take care.

9

THEY SPOKE IN JAPANESE across the aisle between their beds. The lights were low and the din of traffic outside a steady hum as Hanako shifted on her bed. She adjusted the delicate lace on the hem of her nightgown and the flight attendant who shared the room remarked on it, asking where she got it.

Hanako replied that it was purchased from a store in Waikiki by her new friend, the American businessman.

A salaryman? Megumi clarified. And an American at that!

Hanako defended him, but Megumi was strict with her junior colleague. When she changed her tone from sounding too serious to teasing, Hanako calmed down. It was her responsibility to see that the younger ladies did not go too far in bending company rules. The long, overseas flights were particularly dangerous, with all manner of criminals and lechers ready to pounce on her charges.

You are perfect in face and figure, Megumi told her as though it was a list of her faults. You are beautiful to American men. I know Japanese men will be afraid to speak to you, but these Americans, they always are so forward. I worry about you, Megumi explained, because you are the most physically beautiful. They will come to you first among us. You must be careful.

How old are you? Hanako asked her suddenly. She answered by saying simply that she was hoping to marry her long-time boyfriend, a Tokyo salaryman, after she retired next year at the ripe old age of thirty-five.

And you, Hanako, young lady, do not be so quick to indulge in the strange, exotic, dangerous customs of these far-flung ports of call. The repercussions could be serious, not only for you but for all of your flight attendant sisters, and the good name of your company. Be careful, Hanako. Do not be so easily swayed by the fancy words of strangers.

She was not a teenager, Hanako reminded Megumi, she was twenty-four and she would certainly keep her bearing in line with her company's image and her own conservative sensibilities.

Just be careful, Megumi warned her, turning out the light. Be always on guard for your feelings, too.

In the dark, Hanako told her about her second date with Benjamin-*san*. They had visited Waimea Bay this time, and it was the most beautiful beach she had ever seen, much better than Kamakura — or the beaches in Miyazaki, Megumi's home. When Hanako returned to Hawaii on the flight next week, he promised to show her the windswept heights of Na Pali.

American men fall in love easily, Megumi muttered in the stillness before turning over, away from her, speaking the final sleepy words: "*Oyasumi nasai.*"

Hanako spoke no more, but in her mind she was composing letters to him. To *him*. Benjamin-*san*. She had never written to an American before; indeed she had never known one. Not up close. She worried about her English and she planned to buy an English-Japanese dictionary when she was back in Japan.

Hanako came through the gate, pulling her flight bag behind her on a tiny cart. Before she could look around for him, some of the other attendants spoke among themselves with muffled voices.

"*Koibito desho*," she heard them. Her lover, they thought. "*Gaijin-san, ne.*" A foreigner.

We are the foreigners here, thought Hanako.

She hesitated going up to him, standing across the corridor in a pink and blue Aloha shirt, a bouquet of pink flowers in his hands. Her colleagues were with her; she could not endure their teasing. They had begun taunting her when she was coming back late to the hotel where they all stayed. She started declining to go out with them on their off-time. Then they saw her once walking down Kuhio Avenue hand in hand with her *gaijin* friend. It was not illegal, not against company rules to date Americans while overseas, but the other attendants were putting pressure on her to stick to her own kind. Maybe they were jealous, she thought. She almost did not care now; she was too much in love.

Then why did she continue to pretend not to see him and turned the corner with her colleagues? She knew she would see him later. He would never understand the customs of her colleagues. How could he ever accept that she could not do certain things, such as greet her lover in front of her colleagues? He would probably embrace her, maybe try to kiss her, right in front of everyone. She would feel so embarrassed.

He followed them, down the corridor, through the security gate and out to the curb where a private hotel limousine waited to whisk them straight to their hotel. Company rules stated that all personnel must report to their overnight residence before going off duty.

"Hanako-*chan*," Megumi spoke to her. "*Koibito imasho ka?*" I guess he's your boyfriend, isn't he?

She could not ignore him any longer and stopped at the curb as the others climbed into the limousine. She counted to *jû* and turned to face him, aware of the others' curious eyes.

"*Konnichiwa*, Hanako," he called, grinning. He performed his best practiced bow.

She heard the flight attendants giggle, then call her to join them for the ride. Time to go.

"I am sorry, Ben," she said in a soft voice so no one else could hear her, "but I must go to the hotel right now."

He smiled but she saw the disappointment in his eyes and wished she could say something else to make him feel better.

"These are for you," he announced, offering her the flowers.

She took them quickly, forced a brief smile, and climbed into the limousine. The door closed and they drove off. She looked back and saw the puzzled look on his face.

"*Nan desu ka?*" Megumi asked her. What's wrong?

She began crying.

"*Kare-shi wa suteki desu ne,*" Megumi remarked to her, patting her shoulder. Your boyfriend is good looking.

That evening her colleagues went out together while she stayed in her room, waiting for the phone call which never came.

For three weeks she had been stationed in Tokyo for special training.

At the staff lodging back in Honolulu, Megumi ran back to her room and closed the door silently, nudged her sleeping roommate gently until she awoke. Hanako's eyes were full of fright, staring into the wild eyes poised above her. Then she was told that her *koibito* was downstairs waiting for her.

How could that be? she asked.

Never mind that, Megumi scolded. Just go while you have the chance. Go to your lover.

But you are the one always telling me to be so cautious, Hanako replied, puzzled, still sleepy. Why do you let me go to him?

Because I am happy for you, Hanako, was Megumi's surprising reply. I cannot go, so I shall be happy through your happiness. Now go. Go to this man you say is so kind to you. He is still waiting.

Hanako glanced at the clock, nearly one o'clock. But Megumi was pulling her up from the bed. With her help she got dressed and brushed her hair. Then she was secretly ushered into the hallway, and pushed toward the elevators.

Hanako was arguing and Megumi was telling her to be quiet, that it was all right. No one would know, she insisted, and she would keep it confidential.

He bowed deeply when they arrived in the lobby.

"*Domo arigato*," he spoke to Megumi. Thanks. "*Konbanwa*," he spoke to Hanako. Good evening.

She fell into his arms.

"I missed you," he told her as Megumi left them. "It's been nearly a month since I saw you last. I'm sorry it's so late."

Megumi smiled as the elevator doors closed.

"I am sorry, Ben," Hanako cooed, sleepily.

"The flight is delayed."

"I'm too tired to . . . to go on date."

He held her, looking down over her tired face, still radiating beauty, her eyes opening and closing.

"I know you want to go back to sleep, but . . . " he lifted her up into his arms, her head flopping against his shoulder, "would you like to come back to my room? and sleep in my bed?"

A sleepy grin spread across her face as her eyes remained closed.

He gazed at her, wondering about the future, as she slept dressed in only his pajama shirt.

She flopped down beside him on the beach towel, the hot June sun melting the lotion on her back.

"I got a letter today," he told her, pulling it out of his knapsack, "from my parents."

"Is it happy letter?"

"Well, that depends. I wrote about you last time and I asked what they thought about you."

"You wrote about me?"

"What's wrong with that?"

She frowned, her face reddening.

"It is not polite, is it?"

"I just said I met a girl here and we were going out, and that I loved you—"

Her shriek startled him and drew the attention of their neighbors.

"You write you love—me?"

"Yes, because I do. It's true."

In the warm sunshine her pale skin blushed from her forehead down to her white belly. Like him, she did not tan easily. She pulled on her T-shirt, sitting up beside him.

"I'm sorry, Hanako, but I wanted to tell them."

"For what reason?" She was in shock.

"I love you. I want to tell everybody. I want the whole world to know."

She clapped her hand over his mouth.

"It is private thing, *ne*? You not tell all your friends. How many you tell? It is private for us alone. Please don't tell anyone."

Turning away, he thought he heard her crying. She did that a lot, he knew.

"I also wrote that you were Japanese."

She stared at him sternly.

"Maybe it doesn't make any difference," he continued. He could not accept her cross expression. "What is it? Is it because of your parents? What did *your* letter say? You didn't tell me."

"I did not write about you!" she exclaimed.

"Why not?" he asked but knew the answer even as the words fell from his mouth.

He laid back on the towel.

"Well, don't worry. My parents were not enthusiastic about what I wrote. I forgot to tell you something about my folks, Hanako. Maybe I should tell you, but I didn't think it would be . . . polite."

She rolled over to face him.

"Please say what is it."

He gave her a quick kiss which caught her by surprise and her innate response was to wipe it away before anyone saw it.

"My father was in World War Two."

"You said before."

He nodded.

"Yes, but I didn't tell you he fought in the Pacific. Actually, he was an airman. He flew in the airplanes that bombed Japan."

She looked away, painfully.

"He was a bombardier. That's the guy that—"

"I know. It's bomber!"

He waited a moment, then placed his hand on her bare shoulder.

"Please no hands in daylight," she instructed, but she did not remove his hand.

"Hanako, I'm sorry. I shouldn't have told you. I love you, and nothing will change that. If we go further, I would have to tell you anyway. I couldn't go on without telling you. You would have to find out sooner or later. Hanako, I don't know how to say it. Help me."

"Is that all you say?"

He sighed. "No . . . ."

"Please stop."

She waited, cringing.

"Let me finish. I know he flew—at least—two missions . . . ."

"No! I don't want to hear," she cried.

"Over . . . Nagoya."

She sucked in a sharp breath, and let out a long exhale.

"I'm sorry, Hanako. It makes no difference to me where you come from."

Suddenly she spun around. "It makes difference where *you* come from!"

He shook his head. "You're right. You and me . . . we are not those people. We are separate from all that."

Her hands went to her face, hiding her tears. Between her sobs she was telling him something, but he couldn't understand her muffled words.

"I'm sorry, Hanako. I'm sorry."

The subject was forbidden from then on, but it was easy to forget as warm, playful days of July burned steadily through August and settled comfortably in the hazy afternoons of quiet September.

They stopped along the steep trail, where it leveled, just to embrace and then began kissing passionately.

"*O-hisashiburi desu,*" she sighed, wrapping her arms tightly around his shoulders.

"A long time. Yes," he whispered in her ear.

But they had further to go, climbing up the trail to Sacred Falls. It was hidden away in a seductive, beautiful tropical forest, known to tourist guides but too much trouble for most people. Luckily, it was not often visited. During the week, especially after the usual summer vacationers descended on the islands, it lay invitingly virgin, its cool waters welcomed by weary hikers.

Two miles' tough climb up Kaluanui Valley to the cliffs where the cool spring waters plunged down to form mirror-like pools, they sat on a huge rock, watching the waters fall, feeling the spray on their faces. Their boots were off and their feet dangled in the cold pond.

Jungle birds cried around them but no other creatures shared the pool with them. They were alone.

Realizing that, they again embraced and kissed wildly without even an eye turned down the trail for other visitors.

Before the kisses paused, her green University of Hawaii T-shirt was up over her shoulders, his own matching shirt pulled up to mid-chest. His hands cupped her breasts. Her hands held his face.

They parted their lips only long enough to pass their shirts quickly over their heads. Once bare from the waist up, their lips sought each other again. And their hands groped their hips. He lay back against the rock and she dropped against him, her hips pressing hard against him. He was slightly alarmed; she had never been so assertive.

The sun beat down on his forehead through the trees, the frigid waters chilling his legs. Opening his eyes, he regarded the angel posed over him, water dripping off her pale, lithe body, lost in the encircling sunlight of early October.

"*O-hisashiburi,*" he sighed. It was a long time.

For an hour they swam nude in the pool, only the birds watching them. So chilling were the waters that they were happy to lounge on the warm rock in the full sunlight. They dried quickly, dived into the pool once more, and repeated everything.

"This is like *rotemburo*," she remarked to him, lounging in the cool waters. "In Japan we have outside *onsen* we call *rotemburo*."

"What's an *onsen*?" he asked, laying on the rock, his arms dangling in the water below, seeing her white form through the water.

"It is hot spring. We like to go to the *rotemburo* in winter. My grandmother's house is near one. We can sit in hot spring and drink *sake* and see snow falling around us. It is like winter wonderland."

"But this water's cold."

"It's refreshing."

Finally, the afternoon had grown too hot for them and they took refuge in the pool itself, swimming. Or just holding each other and gazing into each others' eyes.

A five day weekend lay ahead of them and they were intent on maximum their enjoyment. The months had not been kind to them, and their schedules had viciously crisscrossed as if conspiring to keep them apart. This time, however, they matched. Each time they met, they planned some way to be together forever. By the end of the fifth day, they had signed the lease for the twelfth floor apartment in a high-rise apartment complex overlooking Pearl Harbor. Never again would they have to seek private pleasure in public forests in the afternoons or on public beaches in the dark. A love nest had been secured.

"Can't talk long, Rich," said Ben into the phone. "I've got a dinner party to go to."

"They can't keep away from you, eh?"

"I'm sorry to tell you but it's not business."

"That's why I'm calling. You haven't sent any reports for three weeks now. Is everything all right there? I would've thought you'd be wrapping things up by now. You've been so anxious to get out of that sinful place, I know, guy."

"Who, me? Leave Hawaii? Are you kidding?"

"I'm glad to hear you're finally enjoying yourself—"

Hanako came up to him from behind and jumped on his back, knocking the phone from his hand. Ben spun around, grabbing her thigh with one hand to steady her and scooping up the receiver with the other hand. Hanako was giggling loudly, Ben catching his breath.

"—the other hotel there."

"What? What did you say, Rich?"

"I said I haven't gotten the rest of the report on that other hotel. I don't even know the name of it, or an address."

Ben shook off his girlfriend, dumping her on the bed where she bounced around in her bra and panties and arrived on her feet beside him again.

"Didn't you get the papers I telexed to you? That was a week ago."

"I'll look again, but I don't think we have them in the office. Barb doesn't have them and the new girl, Kate's her name, doesn't know Jeanie's filing system yet. We're in a bit of a mess here."

"So don't blame me—"

He saw the report folder under a loose pile of Hanako's pantyhose on the corner of the dresser, and slid it out, staring at it.

"Wait, Rich—I have it."

"You?"

"I'm sorry, I thought I already sent it but I just found it here. I'll send it out first thing in the morning."

"All right. You do that, guy."

"Got to run now, Rich."

"Okay. And Ben?"

"What?"

"Don't enjoy Hawaii too much."

"Right."

He hung up the phone and dived onto the bed, pulling her down with him, rolling among the blankets and sheets, slipping out the opposite side and crashing to the floor.

"It's good news?" Hanako asked as Ben picked himself up.

"What? The phone call? That's my boss, wondering why I haven't sent out a report."

"Your boss? It's serious?"

"Oh, no. We're friends."

He kissed her, crawled up to his knees and gathered her up into his arms.

"Come on, you haven't taken your shower yet."

"You haven't, too," she cried, grabbing the door jamb in mock protest.

They both end up in the shower.

It was not a formal affair. Hanako was meeting some of her colleagues at the Monterrey Bay Canner's, a seafood restaurant at the Pearl Ridge shopping center near the new apartment they shared when she was in town. She wore pink Bermuda shorts, which she loved so much that she never wore anything else outside. He wore the lavender aloha shirt she gave him for his birthday. Their friends — *hers*, actually — were dressed in nicer clothes, something he had noticed among Japanese tourists. They always dressed more formally, even if their clothing did not look very comfortable for the relaxed atmosphere of Hawaii. But it was their party, anyway. They could dress anyway they wished.

"Congratulations!" their friends sang out in English, following the *Omedetô* cries.

Hanako blushed, thanking them for coming to help celebrate the one year anniversary of their first date. It was all they had to celebrate. He celebrated the first day he saw her, when he was too shy to speak to her. Hanako told her friends the story, as he had told her, and they were all amused.

"Congratulations, Benjamin-*san*," they cried.

Hanako leaned over and kissed him, full on the lips, surprising him and their Japanese friends. Their eyes were lowered when she parted from him, and no one spoke for a moment.

Hanako was concerned for a second, then laughed and called out "*Itadakemasu!*"

They began eating.

The conversation, mostly in Japanese, was lively as the meal went on. They were happy for her, happy for him. And secretly worried that these two might go and do something that would cause ruin in each of their innocent families.

Yumi, who would be Hanako's roommate now if Hanako was not spending her off-duty time in Ben's apartment, held up a camera and begged the happy couple to pose for a photograph. Hanako was more than delighted, dragging her boyfriend to the side of the parking lot in front of some tropical landscaping.

"Say '*chizu*'," Ben offered.

"No," Hanako corrected him. "It's '*chiizu*'. '*Chizu*' is a map."

"*Warate kudasai*," Yumi called to them, first the couple, then the whole group. Smile, please.

When they received copies of the pictures, Ben saw that none of them had smiled, except Hanako and him. And her smile was the widest, happiest grin he had ever seen in a photograph. She was in love, he could clearly see. And he was, too.

When he returned home from his office one rainy day in February, he found the door to his Aiea apartment unlocked.

Hanako was home early. She was crying.

When he asked what was wrong, she rushed to him, embraced him, and showed him the letter.

Of course, he could not read it in Japanese, but she explained that it announced a change in her home base. Beginning in June, she would be based in Nagoya—the airline's headquarters. Before that, however, she would be in Tokyo for training. It was a promotion.

"What shall we do?" she cried.

She was still in her uniform, her hair still pinned up, cap on. Her hand was rubbing his back through his shirt. Her tears ran onto his cheek.

He set down his briefcase, gathered her in his arms, and escorted her into the bedroom. He pulled the curtains closed and lowered himself on the bed beside her. Her flight wings pin stuck his neck when he pulled her close.

"We'll just have to make the most of the time we have," he said.

They had always known the day would come, but to mention it was taboo. The forbidden subject was in their minds nearly every day, yet they never allowed themselves to think about it, even to make any plans for it. Like a terminal illness, the best remedy was for the patient to die before he knew he was sick.

"Yes," she responded, staring deep into his soul.

Late in the evening they were still on the bed, the moon shining blue through the curtains. The pillows were wet from tears, the sheet hot from their bodies. They lay together, holding each other.

Soon, the south-facing windows looking out over Pearl Harbor let the sunrise in. Exhausted, still in their crumpled clothes, they awoke from their brief sleep. They did not have to speak; they had learned to communicate with each other silently.

Why then, Ben might wonder later, could they not feel each other's desire?

They continued with their planned weekend trip to the Big Island. Now the hike could help to soothe their frazzled nerves, too.

They drove the rental car out to the Hawaiian Volcanoes National Park. Puffs of sulfur steam from air vents on the Kilauea caldera were their first hint that they were driving across the slope of one of the world's most active volcanoes. Stopping at the first lookout point, the trail was misleadingly simple until it rose over a ridge and broke through the trees to the railing at the rim of the huge pit. There before them it lay: two miles wide, and five hundred feet deep. Realizing how small and insignificant they were in comparison to nature, they were in awe.

The park road wound down around the crater, soon crossing it at the far, lower end. As they went, the road cuts in the endless plain of lava rock left them humbly silent. The sheets of dried, cooled lava — a'a, the jagged, chunky kind, and *pahoehoe*, the round-edged, ropy kind — spread across the plain like a lumpy asphalt parking lot. For mile after quiet, desolate mile, they went. Looking back from time to time, the cinder cone of Pu'u Pua'i rose starkly from the end of the barren Devastation Trail.

Finally, the road descended over the ridge formed by the volcano, dropping down to the coast and the brilliant blue sea. They stopped at another lookout point and climbed up the wooden tower there to see the view. The winds whipped past them, whistling in their ears. Beneath the sizzling fire of the afternoon sun, the sheets of lava took on a luster, sparkling in the sunlight. The winds were chilly and they held each other for warmth as they felt the desolation of the place.

Leaving the Kilauea Caldera section of the park, they turned the car northwest and started up the narrow road to Mauna Loa, second highest peak on the island, rising to over 13,000 feet. As the road bent and curved up the slope, zigzagging through cuts in old lava flows and around stands of trees, it grew even narrower. She worried that they might meet another car coming down on the one-lane road. With hairpin turns every few meters, she insisted he honk the horn at every turn. He worried about more dramatic events, such as what they would do or how they would get down from the mountain if it were to suddenly erupt and spill burning lava down the slopes.

Eventually they reached the first lookout, pegged at 6600 feet—over a mile high and yet less than twenty miles from the sea coast. The paved road ended there in a wide circle, but the trail continued up to the caldera rim at the peak. Beside the turn-around was a small, stone gazebo for picnicking. They had brought no lunch but they sat in it anyway. For several minutes they gazed from the gazebo out at the vast expanse before them. The winds blew strong there and the wide, gaping caldera of Kilauea stretched below them like a monster buried in the earth waiting for an unsuspecting giant to step into its open mouth. She was frightened, feeling so isolated, so utterly alone in this primitive place.

There were no other cars at the parking circle, so they believed they were alone. They stood on the porch of the gazebo, set on the mountainside with wild thorn bushes covering the lower slopes. They were just there for a tiny point of time on the calendar of the Earth, he told her but she was not relieved. Did that somehow make their love less significant?

As the sky grew darker, clouds collecting, the wind surging stronger against the gazebo, she wrapped her arms around him, hugging him tightly. He continued gazing out at the ocean far, far below. She went to the car and retrieved the beach towel.

The slopes, yellow with dry, brittle grasses and striped by crooked brown lines of old lava flows, filled him with pride. And fear. He knew his place in the world, as though he had stepped back from the fury of life and examined its flaws at leisure.

When he turned to tell her how he felt, he saw her body shielded by the large beach towel. Her legs were bent up, her arms tucked around her knees, the towel thrown over her shoulders. He joined her under the blanket.

"I shall miss you, Ben-*chan*," she said, hugging him.

"Don't talk like that. We'll figure something out. We've still got six weeks together. At least. We'll be together again, I know. Sometime."

He started to say more but she held her finger to his lips.

"Please, speak no more." Her voice choked. "Hold me."

"No, we *have* to talk."

She shook her head, as though she had been chased and was now cornered, out of breath, too tired to resist, too exhausted to fight.

"It is my blame," she cried. "I should never go dating with you. I know I go away someday, so it is best I never meet you. Now we are sad. Now we will be so sad for long time. I am selfish girl."

"No, Hanako. It's not your fault. It's not anybody's."

Tears coursed down her cheeks.

"I am Japanese. You are American. We cannot be together, never. My family . . . ."

"Yes, I know," he said. He let out a sigh of resignation and a grunt of consternation. "Your grandfather was killed in the war, your mother hates Americans, your brothers would beat me up, your co-workers would kick you out. You've told me before, like it excuses every little thing we do. It doesn't, though. Can't we just be *us*?"

She smiled at him, and at first he thought he had changed her mind and she was in agreement. But the longer she held her smile, the more he knew that she was hiding her true feelings from him.

And they had grown so close these past few months!

"I am Japanese. I must go my home."

"*To* my home, dammit!"

"No, *my* home. In Japan."

He shook his head in frustration, feeling his eyes become moist. That was her answer. And he was American, so he must go home, too. Those were the rules.

"I'm sorry, Ben," she cried. "But I love you."

His ears played tricks on him and he thought she said she was sorry for loving him.

Stars. There were only stars around them as they lay on the sand. There were only breezes, cool breezes, touching them as they touched each other. Some day the stars would not be there. A day would come when he would look at the stars, remember the girl, weep, and swear never to gaze at them again. Solemnly, she promised never to watch the stars again, too.

"Here's a present for you."

"For me?" She was leaning against the balcony railing. "Why do you give me?"

"Because I want you to have it."

"What is it?"

She took the package, wrapped in pink paper with orchid prints, examining it.

"It's pink," he admitted. "That's your favorite color, isn't it?"

"Oh, Ben-*chan*."

"Open it."

Walking back to the living room and sitting on the sofa, she carefully released the ribbon, pried up the tape, unwrapping it as though opening a time bomb. He chuckled at the irony of it. It was a time bomb, because soon she would leave.

"I found it on sale downtown and . . . ."

She was busily engaged in unwrapping.

"What are you doing? Just tear it open. You look like you're planning to re-wrap it after you see it. Just rip it open."

"It's so beautiful, I want to save this paper," she said.

"It's Christmas paper."

"Is it?"

She studied the patterns on it.

"Hawaiian Christmas, I guess. No evergreen and mistletoe, just orchids and palms."

"I like it."

"I decided to give it to you now because I already have it and, well, you won't be here for Christmas. I hope that's all right. I want you to have it now." He let out a nervous laugh. "Maybe you can use it before you go. Who knows?"

The paper fell away, the ribbons and bows at her feet. She slowly pulled up the box top, creating suspense for him, as well. Finally, the top separated from the bottom and her eyes widened in delight. He smiled from the chair across from her.

"Do you like it?"

"Yes, of course I do!"

The box dropped from her lap as she held up her Christmas gift: a short, pink satin nightgown with lacy strips running up the hips and across the chest, stringy straps over the shoulders.

"Oh, *subarashii!*" she cried. Wonderful!

"I'm glad you like it."

"Please let me wear it."

"That's the idea."

"Really?"

"Yes. It's yours."

She rushed into the bedroom, returning a few minutes later.

The gown swept her hips like flower petals, the lace accentuating the graceful figure inside, and her legs became dainty beneath it.

He could not speak, not knowing what words to say. It was not because of the nightie, the pink chemise. It only reminded him of the approaching end. She was dancing around the bedroom, pausing in front of the mirror each time she passed. He stood in the doorway, regarding his little ballerina, enjoying her enthusiasm.

"I love you," he said.

Suddenly her dancing stopped, the unheard music halted. Her eyes were wide, doll-like, but her face was taut.

She ran to him, embraced him, and her tears wet his collar.

"I love you," she whispered against his ear.

10

THE TRAIN SHOOK VIOLENTLY as it came rushing out of the long tunnel, awakening Ben. Around him the hills were spotted with late spring snow. The Japanese writer, Yasunari Kawabata, wrote in his most famous novel: *The ground lay white amidst the night's blackness.* But Ben was not him, nor was it nighttime. However, like Kawabata and the hero of the novel, reading the copy he had bought in the train station's bookstore, Ben had entered the Snow Country.

Being April, however, the only snow was the generous dusting across the hilltops. The hillsides lay as pale as the beaches of Hawaii, as the jagged surf, as the band in her hair, as the soft flesh of her warm belly. He realized where he was, of course, and compared it to the reality of his dream. Not quite full circle, but easily three-quarters.

A smooth coast bordered the railroad for a while, then turned away. Later, a robotic female voice announced the train's arrival at Kanazawa, the principal city of Ishikawa prefecture. Ben remained in his seat, waiting for the country to pass him by, waiting for his station to appear before his eyes. He continued staring out the window at the remnants of winter. The train started off again.

A lake passed. Mountains came at him from the right side, stayed with him until he fell asleep.

At the beginning of the journey, passing northward through Gifu prefecture, the hills were cut into terraced steps, dried now but he could see that in summer each a small pond would be filled with rice. On many of the hills stood tall, orange *torii*, marking the entrance to shrines. Beside another hill a junior high school swept past as though he were watching a program on television, the building surrounded by rice fields brown with winter's waiting. Students, identical in their blue and white sports uniforms, played six different sports on the dry, chalky grounds. None of them waved as they passed him. There were endless tiled rooftops, blue and red or brown, some turned-up at the corners to protect against evil spirits. Many were crowned with thatched roofs which had dried to a bitter gray, sitting silent among the rice fields, beside the dry fields.

At each little station, creaky wooden buildings squatted beside the lonely tracks, bent old women, slightly smiling mothers holding well-behaved children by their hands, out of uniform teenage boys with close-cropped hair, blue-suited businessmen, housewives with their apron uniforms, high school girls with hair braided into pig tails standing in their sailor suits, the rickety station masters looking world-weary behind their ticket gates, their call to board a vacant cry in the wind, the tracks rising, always rising into the mountains.

It looked like nothing Ben had ever seen in America, and he began to feel the strangeness, the bizarre and uneven beauty of this land, feeling the exquisite foreignness of it all. No more the straight lines of a modern city but the curves of a countryside.

The coast arrived suddenly. The crooked shoreline and the jagged mountains. The scent of the sea, the cry of the sea gulls. Then the coast became rough, indented, and the mountains grew more fierce, frowning at him, daring him to continue. Stands of emerald cedars spread down from mountain crests. A long, narrow valley swallowed the train and the shoreline sank away. Stately power line skeletons played tag with the train, pushing it safely into the little town of Nanao and the train stopped at its station.

The endless tracks turned west and another, different coast ran alongside the train. The tracks swung north again and Ben feared they would run out of peninsula before he reached his destination.

"*Noto Nakajima*," the conductor called, and Ben's heart skipped a few beats.

A small, rustic station pulled up beside the panting train. Only Ben stepped out. No one else dared.

According to the girl at the information counter in the Japan Rail office at Nagoya Station, this was the closest train station to his destination. He had shown the girl the return address scrawled on Hanako's grandmother's letter. After a couple minutes of explanation in English, the girl had smiled and written it out in *Romaji*—Roman letters—and told him how to get there. The next part was easy. Ben told her he wanted a ticket to the closest station. Researching through several timetables and other references, she determined that Noto Nakajima was it. Now, he had to continue on his way by bus, cutting back to the west, over hilly countryside to the opposite coast, to some place called Togimachi.

The sky was dark with storm clouds, the breeze strong and chilly. From the station, he walked down the main street, feeling a profound weariness. He was lost in some historical drama, samurai about to step out and confront him. Had he ever been so far from home? The street seemed to extend right up into the mountains. Snow spotted the upper slopes. Snow lay in piles at intervals along the street. On the left was a noodle shop—*udon*, maybe, by its sign. To the right was obviously a *sushi* restaurant. He went there.

Setting down his suitcase, he hopped onto the stool at the bar. The old woman was no doubt surprised to see a *gaijin* in this remote part of the country, but she had a smile for him nevertheless. Ben knew little of the language, even now desperately trying to remember what he had learned in that post-Hawaii college course. He had learned the names of the various types of sushi, so he ordered confidently. But when she asked something about his order, all he could think of to say was the all-purpose "*hai*"—okay.

Never know what you'll get if you answer that way. He could not help but grin. She must have asked if he liked *wasabi*—the hot, hedonistic green mustard dabbed between the vinegary rice ball and the raw fish—because she seemed to have put in extra. Reaching hurriedly for the cup of green tea she offered, his head opened very quickly as though a tunnel was burned through his skull.

The old woman chuckled.

The first time Ben had tried sushi was in Hawaii. It was also the first time, he remembered, that he had taken Hanako's hand without her protesting.

"Where shall we eat?" she had asked.

"I want to try sushi."

"Why sushi?"

"Because it's Japanese. Like you. I want to see what it's like."

"Maybe you don't like."

"Teach me, Hanako."

They walked along Kuhio Avenue in Waikiki, not far from the International Marketplace, notorious haven for entrepreneurs selling island jewelry, art, and beach towels to tourists. He held her hand tightly, so she could not get away. Later he bought her a large, colorful beach towel with a parrot on it, for both of them to share. She gave his hand a squeeze, dodged the disapproving stares of the Japanese tourists on the sidewalk, and pulled him down Seaside Street.

"I take you my sushi shop," she said.

"*To* my sushi shop," he corrected her before catching himself.

"No, *my* sushi shop," she corrected him. They were going to her shop, she understood.

He grinned and let her lead the way.

Arriving on Kalakaua Avenue, which paralleled the famous beach once it passed the Royal Hawaiian Hotel and its newly built shopping plaza, she pointed across the street as they waited at the light.

"My office," she said.

The light changed and they stepped off the curb.

Beside the shiny, glass Japan Pacific Airways office building stood that traditional landmark of devout Americana: a Woolworth's store rising four floors high in the midst of Waikiki.

"Here?"

"Yes."

She led him around the side to the separate, snack bar entrance. Inside, it was not a typical Woolworth's snack bar. The patrons were a collage of Asian nationalities, huddled on stools around the sushi bar. Behind the counter, an old mama-san greeted them in Japanese as they sat at the counter.

Hanako explained to the woman, speaking Japanese, that her date was just a beginner at eating sushi. What was recommended? She smiled at the answer, offered a little dip of her head in thanks. After glancing at the menu, she ordered.

"How can you read all these funny little squiggles?"

"It's easy for me," she grinned, pointing to each item on the menu. "This is shrimp. This is — what do you say? — tuna. This is *ika*."

"What's that?"

Not knowing the English word, she asked the mama-san, who replied: "Squid."

"Squid? Did you say 'squid'?" He turned to Hanako. "How can you eat raw squid?"

"It is cooked, Ben."

"I know what sushi looks like and what it is, Hanako, but I grew up in the Midwest. That's in the middle of the United States. I didn't have any chance to try it. Before now, I had no reason to try it. Anyway, all the fish there is battered and deep fried."

"You're funny, Ben-*chan*."

His first sushi meal consisted of a pair of shrimp *nigirizushi*, and a roll of *teppa-maki* cut into four bite-sized morsels. The shrimp he handled easily. It was like shrimp cocktail without the sauce and with rice. The rice was sweet, too. The *teppa-maki*, a sheet of dried seaweed wrapped around vinegary white rice and a finger of bright red raw tuna, should have made him hesitate, but he was eager to show off. She showed him how to mix the pinch of *wasabi* with soy sauce to make a paste in which to dip the sushi. He was excited. Drowning the first bite in the mixture, he popped it into his mouth like a piece of candy.

"Be cautious," she said.

Then he heard Hanako laughing and he knew in an instant that he needed some water.

After drinking down half a glass to extinguish the fury of the *wasabi*, he could still feel the tingle in his sinuses.

"I think you use too much *wasabi*," she said, giggling. "Try mine, please."

He dipped the next bite into her dish of *shoyu* — soy sauce — and slid it between his lips. This time the pleasant warmth of *wasabi* was delicious.

Then he ordered a pair of *maguro nigirizushi*, the hand-squeezed balls of rice with thick slabs of raw, red tuna meat laying on top of them.

"How do you say 'delicious' in Japanese?" he asked and she told him. Then he turned to the mama-san and cried, "*Oishii* — delicious!"

"He become good Japanese, *ne*?" she remarked to Hanako.

"Maybe so," she agreed.

"What are you talking about?" he asked her.

She smiled, leaned a little closer.

"You are good using *hashi*," she remarked.

"You mean chopsticks?"

"Yes, ze choppusuticksu! You do not drop any sushi in your lap."

"Thank you, Miss Nakamori," he said, proudly. "I've only been practicing every day at lunch."

"Good you."

"Good *for* you," he again corrected.

He threw his arm up and squeezed her shoulders for a second. Only a second. It was still too early in the relationship, they mutually and silently seemed to agree. Even though he was thirty-three, at that moment he felt he was sixteen again and on his first date.

Leaving the cozy snack bar, they had walked across the street and circled through the Pink Palace's tropical garden. They came to the beach. Through the low, gently waving palm fronds, soft gray clouds parted to shower them with stars.

"The same stars that people in Seattle see," he whispered to her, "the people in Nagoya, Japan — your home — also see. It's a small world."

"*So desu ne,*" she whispered, breathlessly.

"So dizzy," he tried to repeat.

She laughed, pleasantly.

He curled his arm around her waist and her body shuddered until she chose to allow his arm there. They proceeded down the beach toward Diamond Head.

Somewhere near the point where Kapiolani Park's greenery began across Kalakaua Avenue from the beach, they paused at the edge of the surf. Barefoot now, shoes in their hands, the cool tide trickled between their toes. He held her in his arms and leaned against her. Seeing her eyes already closed, he pressed his lips against hers. As his eyes fell shut, her lips pressed back and her arms slid around his neck.

"*Sumimasen.*"

He was still daydreaming.

"*Sumimasen,*" the sushi woman called.

"*Hai?*" Yes?

He could not tell what she was asking. Evidently, he had drifted off into memory land and she was concerned. Looking down at the remaining bites of *tako* and *uni,* he realized how far he had come. Now he was eating octopus and sea urchin roe. And he used a lot of *wasabi.*

Finishing the last bite, he paid the bill, then exited to the happy calling of "*Domo arigatô gozaimashita.*"

After a half-hour asking the bewildered townsfolk for directions, he finally got on the right bus, the one bound for Togimachi.

11

PINE TREES HID THE OLD HOUSE from the road, but the taxi driver knew the address. It seemed as though everyone in town knew the house where he was going. They seemed to know him, too, even before he spoke. He seemed to be a celebrity in the bus station.

Feeling equal bolts of excitement and anxiety shooting through him, Ben stepped down the stone path, lifting boughs out of the way, watching his footing on the line of smooth stones leading down to the ancient house.

In the weak evening light, it appeared deserted. Looking back up at the road, at the top of an incline, he saw the taxi had already driven away.

The dirty windows of the house hid the occupants as though they were inmates. Was there to be no warm welcome? Did they not know of his arrival? There was only the silence of a temple as he stepped up to the door, heart beating like the temple's bell. All around him pines were whispering their secrets in the chilly breeze.

The *kanji* on the doorpost confirmed that he was finally home. He recognized the two characters for Nakamori.

Where is my family?

Knocking on the hard, weathered door, he struck up the loudest, most unprivate sound this solemn grove had surely heard in years. That was how his ears heard it. He sat down his bag.

Hearing some sounds inside, he waited, embarrassed at having disturbed the delicate peace here. He roused his courage and knocked again, not out of impatience but nervousness. The face that would greet him when the door swung aside would be that of Hanako.

His heart nearly stopped as the handle began to turn. Then his heart lurched in his chest as the crack of night widened and the warmth of a fire flowed out. When his eyes gazed down into the sad, crow-footed, baggy black eyes of the bent old woman in the brown striped *kimono*, two long pins stabbed through her bundle of hair, his heart was ready to explode.

The woman knew him in an instant, and threw the door wide open.

"Nakamori-*san desu ka?*" asked Ben.

"*Hai*! *So desu yo.*" Yes, of course.

She bent down to place a pair of slippers before his feet. He slid off his shoes and stepped into the small, worn slippers, his heels scraping the floor. She took his bag with some words of welcome but found it to be too heavy and sat it down just inside the doorway.

As he passed within, she began crying although she tried to hide her face from him.

The room was dark, the curtains drawn. The floor was covered with *tatami*—rice straw mats—with smooth hardwood planks at one end where a pale, pink vase stood with its lone *sakura* stem, its pale pink petals warming the room with their vivid mark of spring. At its base a few fallen, withered petals had already collected. This was the *tokonoma*, he recalled from the textbook he had studied, from the sidebar on "cultural notes." The *tokonoma* was the space reserved for beauty in a house otherwise too busy to worry about such aesthetics. Above the vase and its flowers hung a scroll scrawled with *kanji* he could not read.

All was silent.

The woman was Nakamori-*san*, Hanako's grandmother. That is what he presumed. She bade him sit on the cushion beside the low table in the center of the room, his back to the *tokonoma*, the position for the honored guest. He felt honored. He had come a long way to visit this house.

She politely took his coat and disappeared. When she returned, she brought a tray with a teapot and two cups. She set it down on the *tatami*, bowed, then poured the tea so calmly that watching her slow movements caused his tired body to melt into a deep state of relaxation.

He slumped on the cushion, finished his cup with a dozen slow sips. As he finished, she spoke.

Of course, he could not understand what she was saying, so he just smiled and dipped his head every now and then. He added a soft '*hai*' occasionally. What he wanted to know was where his girlfriend was. Where his former girlfriend was. What she was saying did not seem to answer his questions.

"*Sumimasen*," he jumped in when she paused. "Ah, Hanako-*san wa doko desu ka*?"

Her somber face suddenly melted into an awkward smile. It was the same smile as Nakamori-*san*, this woman's daughter-in-law, had displayed in Nagoya, he recognized. The embarrassed smile, to hide the inner turmoil.

"*Gomen nasai*," he spoke quickly to recover their mutual face. I'm sorry.

He got up and went to his bag, dug in it a while and returned to the table with one of the two rubber-banded bundles of letters. The old woman recognized them and her eyes lit up. Pulling the band off, he unfolded them on the table and offered her the first letter. It was the second one that she — the grandmother — had sent to him.

She whispered something that sounded apologetic, apparently reading over the letter.

"*Sumimasen*," he began again. "Is Hanako-*san* still living here?"

She smiled again, in the same pained manner, and her eyes quivered, wishing she could understand him, as though pinching her eyebrows together would strengthen her intellect.

"Hanako-*san wa ima desu ka*?" He was not sure if it was correctly spoken. "No, I mean, Hanako-*san ga ima wa doko desu ka?*"

She paused, gazing directly at his face in very atypical fashion. Then she looked down.

"*Nakunarimashita*," she whispered.

He hesitated, not hearing her clearing.

"*Nani? Mo ikkai, onegaishimasu.*" What? Once more, please.

She looked up, two tear streaks coursing down her weathered cheeks.

"*Nakunarimashita*," she repeated, nearly inaudible to him.

In his brief study of *Nihongo*, Ben had not learned many words, certainly none of any serious usage. More what a tourist might need to know. But from Hanako he had learned the word *naku*, which meant 'to cry.' She did that often, it seemed, so it was a useful word for him to know. It was obvious the old woman was doing that, but he did not know why.

"*Doshite?*" he asked. Why? He realized it did not make sense but it was what came out of his mouth. It obviously confused her.

She stared harshly at him.

"*Wakaru?*" she cried, holding up the letter she had written. "*Kore wa wakarimashita ka?*"

Now it was his turn to be embarrassed. He could not remember the words he used to know and it would be impolite to ask her to repeat again what she said. *Wakarimasu* was 'understand,' he knew. Did he understand? What was he suppose to understand?

"*Gomen nasai.* Hanako-*chan wa nakunarimashita*," she repeated.

"*Doko desu ka?*" was all he could say in his stupor of confusion. Where is she?

The old woman scooted back from the table and bowed low, her head almost touching the *tatami* mat.

"*Ashita, ne. Kanojo no tokoro e zurete itte agemashô, ne.*"

He bowed in return, though not understanding her words.

She rose gracefully, her composure collected and calm, and took away the dishes.

At least he knew something: *Ashita* was 'tomorrow.' Tomorrow, he would see Hanako. Fine. One more day would not hurt, he thought.

Perhaps she was living in town, or she was just not home today but would return tomorrow. It did not matter, he decided. It had already been too long already. He did not think he could take the strain of anticipation much longer. Tomorrow, then. Grandmother would take him to 'her place.'

Ben could hear the grandmother shuffling around the house, a dull swish-swish across the *tatami*, then slippers over the wooden floors.

"*Sumimasen ga chotto kochira ni kite itadakemasu ka,*" she called from the doorway of the room where he was invited to sleep. Again she knelt and bent her head to the *tatami*.

Surprised, Ben turned where he sat at the low table. As the old woman straightened up, she waved her hand up and down as though saying goodbye. Ben knew from Hanako that this was the Japanese gesture for 'come here.' So he followed her, this old woman, this *obâsan*, down the hallway to the last room.

They paused at the doorway, at the sliding *fusama* panel, and she listened a moment.

Turning to him with a knowing grin, she slowly slid open the *fusama*. Inch by patient inch the doorway opened and he finally could gaze into the room. Across the *tatami* floor were several small toys, mostly stuffed animals. The door opened wider, like a magic curtain, revealing a small child of perhaps three years sitting in the center of the room quietly playing with a pile of wooden blocks.

Soon their spying was discovered and the child looked up, her dark eyes regarding the stranger with curiosity and fear. The straight, even line of black hair across her wide forehead contrasted beautifully with her yellow T-shirt and her baggy, red jumpers. Her fat cheeks were rosy circles and her chin had a dimple just like Ben's did. Her tiny fingers held a block with the *hiragana* letter *wa*—in one particular *kanji* meaning 'peace.' Her feet were bare, sticking out of her corduroy pants, and her tiny toes wiggled alternately with the blinking of her beautiful, innocent eyes.

"*Dozo*," the *obâsan* said, gesturing for him to enter the room ahead of her.

Ben stepped inside and the child's eyes followed him, curious, no longer fearful.

She called to the child.

"*Namae wa nan desu ka?*" he asked the *obâsan*, wondering what the child's name was.

She smiled at him. "Aiko-*chan desu yo.*"

He smiled. "Aiko . . . ."

Ben knelt with her, both of them beside Aiko, whose eyes never left him. Nervously, he picked up a stray block, offered it to her. She hesitated a moment before wrapping her chubby little fingers around it. Stacking it on top of the *wa* block without looking, she continued to regard him. She never smiled.

"So . . . I have a daughter," said Ben. A burst of bright sunshine seemed to fill his chest. "And her name is Aiko."

Obâsan was telling him something, motioning at Aiko frequently. He just listened and watched the child playing on the floor. She would never know how much trouble she had caused. He was not blaming her, of course, but she was merely the calm center of a churning hurricane. He was safe now, but soon he would have to pass through the outer ring of winds. On one side of the storm was Addy, who wanted a divorce. On the other was Hanako, who never told him about Aiko. Tomorrow, when he met her again, the storm would hit and he would be drowned.

As he studied Aiko, it gradually began to sink in that this little child, this cute, innocent girl, was his daughter. *Mine*, he thought. *Where had she come from?* It seemed as though he was in a dream, where such magical possibilities became real. Here sat this child, free of all inhibitions, free from all anxiety, free from worry. And yet, she did not seem a happy child. The longer he watched her, the longer she went without smiling. She played, but what ideas were running through her head? Was she going to be an architect someday? She knew what she was doing with the blocks. She was building a wall, block after block, piece after piece. A line was forming, one block tall, like the Great Wall of China. It grew at both ends, longer and longer.

Then, suddenly, Ben realized the wall was stretched between him and the child.

Aiko bent her head upward, staring into his eyes, seemingly challenging him. Then she rolled away to play with a different toy, leaving her wall standing, barring his way, keeping him at bay.

Would tomorrow be the same? He wondered if Hanako had any knowledge he was visiting — since it was the *obâsan* who had written to him. Perhaps his visit was going to be a surprise. He wondered if Hanako knew about her letters, or if she would even approve.

Suddenly, his memory landed on a letter Hanako had sent to him after they parted for the last time.

Was that the one in which she might have told me?

He excused myself, waved goodbye to Aiko, and hurried to the sitting room. Sifting through the stack of letters, spreading them out over the table, he searched desperately for the right letter. He went to his bag, pulled out the second bundle, began sorting them.

The *obâsan* came into the room, puzzled.

There! He quickly unfolded it. He read down half the first page, flipped it over and scanned the back. Here it was, he thought, but when he read it through he found he was wrong. Somewhere, she had written him a letter which hinted that she was going to have a baby. She would have done that, he believed.

"When was she born?" he asked Obâsan, still digging through letters.

"*Nan deshô ka?*"

He realized he had spoken English.

"*Itsu?*" he asked, gesturing like he was pulling a baby out of his womb.

"*Asoka! Ichi gatsu no ni-ju-shichi nichi ni umaremashita,*" she replied.

At least Ben remembered the Japanese numbers. Aiko was born on the twenty-seventh. In January. He counted back. They parted on May twenty-ninth. Nine months from the end of May would have been the end of February. No, nine months from *April*. That's when it started. The twentieth through the thirtieth they were together. They were saying goodbye. It was special because they knew she would be returning to Japan for good and they wanted to enjoy the final days together.

He took off several days to be with her. Those ten precious days were their honeymoon in Hawaii. They did not know what would become of them in the years after they parted. Although they had talked of marriage, they knew both their families would disapprove, old-fashioned as they were. He left Hawaii a few months after she did, never expecting to visit Japan, not knowing if he should even try. They wrote letters, of course. Many letters. But time soon pushed them apart and the letters stopped.

And Aiko was born in January.

She was born one month before he met Addy for the first time. He was amazed at that calculation. And it was fully three months before he and Addy had their first date. Aiko was already two years old before his and Addy's wedding. Hanako never told him anything. Why hadn't she written to him? Why hadn't she told him something so important?

Or was I just too dumb to figure out her hints?

"*Kochira?*" he asked. Was she born here?

The *obâsan* bowed deeply, came up with a proud smile, holding out her two old hands. He guessed that she had delivered the baby. This was the only home Aiko had ever known.

After dinner, the *obâsan* showed him to his room where a *futon* bed had been laid out on the floor. From the way the room was decorated, he immediately guessed that it was Hanako's room. The *futon* was hers. He would be sleeping on it. There was a low desk at the end of the room. He saw the picture standing there. Seeing his stare, the grandmother brought it to him and he smiled longingly at it.

The casually posed picture showed Hanako and him outside the Pearlridge Shopping Mall in Aiea, Hawaii, standing in front of a seafood restaurant. They were celebrating her birthday. She was twenty-four. He regarded her in the picture, wanting to return to that moment, wanting to touch her. She wore pink Bermuda shorts, the ones she had worn on their first date, the ones she always wore, and a pink and white striped tanktop. She loved pink.

That evening, her Japanese friends had joked about them getting married, saying they made a 'loving couple.'

He chuckled, remembering how she had corrected them, saying they were a 'lovely couple.'

But we were a loving couple, too.

They had been dating only a few months when the picture was taken by one of her friends. This was the first time he had ever seen the photograph.

Telling Obâsan how much he liked it, she replied with something that sounded positive.

He smiled and thanked her.

"*Oyasumi nasai,*" she said. Good night.

As she turned out the light, he stretched out on the futon, holding the picture frame against his chest. He would see her tomorrow. His heart began a wild fluttering and he could not fall asleep, despite the long, exhausting day. He thought about the next day deep into the night, long after he heard Obâsan go to bed. Tomorrow he would be taken to Hanako's place.

Then he thought of little Aiko, and smiled.

Ben awoke before dawn, at first not remembering where he was. He could not return to sleep and sat by the smoky window, watching the fog settled among the pines. It was a gray fantasy world, as if the forest were on fire. He could feel the chill through the thin window pane. Outside, the shadows were beginning to take on a pink hue, smudges of early sunlight.

Feeling a presence at the door, he turned and met the *obâsan's* warm eyes.

"*Ohayo gozaimasu,*" she whispered, bowing. Good morning.

He replied in kind and she left. He returned to the scene outside the window. So alone out here in the woods, foggy and silent, he thought. So far away from the world.

After a few minutes, she returned and pulled him away.

Through the crack in the *fusama*, he watched Aiko sleeping on her little *futon* with her pile of small blankets and her tiny pillow. Her face was turned toward them, her mouth agape, her eyes darting about beneath their lids, following dreams no one else would ever know. Her chubby little hand fell out of the covers, grasped at air.

The *obâsan* chuckled. He smiled.

Through the front door's glass panels, the sunrise's warmth struck him. It was going to be a nice day, a warm and comfortable spring day, an *atatakai* day.

Suddenly, it seemed as though his three years with Addy was last night's dream, as though his short time with Hanako was a dream of the night before. It seemed as though this fog-shrouded morning was the only reality. He felt no ties to any of his past. He had not flown to Nagoya. He had not ridden a train through the mountains and up the coast to Noto Nakajima. He had not taken a bus across the peninsula to Togimachi. He was not staying in the home of his former lover's grandmother. And who was Addy? Just someone he had known for a while, some time ago. Nothing had any history here. He had just appeared here, as if being born. His head swam with visions, wet images quickly absorbed into memory's sponge.

An intense sense of *déjà vu* swept over him as he dressed for the day and he tried to grasp it but it evaporated before breakfast.

Perhaps he was just tired, he considered, sitting at the table as the grandmother served breakfast, setting down various bowls from a tray. Perhaps he was changing somehow, becoming calmer. In a different environment, he was forced to leave civilization behind for the first time since he had begun his career. Even in Hawaii it had been constant work — except when he was with Hanako. Perhaps he was learning the fine art of patience.

After a leisurely meal of rice, *miso* soup, and pickles, he waited while she washed the dishes.

Then they climbed up through the pine forest, following a trail that rose sharply at first, then stretched along the side of the ridge overlooking the old house and the road beyond. He helped the *obâsan* with one hand; otherwise, she used a cane. Aiko ran ahead of them, her short legs producing a waddle. She stopped frequently, swinging her hand at insects or stooping to pick flowers. Whenever the adults would catch up with her, she would run ahead. She seemed to know the way.

Not a word was spoken since they left the house. Ben did not think it necessary once he confirmed the final destination over breakfast. They were going to meet Hanako. Perhaps she was in the village or at another house in the forest, he thought. Why she would be living apart, he did not know; he just wanted to see her again. Then he could ask all his questions — like why she never told him about Aiko.

Eventually, the trail turned upward again, a steep incline that made the *obâsan* pause for breath. The pines thinned, opening onto a view beyond the house: the blue sea and the rocky shore far below. Aiko waited quietly for them on the level ground above, a bouquet of wild flowers gripped tightly in her two little hands.

The *obâsan* caught her breath, leaning against a thick pine trunk. Ben waited for her. She spoke words he could not understand.

He stepped aside to let her lead the way once again but she stood her ground.

Ben's attention was drawn to Aiko's voice off to his left, cooing softly, like some children's song. As he listened to his daughter, he turned to regard her, to locate her among all the wildflowers, and his eyes fell across a magnificent defect in the pure, natural composition of the Japanese forest. His gaze became more focused and he took a step toward Aiko.

The *obâsan* spoke again, louder and more firmly, but he did not listen. He was too transfixed on that singular imperfection. The flaw that was glistening in the morning light, its cold, polished corners reflecting the sunlight, as though the sun had been invented just to light up this unnatural thing for him.

Ben stood stiffly, off balance but somehow frozen in mid-step. His eyes tried to burn away the horrible aberration.

Aiko knelt before the stone, trying to stick the flower stems into the black soil. Her sing-songy voice was not so much full of cheer as full of innocence. She did not know what it was, standing erect there amid the peacefulness of the pine grove. Perhaps she did know, he wondered, but simply did not understand what it foretold. He did.

And so he fell to the earth beside the child, joining in her prayers before the headstone of her mother's grave.

12

WHEN BEN FINALLY RAISED HIS HEAD—he did not know how long he had cried with his face down against the pine needles—he saw Aiko sitting atop the mound. She dug in the dirt, still trying to plant her flowers, striking the dirt with the stems. But the stems were too weak to push their way through the hard soil. She faced away from the headstone, lost in her own world. It was a world of play, of clear skies and warm breezes, of kindly grandmothers, of hugs and kisses, of wildflowers, of strange men who speak strange words and have brown hair and blue eyes, of happiness in the heart, and unknown sadnesses. He wanted to be like her: to not know, to not understand. He ached for the innocence she delighted in. But for Benjamin—having passed through the threshold of adulthood—he was now forever barred from it.

He understood. Now, he understood.

His throat tightened the same time the *obâsan's* hand touched his shoulder. She knelt down beside him and he could not hold back his tears. Her words offered no comfort, even if he had understood them. She had not told him, could not tell him in any way he would understand. He never would have known. He had come here naively expecting to meet Hanako—not *this*. The *obâsan* did not tell him. So she had shown him.

"This is why I have been summoned to Japan," Ben muttered. "This is why she wrote to me. Come and claim your child. That's what she had said in her letters. And I didn't know anything. I couldn't read them. I had no idea what they meant."

But what did it mean now? He stared at the gray stone. What did she want from him? He gazed at the old woman kneeling in the grass. What did *she* expect of him? He stared at the child, *his* child, playing so unaware in this family cemetery. He had the answers in his head as soon as he asked them. The answers were simple.

"Aiko is mine now."

The *obâsan* was passing her to him, ever so gently. He saluted her determination but wondered if she really was doing the right thing.

He turned his wet eyes to the big lie.

"Why had she not told me? What harm would there have been in telling me?"

He did not understand. There was no reason he could think of. Except her own vanity. She had plenty of time to tell him. Over two years, in fact. Aiko celebrated her third birthday without him even knowing of her existence. Now she was four years old and in many ways she still did not exist. Not even her sweet, *kawaii* face and her soft, baby voice were enough to convince him of the reality he saw.

"What am I doing?"

He cringed against the ground, the *obâsan's* hand pressing his trembling shoulder.

"What was I thinking?"

He held back another fit of tears as he shook away the feelings.

"What was I doing?"

He shot to his feet, dizzily swaying, and dropped to the ground once more. Picking himself up again, he shunned Obâsan and Aiko, fixed his gaze on the old Shinto shrine nearly hidden in the shadows of the grove. It was a small hut surrounding a stone statue of a Buddha, its shelf strewn with the remnants of many offerings. During his grieving moments, the *obâsan* had lit incense there, giving the grove the musky scent. His eyes were stung by the smoke.

The chiseled Roman letters grew in size, twisting into grotesquely sharp focus, searing, cutting into his scorched eyes:

NAKAMORI HANAKO

21 MAY 1962 – 7 NOVEMBER 1990

And in place of 'Rest in Peace' was simply the *kanji* for peace, spoken as *Wa*. He remembered the symbol on the toy block his daughter had held when he first saw her in the room. They matched.

"Am I going blind?"

The shrine, the grave, the incense, whispered prayers, the innocent child playing, broken wildflowers, the burning morning sun, the melting fog in the corners of the grove, the towering headstone, the Roman letters hewn in the gray stone, the child's calm singing, the weeping of the *obâsan*, the sting of the incense, the girl's tiny voice, the cool breeze, the pine needles, Aiko's innocent song, Obâsan's Shinto prayers, tears drying on his face —

He burst out of the grove, stumbling down the slope, crashing into trees, tearing through the brush, losing the trail, losing his mind.

"She's dead," Ben cried into the phone.

"What did you say?" asked Carmen, raising her voice.

He could think of no-one else to call; he needed to cry in English.

"I said, she's dead. Hanako is dead."

There was silence in Nagoya.

"Oh, no," she said finally. "Ben, I'm so very sorry. Oh, my. What happened?"

It was his turn to be silent, fighting to keep his voice strong.

"I need your help. Can you come here?"

"What's wrong?"

"I'm sorry, Carmen, it's too complicated to explain now. Please help me. I'm desperate."

"Where are you?"

He told her all the twisting directions but she was quickly lost.

"I'll meet you in Kanazawa, then," he suggested. "Is that all right? I'll pay you back for your train ticket."

"I can't come right away," she said. "I have a bunch of Canadian businessmen coming this afternoon. I can't get away until Friday at the earliest. Can you manage until then?"

She heard his tense voice, taking deep breaths.

"All right."

"I'm really sorry," she said. "Are you okay?"

He waited until he caught another breath. "I think so."

"What are you going to do?"

"You mean now?"

"No, for the future."

"The future?" It was the present that distressed him. He was not ready for the future. He had no idea what he was going to do.

"Take it easy, Benjamin," she spoke up after the silence grew too long. "I'll be there in three days. I'm sorry about your friend. Don't worry, Ben. I can find my way to Togimachi."

He sighed. "Okay."

"I'll meet you at Togimachi. Outside the station."

The cafe was called Bourgouisse. That was how it was spelled, at any rate. Ben wasn't sure why there would be a French café in downtown Togimachi, but there it was, looking rather Provençal and quaint with its country trappings and window boxes full of flowers, as though it was lifted straight out of some small village in southern France and plunked down here.

Ben quietly stepped inside, not wanting to draw any attention. The rich scents of coffee filled his nose, comforting him. The decor was a rustic hunting lodge, two deer heads on the walls. Booths along the outside wall with the windows, tables in the middle, the counter against the inside wall. The music playing was some Italian *bel canto* sung by a tenor, maybe from an opera. He decided he liked the place and threw himself down in the back booth. Soon the girl at the cash register brought him a menu.

In twenty minutes, he had not managed to decipher the weird English or *katakana* phonetic renderings of the many English words, so he just ordered coffee. For three hundred yen he got a small cup of coffee. He stared at it, knowing he could down it in three gulps. At that rate, he calculated, he would use up all his cash just getting a normal caffeine fix.

Outside, the afternoon mist had changed into a light evening rain, then a steady drizzle. The rustling wind and prattle against the windows calmed him at first, then helped him slip into depression as he recalled one time with Hanako when a similar light rain fell.

He sat back, watching the waitress serve the other customers. He watched them, too, seeing what they ordered and how they ate it. She reminded him of Hanako, but only because she, like all Japanese girls, had black hair. Actually, the waitress was taller and more slender than Hanako. This girl's long hair was straight in back and gathered into a ponytail. Her face seemed sad—or she'd just a long day serving coffee.

While waiting for the right train back in Nagoya Station, Ben had wandered through the underground shopping arcade and browsed in a couple of record stores hoping to find something to listen to during the long ride. He looked for Akiko Kobayashi, Momoe Yamaguchi, Megumi Shiina, popular female vocalists, or *Off Course*, a male group. It was the music that was most often playing while he and Hanako had fallen in love. Instead, he found a new generation of music: a septet of teenage boys on roller skates called *Hikaru Genji*, a pair of cute preteen princesses called *Wink*, and a sad faced chanteuse named Shizuka Kudo.

The waitress looked like her. Shizuka Kudo had thick, upturned eyebrows which made her appear to be on the verge of tears—which made her good for singing sad songs, he guessed. When the waitress smiled, she sported the crooked teeth that were considered cute in Japan—like Seiko Matsuda, another pop singer whose songs Hanako liked. The waitress did not have a pretty face, he decided, not pretty in the classically Japanese way the female singers had. But she looked attractive in the tight black skirt and loose white button blouse.

He stopped himself. It was perfectly innocent to make note of his surroundings, especially in a foreign country.

There was one last swallow in the cup, he saw. He finished it.

When she noticed him staring at her, she took his order and brought him a second cup of coffee.

He nursed the small cup, thinking of the day. From the sacred pine grove, he had run off wildly into the forest, to a dark corner of the wood where he thought no one had ever been or would likely ever go. Falling among the grass and wildflowers, near a mocking, chuckling brook, his weary eyes regarded the innocent blue sky up through the pine boughs. His back cool against the earth, anguish ran from him like blood from a fatal wound. Somewhere in his confused mind there was the thought that nothing today was by chance, that his subconscious had known it all along.

He lay there until late into the afternoon, thinking, crying, resting. No one came to look for him. No one called for him. Then he stumbled back to the house, not knowing how he was able to find it in the forest.

Inside, Obâsan was stoking the fire in the hearth, warming the house for the evening. She looked up when he entered but did not speak. The house was filled with pine scent and the heavy mood of a funeral parlor. He could not stay there. Visiting the room where he had spent the previous night, he searched for one special photo and one particular letter, or maybe dozens of them. He had to piece them together. He had to learn what had happened. Grabbing the whole bundle, he left.

There had to be clues in her letters, he was convinced. She had to have told him about Aiko, although certainly not straight out. She liked mysteries, he knew, and games, but he could not understand why she would not tell him directly. Therefore, he had to dig. He was certain the answer was hidden somewhere in her letters. He cursed. Why hadn't she sent the photograph which Obâsan had sent to him? Why did she not want him to know?

From Obâsan's house he had walked nearly a mile before he was picked up. The delivery van driver wanted to practice his English, but Ben was not in a mood to chat. Thankfully, the driver understood, and took him into town, nevertheless. From the main intersection, Ben had walked aimlessly down the street, like a ghost, looking for something but not knowing what. He watched the people watching him, no doubt thinking he was drunk. As the evening came on, the streetlights burned and made the moist, foggy air glow in the night.

The green telephone in front of the post office had a slot for telephone cards so he pulled from his billfold the one Carmen had recommended he get at Nagoya station. The card had a picture of Mount Fuji framed with cherry blossoms. He paused to regard it before sliding it into the slot on the phone. The machine beeped and a red digital number 50 showed on the front. He studied the phone number on Carmen's *meishi*, checked his watch, and hoped for the best. Carmen was still in her office.

Now he would have a three-day wait until she arrived. There were questions that needed to be asked and he was unable to form the sentences with the necessary subtlety. Here in *inaka*—the outland, the countryside—there were few interpreters to be found. He had to ask Obâsan important questions.

Foremost in his mind was the question of how Hanako had died. Accident? Illness? Was it quick, painless, at least? Then, he tried to insist to himself as the inescapable future beckoned, he would need to ask questions of the consulate. The future was unfolding now.

The question echoed through his head and his mind's eye began conjuring vividly gruesome images to frighten and intimidate him.

How did she die?

Standing on a street corner, observing the rush of people to their homes, he felt lost. He was a shadow, and anyone who looked at him could see through him. The mist wet his face, dampened his coat and hair. Across the street, appearing like a lighthouse to a sailor, was the warmly lit windows of the coffee shop. He steered for it.

13

AFTER AN HOUR, spending half that time sorting through the letters he had brought, Ben ordered a third cup of coffee. He picked up on the girl's stilted pronunciation — koh-hee — and used it himself.

"*Arigatô*," he said, absently.

"You're welcome," the girl replied.

A moment after she left, he looked up, realizing she had spoken English.

He watched her serve another table, then tend to work behind the counter. When she came to clear the table next to him, he spoke to her: "You speak English?"

She did not look up, continued wiping off the table. "A little."

"You sound pretty good," he told her, but she did not smile or blush. "Where'd you learn it?"

"In school."

"College?"

"Yes, some."

He paused, thinking of something else to say, but she spoke next.

"You are not from here."

"No, I'm not."

"Where you come from?"

"America."

She was either not impressed or just tired from her work.

"Have you been to America?" he asked.

"No, never."

She straightened up from wiping off the table and regarded his with apparent fascination. "Are you English teacher?"

"No, I'm here . . . on business."

He was not lying. He did not say what his business was.

"Good."

"What's your name?" he asked.

She smiled, showing her crooked teeth.

"Tomoko." She held up her hand. "Your name?"

"Ben."

She tried to hide her smile with her hand.

"Excuse me, Ben-*san*."

She returned to the back room, somewhat curtly. Must not get a lot of foreigners—*gaijin*, as Carmen said. He watched the waitress carry away the dishes, then continued his letter sorting. He was in a more encouraging frame of mind now, having been able to communicate with a fellow human being and taking some warmth from that.

He was engaged in arranging the letters in chronological order by the postmarks on the envelopes when Tomoko came back with a cup for the customer across from him. She saw the stack of photos beside the letters and paused to gaze.

He let her gaze, wondering what she would think of this foreigner and his letters obsession.

He sensed a gasp, though he heard no sound from her.

"You know her?" she asked, pointing at the photo of Hanako in the *yukata* holding baby Aiko.

"Yes," he answered, turning in the chair to face her and seeing her grim expression. "I did."

She straightened up.

"Are you . . . ?"

She waited for him to understand her question without having to speak the rest of it, but he was not good at that Japanese game.

"*Nan desu ka?*" he responded, hoping his use of Japanese would relax her. What is it?

She leaned down as if to tell a secret, staring intensely at him in very un-Japanese style.

"I know her."

"You knew her?"

"Yes . . . ."

"But . . . ?"

"*Ju-ichi gatsu* . . . aaa, Novembah . . . ."

He leaned over the table, prepared to catch her precious secret. "Yes?"

She glanced quickly around the shop. "She die."

He sat back with a weary sigh.

"*Shiteru,*" he muttered. He knew already.

"*Gomen, ne.*" Sorry.

She started to get up but he waved her back.

"I only found out she died this morning."

There was shock on her face.

"*Mo shiwake gozaimasen,*" she uttered, adding a deep bow, another apology for . . . something.

"*Dô itashimashite,*" he replied, waving her words into the warm air. You're welcome.

She looked at him more seriously as she rose from her bow.

"You boyfriend?"

He let out a chuckle, embarrassed. "Boyfriend? Why do you ask?"

"Everyone here know her. She have baby. Girl baby. They live with *obâsan,* south from Togimachi."

He cleared his throat. "Why does everyone know her?"

Tomoko glanced around the shop, saw only one customer sipping coffee, unconcerned. Her boss was in the kitchen. Ben took a moment to stare out the window. Outside, the light rain had become a steady downpour and the night had grown darker.

"She have baby of American man. Everyone know."

He stared into her sad, dark eyes. "Is that so bad?"

She dropped her gaze, evidently embarrassed.

"For crying out loud!" The anger he had been suppressing broke out. "A baby is a baby is a baby. They're all cute, so what's the big deal if one is half Japanese, half American? Geez, this is the twentieth century. Why can't people just leave other people alone. Let lovers fall in love. It's nobody else's business."

Tomoko was startled. He caught himself and stopped abruptly, but she was offended. A tear spilled down her flushed cheek.

"I'm sorry," he said.

"*Mo shiwakenai,*" she blurted out as she sprung to her feet, turning toward the kitchen. Another apology? He wasn't sure.

"Wait," he called. "I'm sorry."

But she was gone.

So he calmed himself and, the rain steady outside, resumed reading Hanako's letters, beginning with the first one he received after he returned from Hawaii. There were no obvious remarks in them telling him about Aiko. He tried to read any hidden meanings or any vague suggestions, but there was nothing. She related her love for him on every page, though. Reading those words now, he felt guilty. The same feeling one gets at a funeral, knowing one could have done more for the deceased while she still lived and regretting not doing so. *What was I thinking?* He had just come home from a funeral today. Pangs in his heart signaled his sorrow. The difference was that he would have done more for her, if only he had known. But she would not tell him and there was no way he could guess.

After Ben finished her letter of September ninth, folded it carefully and replaced it in its envelope, Tomoko came to his table and told him the shop was closing. He glanced at his watch. It was nearly ten.

He called to her as she was leaving.

"*Hai?*" she responded. What?

He forced a smile, trying to show friendship.

"Did you know her?" asked Ben, holding up the picture on top. "Personally, I mean. Were you friends with her? Did she ever come in here?"

"I never meet her."

"But everyone knew her, you said."

She nodded.

"November. Last year," he started, then hesitated.

Tomoko's eyes twinkled, as if she knew she had a terrible secret for which she might extract a great price. A reward, perhaps. But she gave it away for free. Seeing his cold, disillusioned reaction was payment enough.

"Do you know . . . ?" he asked.

Her face went blank.

"I don't know. I read in newspaper," she explained. "Newspaper say she die. One night—she die. Everybody know. That's all to say. She died."

The quarter moon glowed at their path as they walked on the Noto Kongo beach. Ben was telling Tomoko the story of how he first met Hanako on the beach in Hawaii. She listened intently, pacing beside him, marking the wet sand with her boots. They both stared out at the murky waters of the cold Japan Sea. He got a little carried away, perhaps making the truth more dramatic. But the truth, he told her, was that there was nothing unique about the beginning of their relationship. She seemed to understand that, and he longed to hear her story. He was sure it would tell him why she was so ready to sympathize with his.

"On our first date, *Koi ni Ochite* was on the radio, the song by Akiko Kobayashi," said Ben. "That was the first Japanese pop song I ever heard, and I liked it. I especially liked it because it made me think of her. I never knew the words exactly, except the verses that were sung in English. But those didn't really make sense."

"I know za song," she said. "You want hear it? I got cassette."

"I don't ever want to hear it again," he retorted immediately. He decided his outburst was silly. "Oh, I like the song, but . . . I don't want to hear it again. It's taken this long to clear it from my head. Hah, just talking about it makes it play again in my head."

"I'm sorry."

"*Daijobu*," he muttered. Don't worry.

They had walked about a kilometer down the beach, away from the town. When the coffee shop closed, they were deep in discussion concerning the major news story in Togimachi. The death of the girl from Nagoya who gave birth to the *gaijin*'s child. Poor girl, they had all said. She should have had an abortion was the popular suggestion, rather than suffer all her life with a half-and-half child. And why did she have to come to Togimachi? They wondered why she chose their village to disgrace.

"Do people really think like that here?" Ben asked.

"Oh, yes," Tomoko said, frowning. "Many old people here, old customs, and no contact with foreign people. Very serious here."

"So that must be why Japan is trying to improve their so-called internationalization?"

She did not understand the comment, so she just continued her explanation.

"Here is far away place in Japan. Here is lonely place, good for think of bad things doing. Many people come Ishikawa to forget, feel guilt, hide from world. Here is place to hide."

He nodded.

"She came here to hide? Is that it? Why? Why here?" He stared at the horizon. "She had nothing to hide."

"She had baby of *gaijin*."

He regarded the moonlight on the dark, dancing waves, and felt Tomoko watching him for a long time.

"Where you go after that?" she asked finally.

A fine February mist fell on the windshield as they drove the rented Toyota up the coast. They were talking cheerfully, with Radio KZOO playing softly under their voices. She was happy to listen to his story, about his first days in Hawaii. Then a new song began to play on Honolulu's exclusive Japanese pop music station.

"This is Kobayashi Akiko," she blurted out to him with a grin as wide as Kaneohe Bay, which they were then passing. "She's famous singah in Japan."

"You like her?" he asked.

"Ah, yes! She my favorite," she replied unequivocally, turning up the volume on the car radio.

"'. . . I am not living in your heart . . .'" she sang along.

Ben listened to her sweet, light voice.

Around the crest of the Waiahole Forest Preserve, past popular Swanzy Beach Park and Mahie Point, the road gripped the narrow cliffs below Mount Kauhiimakaokalahi—called Crouching Lion by the locals—as it bent down into the cool Kahana Valley. From the snaking strip of pavement, the wide bay spread out below, opposite the towering, jagged green peaks of the Hauula range which pierced the clouds that hung in the lush valley. Descending from the steep heights to the lush valley floor far below, the road bent and leveled as it rolled past the wide beach, hugging the horseshoe-shaped bay. There were campsites but since the water in the bay was too rough for swimming, it was usually deserted. A grove of palms covered the camping area, the waving fronds separating the lonely beach from the frolicking campers.

"'. . . Just like a lost child, standing here alone . . .'" she continued.

"You're good," he told her and her smile widened. He pulled into the small parking area, shut off the engine and turned to her.

"This is Kahana Bay, my favorite beach."

"*Kanashii*," she murmured.

"What did you say?"

"It is sad place here."

"Yes, that's why I like it so much."

"Why do you like?"

"The first time I stopped here, I walked along the beach. A cool, fresh breeze was blowing in off the bay, chilling me even with the warm summer afternoon. My mood changed as I gazed out at the sea, far out of the bay—out there," he raised his hand pointing, and her serious face with concerned eyes followed. "Out past those ragged, rocky points, out to the far horizon. It was silent—like it is now—and for no reason I felt melancholy. An agonizing melancholy. From then on, whenever I feel sad, I drive here and walk this beach. Sometimes I just sit in my car listening to sad music." He chuckled, somewhat embarrassed at his confession. "And stare out through the trunks of these palm trees."

She could not catch every word he said, it seemed to him, but she understood his tone of voice.

"Why are you sad?"

Her words were so full of concern that he had to laugh.

"I'm not sad, Hanako. Not now. Not with you here."

She grinned, laid her head on his shoulder.

"Is it always sad here?"

"Every time I've been here, it's been overcast and chilly. Every time. And I've been in Hawaii for about seven months now."

"Please, do not be sad, Ben."

Grinning, he knew he was falling in love. He wanted to kiss her, but he was afraid.

"'Can't stop you, can't hold you, can't wait no mooooore . . . '" she sang softly, still hearing the song in her head. It was barely a whisper.

He bent down and kissed her quickly, before she could react.

When the song was finished, she turned off the radio and jumped out of the car. She kicked off her flip-flops and ran out from the shade of the palm trees, laughing and calling to him. As he locked the car and followed, the clouds he had never known to leave Kahana Bay suddenly thinned and over the course of the next ten minutes or so they parted and allowed the sun to shine through.

Hanako's spirit was released by the warm sunshine. Throwing off her stiff, white blouse, she ran free across the sand in her maroon tanktop, leaving a trail of tiny footprints behind her. She waved to him and he chased after her, easily catching her.

They walked the beach barefoot. At one point, she stepped in the surf just in time to have to scramble back to higher ground. Her pink jeans, rolled up to mid-calf, were splashed by the waves. She ran to him for safety, catching him in an unsteady embrace, hanging by her arms around his shoulders. Her knees were bent, feet dancing in the air as they spun around and around.

"This is not sad place, Ben!" She laughed. "I am happy this place."

He chuckled at her exuberance.

"So am I—now."

When he let her down, she stood on his bare feet, and stretched up on her toes to take his face in her soft hands.

"'I'm just a wom*aaaa*n,'" Hanako sang to him, "'fall in love . . . .'"

"Fall*ing* in love," he corrected her.

"Falling in love," she repeated.

Tomoko's smile was half hidden in the shadows as a cloud passed in front of the moon. Her path converged on Ben's, their footprints mingling in the moist sand.

"I know a book might read that way," he continued his story, "but I swear it really did happen that way. If there's anybody who hates all that meteorological symbolism, the clouds and the sunshine, it's me. It just doesn't happen that way. But it did then, for us. It was no symbolism, it was Fate. I swear it's true. The first time the sun shone in Kahana Bay was the first time I took her there. Of course, I took it as a good omen."

Tomoko laughed, covering her mouth shyly. Mixed with the rustle of the pine trees on the hillside and the hiss of the surf, her laugh sounded delightfully reminiscent of Hanako. Ben studied her, still hidden in the shadows of moon-blanketing clouds. But she was not Hanako.

Staring up at the stars now, he could feel the warm breezes of Hawaii, in his heart and in his head.

Turning to Tomoko, he saw the shadows drift away from her, sailing down the beach.

"Then I asked her what they called a beautiful girl in Japanese, and she said *bijin*."

"'That is right."

"So I called her a *bijin*."

Tomoko smiled, barely more than a pinching of her thin lips.

"She sure was a *bijin*."

"Yes," Tomoko replied.

He gazed at her, trying to catch sight of her face in the beam of moonlight.

Her face became sullen at that moment and he thought he saw a tear roll quickly down her cheek. He heard her faintly humming *Koi ni Ochite*, her mind apparently elsewhere.

14

DESPITE BEN'S SEVERAL HOUR TRIP through the Japan Alps, three train changes, and a lot of shaking, Ben was not used to traveling by train and the rocking of the car was making him sick. He had an intense headache. All he could hope was that the train reached Kanazawa as soon as possible. With luck, he would arrive two hours before he was to meet Carmen.

He had expected to meet Carmen in Togimachi, but she had called at the last minute to say he had better meet her in Kanazawa. She thought she might be able to help arrange an interview for him with the consul there. Honorary Consul, that is. Someone who could handle the paperwork. It was difficult for Ben to explain everything over the phone, but even in his emotional state, he had managed to make her understand that now, with Hanako dead, something had to be arranged for Aiko and that he probably needed to fill out some papers in order to do that. Probably a bunch of papers.

Adoption came to mind. But was it accurate to 'adopt' his own daughter? For that, he would need a lot more time and go through a lot more trouble. The end of his leave of absence from the office was looming ever closer. Carmen was kind enough to offer to contact the American officials and inquire about the circumstances. In her phone

147

call, she said she would bring him *all* the necessary forms. He promised her another dinner for her trouble.

The train finally cruised into the station, just as he was about to lose his breakfast.

He took a taxi to the local KDD office, the long distance telephone company, to place a direct call to the States. He was shown to a private booth. The girl dialed the full number for him, then bowed and closed the door to the booth. He could still see her through the glass door, sitting at her desk.

The phone began to ring and he held his breath, then took a deep breath after the forth ring. Surprised to find Addy still there to answer the phone, he did not know exactly what to say at first.

"She's dead," popped out of his dry mouth.

"What do you mean?" Addy asked.

"She is dead. She died last year."

"What? Are you serious? You mean the girl, or the baby?"

"The girl—woman. Her name's Hanako. She died last November. The baby, a girl—Aiko's her name—is fine. I want to adopt her."

There was silence.

"You want to adopt her? I guess that's what I've been expecting. Remember what I told you before you left? I said you'd have to make a choice when you got there and found out how things were. I guess it's that time now. The decision is yours."

"There's no decision to be made, Addy. The choice is made for us. I have to take care of her. There's no-one else. Hanako's grandmother has been taking care of her but she's old and can't keep doing it. Her family sent her there because of the baby. It's all a big mess. I'm not sure what to do. But I want to bring Aiko home. I have to. I'm the only family she has now."

The hum of international phone line was all he heard on the line.

Is she even listening?

"She's really cute, Addy. You should see her— a roly-poly ball of rosy cheeked, baby fat little girl. She doesn't seem affected at all by her mother's death. But I can't leave her here. I've got to bring her home with me. It's the only home she's got now."

He heard only static on the line.

"Do you hear me?"

"Yes, I hear you. What do you want me to do? You want me to welcome into my home the progeny of your illicit affair? I don't think you're understanding my position. I don't have any ties to her. She may be cute, but she's still *her* baby. She's not mine."

"Come on, Addy. You'll love her. You'll grow to love her. How can you be so heartless?"

"Heartless? Me? Remember who ran out on who. You hurry over there the first instance you can to see your girlfriend again. If that's not love, then I don't know what is. I'm sorry she died, but don't you go blaming me for that, either. You'd better get ready for life after Japan because you'll have to go it alone."

"Be realistic, Addy."

"I am. I don't want your bastard child in my life."

"Wait a minute!"

"I'm sorry I picked up the phone. Actually, I came over only to pack up a few more things. *My* things. The lawyer I got suggested I get my own place, says it's easier for the court if we're apart. So, today's moving day. And if you ever do come to your senses, I'll be staying at Mother's."

"What are you talking about? Are you serious? You got a lawyer?"

"Damn right—pardon my Japanese! What's that other word? Sayonara? Is that it?"

"Wait. Please, Addy."

"Goodbye, Ben. And, I guess, good luck."

Before he could say anything further the phone clicked and the line was silent.

He took his phone receipt to the clerk and paid for the call.

Outside, dark clouds gathered overhead. He was angry, weary of it all.

By the time he returned to the station, he still had forty minutes before Carmen's train was due. Plenty of time to steam over the phone call. He was really being divorced, he realized. She was really going to do it.

He sat with Carmen in Bourgouisse, Tomoko's coffee shop, after traveling by bus back to Togimachi. They discussed the consul's suggestions. He had been happy to see Carmen, Ben's interpreter, and was willing to look into the case. For Ben's part, he received a stack of papers from both the consulate and Japanese Immigration. The instructions ran several pages as well. During the long ride to Togimachi, Carmen explained the details, the procedures of adoption and immigration. And of the long wait for the paperwork to be processed and approved.

He had no appetite, and fidgeted with his coffee.

"It's too much trouble—not that I'm not willing to go through it all," said Ben, "but it just seemed like a lot of unnecessary red tape, a kind of 'let's see how badly you want it' game."

"You've got to remember, Ben, your case is not exactly unique," Carmen lectured from the opposite side of the table.

"I was sorta hoping it was."

"The U.S. Consulate's got loads of paperwork. There are still some military bases in Japan, for example, and who do you think those lonely soldiers date? The local girls, of course. I've seen enough of them around, giving the Japanese here a wonderful impression of Americans. And there are plenty of other foreigners, not just Americans, working and living in Japan who happen to get lonely, too. Do you know how many American men dream of a Japanese wife? Look in *Tokyo Journal* and you'll see the ads of a dozen different marriage correspondence clubs. It's a big business."

"A business, huh?"

"These Japanese girls only want to marry Americans because they think you will be a little kinder to them than the local boys would be. And I tend to agree. But the real matter is the kids. They stand out. And that's what they don't like here: any person who stands out. Except the few that are models or television faces. In America it's not so apparent because we all look different. But here, a mixed child does stand out. The poor children will be ostracized all of their lives, from the first day of school to their last day of employment."

"It can't be that bad. It's the nineties, after all."

"Old traditions die hard."

He shook his head, let out a long sigh.

"But I'm not like them. I'm trying to do the right thing."

"I know, Ben. I can see that. I'm just telling you that you've got a wait ahead of you."

"I've gotta be back in the office in a week."

"You're lucky you have that much time. Maybe you'll be able to file the petition before you leave." She chuckled, cynically. "You can come back later to get the child."

He shook his head again. "I won't leave without her."

"Noble, yes. Smart, no. If you lose your job because you didn't want to leave without her, what good would that do you in adopting her?"

"That's what I came here for."

"Come on, Ben. I can see right through you, like all the other men who come to Japan. You came back because of your hard-on. I know what I'm saying 'cause I've lost boyfriends to Japanese girls before. I know that's why you're here. You wanted to be with her again. Come on, admit it."

"I don't know what you're talking about." He stirred his coffee. "I came here to see my child. I had to see if it was true. She's my first, my only child. I want her, no matter what I have to do. Can't you understand?"

"Of course, I do. But what about your wife? Haven't you told her?"

"Yes, but like I said, she practically hung up on me—after telling me about her lawyer—so I guess nothing's changed. I'm going to be divorced soon and I don't know what to do. If I bring Aiko back with me, I'll be raising her myself. And if I don't, then what will happen to her—and maybe she'll still divorce me for coming over here."

"She's a woman. Like me. That's why we think alike. Haven't you figured that out by now? And the proof is in the act, isn't it? You did come here, so that proves where your heart is. What can you do? Not a whole lot, as I see it."

"Let her divorce me then. I think she's just bluffing, anyway."

"I don't know, Ben, you might have trouble pushing the papers through as a divorced man."

"Dammit! What does the world want? They want to keep us apart, don't they? What the hell is wrong with this place? They go against everything that flows naturally. Isn't it enough that I spent all this time and trouble, not to mention the expense, to come and get my daughter? They won't let me have her just because my wife is not her mother, and therefore she doesn't want the child—or me? That's absolutely the most ridiculous thing I've ever heard."

She slapped the table.

"That's the reality of it, Ben. I'm just saying it for your information. I came up here to help you, after all. I thought we were friends: the Mutual Cynics Society. Remember? Two lonely hearts?" She folded and unfolded her napkin. "I didn't have to come here, you know. I wanted to see you, too. You seemed like a nice guy. Maybe I wanted to get to know you better, married or not. There are so few of you types here. Ah, hell, I just wanted my raincheck dinner. All right?" She tossed her napkin on her plate. "Lighten up, will you? Don't get all wound up. And don't kill the messenger. Okay?"

"I'm sorry," he mumbled.

Feeling anger still boiling inside, Ben tore himself away from the table, headed for the restroom.

He stared into the mirror, studied the red-faced maniac bending over the basin. He had no choice; there was nothing else he could do.

"If I want to win the game," he mumbled to the man in the mirror, "I have to play the game. If I want to play the game, I have to play by the home team's rules. Even with the referees paid off by the home team. That's the only way. Otherwise I automatically lose."

He gazed sternly at his reflection, feeling helpless.

What am I doing?

He was sending everything in his life to hell for the sake of one child. Sure, that was a noble thing to do, but it was not all that smart.

What if she were not really his child after all? Yes, he counted the months, but what if? Sure, he could leave her to her fate. He could fly back home, hope Addy was still there, and go on with his life as though he had never even thought of going to Japan. He could do that, he told myself. But he would carry a perpetual heartache inside for the rest of his life. Having looked into those beautiful dark eyes, he could never forget them.

"Does she make you think of her?" he recalled Tomoko asking, referring to Aiko. He wondered.

Could I have been lying to myself again?

Perhaps he was so determined to save Aiko for the simple reason that the child brought back to his consciousness so many pleasant memories. Through Aiko, his dear Hanako still lived.

"That is why you come here, isn't it?" Tomoko had forced him to confess. His words haunted him.

"Yes, a child is still a child. I can feel commitment. I can believe in responsibility. I can be compelled to see justice done at the expense of convenience. But was I a little more concerned with the possibility of once again being with Hanako?"

He splashed water into his face, pulling his facial muscles taut.

The question: Hanako or Aiko?

He wiped his eyes as he stared at the strange image in the mirror, he mumbled the sobering answer.

Hanako.

He had to be honest. He had to be brutally and cruelly honest. Staring into the mirror, there were no witnesses, no judges, no juries. It was safe to tell the truth. And the truth was that he had not forgotten her. Not really. She had never left his heart completely. He had just pushed her deeper inside when he came home, when the letters stopped arriving, when he met Addy. When he married Addy. Not thinking he would ever be able to visit Japan, he resigned himself to forget her. Over time, it seemed to work.

"Then why did I even go looking for someone else," he asked the mirror, "someone who eventually became Addy? Why didn't I plan to go to Japan to be with my Love?"

It was simply inconvenient, he admitted after a minute.

"If she had come to the States to be with you," he asked the man in the mirror, "would you have taken her in?"

He did not have to ponder it. *Yes, of course. Certainly.*

"Then, it was just a matter of convenience?" He could not hide his answer. "I supposed so."

He did not want to go to all the trouble of going to Japan, filling out the visa papers, paying the cost of the tickets, going through the hassle of arranging a wedding and more visas, or dealing with the suffocating, nervous feeling of losing his personal freedom by quietly submitting to the confines of marriage—was that it? The perpetual bachelor syndrome. Isn't that what every young man wants? The security of marriage with the carefree lifestyle of the single playboy. At the same time, in fact. *Quite normal, yes, but . . . .*

After everything, it was a simple matter of convenience.

"But here you are, having paid for the tickets which cost more now, having taken the trouble of coming to Japan, and about to fill out the endless immigration papers to bring the little girl back home."

It was exactly the same as what he would have done for Hanako. Now it was for Aiko.

"If you were willing to do all this, make this trip, only five months earlier—"

Ben looked up, frightened by the pathetic scoundrel he saw staring back from the mirror.

— then all of this senseless tragedy might have been avoided.

He let the tears fall as he slammed his fist down on the counter. Guilty as hell, selfish bastard. He crashed his head against the tiled wall beside the basin. It hurt, but that was what he wanted. He wanted to punish myself.

There was a tapping at the door.

"*Chotto matte,*" he called out in a weak voice. Wait a moment.

"Ben? Are you all right?" Carmen called.

"Yes, fine. Be out in a minute. I'm just not feeling so good right now. I'll be okay."

He waited another five minutes, clearing his head, wiping his face, calming his temper, before he returned to the public.

"Let's go," he said brusquely to Carmen, who had ordered another cup of tea while he was gone and also finished it.

She pulled on her coat as Ben went to the cash register to pay the bill. Tomoko, the only one in the shop, stepped up. Her eyes were lowered, maybe in sympathy for his red, tear-stained cheeks.

"*Issen kyu hyaku'en*," she said in Japanese. One thousand nine-hundred yen. She stared at him, up from under her eyebrows.

"She your new *koibito*?"

He was in no mood for interrogation.

"What?"

"I guess you *gaijin* all same, *ne*."

"I'm sorry," he snapped, throwing two *sen* yen notes down on the counter.

She took the thousand yen bills, then flipped up the change from the drawer.

"I don't think it matters to you."

"You *gaijin* is . . . stupid!" she said, slamming the drawer closed. Her dagger eyes cut into him.

"Gee, relax, will ya?"

He turned away, joining Carmen at the door.

The taxi ride from the town out to Obâsan's house was silent. Once there, Ben introduced his guest to the woman of the house. He was ignored as Carmen and Obâsan began the customary ritual of exchanging bows, each one trying to bow lower than the other. Finally, Obâsan won by dropping to her knees on the tatami floor.

He had not told her that Carmen was coming, so he could not know what she was thinking. Perhaps she thought Carmen was his wife—if she even wondered whether or not he *had* a wife. Obâsan always smiled at him so there was no way he could ever guess what deep thoughts lay behind her kindly, gentle eyes. Then he bowed to her, from the waist.

Carmen introduced herself. She was Ben's interpreter, come all the way from the Nagoya International Center. Carmen handed over a *meishi* with both hands extended, a gesture of respect. Obâsan seemed surprised. Why did they need an interpreter? They communicated effectively with their hearts, and sometimes with their eyes or with gestures?

Then they met Aiko.

He could tell Carmen was in love from the first instant. She quickly dropped to the *tatami* to play with his daughter and they had a good time as he watched. They built another wall with the blocks, but this time it did not separate the child from the stranger. Rather, it stood between them and the far wall of the room. Carmen picked up Aiko. She was giggling, rosy cheeked and bright eyed.

"Here you go, Ben," she called, holding out Aiko for him to take.

He hesitated.

Being an only child himself, he had always had few playmates. His cousins had their own children now but they were not his so he did not feel as though he should get down and play with them. It was not that he did not like children. It was that he was nervous around them. He was fearful that he might accidentally hurt them, or frighten them, or say or do something that might disrupt their normal childhood growth. Now he was holding his own child and he did not know what to do.

"See, Ben, it's easy."

He chuckled. "Easy for you to say."

As he held Aiko, they stared at each other. He wondered what she was thinking. Did she know who he was? Was there some genetic trick that enabled her to know they were related? She wasn't as giddy in his arms as she'd been with Carmen. Perhaps living only with her mother and great-grandmother, Aiko had little experience with men. He was bigger, his head bigger, his face had a larger nose and he had whiskers. Who was this monster?

He tried to smile, worried it would look like the evil grin of a troll. He stretched his grin as wide as he could, trying to get a reaction from Aiko.

She suddenly burst into tears, struggling to get free from his grasp.

"Here, let me take her," said Carmen.

Obâsan seemed worried.

"Are you sure you're cut out to be a daddy?"

He stared back at Carmen, his eyes showing apology. He assumed Carmen meant what she said with a sense of humor.

"I'm prepared to try . . . as hard as I can."

She held out Aiko again for him, now calmed.

"The first step is to hold her without making her cry. Okay? Let's try it again."

He took her once more, gathering her in his arms as Carmen had done, but he did not stare at her, did not force any smile, did not try to get any reaction out of her. Instead, he just held her comfortably as he talked with Carmen and Obâsan.

After a while, Aiko reached out and tugged on his nose. Lightly at first, curiously. Then with a firmer grasp with her stubby fingers. He reacted. Carmen and Obâsan laughed. Aiko laughed.

15

BENEATH THE WARM GLOW of the desk lamp, set on the tatami beside the futon, Ben began filling out the stack of paperwork necessary to claim his daughter. The house was almost silent, but he thought he heard Carmen talking to Obâsan in the sitting room. Aiko was surely asleep at this hour. He longed to go peep at her, but he had to get the papers filled out and turned in as soon as possible. Then the waiting could begin.

Ben looked at the heading: PETITION FOR ALIEN RELATIVE. He read the instructions, telling him to read all of the instructions.

Who can file? read the instructions. *A citizen or lawful permanent resident of the United States can file this form.*

Well, that was good, he thought. At least he was allowed to file the damn petition.

"For whom can you file?" he mumbled, reading the form. This was the important part. "If you are a citizen, you may file this form for your husband, wife, or unmarried child under twenty-one years old."

That checks out. "I am allowed to file for Aiko," he muttered, as though he had not been sure of it.

He read through the instructions worded for lawyers, deciphering the legalese *contained therein.*

Number seven. What documents do you need to prove family relationship?

That sounded interesting. And it might even be applicable to him.

You have to prove that there is a family relationship between your relative and yourself.

Well, that seems reasonable enough, he thought.

Find the paragraph in the following list that applies to the relative you are filing for.

He turned the page over.

If you are filing for your . . . . Letter A, no. Letter B, . . . *child and you are the mother* . . . no. Letter C, . . . *child and you are the father* . . . . Bingo. That's it. *Give the child's birth certificate showing both parents' names and your marriage certificate.*

That would be difficult.

He sat back on the *zabuton* cushion and let out a sigh that must have been heard by the ladies out in the sitting room.

"We weren't married," he spoke to the papers, "and I don't know how birth certificates are done in Japan." Maybe she did not list his name on it.

He read on.

. . . *Child born out of wedlock and you are the father* . . . . Here it is. *Give proof that a parent and child relationship exists or existed.*

What in the world did that mean? How could he do that? He just learned he was a father.

The child's birth certificate showing your name and evidence that you have financially supported the child . . . .

He was sunk. Not only did he not know if a birth certificate even existed, but he certainly had never been financially supporting the child. He had not known 'the child' existed until a few months ago. Ben grumbled, shaking his head.

For crying out loud, what do they want? Why does everybody have to make things so difficult – needlessly difficult?

First, he had to find the birth certificate. As for establishing the relationship, perhaps he could show them some photographs of him with Hanako. He would show the consulate officials the pictures of the two of them in Hawaii, then the pictures of Hanako and Aiko in Japan. Hopefully, they would see that the girl was the same in each. He would establish that Hanako was with both him and then later the child. Two plus two. Simple. Actually, one plus one equaled three. They would see how it made sense. The way such things usually worked, they would understand that her being with him would come first, baby second. The natural order of things.

Then again, he wondered if they would see any resemblance. Aiko looked like a carbon copy of her mother.

It was hopeless. That was enough for tonight, he decided and got up to stretch. A groan escaped his lips.

He stepped into the hallway, moving softly toward the sitting room where light filtered through the *shoji*, the paper wall panels.

Low voices were speaking Japanese. Wondering what was being said, he crouched behind the *shoji*, trying to understand.

Carmen sat unmoving, listening to Obâsan's tale. Ben could see the intensity reflecting on her face. He did not know what they had been talking about, but it must have been serious. Obâsan seemed to be near tears. He could not disturb them now.

Returning to his designated room, he changed into the *yukata* laid out for him and headed out to the *ofuro*, a separate shack behind the house. The cedar wood tub was wide enough for three or four people to sit in it and deep enough to sit with his shoulders submerged. The once log-burning stove had been modernized to use kerosene to heat the water. He filled it from the tap and flicked on the gas.

Through the windows, he could see the moon rising above the pines. It was almost full, but the cloudless sky let it seem to shine brighter. He stood in the doorway of the hut, breathing the cool April air, waiting for steam to start rolling off the water. It was a long wait.

He stared out of the hut's doorway back at the dimly lit window in the house.

As he watched and wondered, the steam began to curl around him, warming his back while the night air cooled the front. Turning inside, he closed the door and pulled off the *yukata*. Standing naked beside the tub, he tested the water with his hand. Hot enough, he decided, but still below Japanese standards.

He climbed in, standing knee-deep in the tepid water, waiting for his tender red flesh to get acclimated. Slowly, he settled down to the bench around the sides of the two meter square box. The water swam up around his shoulders, then up to his chin as he immersed himself.

Worries melted away, muscles relaxed, blood ran smoothly through his body, and his mind became dull. He never wanted to leave.

Hanako was filled with joy: a new letter had come for her, the *obâsan* explained to Carmen. Sent all the way from America, the letter was precious. She touched the colorful stamps gingerly, respectfully. She slit the end of the long envelope, let the crisp, white pages slide out onto the low *kotatsu* table. Her grandmother quietly left the room, giving the girl the privacy to read her love letter.

Her grandmother knew of her happiness, wished her even more.

When would her *koibito* come for her? It had been more than a year since she had come home from Hawaii, and though the letters came without fail, he never did. She wondered how long her optimism would last. How long would it be before she would realize that he was not going to come for her? When would she have to tell her?

The *obâsan* knew about Americans from her experiences with the Occupation Forces. Some were kind, but most seemed interested in only one thing: the beautiful, exotic girls of Japan. And she was one of them. Yes, she had a son and a daughter, but she had lost her husband in the war, on some Pacific island whose name she did not know or want to remember. When the American soldiers came, she and the other women of the town hid themselves in their homes, fearing the gazes of the blue-eyed men in khaki or green uniforms. As the days went by, she became bold and ventured out into the street. She did not worry about herself, being thirty-seven years of age, but she did worry about her daughter who was eighteen.

Nothing happened to her or her family, but she was always filled with the dread that something might. Still, the soldiers in their district did seem to be kind generally. But there were certain girls in her town who had become friends with the Americans. They flaunted their relationships, profiting from the soldiers' presence. A few months later, though, they had babies with round eyes. Some girls were sent away, never to return. She recalled one father who took his daughter's newly born half-American baby from her and tossed it, crying, into the sea from a rocky point of land jutting into the sea. That was the most serious incident that she could remember.

Many of the soldiers were young, young enough to have soft hearts for their Japanese girlfriends. She saw the couples on the streets holding hands, and she heard the girls promising to wait for them to return. The young men seemed sincere, and she had no doubt looking into the faces of the girls and the soldiers that they were truly enamored by each other. And yet, none of the soldiers ever did return. The girls waited and waited, though a few were fortunate to find a Japanese man who would marry them. Most lived their lives in solitude and shame, their only companions being the other women with which they shared their sin. They had only the love of their children.

She held no ill feelings for Americans; she had no bad experiences with them herself. But she learned from that time that Americans never came back, and when her granddaughter arrived from Nagoya with her belly swollen and her heart palpitating, freshly exiled by her parents — she knew exactly what to do. First, she tried to encourage her, to keep up her spirits while she was pregnant. That was the best thing for assuring a healthy birth. But once the child was born, she gradually tried to make her understand that, like the others, her American *koibito* would never come for her, no matter how much she wanted or hoped he would, no matter how many letters she received, no matter how many times he wrote of his love for her.

Finally, her granddaughter received the last letter, and she knew she would not have to tell her granddaughter again that he would not come. He had told her himself. He wrote that he had met another girl, a Western girl with blonde hair and blue eyes. One of his own kind.

That would have been best under normal circumstances. But this time there was a child involved. It was then, seeing her granddaughter's torment, that she came to feel sorry that she had turned her against him. There was nothing to be done now. It was finished. Like the other girls, she would live out her life alone, with only the love of her child.

Her name was Aiko, she had said on the last day of the month after the child was born. She was a child born from love. She was not like the children of other girls, who were born out of their mothers' lust. No, she was in love when she conceived, and she was in love with him when she gave birth, so her child was a love child. And that was her name: *Ai* — Love, *Ko* — Child.

Ben was on the edge of blissful sleep, floating like a Styrofoam paddle board, when the door opened and in stepped Carmen, wrapped in her own blue and white yukata, her hair pinned up.

"*Konbanwa*," she said. Good evening.

Ben replied in kind, eyes closed in his deep relaxation.

"Thanks for heating up the bath for me," she said with a slight hesitation in her voice. "I've never had a real *ofuro*, I mean like this, in a little outhouse, in a wooden tub. How is it?"

"It feels great."

He sat up, eyes open, and reached for the tiny washcloth, brought it down into the water to cover his lap in proper Japanese modesty.

"Good. It's all right if I join you, isn't it? Obâsan invited me to use it. I guess she didn't know you were out here."

He was so relaxed that he could not formulate a reply.

"I can come back later," Carmen offered.

He shook his head, too numb to speak.

She hung her towel on the hook and turned away from the tub.

"Look away," she said.

With her back to Ben, she untied her *obi* and slid off the *yukata* with the grace of a *geisha* preparing for bed. She glanced over at him, checking that he was looking away; his eyes were closed. Next she squatted on the stool before the floor-level spigot and filled a plastic bucket with water. In Japanese fashion, she poured the water from the bucket over herself, rinsing her skin off, perfectly poised to restrict his view of anything more than her back.

"You still alive?" she asked.

"So hot . . . " he muttered, "so relaxed . . . ."

He opened his eyes then and studied how she carefully applied soap to herself, working it into a sudsy lather that covered her body. She lifted another bucketful of water over her head and poured it over herself, washing away the suds. Then she set the bucket back in place with the soap, reached for her washcloth and held it in front of her lap.

"So that's how it's done," he managed to say.

She stood, her back to him, and his eyes dropped down to her feet. Maybe it was just modesty, or maybe he really wanted to peruse her completely. As she turned toward the tub, his eyes moved without hesitation upward along her legs to the small towel she held in front of herself. He dared not raise his eyes higher.

"Did you look?" she asked, feigning shyness.

He looked away, staring down at the water in the tub, hearing her stepping across the wet boards to the tub.

Before he could look up again, she had stepped into the tub and sank beneath the waters, settling on the opposite bench. The towel remained in place.

Ben regarded her, now that it was safe.

"Hello," she spoke in a low, husky voice.

"Yes, hello," he replied.

"It does feel great."

He nodded.

"What've you been doing tonight?" she asked.

He let out a long sigh. "Well, I was trying to fill out those forms, but I got tired of reading all the instructions. I don't know what to do. Maybe it's hopeless."

Carmen sat back, relaxing against the smooth cedar boards. "Don't worry. At least not tonight."

"But there's so much to worry about here. So many rules and regulations. Too many to remember. In fact, I've got a confession to make."

Carmen frowned. "Oh, I think I've heard enough for one night."

"What do you mean?"

"Talking with the *obâsan*. That was a sad story she told me."

"What was it?"

She shook her head. "It's private."

"About me?"

"No, about her life. Life after the war." She adjusted her position in the tub. "What's your confession?"

He sighed, cleared his throat. "Well, I don't know how to tell you, but . . . I forgot to sit on the stool and wash myself before getting into the tub."

She burst into laughter.

"Oh, yuck! You'll never make it as a Japanese. I guess we'll have to empty this polluted water and start over again."

He gazed at her breasts, bobbing in the water like a pair of apples.

"If we let out all the water, then I'll be able to see you," he said.

She grinned and slid lower into the steam-shrouded water, hiding.

"We can't just sit here and stare at each other, can we?"

"Then tell me what Obâsan said."

When she had finished, the solemn silence filled the air of the hut, held aloft by the swirling steam. He had heard the tale of Hanako, not of her grandmother. Ostracized in her own town, she kept to herself and began the long spiral down into depression. What a change, he sighed, from the care-free young lady he had known in Hawaii. She was so full of life that she was continually lifting him out of his melancholy.

His mind faded in and out of memory as he struggled to perfect a crystal clear image of a special day.

"What're you thinking of," Carmen asked, lifting her towel from the water and wringing it out over her head, then replacing it.

He realized how much better he felt. Relaxed, yet feeling energetic, so inspired he wanted to leap up. Then the swirling fog of his daze lifted and he knew where he was. Happy times were in the past, in the far away days of four years ago. It suddenly seemed blasphemous to have pleasant thoughts.

"I was just thinking."

"Oh?"

"Back in Hawaii . . . ."

"Of course. Go on."

"One time we went on a hike up to a spring in the mountains. It's called Sacred Falls—there's a waterfall there, naturally, surrounded by a lush tropical forest. It's popular with hikers but it was not the tourist season then so we had it all to ourselves. We were so hot and tired from the hike that we pulled off our clothes and dived right in—no swim suits. Skinny-dipping. That water was as cold as this *ofuro* is hot, but we sat on the rocks in the sunlight so it wasn't too bad. She had been away for two weeks, I think, and I had a surprise for her. She said that pool reminded her of an *onsen*—is that it? an outdoor hot spring?"

"Yes, that's it, but it's called a *rotemburo* if it's outdoors."

"It's kind of strange, I know, but now, being in this *ofuro* reminds me of that icy pool in the jungle."

"What was the surprise? You said you were going to give her something."

"Well, not a thing—a place. That was the first week of May—she had some holidays back in Japan—so we were intent on maximum enjoyment. You see, our schedules were always crossing like the world was conspiring to keep us apart. This time, though, we finally matched."

"So what did you do?"

"Each time we met, we always tried to plan some way for us to be together forever. By the end of that week of vacation, we had signed the lease on a high-rise apartment overlooking Pearl Harbor."

"I see."

"Never again would we have to seek our private pleasure among public forests or on public beaches in the dark. A 'love nest' had been secured."

"That's poetic," she said. "But it didn't last, I take it from your more recent history."

The memory stopped like a film reel running out of movie, and Ben suddenly remembered where he was and why.

"What's the matter?" asked Carmen, noticing the pause. "What are you thinking of?"

"Her," he replied, finally. "I'm thinking of *her*."

"I thought so."

She did not seem surprised or offended.

"Did you two go to the *ofuro* together?" she asked coyly.

"We didn't have one."

"Then why does this make you think of her?"

"Everything makes me think of her."

"How do you mean?"

He shook his head, momentarily bewildered.

"Everything. Every cloud, every sunrise. Every brush of the breeze on my cheek reminds me of her gentle caress. Every tossing of the waves in this bath makes me think of Hawaii. Even you. Watching you washing over there, I was reminded of her. Your long, black hair, your smooth, curved back—I thought of her. I thought what I would be doing now if I came in here and she were here in this tub. I'd be sitting here in this *ofuro* with her. Actually . . . ."

He stopped to look around the room, examining the tub. His hand swung over the tub from left to right.

"This was her *ofuro*. The one she used. She sat right here—or there, where you're sitting."

He froze a moment. His face was wet from the steam but there might have been a tear rolling down his cheek.

"Ah . . . ."

Carmen slid around the bench until she sat beside him. She laid her arm around his shoulders. Her other hand patted his head then came to rest against his near shoulder.

"Instead of you, it would be her," he mumbled, his voice wavering out of control. "If she hadn't . . . died, I'd probably not even be here—

stupid fool that I am. I'd be at home watching television, blissfully ignorant. And perpetually bored—while someone I thought I'd like living with was off in another room reading a book or something else that . . . that would keep us from doing things as a couple. You know what I mean?"

"I think so."

Looking beyond the edge of the tub, he watched her chest rising and falling under his head. Her heartbeat echoed in his ear.

"Carmen, I have only been in love once in my life—if I know what real love is. It was her. She is the only one I've ever loved. I don't know why I even looked around for another. And I sure don't know why the hell I chose Addy."

"Go ahead, Ben," she whispered. "It's okay for a man to cry."

"No, it's not," he said. "I'm not crying . . . am I? I've haven't cried since I was a kid."

"You've been through a lot in the past few days. Let it out."

"Too much to deal with all at once, I guess."

"Let it go," said Carmen. "You can let all those emotions out now. I'm here and it's all right."

He lifted his head, his cheek brushing hers, suddenly so close. They regarded each other at eyelash range.

"I guess I'm as good as divorced."

Someone else said that, not me. He realized it instantly, even though it was his voice he heard echoing through the steam.

She smiled faintly, as though replaying his words in her head. For a moment, the expanding silence threatened to burst the hut.

He blinked, wanting to take back what he had said, along with what it implied. Their voices became whispers, automatically shifting into secret mode. There was no one to hear them though.

"You're very emotional now, Ben." She licked her lips. "It would be easy, but I don't want to take any advantage of you. It would be wrong, you understand. You're caught up in anger and frustration, your love for her, and I . . . I hope I don't get in the way of your plans with your little girl."

She gazed at him through the steam with a sad, pouting face, and her hand slid onto his thigh under the water.

"I think you understand."

"We're strangers sitting together naked in this tub, talking about love," he responded. His heart was pounding. "I can't—I still can't, Carmen. Yes, I understand."

She grinned, and he thought she might be about to lean over and kiss him.

"Don't worry, Ben," she said, "*Ofuro* secrets are never repeated."

16

THE LINES AT THE TOWN HALL were unusually long for such a small backwater place, but they stood there anyway. Ben had to get proof that Aiko was born. Obâsan had no birth certificate and he doubted that the authorities would accept photos. So they stood in line at the records office. Aiko alternately hid behind Obâsan and held Carmen's hand. When it was their turn at the counter, Carmen interpreted and Obâsan—on her weekly trip into town for groceries and gossip—verified the information. For a fee of six hundred yen, they received a copy of the certificate.

"What's this character mean?" asked Ben, pointing to one box.

"That's the *kanji* for 'father,'" said Carmen.

"I guessed. I know the *kanji* for mother: the *kanji* for woman and the one for child smashed together."

"That's one way of describing it."

He stared hard at the wilted paper. "What does the *kanji* there mean? Doesn't look like my name. I mean, shouldn't my name be in *katakana* characters, the phonetic spelling?"

Carmen coughed. "That *kanji* means 'unknown.'"

He looked again. There, in carefully handwritten script, the father was marked as 'unknown.' In her joy, wouldn't she be proud to name him as the father of their lovely daughter? He wanted to be able to show his *katakana* name to the authorities. But it was not there.

Anger boiled inside him and Carmen, seeing it rising to a critical level, cut him off with a soft tap to his shoulder.

"I'm sure the doctor can verify it," she said.

"If we can find the doctor. If he was told the father was 'unknown' before, why would he believe me now?"

He looked down at Aiko. Her face was solemn but her eyes were quizzical, concerned.

"Look at her. She's beautiful—but only because her mother was beautiful. She doesn't look like me very much—or at all. How am I going to prove I'm her father? What can I do?"

Carmen smiled, then bent down and picked up Aiko, holding her close to him.

"Look, Ben. See how she looks at you? She knows you're her daddy. Calm down. Let's go find the doctor. Then we can figure out what to do."

"You're right."

They all exited. Outside, Carmen asked Obâsan where the doctor's office was and she gave a vague answer. After another try, they had the directions straight and took a taxi across the town to Dr. Kotani's office.

The handsome middle-aged man in the white lab coat greeted them with a frown, at first seeing only the two *gaijin*. Then he apparently recognized Obâsan and let all of them in.

Inside, they saw that it was a one man operation, though a woman dressed as a nurse came and went several times. Probably his wife, Ben said to Carmen.

"Yes, I remember Aiko-*chan*." He grinned down at her. "It's almost time for a check-up, isn't it?"

Ben was surprised the doctor spoke English.

"I had my residency in Indiana. It's in the east, near Chicago," he replied.

"That's good. I guess I can speak in English here."

"Unless you want to say a lot of medical terms. But what shall I do for you? Shall we check Miss Aiko today?"

"That's kind of what we came for." Ben paused, thinking.

Suddenly Obâsan spoke up, delivering quickly strung sentences that seemed to explain the whole situation to him. Ben caught some of the words, as she was telling the relationship between him and Hanako. The doctor rubbed his chin and nodded.

"Did you know Hanako very well?" Ben asked the doctor when Obâsan had finished speaking.

"Yes, I believe so. It's a small town."

"She died last year and I came all the way here to Japan to see my daughter." He glanced at the little girl. "I'm sure she is my daughter. Her mother and I were . . . . We lived together in Hawaii and . . . . Then Aiko was born." He looked back at Dr. Kotani. "You helped deliver her, at Nakamori-*san*'s house, right?"

"Yes, I remember. But I did not deliver her. Nakamori-*san* helped her. What's the difficulty?"

"We just came from the records office, trying to get a copy of the birth certificate. But it doesn't give my name as the father."

"Whose name is on it?"

"Nobody's. It says the father is unknown."

"Unknown? I don't think that's right."

"Didn't you fill out the certificate?"

"Yes. I wrote what the girl told me to write. She was a little delirious, perhaps, but I thought she knew what she was saying."

"Did Hanako say 'unknown'?"

"She must have. But that was four years ago. I'm sorry, but I can't remember. There have been many children born since then."

"I need a certificate with my name on it. It's for immigration and adoption. I'm going to take Aiko back to America with me."

"I'm sorry, Mister Pinkerton, but there is nothing I can do if the certificate on file is not satisfactory. I cannot change it."

"That's not what I meant."

Carmen took Ben's arm, another signal to watch his boiling point.

"How can I prove that I'm Aiko's father?"

"Are you sure you want to? How can you be certain she is your daughter?"

Ben's face suddenly paled. Carmen gripped his arm.

"Dammit, I know she is. I just know it." He pointed to Obâsan. "That's why she wrote letters to me to come here. There could be no-one else, Doctor Kotani. There just can't be."

The doctor sighed. "We could try a blood test. Of course, it can only prove you are not the father, not that you are. Will that help?"

"Anything is a start."

The prick of the pin sent Aiko's face to full red and her eyes teary, her expression frozen for a minute before the bawling began. Ben felt her pain, knowing that even this small act was caused by him. He rationalized that it was ultimately for her own good. The cut would determine that she was his daughter. That would open the way to her immigration to America and a comfortable future. Only Obâsan could hold her still and calm her during the operation.

Aiko had the same blood type as her mother, which was the same as Ben's. Therefore, nothing was proven. He was still a candidate for fatherhood, but only a candidate.

Dr. Kotani repeated his statement that what was written on the birth certificate was what was official and could not be changed.

"Can you write some kind of deposition saying that I am her father?" he asked, growing desperate.

"I cannot be certain that you are, Mister Pinkerton." The doctor's face was stern. "Please understand. Given Japanese culture and our customs, it would be better if Nakamori-*san* wrote such a statement for her granddaughter. She was present at Aiko's birth, and knew her mother far better than anyone else." He turned then and told Obâsan what he had just said to Ben.

At first she frowned, then smiled at the last sentence.

"What did he say?" Ben asked, leaning over to Carmen.

"He said he thought he might have a duplicate certificate here somewhere and he'd look for it, but he couldn't promise anything."

"Of course."

Ben thanked him nevertheless for all his trouble.

He carried Aiko, her finger freshly bandaged, and took her for an ice cream cone to soothe her damaged spirit. It worked very well.

At the post office, he decided to send out the papers anyway. The lengthy instructions stated that if a certificate was not available that the sworn affidavit of two witnesses would suffice. He would get those, but for now he wanted to send the papers on their way, to get the process started.

"Let's get that red tape rolling," he sang.

He and Carmen gave the papers a last minute check, the original and two copies. He was thrilled to show them the picture of Aiko they had gotten in the photography shop, one print stapled to each application form. Holding Aiko in his arms while they were in line, he realized what a good job Obâsan had done so far. He respected her even more.

Then he sealed each envelope, had them weighed and paid the postage, and dropped them noisily through the slot in the wall.

"The waiting's the worst part," he chuckled to Carmen, who gave him a sly smirk.

April tenth was warm day, a nice change from the previous week's second winter. Still, there was frost on two mornings in this northern clime. Ben breathed in the spring air and felt rejuvenated. But for Obâsan, the fresh pollen was too much.

After carefully packaging all the papers and mailing them off to their respective destinations—Japanese Immigration and the United States consulate—the three ladies took a taxi back to the old house. Ben remained in town.

Carmen suggested he had at least a two week wait for any reply— even with the big EXPEDITE stamp on the official envelope, courtesy of her friend, the honorary consul down in Kanazawa, himself husband to a Japanese woman. By then, all Ben's leave from the office would have expired. In fact, he would be nearly a week over. He was already late.

That did not matter, however, as he scanned the computer printed numbers on the first thin page of his airline ticket. His return flight was in four days. He had allotted himself only a two week trip. After all, he was not expecting to have to deal with paperwork. There was nothing more he could do. Past business hours, he promised himself to call the airline the next morning.

With time on his hands, he was anxious to be doing something productive. Instead, he was free to worry, free to contemplate why he was here. Most of all, he wished to contemplate the multitude of hidden meanings he suspected lay behind every view seen and every sentence spoken. He wanted to know all that had happened before he arrived in lonely little Togimachi.

Now, though, he was free to go exploring. Not knowing why, he wanted to stay outdoors until darkness fell. He wanted to enjoy the day to its end. There was a kind of peace here that he had never known back in Seattle. It was similar to some of the days in Hawaii, he recognized.

Obâsan mentioned through Carmen a few places where Hanako often went. He had a strong desire to visit them, as if doing so would soothe the restless spirits there. Maybe his restless spirit, too.

The sun had dipped low in the sky and the bright afternoon was coming to a close as Ben walked the streets of Togimachi.

He passed Bourgouisse and saw Tomoko cleaning off a table.

Beyond the main intersection, he walked to the top of the next hill and passed down an alley to a small bookshop. Obâsan said that Hanako used to go there to buy English books. Also, writing paper.

Inside, it was musty, like a good library, and the aisles were not wide enough to turn around in with an armful of books. They stretched to the ceiling all around the tiny shop, its total floor space not more than an eight-*tatami*-mat room. An elderly man stood in the corner, glasses perched on the end of his nose, reading one book while balancing two others underneath. At the cashier counter, an older woman sat on a tall stool, apron hooked around her neck, reading a small, yellowed paperback.

Neither of them looked up when Ben entered.

"*Eigo no hon wa arimasu ka?*" he asked after practicing the phrase outside a few times. He wanted to find the English books.

The woman glanced up at him over the top of her glasses, smiled, and nodded toward the back where the man was.

Over his shoulder, Ben saw it was an English book he was reading. A novel. He tried to read the book spines on the shelves in front of him, and the man never seemed to feel he was in Ben's way. Most of the books there were used books, only a couple of the books looking fresh from the publisher. He was not looking for books, anyway. He was looking for memories.

Returning to the old woman, Ben asked, "Nakamori Hanako-*san wa shirimashita ka?*" Did you know her?

"*Hai. Dare desu ka?*" Yes—who are you?

"Benjamin Pinkerton *desu*. America *kara kimashita*. Hanako-*san no tomodachi desu*." He had practiced his basic introduction a few times, tutored by Carmen, and seemed to have spoken the phrases correctly.

She perked up.

"Ah, *so deshô ka!*" she exclaimed. She called to the man in the back.

The woman and the man talked for a minute, no doubt deciding his fate, then she turned back to Ben.

"Excussa me," she said in heavily accented English, "you Hanako-*chan Amerika no koibito?*"

He nodded. Yes, he was her lover.

"Hanako-*chan* . . . ." She could not finish and glared at the man to help her. He came to the front of the shop.

"She's dead," said the man, speaking in good English. "She died last year. November, I think."

"You speak English."

"I used to be English professor . . . at Kanazawa *Daigaku*. I'm retired now. Are you English teacher?"

Why does everyone here say 'English teacher' with the same tone of derision? He studied the man a moment.

"No, I'm not. Why do you ask?"

"We are curious, that is why. Most foreigners here are English teachers. We have different ones each school year. They come and they go. But the students stay, and never learn to speak English."

"Well, I'm not an English teacher. I'm a businessman. Actually, I'm in the hotel business. I can set up hospitality management but I can't tell you what part of speech a word is."

"Please, take no offense at my inquiry."

"None taken."

The professor gathered his books from the shelf, took them to the cashier counter, nodding at the woman to ring them up.

Ben followed him.

The professor handed over some yen and took the sack from the woman. He turned to Ben. "You asked about Miss Nakamori?"

"Yes. Did you know her?"

"I did know her. Not so well, though. I met her in this store on some occasions. She read many books, and she always bought much stationary. We spoke in English. She said she was writing to a man in the United States. They were going to be married some day. That is what she always said. Perhaps it was you? That never did happen, I presume. That must be why she was so sad. Yes, a very sad young lady. Oh, I'm sorry, you must be sad now, too." He paused to scratch his neck. "Ah, I recall her. She was very good in English. She studied very hard. She said she was going to America, so she wanted to learn English very much."

"I see."

"Hanako-*chan* not go America," the woman spoke up, her weary eyes avoiding mine.

He hated the silence that always followed the pronouncement of her name.

"I know that. Thank you for telling me. I only came here to see what this shop looked like. I heard you had English books here. And you do, as I see."

"*So desu, ne!*"

Ben glanced around the shop.

"Where's your stationary? Your writing paper?"

The professor translated to the woman.

She came out of her booth and led Ben to the right shelf, kneeling, pointing at the packet of lavender paper of 'just the right size and weight' — its packaging said so in English.

"Hanako-*chan no dai-suki*," she told him happily.

"She said, 'That's the paper she always bought,'" the professor interpreted. "Her favorite."

Ben knelt beside the woman as she showed all the items.

"I hope you will have a pleasant stay in town, Mister . . . aaa?"

"Pinkerton. Benjamin Pinkerton."

"Good luck to you."

"Thank you. I think I'll need it."

"Oh? And why is that?"

"Because . . . . Her daughter, Aiko. I'm going to be taking care of her from now on. That's why I'm here. What I mean is that's why I came to Japan."

The professor frowned, nodding his head as if seriously doubting Ben's parenting ability.

"Good luck," the professor repeated with a quirky little twist of his lips that passed for a smile. He left the shop and the bell on the door rang as it slowly swung shut.

The woman was still talking, telling Ben about everything Hanako used to buy. She invited him to see her writing paper, so he reached out and touched it. Feeling the paper's slightly rough texture—a 'suitable thickness for ink' the package stated in English—he knew it was the same paper she used to write her letters. He picked up a sheet. Why he wanted to examine it so closely, he did not know. Perhaps to make certain it was not somehow a forgery.

The woman pointed out the ink pens she always bought, the envelopes she used, and he recognized them. She showed him a few of the paperbacks she had read and returned for resale, and the new hardback book she had wanted to buy but was too expensive.

Ben smiled at everything and bought it all.

17

TOMOKO SAW HIM THE MOMENT he walked into the coffee shop but pretended not to notice him. Ben went to what was becoming his usual booth in the back and studied the menu, hungry as well as thirsty. Long after he had decided, she still had not come to take his order.

"*Sumimasen,*" he called out. Excuse me.

After a long pause, she sauntered over.

"What's wrong?" he asked after he ordered. "I don't know what you're so mad about."

"You *gaijin* all so stupid!" she blurted out.

He had no idea what she was talking about and told her so.

"That why you all so stupid."

He had to guess, as was the custom in this land.

"You know about me, Tomoko. You know I was the boyfriend of Nakamori-*san*. You know I am the father of her daughter. You know everything, and yet you still act like I've done something wrong to you."

"That girl . . . ."

Ah! A hint.

"You mean on Friday? My companion? She's from the consulate."

He lied not out of a desire to deceive. It was just too complicated to explain.

"She's not my girlfriend, if that's what you mean. She's helping me with government business." He studied Tomoko. "Is that what's got you so angry?"

She pouted like a little girl. Some girls in Japan never grow up, it seemed, no matter how old they were. Part of the "cuteness" culture.

"I can't believe that you . . . ." *How to phrase it?* "Were you thinking she was my girlfriend?"

Again she nodded, and he saw what appeared to be a tear settle in the corner of her eye. What an act! He grinned.

"I'm not your boyfriend, either, Tomoko."

She wrote something on the order slip, sniffled back the tear, and turned away, stalking back to the kitchen.

He did not know what he had done, and he did not know how to undo it. Girls were confusing enough, but being in a different culture with a different language made it even more impossible for him to figure them out.

Ben sat back with a sigh. He did not have any such difficulty with Hanako, despite the culture and language barriers. They connected right away.

Tomoko brought him some curry rice: a plate of white rice with a brown gravy poured over it, a few pieces of meat and vegetables in the sauce, with red pickles on the side. He ate leisurely as he watched her at the counter. When she raised her book once, he saw the two *kanji* for 'English' on it. She was busy studying English.

He was not sure, but she was acting as though she was jealous of Carmen. She seemed to be angry because she liked him but he was ignoring her. That possibility was wholly unfounded. Then he recalled the night walking on the beach with her, talking. He thought of her softly humming *Koi ni Ochite*. Was that a date? Was that the reason she thought he owed her some attention?

Suddenly, Tomoko held out the bill for him to take, staring into his eyes. Her face was frozen in anonymity. He took the paper and she left before he realized that she had left the bill earlier at the same time she had brought his dinner. This was just a note written on an order sheet.

Plees see somethig Hanako after finees.

Well, that was a bizarre message, thought Ben. However, under the circumstances, he knew how to translate it. She had something of Hanako's that she wanted him to see after the shop closed.

He glanced at the clock. Closing was still an hour away.

The old apartment building stood at the top of the hill, on a back street overlooking the town and the sea beyond, crammed between three two-story houses that looked in no better condition. Pine trees on the hillside behind the house formed long shadows that bathed the neighborhood in an eerie mood.

A few blocks away, the sound of breaking bottles and drunken laughter of late-night fools echoed through the streets.

Ben stopped at the intersection at the top of the street, to catch his breath, and the dilapidated building was only two lots further.

"*Baishunfu!*" someone called.

Turning, he and Tomoko saw four young men staggering along the street, hanging onto each other. In their drunken state, they were of little danger. Or a lot of danger.

"*Gaijin no baishunfu!*" one shouted, pointing at Tomoko.

"What's he saying?" he asked.

Tomoko took his arm, pulled him along with the force of a mother dragging her son home for a spanking.

"Bad name," she replied. "Sorry you hear."

He followed her up the rickety, clanging metal staircase as the drunks turned down the street still laughing among themselves. Up to the third floor, passed two lighted windows on the second.

"Papa is awake," she whispered, motioning at the windows.

He nodded, pressed his finger to his lips to assure her he would be quiet. Then he wondered what her father would think of her bringing home a *gaijin*, especially so late—or what he might do about it.

She unlocked the door and stepped into the darkness while Ben paused in the doorway. He was amused, ready to receive cries of "Surprise!" from the hidden guests waiting in the room. Instead, she turned on a light in a back room and returned to the front door for him.

Surrounding him when he stepped into the sitting room were a dozen paintings, half on easels, the rest leaning against the walls. Cloth and plastic sheets covered the floor and art supplies lay across a table, a desk, and two shelves of a mostly empty bookcase. Hanging on the walls were six unframed paintings. Ben was impressed. He was also amazed that she had never mentioned her hobby.

"You're an artist, aren't you?"

He was immediately shushed.

"Please here wait."

She exited, stepping lightly.

Returning, she carried a large bundle in one arm and a shoe box in the other. She extended the box and he took it automatically. The bundle, he saw, was a sleeping child of five or six.

"He name Shunichi," she said. "That mean 'only son.' He father England man."

Ben nodded, understanding. No wonder she had such an aversion to this *gaijin* who kept coming to her coffee shop seemingly just to taunt her. He wanted to apologize, but he did not know how to begin.

"He take care by uncle's daughter." She gestured to the next room, separated by closed *fusama*. "She name Miho."

He nodded again. "Your cousin . . . ."

"You hold?" she asked, offering her son to him.

They exchanged their packages and she showed him to a stack of *zabuton* cushions where he could sit. Then she disappeared again.

Tomoko's sleepy son was heavier than Aiko and as Ben sat down on the floor holding him in his lap, the boy squirmed, sniffled, brushed his face with his hand, tried to roll over, and finally lay still again.

Ben stared back into the sitting room art studio, trying to see what he could of her paintings in the dim light. At that moment, he felt as though he was in a whore's workplace. Here was her illegitimate son sleeping the night away, remnants of past lovers captured on canvas, aids to her memory. There was one painting, not yet finished, which he could see well enough in the poor light to be intrigued. Before he could examine it more closely, she returned.

The *yukata* looked unsettlingly familiar, but its blue and white patterns were different. Ben was relieved. However, the similarity made him uncomfortable. Tomoko had pinned her hair up and tied her *yukata* with a brown *obi*. Even in the dim light from the bare light bulb in the tiny kitchen, she brought Hanako clearly to mind.

"What are you doing?" he asked after a moment of inspection.

"For you," she replied.

"What do you mean?"

"I do for you. To make you happy."

She came and took her son in her arms, then moved in front of the bookshelves in the sitting room. The hidden lights were activated, blinding him and bathing her in golden halo. Posed like the photo Obâsan had sent of Hanako holding Aiko, she regarded him with a half-pout and eyes that seemed about to cry.

"Why?" he asked.

"You happy? I happy. We happy be together."

He jumped up, went to her.

"You said you had something of Hanako's to show me after work. Is this what you meant? Dressing like her?"

Unwittingly, he had offended her and a tear sprouted in the corner of her eye, fell.

"I'm sorry," he said, "but I didn't expect this. You look pretty dressed like this, and it does make you look like Hanako, but . . . . I thought you had something to show me that was Hanako's."

She lowered her son to the cushions on the *tatami* floor. He stirred but not awaken.

"Yes, I can."

Her free arm swept around the room. At the paintings, he guessed.

"These?"

She nodded, curling into the bent-knee *seiza* sitting position.

"They're very nice. I didn't know you were an artist. Why didn't you tell me?"

"Maybe you not like."

"Not like? But why? I think they're great. Do you sell them?"

"No person buy. So I keep."

He started to study them, partly to make her feel happy, but also because as he looked at them he realized they really showed talent.

"*Mite, kudasai,*" she directed, pointing at the easel in the center.

It was the same painting he had started to look at before, while he waited for her to return. As he went to it, the image was a strikingly familiar one. Before a wide beach, a young lady stood calf-deep in the gentle surf. She wore not a stitch of clothing, yet her hips were obscured by a carefully placed spray of water. Her arms were bent upward, and as he looked, they held a baby. The woman's hair was tugged by the breeze and the sun was golden over her right shoulder. White clouds floated in the warm sky. It seemed an almost mythical portrait, with the colors too fantastic to be merely the reproduction of an actual scene. He was reminded of a painting he had seen years before in a book: Venus being born out of the waves. This, however, was mother and child, born out of the waters. Or perhaps descending into them. He could not tell which, except that the woman was Hanako and the child could only be Aiko at perhaps six months.

He was transfixed by the portrait, lost in the warm glow of its sky, soothed by the calm, cool blueness of its sea, excited by the sensuous beauty of the woman and child.

His view was disturbed by the flicking of a card in front of his face. His eyes shifted, focused and he saw it was a snapshot. He took it from Tomoko's hand and turned it over.

He stared at the picture, then at the painting, then back at the photo. They were the same.

"Where did you get this?" he demanded.

"She give me."

"Why?"

"For painting. She want painting for you. Give you big present when you come. But you not come. So I paint anyway because I like picture."

"But what about the photo?"

"I take picture."

"You . . . ?"

"I take picture for her. On beach we walk. Her thought — idea, *ne*. She want picture for you. She want you see *akachan*."

Stunned, he could not think of what to say.

Tomoko hung her head.

"I was *bijutsu* teacher," she spoke after a moment, her soft voice wavering with emotion. "That mean art teacher. I was art teacher of Kanazawa *chugako* — middle school." She flashed an apologetic smile. "One day come English man and teach English to students. He come three day every week. Every day he talk to me. He call me *bijin*. He like me, so we go out. I like him, so we be friends. We good friends. We go to bed. Then he work finish. He go England. Say goodbye and smile. Baby I get in six months."

"Now I get it — "

"I can't teach school. Not good girl, anymore. He never write letter or come back. Family send me to uncle's house, here in Togimachi, *ne*. I paint for some people and they pay to me. I work coffee shop. That how I take care Shunichi, my only son. When I go coffee shop, Miho take care him. *Gaijin* all same. Love *Nihonjin* girl, say bye-bye, go home. Hanako-*chan* and me same so we friends. She tell me you come for her. Some day, she say. I think no, she say yes."

"So she told you about me?"

"She want gift for you. She think make a picture like *tanka* poem — she write you in letter, *ne*? You know *tanka*? I paint Hanako-*chan* and *akachan*. It's for you."

Her eyes seemed to be wet.

"She want it for you. For you, Mister Benjamin. All for you."

She looked up and tears were streaming down her cheeks.

"This for you. Please take."

"I can't do this, Tomoko."

"I not Tomoko."

"What?"

"Tonight, I am Hanako."

She came against him before he knew he was accepting her into his arms. Her face was pressed against his neck.

"I'm Hanako for you. You, Peter for me. Please, tonight I Hanako, you Peter."

He patted her shoulders. Her sobs were louder than her words.

"Please," she whimpered.

"I can't. I really can't, Tomoko."

"Hanako-*chan*!"

In his arms, she was shaking. Through the thin *yukata* he could feel her breasts panting. Her skinny arms were wrapped around his neck and amid her sobbing she was kissing his face. The scent of her hair filled his head and suddenly he believed her. She was Hanako. For tonight, in darkness, in anonymity, they could be each other's *aijin*. And the fantasy seemed real as she carried her sleeping son back to his room and pulled Ben into her room where the *futon* quilt was turned back, ready for them, like a maid had prepared it.

"I can't," someone's voice mumbled, even as Ben embraced her illusion.

"*Aishite*," she sighed. Love me.

18

"DO YOU LOVE HIM?" Obâsan asked Carmen, speaking in Japanese, eyeing her across the table.

In the silence, she briskly stirred the dull, emerald powder into a full froth and set the whisk on its handle. She passed the oversized tea cup to her guest.

Carmen took it, turned it three times in her hand and sipped the green tea. Holding it in her two hands, the *cha* warmed her from the evening's chill.

"It's hard to say," Carmen replied finally, in polite Japanese. "He seems to be a nice man. He wants to be a good father, I can tell. I don't think you have anything to worry about."

"I'm sorry, but that was not what I meant," said Obâsan. "Forgive me for noticing, Carmen-*san*, but you were late in bathing. I worried."

"I'm sorry."

"No, it is I who am sorry . . . for disturbing your peace. I only wanted to assure your comfort. If you did not wish to bathe with him, you only needed to say so. I would not have been offended."

"It's all right. Really. He and I are friends, so . . . ."

"My great-granddaughter would have a good life, I'm sure, if she were to be with you and him. You look like a handsome couple. You are not Japanese? Yet you are like Japanese. I could think of you as my Japanese granddaughter-in-law. Then I would be happy. I would not worry then. This old woman could die in peace."

"Please don't think of such things. She will be in a good family with Benjamin-*san*."

"If he is such a good man, why do you not wish to be his wife?"

Carmen chuckled, her face flushed.

"Oh! I'm so sorry. Forgive an old woman."

"It's all right."

Obâsan refilled Carmen's cup.

"I don't know what I should say," Carmen replied.

"To him?"

"No. About him."

"What do you mean?"

"He is—" She sought the best words. "He is married already."

"Is it so? But I thought—I thought he was a single man. Why did he—how could he fall in love with my granddaughter if he is married to another woman?"

"No, no. I'm sorry. He was not married when he knew your granddaughter. It was after they parted that he met the other woman. He did not know Hanako-*san* was carrying a baby. She did not tell him, as I understand it from him. If he had known, I'm sure he would have . . . well, done something about it. I think this is what he wanted me to tell you. That is why I came to Ishikawa."

"It is so? I still do not understand. Is that how all these Westerners are? I should have followed the wisdom I learned back during the Occupation. I tried to tell her that he would not come back for her, but she was so insistent in believing his romantic words. In the end it was true. Now I am ashamed of myself."

"It wasn't your fault."

Carmen politely mixed fresh *cha* for Obâsan and, bowing, offered her the cup.

"She told me nearly every day about her life with him in Hawaii," Obâsan spoke after three sips. "They met on a beach, the famous one, and they were swimming in the sea together. She was wearing one of those very small swimsuits which are certain to attract men. I think he must have loved her then — with his eyes. Then he talked to her with his romantic words and maybe persuaded her to be his lover."

"I don't think it happened that fast."

"It's true! She told me that he took her to get drunk in a bar, then they walked along the beach until they found a dark place to be together. It is a wild, barbaric place, this Hawaii!"

"I'm sorry. Please let me tell you how it is in America. It's very common for men and women to go to bars to have a drink. It is for relaxation. It is not a bad thing for them. It is very popular."

"In Hawaii, she learned bad American customs, I think. Did you know they lived together without any marriage — in an apartment for nearly a year? I do not know how she could not feel ashamed, living like his mistress. It is outrageous! What if she had the baby there? She would not have the care of her family. It's just as well. In Japan, she would have been thought a whore, but in America I hear they believe it is a good thing. They have their values reversed, I think."

Carmen smiled politely.

"He told me about the apartment, but he said it was *his* apartment. She was only there when she flew to Hawaii. Wasn't it something like four days out of ten? I think so. He said they talked a lot about getting married."

"Then why didn't they? He is just like all the foreign men during the Occupation. Sometimes I shake with anger when I imagine my granddaughter being that immoral. I imagine her sleeping with him whenever she was in Hawaii, as though they were already married."

"It's not considered immoral there —"

"Many men call her a whore when she came to Togimachi. Where did she learn such Western habits? She should have stayed there with him and never returned to Japan. Then this cruel tragedy would not have been. Pity! Instead, she did return to Japan . . . to fly the domestic airplanes. Soon, she saw that she was filled with a child. The airline company could not have her working while she was pregnant. And she was unmarried, too. It is a great shame. They asked her to resign and she did. My son and his wife were not kind. They would not care for her. They were greatly shamed. Their neighbors spoke of them in words too awful to repeat. So they sent her to me, to care for her, to care for the child, to live some kind of life."

Carmen was silent.

"I wish him well," Obâsan continued, "as he takes care of Aiko-*chan*, but that is because she has no other. My daughter-in-law will not accept such a mixed blood child. I am ashamed that my daughter has become such a harsh mother herself. It's all my fault. That is why I took my granddaughter in, to care for her because no one else would. I delivered Aiko-*chan* myself, did I tell you? She is such a beautiful child."

"Yes, she is."

They drank their tea in silence.

"Would he marry Hanako-*chan* now if she were alive, I wonder?"

Carmen grinned. "I'm certain of it."

"Ah, but would he divorce his American wife to marry Hanako-*chan*?"

"I'm so sorry. I do not know about that. But, he told me his wife has already asked him for a divorce. When he got your letter with the photograph, she saw it and became very upset. She did not wish to care for the child—because Aiko was not her child—and did not like the fact that he had loved another woman first."

"Ah, it is so?"

"When he met me in Kanazawa, he had just called her and she still wanted the divorce. He is so determined to care for Aiko that he will allow his wife a divorce. He loves Aiko very much. He wants to do everything he can for her."

"That is good, I know, but maybe he hoped to see Hanako-*chan* once more. I wrote in the letter about her death and about Aiko-*chan* needing to be taken care of, yet when he arrived he seemed not to know about her death. I was surprised. When he asked to see her, all I could do was take him to see her grave. He was so upset, he ran away. It must have been a terrible shock for him."

"I'm sorry to hear that. When he called me—it must have been the same day—he was quite emotional. Of course, you know he cannot read very much Japanese. He could not read your letters, yet he came to find his daughter. He guessed that much."

"I know that now. But all I could write was Japanese. I don't know his English. I hoped he could find someone to read it to him. If it was not so, that was why I sent the photograph, to tell him in pictures."

Obâsan lowered her head.

"I have been rude," said Carmen, "but you see, he came all the way here to see his daughter—and he didn't even know all the facts. This certainly shows how dedicated he is to Aiko's happiness."

Having looked up as she spoke, Obâsan again dropped her gaze, swirled the remaining green tea in her cup.

She was embarrassed, Carmen could see.

"If he is dedicated, where is he tonight?"

Carmen sighed. It was becoming more difficult to defend him. And it was not her job, even. Where indeed was he tonight?

"You heard him when we were in the town hall. He said he would like to visit all the places she went to. Like that old bookshop, and that art gallery you mentioned. He wanted to get to know everything about Hanako, about her life here in Togimachi. He wanted to see the beach where she went to write her letters. Maybe he became lost. He might have decided to stay in an inn. But I'm sure he'll find his way home soon."

"I guess he is a romantic fool," Obâsan sighed, smiled, reached for the canister of powdered tea.

"He is that, I'll agree," Carmen laughed. She started to mention their dinner date in Nagoya, his sense of humor, but thought better of it. There would be no humor in the telling for Obâsan.

Pressing forward another freshly-mixed cup of tea, Obâsan bowed deeply.

"*O-cha, dozo.*" Please accept this tea.

Carmen bowed her head, taking the cup carefully in both hands.

"*Domo arigatô gozaimasu.*" Thank you very much.

19

IT MUST HAVE BEEN ABOUT NINE when Ben awoke. The sunlight had risen high enough to penetrate the window curtains. The room was warm and the quilt became too hot to sleep under. One leg slipped out and caught the morning coolness.

Tomoko was still asleep, he saw, laying on her belly beside him, her head turned away from both him and the sunny window.

He watched her sleeping, thinking how much she did resemble Hanako, from her tangled black hair down her smooth shoulders, across the gentle curve of her back. He was torn between maintaining the illusion that she was indeed Hanako and the growing anguish that he had committed a crime. As long as he accepted her as Hanako then he felt no guilt. In the clarity of the morning light, however, the falseness of the idea rang like a whole belfry of chimes, drowning out cries of innocence with their fateful resonance.

Leaping up, his stomach was tight. He was sick. He pounced into the bathroom, hunching over the toilet set even in the floor, no place to sit down. Waiting to vomit, he only expelled moans.

"When I met you," he remembered asking during the night, "you said you had never met Hanako, but you really were friends."

"Sorry," she had cried. "I not know if you good man or bad man."

"I am a bad man," he said, hoping to be believed. "That's why I'm here in Japan. I'm trying to atone for my sins."

She frowned. "What is 'sins'?"

"Bad things."

"I do many sins," she said.

"Don't say that. You're a good girl. You just happen to be in the wrong country."

"*Domo arigatô.*"

She had kissed him.

"Ishikawa is place where people come to forget," she told him. "It far over mountains, far from everywhere. It good place to hide away. Forget trouble. Forget the things you call sins. Be forgiven maybe. It place people go when do bad sins. Ishikawa is cold, cold place, lonely place. Good place to go. People feel much guilt in Ishikawa. Many people come Ishikawa, want to feel much guilt. We can feel most guilt in Ishikawa. It is like sent away to feel shame. It is like punishment. It is my punishment."

There was nothing he could say that he thought would make her feel better, so he said nothing.

"When you come take Aiko-*chan*," she said, "you be lonely still with no wife."

He had not the heart to tell her, but she had insisted.

"Actually, in America, I have a wife."

She pulled herself up beside him.

"But we are getting a divorce," he finished.

"You get divorce? Why?"

"She doesn't want Aiko. She doesn't like my past relationship with Hanako. As soon as I told her why I was going to Japan, she told me she wanted a divorce."

"I'm sorry, Ben-*san*." She kissed him. "I'm sorry for you."

He was gazing into her eyes when she popped the question.

"You have *akachan* now. You need wife now."

"Yes, I guess I do," he had replied, without any thought.

Now he wondered if she was thinking he meant that he wanted her for his new wife. Was she referring to herself when she made that statement? With a caress of her warm, soft flesh in the morning light, he was not sure it mattered. He tried to remember what they had done, then spied the condom packet on the *tatami* beside the *futon* — unopened. He rubbed his head, feeling the hangover from the *sake* they had drank. The rest was a blank.

Quickly, before he could think another thought, he returned to her room and pulled on his clothes. He was frightened of what he had said, terrified of what he might have done.

He passed an open door, saw Shunichi snoozing soundly in his little *futon*. Splashing some water on his face in the bathroom, his feet were squeezed into the special red rubber slippers with the drawing on them of a little boy going number one. He regarded the portrait of Hanako one last time because he knew he could never return to this apartment.

He had to flee. He had to forget whatever happened during the night and call it only a dream. He wanted that portrait, he decided with that last glance, or perhaps he merely wanted to have in his arms once more the woman who was its subject. Then he would have to come back for it. Tomoko — that was her name, he reminded myself, not Hanako — she promised he could have it. He had to take it. And if he did then some day Aiko would see it and remember her mother.

He quietly closed the door behind him.

"Well, *ohayo gozaimasu*," Carmen greeted Ben at the door, wearing a distinct sneer.

She let him in as the taxi drove off.

"Boy, are you in some deep shit," she barked. "I don't know where you've been or what you've been doing all night, but Obâsan's been worried about you. She says there are some rough guys in town who don't dig *gaijin*. We thought maybe you were laying face down in some gutter."

He shrugged his shoulders, embarrassed. "Sorry I'm late."

"Late, hell. You think you're so smart? Well, you just about blew the whole deal. You can't go around being so damn crazy. I don't want to have to defend you to Obâsan. If you really want Aiko, you still gotta be a little sensible, you know?"

"What do you mean by that?"

She folded her arms, blocking his way in the *genkan*, the entryway.

"Are you trying to prove how irresponsible you can be? For Aiko, much less for yourself? Sure, it's none of my business where you go or what you do, but since I did come all the way up here to help you, I'm gonna help you now by telling you something you don't want to hear. Do you want to know what Obâsan told me last night about your girlfriend?"

"Look, I said I'm sorry."

He tried to press past her and she held out her arm to stop him.

"Where were you? Did you stay with the girl in the coffee shop?"

He stepped past her. "What makes you think that?"

"A hunch."

She followed him into the sitting room.

"Listen, Ben," she said. "Personally, I'm glad you got some loving. You seemed uptight in Nagoya, understandably. And I'm sure sorry we couldn't oblige one another the other night, out in the *ofuro*. But, you're obviously a lot more relaxed now. Besides, I believe a person should get whatever they can. But don't quote me on it. Mama would have a fit."

He did not know whether to laugh or feel insulted.

"I did find out some things from her."

"Oh, so you were just playing detective, were you? What was that? Was it so important you had to stay overnight?"

He sat down at the *kotatsu*. Carmen dropped to the *tatami* opposite him.

"The girl from the coffee shop, as you call her, she and Hanako were friends. She's a painter. Hanako had her paint a portrait of her and the baby. I saw it. She painted it from a photograph she took."

"Yeah?"

"The photo, and the painting, are of them on the beach. Without any clothing. Kinda like Botticelli's Venus."

He paused, stared at Carmen.

"Well, don't look at me," she snapped. "She's your girlfriend. Maybe you didn't know what kind of girl she really was. It sort of fits what Obâsan told me last night. Do you wanna hear it or not?"

"She's got a son."

"The coffee shop girl?"

"Of course."

"Not yours, I hope."

"Not quite. He's half and half, right? She told me about the English teacher who came to town when she was an art teacher in Kanazawa. She got pregnant and was fired. Then she had to come to Togimachi and live with her uncle."

"Yes, it's sad. But are you going to save every poor girl who falls in love with a *gaijin*? That's an awfully mighty task, if you do. Why don't you just stick to your own case. It's hard enough, isn't it?"

He was put securely back in his place.

"So what did Obâsan say that was so earth-shattering?"

"Your girlfriend maybe wasn't so innocent."

"What do you mean?"

"You said yourself she posed for nude pictures."

"Art. For art's sake. She said Hanako wanted the painting for me. As a gift. When I finally came for her."

"A girl's gotta make some money . . . ."

"By the way," he asked, "what does *baishunfu* mean? Is it anything like *bijin*?"

Carmen was surprised.

"Don't you know? It means 'whore.' Actually, 'prostitute.'"

"Oh."

"Why?"

"Just a word I heard in town when I was with Tomoko — the coffee shop girl."

"Well, I guess so!"

"Listen, Carmen, I made a mistake. I did the wrong thing and I'm feeling guilty. I can do that all by myself; I don't need you to heap more shit on me. But I'm back on track now, and it'll never happen again. I swear."

"Just like that?"

"It was a mistake, that's all. An accident. I was—what you said—caught up in my emotions, and—and she was—she came to me—and she threw herself at me. She wanted to be Hanako for me and me to be that British guy for her. That's what happened."

Her crossed arms and stern face stood before him, melting his self-esteem. "Did you speak with an accent?"

"No. I only . . . ."

After a moment, she let out a weary sigh. "And ?"

"I'm not sure what happened but I don't think we *did* anything."

"So you slept together and actually slept?" She laughed. "What a Boy Scout!"

He nodded, brow furrowed and eyes squinting like he was trying to see into the past.

"Well, I have to get back down to the office, so I'm gonna try and catch the three-ten train at Noto Nakajima. I think you can handle it from here on out. Just wait until you get a letter telling you when and where to go for the interview."

"Thanks." He looked up from under his eyebrows.

"Better wear a suit."

"I will. I do appreciate your help."

"It's been real . . . well, it's been *real*. No more mistakes now, okay, or you'll lose her."

He extended his hand, nodding.

"I can't accept your hand, Ben. Not after we've shared the *ofuro*."

She crawled around the end of the table on her hands and knees, reached up and kissed his cheek. Their eyes met, then parted quickly.

"Where is Obâsan now?" he asked.

"They went up to the shrine. They go every Tuesday. Don't you know? The anniversary."

"I'll go meet them."

"She's a bit upset, I'll warn you. You not coming home last night. I guess she can figure things out, too. Maybe you should wait here for them to return."

"No, it's better if I go meet them there."

"Sure you can handle it?"

He nodded.

"Then, good luck," she said. She grabbed him by the shoulders and hugged him.

He grinned.

"Look me up if you're ever in Nagoya and maybe we'll do lunch or something."

Aiko was playing quietly in the dried leaves when Ben arrived at the shrine. The air was already thick with incense. Obâsan was kneeling before the stone statue set in its little wooden house. Flowers were draped over the mantel.

He knelt before the gray headstone.

Bowing low, he whispered a prayer of apology. Ben was not a religious person even though he was raised in a Christian family. He doubted that she was still there, in the grave, or that her soul was anywhere nearby. At best, she was a free spirit sent to roaming the universe. At worst, her body was laid into the ground to decay and fertilize the soil. In either case, she was lost to him. But for Obâsan's sake, he said a prayer. And just in case she was somewhere, somehow listening in the pine grove this morning.

The incense was thick in the grove, stinging his eyes, making them water.

Or am I crying?

Obâsan clapped her hands, climbed up from her old, weary knees, and turned toward him.

From the knapsack, Ben pulled out the offerings he had gathered in previous days. A package of lavender writing paper suitable for ink, still wrapped. Two fine point pens, blue ink. A white and pink Hello Kitty writing board, the same as she had used in Hawaii — so the indentions of the pen would not score the following page. Two old paperbacks the woman in the bookshop swore Hanako had read and returned, one in English, the other Japanese. The new hardback volume that was supposed to be too expensive that she did not dare buy. A few stems of Japanese flowers which looked pretty in the shop window but whose names he did not know. One photograph of himself which had been taken by her in Hawaii showing him at Haleiwa Beach with sailboats behind, his face grinning so wide and happy — *She'd just told me she loved me for the first time, using those English words.* And a cheap gold ring with her birthstone set in it, her size, made to order in a kiosk at the Ala Moana Shopping Center in Waikiki and worn around his neck since then — until he met Addy.

He set them in a carefully balanced pile in front of the headstone. Aiko came over to see what he was doing and what the things were that he had brought. He told her about each item and the child stayed interested, touching them curiously.

Then he sensed Obâsan's presence behind him.

He gathered the offerings, stood slowly, and took them to the Shinto shrine a few steps away.

There, he set them down on the alter, beside or on top of Obâsan's flowers and incense sticks. When he stepped back and turned, he met her curious eyes. He did nothing to show he acknowledged her concern. Instead, he let the collection of mementos serve as both offering and explanation for his absence.

She was puzzled, and said something he, of course, did not understand.

Stepping across the pine grove, he caught Aiko and heaved her up to his shoulders. She laughed as she tottered precariously on the back of his neck, her legs dangling against his chest, the mud on her shoes soiling his shirt. They started down the trail and Obâsan joined them.

He had given his offering and felt much better, much less guilty. Then again, he had no way to judge the effect it had on the entities hovering among the pines.

During the afternoon, Ben played with Aiko, first with the building blocks, then with the stuffed animals in her room. She enjoyed his company, it seemed, and he was encouraged. He sat on the floor. He crawled on his hands and knees. He talked and played at her level and she appreciated that. He could tell—as measured on the informal 'genki' rating scale. *Genki* was the word for 'good spirits,' as used in the phrase *O-genki desu ka*, meaning 'Are you in good spirits?' It was his own idea to call the measure of Aiko's spirits the Genki Scale. At the peak of the afternoon she hit an all time high of seven—as compared with his first visit which was in minus figures.

When Aiko tired of play, they napped together. She slept while he held her, watched her, thinking about both Tomoko and Hanako. They were so alike, and yet were so different. In some ways they were the opposite sides of each other. But in every other thought, they were mirror images. He was even more confused than before.

He wanted to return to town. He had to check with the doctor, to see if he had found the duplicate copy of the birth certificate. And if one could not be found with Ben's name printed on it, then he would need two witnesses to state that Hanako had said at one time or another during her pregnancy and after that Benjamin Pinkerton was indeed Aiko's father. Obâsan would be one, but who else other than her best friend, Tomoko? If he ignored her because of his guilt, would she still give him a signed statement? He wondered.

He had to talk with Tomoko again, despite his vow not to. He had to ask her more questions, and hopefully receive more answers. She knew a lot more than she let on, he sensed, and he intended to find out everything. And if his efforts resulted in another meeting, then so be it. He was divorced—or as good as divorced.

But he knew that Obâsan would not allow him to run free around Togimachi. She would be just as upset if he saw Tomoko again, and with Carmen gone, he could not explain to her. It was still her final say whether or not Aiko came home with him. Even now, they were planning the trip to Kanazawa for the interview, whenever it might be. They were still waiting for both letters, from the Japanese and from the Americans.

But how could he pass any interview if his heart and mind were not squarely focused on the most important issue, that being Aiko? It was crucial to clear his head of all the confusing, nagging questions.

How did Hanako die?

He awoke from the nap he eventually slipped into with that one question flashing before his eyes.

How did she die?

In his busy schedule during Carmen's visit, he had forgotten to have her ask Obâsan.

Aiko was still asleep, her tiny mouth agape and gentle puffs of breath brushing his ear with every soft exhalation.

Obâsan entered the room. In her hands was the scuffed brown suitcase which, after a few seconds, he recognized as Hanako's. She motioned with her head for Ben to follow.

Back in Hanako's room, she set it down.

"*Kore wa nan desu ka?*" he asked, confident in his pronunciation. What's this?

She bowed politely, as if accepting his apology, his offering at the shrine, excusing him in her suspicious thoughts. Upon straightening up, she produced a pair of keys from her pocket.

"*Dozo,*" she said, offering them to him.

He took them, still baffled, and watched her step out of the room. Maybe she was still angry. He could not be sure. Why the suitcase? Did she want him to pack and leave? Or was there something in the suitcase that she wanted him to see?

It seemed hours, long past dinner and far into the evening, before Obâsan checked on him. In all that time, he examined the contents of Hanako's old suitcase. Inside were priceless memories. When the seal was cracked, he gazed down upon neatly folded garments—hers.

Every piece was another key in his mind's lock. On top was the sexy pink chemise which he had bought for her in Hawaii. She wore it their last night together—at the beginning, anyway. Beneath it were several pink and white panties. He ran each of them through his tense fingers, recalling the way they had felt when she had worn them.

Several bras, and two pairs of panty hose. There were neatly pressed blouses and skirts. There were several T-shirts and tanktops which had touched her body. There were other articles he recognized. He held each item, as though it was a part of her, trying to extract what residual aura might still be there.

At the bottom of the suitcase, under everything else, were the wonderful pair of pink Bermuda shorts she had always seemed to be wearing. He held them up, examining them, then pressed them to his cheek. His throat tightened as he revisited every occasion she had worn them.

He was filled with ecstasy. They were the actual clothes she had worn! Not merely duplicates, but the real ones. He breathed in their scents, locked in the suitcase since last year, when it was warm enough to wear them — or possibly longer, perhaps unworn since she left Hawaii, since May twenty-ninth, 11:33 in the morning, Japan Pacific Air flight 06, departing from Gate 21.

Searching the suitcase's pockets, he found miscellaneous American coins, safety pins, lipstick tubes, a packet of sanitary napkins, a key ring with a plastic talisman enclosing his smiling photo, a cassette of *Kokoro no Mamani*, the album of pop singer Akiko Kobayashi which contained the song "*Koi ni Ochite*" sung in English.

And the farewell card he gave her.

There was a stain on the flap of the envelope, another at the corner where she had torn it open. One was a tear drop, the other a smudge of lipstick. He could not bear to read it now, but he forced himself.

To my best Bijin,

He remembered the day he wrote it. He guessed this was supposed to be his punishment: to relive the past under the new set of rules.

I love you with all my heart, and no words — English or Japanese — can tell you the same thoughts as I have for you.

All I can try to say is that I hope you will have the best of luck forever and that I'm sure good fortune will follow you all of your life. If ever we meet again—and I'm hoping it won't be long until we do—I know we'll never again part.

Sweet dreams, my Bijin.

I'll love you forever.

20

WHEN THE LAST DAY CAME, the sun rose as usual and Ben awoke early to fix her breakfast. Hanako said she was not hungry, but he insisted she eat something before the long flight. The eggs were half finished, and one biscuit was gone when she went to get dressed. He washed the dishes, then dressed casually in slacks and the lavender aloha shirt she had bought for him at Christmas.

She emerged from the bedroom in navy blue uniform, red-white-and-blue scarf around her neck, her long, lush black hair tied up with pins and ribbons into a tight bun, her slender legs looking sexy with calves taut, wearing the matching blue pumps.

"You look beautiful."

Her face was expressionless. He could see she was holding back tears. They would only ruin her make-up.

"*Ikimashô ka?*" she asked with little happiness. Shall we go?

He stared at her a moment longer as she avoided his eyes, head lowered, breathing quickly.

"All right. Let's go, then."

The airport was crowded so he dropped her off at curbside and went to park the car, promising to see her off. She begged him not to come inside, but he told her he must see her up until the last moment.

He had bought a card, but with her in the apartment, there had been no time for him to write the few words he could think of. There were a few minutes now, so he worked quickly. He struggled with the first line, wanting so much to write something poetic, something meaningful, words of importance rather than trite rhymes. Then he rushed from the car into the terminal.

It was May twenty-ninth and Japan Pacific Air flight 06 was about to depart from Gate 21. He regarded the flight information monitor. It would be set in his mind forever.

His heart was beating feverishly when he arrived at the gate, and he had to pause and clear his head. He had to fight the lines of passengers waiting for boarding. Three uniformed Japanese ladies stood behind a tall white counter next to the doorway and, mixed in the crowd, he did not find her immediately.

He held the card firmly in his hand, his camera dangling from his shoulder. Yes, he had taken many pictures of her, but never the last photograph. There could be only one last picture. He stood in line trying to decide which to do first, take a picture or give her the card.

Watching her busily handling all the check-in procedures, he saw glimpses of her face. She was trying to hold back tears. He waited his turn; he did not have a ticket. There were so many people around them, he realized, and none of those people knew of their private torment. They had said their goodbyes already, the night before, but he silently begged for one more moment free of distraction. Time is fleeting, he cursed at the line. *Come on, people!*

He grew impatient and raised his camera, snapped a picture of her over the heads of the line of people. Several of the passengers in front of him were startled. Others stared at him: one of those Hawaiian perverts always taking pictures of pretty girls.

Hanako glanced up at the flash, an embarrassed smile on her tear-stained face.

"Look at that," one tourist remarked to his wife, "she's crying."

Ben he did not care about them. They did not know the truth. No one knew his heart was aching, would soon be torn from his chest by the thrust of a jet plane.

"Somebody oughta call a security guard," another passenger said. "Look how she's crying. That creep's harassing her with his camera."

Once the pre-boarding area was cleared, she had a moment to pose for him. Her colleagues saw them and left them alone. Her friend Yumi dipped her head in a polite bow to him. Hanako stood stiffly at attention in her crisp blue uniform for him. She saluted and tried to laugh, tried to be cheerful, but a tear dropped down her cheek. She had tried to keep a smile on her face but after that, she could smile no longer. Tears flowed freely down her cheeks and she took a tissue from her pocket.

Face cleared, she pursed her lips, with great effort attempting a grin, a smile, anything positive. He took his last picture of her, and she slipped his card unopened into the outer pocket of her flight bag. Then she turned in the waiting area and waved back at him.

As his eyes met hers in that last, long glance, he lost his nerve, and tore himself away. He rushed out of the waiting area and around the corridor to the wide windows looking out on the giant aircraft.

Feeling guilty about his sudden escape, he pushed his face against the glass, searching desperately for a porthole window along the fuselage where he might see her. Even though he knew he could not see inside, he hoped she might happen to look out and see him standing there, looking for her.

He took long, deep breaths as the plane backed away from the gate. Then, as he watched the big silver and red plane arch into the bright, tropical sky, he thought of only one thing: she did not know what his farewell card said in that last moment before they ceased to gaze into each other's eyes. He tried to conjure the feeling he'd had moments before, staring into those beautiful eyes, fearing it might be the last time.

"Don't cry," he had told her as they stood by the check-in counter together, the eyes of her fellow flight attendants careful averted. "You always cry," he'd told her and they shared a laugh. He could see her make-up smearing as a few tears ran down her face. "We'll see each other again."

She was too choked up to reply so, despite being on duty, she slid her arms under his and hugged him, laying her head against his chest for one full second.

"I can't live without you, Hanako," he whispered into her ear. "I'll come for you — some day. I don't know when, but some day. I'll study and learn Japanese. Then I'll come for you. Then we'll be together forever."

He realized they were trite words, but at the time he was so filled with emotion he could not think of anything more original. So he uttered the words he thought were expected. He wanted to believe them. Long after they parted he still believed them. But words left unwritten fade all too easily, he discovered, although in those final seconds, there was nothing else he could have done.

She was gone.

And six lonely months later he returned to Seattle, where life began again.

In the spiritless days that followed Carmen's departure, Ben spent hours every day playing with Aiko and reading through the letters. He did not sleep much, and barely ate. His heart and mind ached. He lived his former life again through the letters, even as he prepared somehow for a new life. Hanako would live again, hidden in a four year old body.

In the evenings, he ate silently with Obâsan and Aiko, then he would retire to his room — to Hanako's room — and continue his investigation. He was reading through the letters again, the letters he'd sent to her. He looked through the photos. He studied the handwriting, the choice of words, the grammar, the sentence structure — everything. Often he was up until dawn, though usually he could stand it no more by three or four.

The dark moods that came and covered him in those late evening hours frightened him. Left on his own, he was sealed in the room, surrounded by the memorabilia of Hanako. He felt locked in a prison specializing in psychological torture.

Sometimes, if the afternoon was warm, Ben gathered up Aiko and took her to the shrine. Always eager to go outside, she was eager to play in the forest. She liked the variety of playthings available there — the flowers, insects, stones, pine cones, grass — anything available to play with. They went to the shrine and he would sit and watch her playing. His mind usually drifted back to the happy, sad days in Hawaii. As his eyes observed his daughter, his dulled mind thought back to lonely Kahana Bay. He desperately wished to return there to revel in his melancholy. That was where he could feel the most guilt.

Instead, he was lost in Ishikawa — where people in Japan came to feel the greatest guilt, as Tomoko told him. It seemed to work for her. But he knew he would be going home soon. Then he would have a schedule, and he would have a direction, a course for his life. Then he would be free of this time-stopping, reality-bending fantasy world where he was but a shadow, or someone else's bad dream.

As it was, the days were already blurring into a mystic period of isolated chasms of pain and windswept peaks of ecstasy. He never knew when he was heading up or down. Sometimes he did not know even after he'd gotten there.

"Aiko," he called to her on one of the days they went out. He sat with his back against a pine tree, facing the gray headstone as he kept an eye on her playing in the grass. "I don't know how you can be so beautiful, but please don't ever lose it. You're so innocent now. I wish it would last forever, but I know it's impossible."

She looked up at him from across the grove, a mask of curiosity on her face like she was really trying to understand him.

"I hate the thought," he continued, shifting his eyes around the grove then up to a family of clouds strolling by. "Some day you'll want to know why you do not look like your father. You'll want to know where your mother is and all I'll be able to do is show you pictures of her. Will you know who she is? I can only imagine. Will you remember her in years to come? It's been four long years since I last saw her, but her face is as clear in my mind's eye as if she were standing here now. I hope you can remember her that way in the future. I want to tell you about her. I want to tell you everything.

Then you'll know why you're so special."

He waved at her and she wandered over to him, a tiny bouquet of wildflowers in her chubby hand.

Smiling, he sat her on his knee.

"I love you," he whispered, gently pinching her shoulders.

She thrust the flowers up to his face. He sniffed them and when he made an ugly face, she giggled. Her laughter was sweet music in the pine grove.

Ben stood up straight and with a quick thought adjusted his necktie. It was warm enough that he decided not to wear a sportcoat. His dress trousers had wrinkles from being in the suitcase for so long but Mr. Kubota assured him that he looked fine.

"Hello," said Ben in an even tone that was carefully calculated. He added a smile almost as an afterthought. "My name is Benjamin."

"Harrow, Mistah Benjameen," the classroom of thirteen-year-olds responded in unison.

They giggled and he also laughed.

"That's very good," he said, relaxing.

Never before had he spoken to a room full of children but now that the ice was broken he began a wonderful dialog with the students. They asked him questions in English and he answered. At first, the answers were easy. "Do you like baseball?" one boy asked, not too confident in his English. Ben had replied in textbook fashion: "Yes, I like baseball."

Around the room they went, Mr. Kubota pointing to a student and the student standing up beside his or her desk, smiling in fear or giggling too much to speak or being too shy to go further. Two girls were allowed to sit down without asking the visitor a question. Finally it was Ben's turn to ask the questions. Again they went around the room and he asked the same kind of questions of the students and listened patiently as they fumbled with their answers. He was happy and when the class ended and the teacher stood beside him for the final bow of the class period, Ben was sad to leave.

"Thank you, Mister Benjamin, for visiting my class," said Mr. Kubota as they arrived in the staff room.

Unlike American schools, Ben noticed, this middle school consisted of one large room for the teachers—an open arrangement that allowed both colleague collaboration and whole group meetings with a minimum of distraction. He liked it and thought to mention it to Rich when he returned to Seattle. The classrooms were different, too. The rooms belonged to the cohort of students; different teachers came and went according to the subject of the hour. Art, Science, and Physical Education were the only subjects where students had to leave their particular classroom.

"You are the first American they have met," said Mr. Kubota.

Gesturing for Ben to sit in the chair of the desk beside his own desk in the staff room, he explained how Japanese students begin learning English in the first year of middle school, when most were twelve or thirteen. It was a required subject and they would be tested on English at all levels, just like their other subjects.

"We want to be international," said Mr. Kubota, "like all you in America."

"I appreciate that," said Ben. The school secretary arrived with a tray of green tea in small cups for the two of them. "I had fun today." He glanced at the secretary, old enough to be his mother, who smiled in delight, as though meeting a celebrity. "*Domo arigatô,*" said Ben and the secretary bowed her head and departed with a giggle.

"Ah, you know some Japanese," said Mr. Kubota—Kubota-*sensei* to his students.

"I took a class, but I wish I had stayed for more. I never expected I would ever visit Japan when I took that class. But . . . here I am."

"I and my students enjoyed your visit. Please come again any time you like."

Benjamin had been walking in the town and had stopped by the bookshop again. A customer there had struck up a conversation with him. It was Mr. Kubota, a tall, rather thin young man with a prematurely balding head who taught at the middle school, two years out of teacher's college. His subject? English, he announced proudly. They had a good talk and he was subsequently invited to visit the school. The next day Mr. Kubota arrived at Obâsan's house to pick him up and drive him to the school.

Ben spent the whole day there. He visited three English classes, one for each grade year, and observed an Art class and a Music class. Everywhere he went in the school—wearing indoor slippers—or on the school grounds, he was treated as a celebrity.

Some students asked him for his autograph—"Sign, please," they would say, holding out a notebook or piece of paper.

Others would dare each other to speak to the foreigner. "How are you?" was their most common question. Ben started responding with "Fine," then "I'm fine, thank you," but eventually replied "I'm not doing too badly but perhaps I'd be better off with a somewhat heartier breakfast next time and a bit more sleep." The students stared at him, baffled by the long string of words.

He ate lunch with the teachers in the staff room: rice, pickles, fish, soup, and tea. And he stayed after classes to watch the boys' baseball team and girls' softball team practice. The boys let him take an at-bat—he was struck out—and he flied out for the softball team on what he thought was a sure double. When the day finally ended, Mr. Kubota drove Ben home. It was well after seven.

Ben was ready to slump on the futon and call it a day but Obâsan had dinner ready. After eating, he relaxed in the *ofuro*, then went to bed, glad he did not have to get up and go to school again the next morning.

Word got around quickly in the town and he was invited to visit the high school, where the students were quite bored with their English instruction. Ben thought up some games to play and the students began to smile, one by one, and by the end of the class his host teacher, Mr. Fukushima, a short, chubby man with glasses whose thick accented English was difficult for Ben to decipher, was pleased.

And rather surprised. The students needed to study hard for exams to get into colleges. They had no time for games.

Another English teacher, Reina Funatsu, was more gracious. She was happy to see how Ben interacted with her students, even flirted with the girls and encouraged the boys. They had a good discussion of educational differences between their countries over the lunch hour. He enjoyed talking with her so much that he thought of asking her out to dinner but saw the wedding ring on her finger.

An older teacher, Mrs. Hirata, showed him her class of Math students and he patiently watched them doing worksheets for fifty minutes. She beamed proudly.

After a late afternoon staff meeting where he nursed his cup of tea as long as he could, he spent the after-class time with the soccer team and became dreadfully sweaty running up and down the field with them.

He was scheduled for the elementary school next—the one where Aiko would go the next spring if she remained in Japan, in this town.

Watching the children playing during recess time, he wondered what he would do next.

He had missed so much time. Suppose he had no job waiting for him when he returned. Rich would grow tired of waiting for him, this once reliable now crazy hospitality manager. He needed to call him, just to touch base, to get a feel for the possibility of his future with Prime Properties. So he stopped at the NTT office and chose a booth.

"Benjamin Franklin Pinkerton!" Rich's baritone voice had mused over the steady hum of the international phone line. "How the hell are you? Long time no talk, huh?"

"Yes, I'm still here," Ben had responded. He asked for updates on the current projects but could not feel any connection to the day to day tasks he used to deal with easily and effectively. He explained that he needed more time—he had glanced at his watch, 300 *Yen* per minute—time in Japan, that is.

"Take all the time you need, but nothing stops here and waits for you," said Rich.

"And I was wondering if you could advance me some money."

"Advance you?" Rich laughed. "You tapped out already?"

Ben gave him a summary of the situation, how he was waiting on paperwork to go through the system. That could take months, years. Meanwhile, he was investigating how his former lover had died.

"I understand," said Rich. "You have to deal with . . . what was her name? started with an 'H'?"

"Hanako."

"Yes, that's it. And now you have a Tomoko?"

"She's Hanako's friend. She's helping me with my investigation."

"Hanako. Tomoko. The Ko sisters."

"Come on!"

"I don't know what you've got going over there, buddy, but we can't keep doing this, you know. Life goes on. Projects go on. You're going to have to choose where you want to be. Sooner or later."

He had committed that phrase to memory: *Choose where you want to be.* Now he was trying to answer it.

Ben paused to kick back a ball that had rolled his way.

If he had to, he considered, looking around the yard at the happy children, he could stay in Togimachi. He was getting a feel for the place and it was growing on him. He liked the slower pace, the fresh air, the view of the sea and the mountains. And everyone was kind to him, more or less. The town had a mysterious aura, however. People glanced at him as though they knew his secrets. As they had secrets, too. A town full of secrets!

He thought of Aiko and imagined how she would grow up here, starting at this primary school, then learning English in the middle school. Of course, he would teach her all the time, anyway, so she was bound to be the best in her class. And then she would be in high school, studying for the college exams. Then college. A career. A family of her own. And he would be the grandpa. He knew he was getting far ahead of himself, but he had to think of that option.

What if I stayed here?

He could be an English teacher. He spoke it fluently, after all. He could visit the schools and talk to students in their classes and grade their exams. It would not pay much, he guessed, but it definitely would be something he could do. Everyone needed a place to fit in, it seemed in Japan. He could keep living with Obâsan, and take care of her when she became too old to care for herself. Meanwhile, Aiko would have that kindly face watching her grow up. And he would be at peace in this lovely forested hillside next to the sea.

And he might also see that crazy waitress again. Tomoko. She was moody but generally a kind person. They had something in common, too. Hanako, he sighed. That's what they had in common. He thought they might make a good family, his daughter and her son. It could work. He was willing to try to make it work. He laughed, wondering why Addy couldn't extend any effort to try to make it work.

That was a different world, he knew. Suddenly that truth settled in his gut. He wondered if he really could return to that life. Or whether it was better to stay in Togimachi with his daughter.

21

THE DAY THE LETTER ARRIVED was one of the most beautiful days Ben had ever seen: bright, golden, cool and warm, bursting with life, Spring at its finest. The letter was from the Japanese authorities requesting additional information, which at that instant he feared he could not give them. The following day, however, drew in dark clouds full of rain. As the showers fell, he brought in the second letter, perfectly timed, arriving from the U.S. Consulate in Osaka. They needed more information, too. The day was complete.

At first Ben hid the letters from Obâsan, vainly believing that their presence would be an admission of his failure. He needed assistance. He gradually mentioned them to her in his best dictionary-translation Japanese. The letters were in English so she could not read them for herself. Both wanted sworn statements and most of all, the birth certificate. Both agencies demanded the original copy. That would be a neat trick. If it was not lost in the mail, then he would at least have to send it to one place before the other, and each of them might keep it for several weeks. His vacation was over, and he had to go back to work — not to Seattle but in Togimachi.

Two weeks wasted! Ben settled into the paperwork routine once more, trying to decipher the language of the government. He quickly became tired and reached is limit.

There was only a little more, he found as he looked in his wallet, pausing to check his cash resources. It did not cost much to stay in Togimachi, especially living in Obâsan's house for free, but if he had to fly down to Osaka and back, staying in a hotel—that would push him to the end of his budget. After that he would be forced to pull out yet another credit card. He had maxed out his Visa.

After completing some new forms from the Japanese office, and redoing one from the U.S. consulate, he gave himself a break. Before he could send them back, he had to make a trip into town. It was time to visit the doctor. It was time to meet Tomoko again. And someone else, if he could even find him: that English-speaking professor from the bookstore.

While he waited, Ben had puttered around the old house and found a rusty bicycle in the storage shack out back next to the *ofuro* hut. With some repair, he was able to ride it into town. Some high school boys laughed at him, trying to pedal the bent machine.

Ben arrived on the main street breathing hard and feeling streams of sweat running down his back. But he was in town at last. Nothing else mattered now. He headed to the doctor's office.

As he approached, he saw a tall figure in the shadows of the curtains whom he recognized as Dr. Kotani. Then, as he crossed the street, the figure stepped away and a mysterious hand flipped around the sign which he presumed read 'closed' in Japanese.

Reaching the front steps, Ben hesitated, wondering if the doctor intended for him to think the office was not open, or that seeing Ben on his way, he turned the sign to keep out other customers so he could deal with the intrusion.

He passed through the door to the cheerful calling of *"Konnichiwa"* by the two nurses.

"Konnichiwa," Ben replied, expecting them to know he wanted to speak to the doctor.

But they did not guess. He was forced to dig into his brain and pull out some more Japanese. To the delight of the receptionist and the medical assistant, both he guessed to be in their early twenties and to whom the first place prize for international giggling would definitely go, he shuffled through his request. After a second try, one of them understood and left to retrieve the doctor.

Thirty minutes later, Dr. Kotani appeared, acting as though Ben had dared call him out of surgery.

"Did you ever find that copy of the birth certificate?" Ben asked.

"Birth certificate?" the doctor replied, squinting.

"Don't you remember?"

"I think I gave the birth certificate to you."

"But it didn't have my name on it. The place for the father's name said 'unknown.'"

"Yes, that is true."

"But you told Nakamori-*san* that you might have a copy in your files which would name me as the father."

He turned away, spoke to his assistant who left immediately for the back room.

"Did you find it?"

He cleared his throat.

"The copy of the birth certificate has the *kanji* for 'unknown' — like the original."

"Kotani *sensei*, what happened that night? Did she tell you my name? Was she conscious?"

"It was four years before now, and my memory is not clear. Her grandmother delivered the baby, and I came only the next day."

"What happened?"

"It was a difficult birth, she said to me, but no serious problems. The baby was large—" He glanced at Ben, head to toe. "—as you are, and she was very weak. Her strength was low and she . . . she was in and out of consciousness a few days."

"But she was all right, then, right?"

"Yes, of course. She recovered quickly."

"But what about the certificate?" he enunciated each syllable with gritted teeth.

"Nakamori-*san* helped. She told me the answers to my questions, from the words of Hanako-*chan*."

"And she told you to write 'unknown'?"

"No, Mister Pinkerton."

The doctor stepped back, then motioned for Ben to follow him down the hallway, turning into the back office. He sat at the patient's chair beside the desk. The assistant had laid the file there. He could read the *kanji* of HANA-KO NAKA-MORI on the white label.

"I must tell you, Mister Pinkerton," Dr. Kotani continued without sitting, "in our culture it is not common for a woman to be pregnant outside of a marriage. Not officially. And to be joined with a foreign man is . . . ."

"I understand that. But who said to write 'unknown' on the birth certificate?"

The doctor sat down finally.

"It is customary to write 'unknown' when the man who is the father is not the husband of the woman who is the mother."

"What?" He stared at the folder. "Why . . . ?"

"It is customary. If the relationship is a secret one, it protects the identity of the people."

"And what about my case?"

"Yes, it is customary when the father is a foreigner—"

"A *gaijin*, you mean."

He nodded slowly, contemplatively.

"So, in other words, you lied to Nakamori-*san*, telling her—and me, too—that you'd find this copy of the certificate just to make us happy. It's all to keep your face, isn't it? And our faces, too, huh? That's it, isn't it? There is no copy with my name on it. Did you even ask Hanako what my name was?"

"She was unconscious at the time, sleeping."

"But it's been four years, Doctor Kotani!"

Ben jumped up, rattling the chair. Both girls came to the door and the doctor waved them away.

"What's going on here?" Ben glanced around. "Why is everyone trying to make it so hard for me? Did they want to get rid of her? Did you want to hide her sin under an anonymous *kanji*? Why did you not let her give you the answers?"

"Mister Pinkerton," the doctor cut in, just as Ben was losing focus, beginning to rant about all of his frustrations. "I'm sorry. There is no certificate with your name on it. And I cannot falsify a duplicate certificate."

Ben shook his head slowly, rubbing his eyes and found his way toward the door.

"Did Hanako ever tell you my name?"

"No, I don't remember if she did, but I don't think so."

He spun around to face the doctor.

"In four years, Doctor Kotani?" Ben shook his head. "You visited her. You gave Aiko her check-ups. You took care of Hanako. You also treat Obâsan for a variety of disorders—rheumatism, osteoporosis, whatever. For four years. And never once, not a single instance, did you hear them say the name of Hanako's daughter's father?"

The doctor's face was frozen, not used to the aggressive style of American complaining. He could not speak.

"That sounds a little bit suspicious. It sounds like a conspiracy." Ben took a breath. "I know this is Ishikawa, where people go to forget and be forgotten, but this is still a place where people can show some compassion, isn't it? Damn if I see it anywhere. I'll just have to find another way to prove my paternity, doc. Good day!"

Ben's phone call to Addy went right through from the NTT office. At least something worked right this week. Except there was no answer. Maybe that was for the best, he decided. His heart still beat hard from his anger, his breathing heavy. The ringing time allowed him to calm down.

Eventually he hung up the phone. No charge. Then he went on to Bourgouisse.

"Ben-*san*," Tomoko cried out when he entered, no concern for her customers' peace. "Why you no come see me long time?"

He could not tell her the real reasons.

"We need to talk," he told her in a low voice.

He sat at the counter and after she had served one table, they talked.

"It's a very difficult time for me," he explained. "I've been busy. I've applied to Japanese Immigration and the U.S. Consulate to bring Aiko home with me. We will have an interview soon—I hope. But now there's a problem. I think you can help me, and I hope you will. Okay?"

"Okay," she said with a smile.

"The important thing is that I will be going back to America—sometime soon. And I don't want to leave behind any bad memories. Do you understand?"

"Maybe—I not sure."

"I want you to understand. I hope there's no misunderstanding between us. What happened that night was just a mistake. I did not mean to hurt you, or to lead you on. I want to settle that because I need your help. That's why I need to talk to you today."

"What does mean 'lead on'? I not understand."

Either she was playing dumb, or she really did not grasp the meaning of what he said. He wanted her to know that he did not have any feelings for her, not any real feelings. What happened was an accident, and he had to make that clear to her.

He told her using simple English and she seemed to understand. She was pouting and squinting her eyes as though holding back tears. That was a good sign she understood.

Then her boss called her to get back to work and she jumped up to go take an order.

"Will you come tonight?" she asked between orders.

Didn't she hear what I just said? Ben sighed. Or was her steady *'hai, hai'* was the Japanese way of saying 'still listening'?

"I can't," he said.

She brought out food and took it to a table.

"You want painting of Hanako-*chan, ne*?" she asked, returning his way.

"Yes," he decided then. "Of course, I do."

She continued on to gather more dishes from the kitchen and

deliver them to customers.

He had no idea what he could do with such a painting after he brought it back to America. If he were really divorced, he supposed he would simply hang it on the wall and stare at it every day to be reminded of his failures. And if he were somehow not divorced, then he certainly could not hang it on the wall with Addy living there.

"You come tonight?" Tomoko checked once more.

Maybe if he remained kind to her, she would write a statement saying that Hanako had told her that he was Aiko's father.

"All right. I'll try."

22

OBÂSAN WAS NOT PLEASED that Ben was going out again after dinner. It was the first time he had ever seen her angry. She only spoke a few words but her tone was angry. He could also see it in her eyes as she cleared the dishes. He was dressed to go out, not to relax at home.

She brought Aiko in to sit with him. Maybe she wanted to remind him of his duties. He wanted to tell her that he did understand his duties. However, with Aiko eventually tucked in her *futon*, he was free to take care of his business. By then, his mind was too dull to put together any sentences in Japanese to explain that he was trying to get Hanako's friend to sign some statement. A statement that might not be true, he began to ponder.

Perhaps there was another reason. At night, Tomoko transformed herself into Hanako. Was it an affair? Naturally to Obâsan, it was hurtful to her granddaughter's memory. He could see that, but still he had to go.

He kissed Aiko goodnight—she was already asleep—and left for town on the bicycle.

The five kilometer ride was becoming easy, but the hill he had to climb up to Tomoko's apartment was a difficult task. He gave up and walked the bike the rest of the way.

Someone waited on the steps below her place. A man was sitting on the first step, smoking.

Ben's first guess was that he was her infamous uncle, but as he approached, the man resembled one of the drunks from the night Tomoko first brought him to her home. In a black shirt and white tie, he had his glossy blue jacket folded over his knee. He was not a very friendly-looking fellow.

He was watching Ben.

Parking the bike at the foot of the stairs, Ben proceeded to mount them.

"*Sumimasen,*" said Ben. Excuse me.

The man did not move.

Instead, he looked up from under sprouting locks of his permed hair-do, regarding Ben with small, squinting eyes set in a sideways stare, blowing smoke from his nostrils.

"*Sumimasen,*" Ben repeated, stepping on the stair where he sat.

The man stared at him a moment longer, dragging on the cigarette. Then, the man slid over an inch begrudgingly, blowing more smoke from his nose.

When Ben arrived up at her door and looked back down the stairs, the man had turned where he sat and was still watching him. Now he was exhaling smoke rings.

Tomoko quickly pulled Ben inside, wrapping her arms around him, planting a kiss on his lips. He was surprised.

"What's with your bodyguard down there?" asked Ben, prying her away. He pointed out the window.

"I not know. He sit there every day."

"Is he watching you?"

"Maybe he watch *you,*" she replied.

That was possibly true, as popular as this foreigner.

"Don't you have to work tonight?"

"No tonight. We have much time."

"I don't have much time. That's what I was trying to tell you at the coffee shop. I'll be leaving Togimachi soon, I want you to know. But I have to get these papers back to Immigration first." He showed her the sheaf of forms. "I need your help, Tomoko. Will you help me? I just need you to write a letter. Can you do that?"

Only then did he notice that she was again wearing the *yukata* that was similar to the one Hanako wore in the photograph. As he held Tomoko loosely in his arms, he could feel that the yukata was all she wore. He wondered if it really was a night off, or if she had made some excuse to be off. What did she have planned?

She kissed his neck as he regarded the finished painting standing on the easel before them.

"It's done?" he asked, feeling nervous. "The painting?"

She looked up.

"Yes. It finish. For you now."

They had settled on a price the last time he was there. It was sometime during the night. He really liked the painting and although it was supposed to be a gift from Hanako, she had not paid for it. He asked her what she wanted and she insisted he take it as a gift. He thought *ichi-man* yen was fair, about a hundred dollars. It was worth more to him than the average buyer, but he had limited funds.

She held his face tenderly in her hands, as though he had always been her lover. It was the same way Hanako had done in Hawaii.

Her words were full of soothing sweetness.

"We got all the night."

"All night?" He was stalling, thinking.

"You not happy? We together all night. We go together all night in America, Ben-*san*. Okay *desu ka*? Then we good family."

"What are you saying, Tomoko?"

"You get girl now. No wife, you said, so we be good family. You said last night."

"Not last night. You mean the last time we were together. Here."

"Okay, last time here."

"I don't think I said anything about you and me being a family."

He must have looked too serious to her.

"Please, not worry, Ben-*san*," she whispered into his ear as her fingers unbuttoned his shirt.

"I'm not worried. I'm feeling guilty."

"Not feel guilty."

"I have to. That's my job here in Ishikawa. I came here to feel the most guilt. That's why people come here, isn't it? You told me that. But I—I can't do this. I've got to tell you, Tomoko, I can't—"

She put her finger to his lips, silencing him.

"I can't take you to America."

She appeared not to hear him. "Make you happy."

"I can't—"

They were at a doorway, but he realized it was a different room than before. The *futon* was laid out so immaculately, the quilt turned back and the blanket folded like *origami*. Two pillows sat on each corner. The six *tatami* mats looked so fresh. A plum blossom laden branch sat in a short, squat vase at the far end of the room. The air was filled with its tangy scent.

"Special for you tonight," she spoke excitedly, holding his hand.

"It's like that painting in the other room," he remarked, turning back and searching for it. "The one by the front door. The girl on the futon with the open *shoji* behind her, and the branch of a plum tree hanging down from the garden . . . ."

She tried to hug him, regarding the room with him. "It is same. For you."

He ignored her flirting. "And the girl in the painting?"

"Hanako-*chan deshô*," she cooed. "Maybe it is me. Can't you guess? Can you know za difference? It is me, or maybe Hanako-*chan*? If light is gone how do you know?"

All he came for was the painting and a letter. Now she was making her bedroom into a painting in which they could be together.

"Tomoko, will you help me with the papers?"

She rose up and kissed him like she had been waiting years.

"*Hai*. I help you anything."

The bright sun was almost hot, but the hike was less arduous than Ben expected. He followed the trail past the shrine and the headstone, up through the pine forest, rising and rising to the treeless hillside above. As he hiked, the increasing elevation made him think back to a day on Hawaii's great Mauna Loa and he was once more filled with exhilaration. Yellow, knee-high grass lay like a sea before him and he waded through it to a higher summit. A lone tree, bent and twisted by wind and time, offered some shade from the burning sun. He sat down with the knapsack, slipped out the *bentô* box lunch Obâsan had prepared. He laughed when he saw she included a fork, though he had no trouble using chopsticks.

From the heights, he could hear no human noise. He could see no human things, only nature. The deep blue of the sea stretched out from the rocky shore far below, laying smooth as silk. The horizon was very distant in every direction. To the left, he could make out the twin rocks of Noto Kongo, where local people, believing the rocks to be married had tied them together with huge straw ropes, the big one to the smaller one. A few bent pines grew on the larger rock.

Ben felt nothing but peace there, sitting above the confusion and frustration of the world.

It was a small *bentô* and he finished the fishcake, pork slices, lotus roots, bamboo shoots, carrots, and some pickled seaweed in short order. Half the box was filled with rice, of course, and Obâsan had sprinkled sesame seeds over the rice to give it flavor. A fat strawberry tucked in the corner was dessert. Finished, he popped the tab on a can of something called Pocari Sweat—an 'isotonic drink,' the can said—and tossed it down the lemony liquid.

The sun felt hotter after he ate lunch and he lay back under the tree to rest. In his back pocket was the crumpled paper that was his airline ticket. With a quick jerk, he retrieved it and unfolded it, holding it up. The date was correct, so was the time. He checked his watch and knew that down at the Nagoya airport, a big jumbo jet had taken off for America. This bunch of onion skin forms with carbons stuck between them, all clipped together at one end was as worthless as Yen in Kansas City. He would keep it for the memory, someday show it to Aiko—when she was old enough to understand all that her father had done.

He dropped his head back, allowing the ticket to fall onto his chest. A breeze picked it up, tickled the pages, tugged at them. Closing his eyes, he willed the wind to carry it away, but like most things this month it did not happen to his satisfaction. Instead, it only blew off his chest and caught in the nearby grasses.

At least I have my letter from Tomoko. She had written it in Japanese, of course. After they had talked about Hanako. Since she and Hanako had been best friends, they spoke privately many times, and Hanako had told her that the name of her lover in Hawaii was Benjamin Pinkerton. Tomoko had no hesitation in telling him so. He could not understand why the others were so reluctant to admit that this union between one of their own and an unscrupulous foreigner happened.

Obâsan was waiting for him when he returned in the morning, her eyes burning with a hatred she likely had thought put away for forty years. He was caught. Even though he showed her the letter, she remained quite stern and refused to let him see Aiko, who was still sleeping. Not wishing to argue with her — they had no language in common, anyway — Ben retired to his room — to Hanako's room — and collected all the papers.

If he had not gathered her sworn statement before last night, he was sure there was no way Obâsan would give it to him now. But didn't she still want him to take Aiko? Carmen had warned him, and he took it on advisement without really believing he would confront that possibility. If Obâsan meant to change her mind, she was hiding her feelings. But then, all Japanese hid their feelings, Ben had learned.

He rolled over in the grass, tired already.

Rising early, he had gone to mail the packets of papers, riding the beat-up bike into town again to catch the opening of the post office.

Propped up on his elbow now, he watched a fishing boat making its way toward the Togimachi harbor up the coast to his right. All he could make out was a small, white square with a jagged, white line cutting through the dark water like a knife.

The breeze stirred the grass.

I am nowhere. Content in this place and time, he felt free, unstuck from the roller pins and machinery of life. Unbounded by rules, by opinions, by timetables, by corruption, by fear, his only concern was for food, rest, and perhaps love. *That's all I need.* The only thing he was bounded by was death. *Not mine. Hers.*

That was the one thing he could not know. If he knew who to ask, or where to look, he would still have need of an interpreter like Carmen. He dared not ask Obâsan, even if he could get across the idea, no matter whether it was delicately phrased or not. Her peace had been disturbed enough already. If she were to try and tell him about Hanako's death, he believed she would break down, maybe fatally. He did not want that.

He gazed out at the world, eyes skimming the sea of grass.

A bird flew by, cried, continued on.

This was the hillside meadow where the *tsuru* danced in autumn. Hanako had told him many times, he recalled. The long-legged snow cranes mated among the winter grass and the marshy ponds of the alpine ridge. The tropical forests of Hawaii were so opposite to her wintry homeland that she used them as a metaphor for Japan. When she was sad, or homesick, she would hold him and say she missed the *tsuru*.

But it was spring now, and he would not see the dancing snow cranes.

The sun was warm on his legs, so he pulled off his shoes and socks, rolled up his pant legs.

The sea looked so inviting below, so pure, so cool and blue. He wanted to go for a swim, but he knew that up close it would be green and dirty. He tried to never look too closely at anything.

As he lay back, he thought of the night in their condo in Aiea, when they slept in their clothes, too upset to make love.

He wanted to slap himself — again. Why had he not broken the taboo and discussed getting married? That was the turning point. They knew they would be sent apart. Why did they never even try to go counter to that foregone conclusion? It was as if they believed they had no choice. 'We're together for now but only with the promise that we'll eventually part and go our separate ways.' That was the deal. But no one ever expressed that. No papers to that effect were ever signed, much less drawn up. There was nothing that made it so. They passively accepted it.

We just let it happen.

Writing letters was not a means to keep us together, he concluded. It was a way to lessen the pain of parting. They said goodbye to each other for two years. And they might still be saying farewell if he had not met Addy.

"But we had a child," he explained to the breeze, "a beautiful little girl, and if she had told me she was pregnant, I would've been on the next plane to Japan. But she said nothing. Even after Aiko was born, she wrote nothing about her."

Was it some Japanese custom? He dared not believe it was common for a woman not to tell her lover about the birth of their child. The only reason she might not have told him was that she simply did not want him to know.

But why?

Her family was probably insisting on an abortion. They wanted to kill the baby, pretend it never existed. If she had gone ahead with it, he would not be here now. For whatever reason, she had decided to give the baby life. That meant being exiled to Ishikawa. Then, after the birth, she was joyful, he presumed. Until . . . .

Why would she not want me to know?

"You want to know what Obâsan told me about your girlfriend?" Carmen's cold words came back to him.

The afternoon sun had fallen into the jumbled clouds on the horizon and the sky had melted into a somber hue. The ship had reached port. The rocks were still married. The breeze was cooler, the grass softly rustling.

He packed up the knapsack and descended into the pine forest.

Behind him, he imagined hearing the wild cry of the *tsuru*, calling him, calling Hanako.

23

BENJAMIN'S CALL TO ADDY was answered by a long series of rings. He hung up and dialed again. More empty rings. She was gone. He could have called her parent's house — where she would have gone — but he did not really wish to speak to her, anyway. He would only receive abuse. Or legal trouble. His curiosity was satisfied none the less; she had left the house now.

Then he turned to his office number and dialed. The phone had an unfamiliar ring, but finally it was answered. He recognized their secretary's Southern accent but it took a moment to begin thinking in English once more.

"Hello, Cheryl. This is Ben Pinkerton. Let me speak to Rich, will you? It's long distance."

"Good morning, Mister Pinkerton! How are you? You're still in Japan? We've missed you here."

"That's nice. I'm sure Rich's paid you to say that, hasn't he?"

She laughed and after an expensive minute, his boss was on the line.

"Ben! How the hell you doing? What's happened to you? I give you a couple weeks to visit Japan and then nothing. Are you all right? I mean, when you didn't come in last week, I called your house and

Addy said you two were getting a divorce. Is that true?"

"Unfortunately, yes. But this is long-distance, Rich, so let me get to the point—"

"You really calling all the way from Japan? As frugal as you are, must be bad news."

"Not quite. Well, I've got some good news and some bad news."

"Which do I want to hear first?"

"The bad news is that I need another two weeks probably."

"Two weeks? Good God, Ben. We were expecting you back a week ago. When I talked to your wife, she said you went over there to reunite with your old girlfriend. But I knew you said she died. Does Addy know that? She's sure you're not coming back. Hell, I thought you weren't coming back. I already hired someone."

"What?"

"We have work to get done."

"What are you saying? That I don't have a job anymore?"

"Well, yes, Ben. What am I supposed to do? You were supposed to be back a week ago, and I hear you're staying with your, uh, mistress. Is that right?"

"I told you: she's dead. I'm trying to bring our daughter back to the States. I'm not living it up here. I'm staying in an old house with an old woman and trying to get the damn paperwork through the right offices—"

"I remember you talking about here. Hanako? Tomoko? Some girls like those. Doesn't sound like you're coming back to me. At least not taking your job very seriously. What do you expect me to do?"

"I expect some loyalty, Rich. You knew I was coming here to work out some personal problems. Can't you give me a little flexibility?"

"What the hell's going on over there? Really."

"It's difficult to explain, Rich. It'd take too long over the phone. But, you remember the trouble you went through to adopt your son? Well, I've got the same problems, only times two because I've got to deal with Japanese Immigration *and* the U.S. Consulate. And that's double the red tape."

"Is that so. The girl *is* your daughter?"

"Yes. It was the grandmother who sent the letters. I've sent in all the paperwork—what a headache, let me tell you. Now all I can do is wait. Then I'll have the interview and I'll be home. *We* will be home. I don't know when that will be exactly, though."

"Are you sure about that? I mean, we needed you here and you keep playing hooky. Ben, you know you took off right when we were starting Royal Gorge. I had to give it to Charlie—"

"Yes, I know. I'll work weekends all next year. I can't quit now and I don't want to lose the job. I have to see this through. Only then will I know that it was the right thing to do. I'm counting on you to understand."

"Well, I hope so. No other hidden family out there?"

"Give me a break."

"Seriously, and personal problems aside, you've got to get back here. I'll be forced to make this guy permanent. You hear me? Addy said she already moved out of the house—did you know that? I don't know what the hell you're doing over there, farting around for all I know. All I can say is cut it out and get back here. I'll give you a week—that's the best I can offer. I've got work here and if you're not here I'll need someone else."

"Dammit, Rich! I've got personal problems to take care of. Didn't you hear me? Can't you be more reasonable. I'm not staying with my ex-girlfriend, no matter what Addy said—that's why we're getting the divorce—that's why she's getting it. It's out of my hands now; I'm waiting on the damn paperwork to go through the red tape. If this is all the loyalty you can offer me, then I think maybe I can do better elsewhere."

"Ben, what are upset about? I said I'd—"

"Do I have a job now or not?"

"Well, if you put it that way, if you want to force the issue, then I guess you don't have one."

"That's what I thought."

"Ben, wait a minute—"

"That's it. I'm screwed in every direction!"

"Calm down, Ben. You're overreacting. Why, just the other night,

Addy was saying she might be having second thoughts."

"The other night?"

"Yes, we met for dinner. As old friends. No harm in that, is there?"

"No harm? Just because you dated her before I came back from Hawaii? You're a bastard and a jerk, Rich. You can keep the job, and you can keep that bitch, too. Addy, second thoughts? Not about me, about you!"

"Ben, you're not taking me seriously, are you?"

"Go to hell."

"Yeah, well, don't enjoy yourself too much."

"Don't worry."

Ben slammed down the receiver hoping to break it but he did not succeed. The manager of the NTT office complained. Ben bowed to be polite but he was seething inside.

"Why she want divorce?" Tomoko asked, using her hand to shield her eyes from the afternoon sun. She gazed at Ben as he told her about the phone calls earlier that day.

He took Aiko's hand, led her across the street.

"As I told you before, she's jealous of Hanako. She's jealous of Aiko. Now my boss told her I'm dating you."

Tomoko pulled Shunichi up onto the curb.

"But Aiko beautiful child."

"That doesn't matter to her. She's not interested in that."

It was not until they entered the small park across from the post office — a patch of grass with swings and a wooden jungle gym, a few trees, and a drinking fountain — that he realized why so many people had been staring at them. The four of them were the "perfect" family. Japanese woman, American man, and two half-blood children, a boy and a girl. Perhaps they already knew Tomoko as the artist-whore and Ben as the traveling *gaijin* daddy.

Tomoko noticed, also.

"You see, we good family now."

She and Ben sat on the bench and watched their children playing together in the grass. He stretched his arms, laid them across the back of the bench, one arm behind her.

"Do you think anyone saw us walking together?" he laughed. "I guess someone may tell the police."

Tomoko snickered, leaned quickly against him. "I not afraid."

"Me, neither."

"When you go America?" she asked after a moment.

"I'm not sure. I can't leave until we have the interview. I don't know when that'll be. I'll have to go down to Osaka."

"Osaka, *ne?*"

"Osaka. That's fifty thousand yen I don't have to spare."

"*So da no.*"

Her cheek rested against his collar, her hand on his leg. Before he could object, the question fell from her mouth like a lead weight and hit his foot, breaking a toe.

"You take me with you in America?"

"What's that?"

"Please you take me America?"

He had been readying himself for that question, just as she had been leading up to it, almost since that first night together. But he still did not have an answer prepared.

"You take Shun' and me America?"

He drew a deep breath.

"I don't know if I can," was all he could manage on short notice.

"We be good family. America *ni* we good family. Please."

He shook his head, squinting in the sun.

"How can you ask like that? Like you're begging?" He watched Aiko offering a bouquet of grass to Shunichi. "Besides, it's not that easy. I'm trying to arrange to take Aiko back to America, and that's hard enough. And she's my daughter. To bring you, I'd have to file again and they may get suspicious if I file a second petition. Besides, my divorce is not final yet, anyway." And he added, for himself, that he was clinging to some small hope that he could have some kind of reconciliation with Addy.

Tomoko bowed her head. "I sorry, Ben-*chan*."

"Oh, don't be that way. Sure, I want to bring you to America. You sure don't have any kind of life here in this sad place. But it's not something that can be done so fast. Don't you understand?"

"*S'koshii*," she replied, pinching the air with her fingers. A little.

"Hell, I don't know how to tell you."

"Tell *nani*?"

There were no words in the language that could be adequately put together in sentences which would convey the complex feelings Ben had. Although he'd had the thoughts before when he was with her, he had never allowed himself the time and energy to moralize over his actions. He knew the first time they were in bed together that he was would not get involved with another Japanese lady. He knew he was not going to bring her home with him.

Tomoko was dressing like Hanako now, maybe to subconsciously persuade him that she could be a credible substitute to his lost *koibito*.

"Do you want to live in America?" he asked.

With a smile as big as the Pacific Ocean, she nodded her head.

"Bery much."

"What will you do there?"

"I be your wife. Take good care you."

"Yes, yes, I know, but what will you do? I mean, will you keep on painting?"

"I paint if you want me paint."

"Yes, I want you to paint. You should keep on painting. You're very good. I think you could be a success in America."

"*Honto ni?*" True?

"Yes, of course. I mean, I'm no art critic, but you do have talent, that's for sure."

"*So desu ka?*" Really?

"Oh, yes. You could make it in America."

She hugged him, kissed his cheek in the full daylight.

"*Domo arigatô gozaimasu!*"

"You're welcome."

They looked out at their children.

Shunichi's sand castle was nearly finished. Aiko, bending over on her stubby legs to pick up a beetle, backed into it and fell. The castle was destroyed, and Shun' immediately began crying.

Tomoko rushed to him.

Framed in the golden glow of the late afternoon sun, their figures became silhouettes and in their anonymity, he saw Hanako and Aiko, and the son they might have had later, playing together as a family.

Perhaps we could make a pretty good family, after all.

But the hallucination evaporated just as quickly and Ben was left contemplating the fantasy of the present and the unknown future. It was all like a movie he was watching. The music was swelling and he knew something exciting was about to happen.

24

AFTER TWO SHOWS AT THE KAMEHAMEHA II DRIVE-IN — a silly romance and a stupid comedy — they pulled out in their rented Toyota and headed north from Aiea on the old Kamehameha Highway. In the darkness, the full moon lit a path across the wide sugar cane fields to the peaks of the Waianae Mountains. The road turned up a steep incline a few minutes later and they entered the little town of Mililani where the only noise was some teenagers parked at the McDonald's.

The car continued north across the central valley of the island of Oahu, the two passengers content from the large super pizza and the six pack of guava juice consumed during the movies. The lights of Wheeler Air Force Base came up on the left and they slowed to exit the old highway and merge onto the new freeway which itself ended at the entrance to Wahiawa. Schofield Barracks was closed on the left, twisting Wahiawa Lake on the right. The black-top road descended through pine forests and up to the plateau where the pineapple fields stretched under the moonlight from the foothills of Mount Kaala to the shadows beneath the crests of the Koolau Range.

Ben open the window a crack to let in the early April breeze. The air was scented by the sea. Hanako lay her hand on his arm.

The plateau rose gently, then broke into a wide panorama of the

North Shore. Through the sugar cane stalks, the ivory beaches curved like a long pearl necklace, glimmering while the white caps rolling in reflected the moonlight.

Dropping down from the plateau, the road ran into the Haleiwa roundabout, where the compact car circled to the right and cruised into the dim lights of Haleiwa, the artists' village, closed for the night. Her hand fell onto his thigh as he shifted the gears. The still harbor appeared on the left, then disappeared. They were heading for another beach down the road. Beach houses stood on the left, on the right, rising pine-covered hills, the din of crashing waves everywhere.

Past Kapaeloa beach, the road bent sharply into the canyon of Kamananui Stream, winding around the open expanse of Waimea Bay and its wide, golden beach. Below the cliffs, the Rock stood firmly against the waves. On the far end of the beach, up on the cliffs, stood the Spanish tower of the Sts. Peter and Paul Mission. Between the two landmarks, the beach lay quiet and fluorescent.

The white hatchback turned into the parking lot, found the gate barring the way, and circled back out and onto the highway. They paused to kiss.

Then the car groaned up the steep incline and veered to the side of the road against the guardrail, high enough to scan the beach where they had spent so many sunny afternoons but never a night. They climbed out the driver's side, collected their knapsack and the plastic rings holding two last cans of guava nectar, locked the doors and leaped over the bent guardrail.

Breaking through the trail brush, they burst out onto the grassy yard surrounding the dressing house and lifeguard stand. The waves surged against the beach. A wide beam of creamy moonlight guarded the beach. Lest anyone notice them, they moved cautiously along the edge of the cliff's shadows. They followed the rocky cliff, kicking off their rubber flip-flops and stepping out barefoot into the sand.

There, the Rock towered over them like a castle, throwing a thick, welcome screen of blackness over their stretch of beach.

Between pairs of stones rising from the sand they spread out their blanket, weighed the corners with their shoes and knapsack.

With restrained modesty, she pulled up her oversized T-shirt, the words SURF NAKED emblazoned so unabashedly in brilliant letters across its otherwise white surface crumpled in her arms. Beneath it, her barely tanned breasts were held in the cradle of her cobalt blue string bikini, a fashion she wore only for him.

He tugged at his shirt as she unbuckled her pink Bermuda shorts and slipped them off. The metallic blue bikini bottoms caught the moonlight like a mirror, sparkling. He stood before her, straightening his swimming trunks as she neatly folded her clothes and sat them high and dry on a rock.

She gazed up at him as she collected her straight, black hair and tied it together with a white hairband. Her white belly felt cool in the breeze. She rubbed her bare legs, whispered something to him about happiness.

He went to the water, tested it with his foot, waded in to mid-calf.

Adjusting her suit, she went in after him.

The water was not as warm after midnight as it was at their usual afternoon swimming time. They embraced in the chest-high water, his feet planted at the bottom, hers bobbing in the calm surf. They kissed again, words were exchanged, followed by more kissing. His hands settled lower on her body. She wrapped her arms around his neck, pressed against him. His fingers pulled at the strings of her top and it fell free. She pulled him close, kissing him, and his hands cupped her face.

"You're beautiful!" he whispered into her ear, then took her by the hand and led her back onto the beach.

On the beach towel, she slid down his trunks, brushed away stray grains of sand, and stretched out beneath him. Braced himself on one elbow, he reached for the knapsack, pulled open the outer pouch. He reported the pocket was empty.

She covered his hand with her hand, then pulled him back over her. His eyes asked if they should continue.

"You're *bootiful*," she whispered, opening to him.

Ben shook when he awoke, not knowing where he was but sensing the sweet air of Hawaii, the breeze of the North Shore, the touch of Hanako's hand.

It was Tomoko's hand. And he was napping on her *futon* while she prepared dinner.

He glanced over at the clock, calculating he had slept for an hour.

The dinner was simple: steamed white rice and baked salmon, a dish of pickles and, of course, rice and soup.

Aiko loved *miso* soup, Ben noticed, indulging herself in the thin, brown broth made from soybean paste, a few squares of tofu and several bits of clam and seaweed added. It was delicious, he agreed, finishing the bowl. He watched the children and recognized that their tiny fingers were already more adept than his at manipulating the short, lacquered chopsticks.

"You stay here tonight?" Tomoko asked, clearing the table.

"I think I'd better get back." He exhaled loudly. "Aiko's probably a tired little girl."

Tomoko was disappointed, but he really had to return or Obâsan would be angry again.

She was.

Barely flinging the door open, he was confronted by a wild stream of Japanese he could not understand. But her meaning was clear. He was wrong in seeing the woman called Tomoko. He caught part of her words; she tried to speak standard Japanese so he would be able to understand. Someone had seen them in the park and told Obâsan. Yes, they had sat together on the bench. They had walked together along the street, too. What a scandal!

Ben stood in place and took it, quite shocked himself that he had caused this fine old woman, this kindly lady to show her rage at his transgressions. He was startled, but he let her vent her anger, even as she scooted Aiko away to her room.

"*Gomen nasai, gomen nasai,*" he uttered, bowing from the waist.

Then, suddenly, she rushed from the room and brought back the paperback Japanese-English dictionary from Hanako's room, an old pencil carved to a point by a knife and a tiny yellowed pad of paper.

"*Nan desu ka?*" he asked, curious.

She flipped through the book, landed on a page with a slip of paper to mark the place. Her face reddened as she dug the pencil point into the paper, almost tearing it.

As he watched her shaky hands draw the lines, he saw the word form. The *kanji* for 'love,' then 'child,' and he knew she meant Aiko. Then a letter formed which became a crooked 'N' with the diagonal going the wrong direction. It was followed by a tensely drawn 'O,' and the message became clear.

She pointed at him, speaking too fast and frantic for him to follow, jabbing her pencil-holding hand in his direction. He so overwhelmed her in size that he was embarrassed and frightened of becoming angry at this bent, old woman with the fire in her heart, scolding him, condemning him. He had proven himself beyond any doubt to be an immoral man — as was her suspicions when Hanako had first come to her from Nagoya, he guessed — and Obâsan believed it would be wrong to give up Aiko to this — this *American*!

He hung his head in shame as she swept out of the room, the force of her words echoing throughout the old house.

The paper she had written on had been blown off the table in her departure. He bent down and picked it up, held it gingerly in his hands, feeling his saddened heart quivering. He knew she was right. He could invent any number of excuses. He could rationalize everything he'd done for days. But it would not change anything. Did he even have a second chance? Was Obâsan expressing her final ultimatum, or was it a warning?

Whichever it was, he sank to his knees and pitched forward on the *tatami* mat.

"Hanako, my *koibito*," he whispered. "Why didn't you tell me? Why didn't you tell me we were going to have a child?"

His throat tightened and he could only think solemn thoughts.

Hanako, why did you die?

25

THE SEA WAS A SHEET OF DARK GREEN GLASS as Ben sat gazing out at the harbor.

While waiting to meet Tomoko after she got done with work, just to tell her he could not see her again, not if he was still going to be allowed to keep his daughter, Ben passed the time gazing at the sunset over the harbor. He thought about life, death, and the strange variety of tomorrows ahead of him. And the terrible, deceitful world that was slowly and steadily crushing him. The loyalty of friends, the faithfulness of a wife who didn't want to be his wife, the bureaucracy which conspired to drive him insane—all of it. He was very weary now. He had found melancholy once more with Obâsan disappointed at him and threatening to not give up Aiko, the hassle of the endless forms, the uncooperative doctor, the suspicious townsfolk, his wasted airplane ticket, his lost job—because Rich was an ass and had no patience—and Addy divorcing him because he happened to fall in love before he ever met her.

What the hell am I trying to do here?

Reality often had trouble finding him, lost in Japan.

Thank goodness for a beautiful day to lift his spirits! He welcomed the warm breeze crossing the harbor. When he was surrounded by the harmony of nature, he could believe everything would work itself out. A bright day turned him into an optimist. He was in another world, and all the events of the past month were mere dreams. He only needed to wait out the sunset, the darkness of night, and the new sunrise, and maybe all the misfortune he was party to would be magically undone.

He heard footsteps on the wharf behind where he sat.

Ben looked up to see three young men approaching with a casual, self-assured walk. Their hard soles clicked against the wooden planks and their mod-styled suits and permed hairdos like curly monkey fur, or the James Dean impersonator among them, left no doubt they were some of the local boys known as *yakuza*. Or perhaps they only wanted to be seen as gangsters, thought Ben.

"*Konnichiwa*," the James Dean wannabe called to Ben as he stood and brushed off his pants.

"*Konnichiwa*," Ben replied.

"*Nihongo wakaru?*" he inquired. Understand Japanese?

"*Eigo wakarimasu ka?*" Ben responded. Speak English?

The tough guy laughed, glancing down as if grinding a butt into the planks of the wharf.

"You good friend . . . Kaida-*san*?" he spoke in fairly good English.

"Well, that depends."

Under the circumstances, Ben thought it was the only appropriate answer.

"You good friend . . . Nakamori-*san*?"

"I knew her, yes. I don't know what you mean by 'good friend,' though."

The leader sneered. "You go with her?"

"Go with? You mean like 'going steady'?"

"Did you stay night with her?"

Ben paused, the answer caught in his throat.

"I actually don't think that's any of your business. Why are you so concerned?"

He cleared his throat then, the toe of his shoe digging at a knot of wood, his hands comfortably shoved into pockets. When he looked up again, he squinted and spoke louder.

"Why you come here?"

Ben put on a smile. "On business, of course."

"*So, ne.*" Is that right?

"Yes, it is."

"Business do not take three weeks. Not here in Togimachi. What business you do?"

Ben knew this conversation was not likely to end well, so he slowly stepped to the side, intending to walk around them. It was slow enough that they seemed unaware he was actually moving.

"Personal business," Ben answered, moving a little quicker.

"You know Kaida-*san*?"

"What is this? Twenty questions? I know a lot of people."

James Dean's mood turned aggressive.

"You go to bed with Kaida-*san*?"

Even in America such a question as that usually would have been considered forward and impolite. Ben told him so but the guy was not dissuaded.

"It not good thing to do here."

Ben forced a chuckle, believing him. "Yeah, I guess not."

"Go away," he spoke in a calm, even voice.

"Pardon?"

"You go away—now."

"What do you mean?"

"Go out Togimachi. Never come back."

"That is my intention, I assure you. But first I have to finish my business."

James Dean became angry.

"You go away from Kaida-*san*!"

Ben rubbed his chin, thinking of a cute answer. "Are you by any chance related to her?"

James Dean had to stop and translate in his head. "You should not go see her."

He pressed his index finger into Ben's chest to make the point.

"You mean tonight?" asked Ben.

"Every night!"

Ben was near the end of the wharf now, just an easy leap over the railing and away with his escape.

"I guess that would be prudent, wouldn't it?"

James Dean nodded his head and the others, not knowing what Ben had said, followed suit.

"Thanks for the tip," said Ben. He took a step to the side, intending to walk around the trio.

Ben felt a hand on his shoulder, and in that breath he knew what the next two minutes would entail.

It was James Dean grabbing him, and as he spun Ben around, his fist struck Ben's jaw. Ben fell onto his side and the two gangsters each kicked his stomach. Ben cried out for them to stop, but they did not understand English. And they were too busy dragging him the length of the wharf by his legs. Once they released him, Ben continued to slide along the rough wood until he came to the end and tumbled off the wharf, down into the murky harbor waters.

Faint music wafted from somewhere. It was a song Ben knew, the English words sung by a female voice. Maybe he was in heaven, he thought. He couldn't be if he hurt so much. It was the voice of Akiko Kobayashi, he realized, so he felt safe.

A soft hand caressed his cheek. It was their song so it had to be Hanako's hand. Ben smiled.

When he opened his eyes, however, there were eight eyes staring down at him. Fuzzy as his vision was, he was able to recognize Obâsan and Aiko. The other eyes looked like those of a boy and a young lady. Maybe Hanako, he thought.

As he gained consciousness, he saw the image shift into the plain, narrow face of Tomoko.

She told him what had happened and he slowly remembered. After the punks had punched and kicked him, and thrown him off the wharf, he had pulled himself up from the mud of low tide and lay resting on the wharf. Eventually a man found him and helped him into his shop alongside the dock, where he telephoned his friend, who called his brother.

That was the retired professor Ben had met in the bookstore, the only citizen of Togimachi known to speak English, apparently, and therefore the only one qualified to assist this misfortunate *gaijin*. After all, Ben was an honorable guest in this country, eligible for all manner of sympathy like a wayward child. The professor came and examined Ben, then went to get Dr. Kotani. The doctor was away on a house call, so the nurse suggested the professor contact Tomoko. So the professor went over to Bourgouisse and brought Tomoko back to the fish factory by the wharf where Ben lay delirious and dirty.

Ben sat up, feeling the ache in his gut, and gazed around the room and into their warm faces.

Obâsan was surprised to meet Tomoko, who had a bad reputation in town. She was the town whore, even though she swore she never slept with anyone except Shunichi's father. No doubt if he was going out with this immoral, scandalous girl, then what must he have thought about her granddaughter? Ben imagined Obâsan thinking he was just playing with Hanako. He was just a playboy.

They left to drink tea in the sitting room.

As Ben listened to them speaking in Japanese, he climbed off the *futon*. Shun' and Aiko waited for him, entertained by his grunts and groans. They giggled. In his wavering consciousness, he had been undressed completely and had an icepack on his belly. The children watched as he stood up slowly and put on the *yukata* folded on the bed. They were more concerned about him than the adults, it seemed. Ben smiled at the children, gave them a wink.

Aiko rose from the floor and tugged on the robe. She wrapped her chubby arms around his leg, hugging his knee.

Again Ben sat in the *ofuro*, his sore belly and scraped back soothed by the boiling waters.

"You want to know what Obâsan told me about your girlfriend?" Carmen had said before. The words haunted him.

Tomoko and Shun' were staying the night since it was too late to call a taxi. Obâsan seemed to adapt to her presence comfortably. They drank tea late into the night, and talked at length. Perhaps Obâsan was simply grateful to her for delivering Aiko's wayward father back home.

He soaked for an hour and a half before Tomoko came to fetch him. After all, some people were known to shrink completely out of sight if they sat in the *ofuro* for too long. That was something he remembered Hanako telling him a long time ago. At that point, he had not shared the *ofuro* with her. Now he had used the same tub she had used, but she was gone.

Tomoko brought a towel and held it open for him as he climbed out, then smothering him in its folds like a little boy. Once he stood warm and dry on the wooden plank floor, she took away the towel. He shivered, naked, until she gave him the *yukata*. Then, tossing away any modesty, she slipped off her own robe and sat down on the stool to wash herself prior to bathing.

No sooner had Ben tied the *obi* belt than Obâsan called to him from the house.

Ben rushed back to watch over the sleeping children while the old woman went to the *ofuro*.

He drank down a cup of tea, and went to check on the children. He tucked in Aiko's covers and she said something in her sleep he could not understand. Shun' was already fast asleep beside her on a bed of folded blankets. They were so cute, so *kawaii*, with their dainty nocturnal expressions.

Hearing the two women chattering away out in the *ofuro*, Ben decided to get some rest. It was the first time in nearly ten days he had turned in before midnight.

In the morning, the letter arrived.

26

THEY GATHERED AROUND THE *KOTATSU* TABLE, examining the pages of the Consulate's letter — which also contained the red-stamped letter of approval from the Japanese immigration authorities. Ben anxiously searched for the words that would tell him the results of his long application.

You are scheduled for an interview . . . .

Obâsan and Tomoko practically danced as Ben jumped up and cheered wildly. He knew he was nearly finished. The interview was in one week, at the honorary consul in Kanazawa. He didn't have to go to Osaka. However, the presence of Aiko and two witnesses were required.

A visa may be granted upon the conclusion of the interview . . . .

Ben grabbed Aiko and told her they would soon be going home. To her new home. In America!

The room was suddenly still. Tomoko had lost her smile. Obâsan was quiet, too. The sooner he left with Aiko, the sooner they would be alone, all of them realized. The letter was not joyful news for them.

"I'm sorry," said Ben.

After having a lunch that they were too excited to eat, they called for a taxi and went into town. It was Obâsan's day for groceries and gossip, but Tomoko had to get back for work, too. Ben was eager to call Carmen and tell her the good news.

The two women were busy continuing their talk in the back seat all the way into town.

He left Obâsan at the supermarket and went to his favorite phone booth at the KDD office with a new *denwa* card in hand. Tomoko took Shunichi and headed to their apartment, talking in happy words to him about something.

"*Moshi moshi,*" Carmen spoke on picking up the phone.

"It's me: Ben."

"Are you still there?" She took a breath. "I thought you would be long gone, back home. Did you get a letter from the consulate yet?"

"Yes, got it today."

"Well, good for you. When's your interview?"

"In a week. It's in Kanazawa—at your friend's office. He is still your friend, isn't he? I hope so. And the notice said a visa could be issued upon conclusion of the interview, if we pass."

"I believe so."

"Then we'll be on our way home—finally. It's been the biggest hassle of my life, I want you to know. I am out of money. I've lost my job back home and probably my wife, too. But I've got a daughter!"

"I hear you."

"We'll have to have a big celebration dinner, Carmen. I couldn't have done it without you. I've got to thank you somehow. I mean, getting the red tape rolling, and bending the ear of your consulate guy."

"Yeah."

She was not her usual peppy self, it seemed.

"What's wrong, Carmen?"

"Nothing. Just being cynical today."

"Come on. What about the Mutual Cynics Society, huh? I don't know if I can be a member any longer. I'm so excited, some of it will probably rub off on you if you just let it."

Again she was silent.

"Hey, suit yourself," said Ben, too happy to be quiet.

"Ben—"

"By the way, I'm suppose to bring two witnesses for my character. And even Aiko has to have two witnesses. Of course Obâsan has to go, to verify the records. I thought she'd be my witness, too. And there's another girl, the one who was Hanako's best friend here, you know. And . . . I was hoping you'd be my other character witness. Can you?"

"Ben, I'm pregnant."

That was not the reply he was expecting and it took a moment of silence for it to reach his brain.

"Say that again?"

"I'm pregnant."

"Are you sure? I mean, have you seen a doctor?"

"No doctor yet, but my period is two weeks late. It's got to be either Yoshio Furukawa or . . . I don't know who."

He had to pause to sort out her words.

"I'm sorry, then. Why is the discovery of a pregnancy always greeted with sadness and shame?"

"Because everybody knows you've done the great, universal sin. If I was married, I'd be jumping for joy. But here in Japan, a single woman cannot have a career and a kid. It just doesn't work here. They won't let it work."

"Then go home."

"Nagoya is my home."

He sighed. "Then what are you gonna do?"

There was hesitation in her voice. "Do you believe in abortion?"

"What do you mean 'believe in'?"

"I want your advice, Ben."

He had no quick answer for her.

"Have you talked to this Yosha Fukagama?"

"That's Yoshio Furukawa. And no. He'd be even less sympathetic. That's why I'm wishing it was your child. You have a good heart."

"How kind."

"If I don't get it done there'll be another baby in Japan to worry about. That's the fact of the matter, Ben. Isn't going through all that hassle once enough for you? Who else would want to do it?"

"All right. Do what you think is best."

"Listen, I can be in Kanazawa next week, if you like. Then we can kill two *daruma* dolls with one *mochi* ball—as they say. I'll go to your interview. Then we'll take care of the abortion. That's where I went before."

"Before?"

"Yes, last time."

Ben said little in closing except the time and date of the interview.

Laughing sadly, he reminded himself how little he really knew about women. Thinking of Carmen as some kind of puritan soul had led him astray. Where was the dividing line? Was there a line at all? Tomoko seemed like an innocent girl and he was glad she took an interest in this lonely *gaijin*. But for the townspeople calling her *baishunfu*, he never would have known. Still, she was a warm person.

Hanako was pure when he met her. She told him she was a virgin the morning after their first night together and that made him feel special. But after that night she was no different. She never lost that lovely aura of innocence, or the vague impression of purity.

"That's just a hang-up men have," Carmen had said back in the *ofuro*. "The reason all you Western guys go for these Japanese girls is that they are just about the closest thing nature has to the type of women that the average American male has on a pedestal. She has an innocent appearance, baby-faced cuteness that's appealing to Western men, because it suggests youth and innocence. They have smaller bodies and delicate features—like a young Caucasian girl of fourteen or fifteen years—so they have the appearance of 'forbidden fruit' which is, however, accessible."

"Maybe so, Carmen, but Japanese girls are also more willing to be feminine and show off their femininity compared to most Western women."

"You mean Japanese women are not feminists?"

"I don't mean that. As you just said, we like that innocence. The illusion of it, anyway."

"Ben, you forget one very important aspect of your perversion."

"And what's that?"

"That foreign men are often attracted to Japanese girls because they pity them. Maybe pity's not quite the right word but—I mean, it's a pity that when viewed from a certain perspective, pity may feel like love, but it really isn't. And I'll tell you, Ben, a lot of this pity is just a bunch of selfish egotism, built up by the foreigner who believes that the girl is naive, soft, sensitive, helpless, and wouldn't be able to live without him. Isn't that right, Benjamin? You thought you were rescuing her. Right?"

When Ben started to climb the hill, he saw furniture being carrying down the stairs by several men in gray coveralls. The line never stopped as they hauled out one piece after another. Two neighbors stood in the street watching the progression.

"What's going on?" he called up to Tomoko from the bottom of the stairs when she stepped out of the apartment at the top.

"Move out," she called down.

"But why?"

He was pushed out of the way by two descending movers with the wooden easels folded in their hands.

She stepped inside while she gave instructions.

My goodness! Ben shrieked inside. *Was she already packing to come with him to America?*

That could not be true. He had to make certain she understood what he had been trying to tell her for the past month.

He ran up the stairs once they were clear.

"Tomoko, we've got to talk."

"No time. Move now," she said, and turned away to pack some dishes into a cardboard box.

"We have to make time. I don't want you to misunderstand me. I thought I told you so you'd understand. You said you understood."

"Understand what?" she asked, wrapping cups in newspaper.

"About moving. I'm going back to America in about a week. Is that what this moving is all about?"

She looked up with a wide grin on her face.

"Yes. Move out today, never come back!"

Forget politeness, ignore diplomacy, and just be damn direct, he shouted at himself.

"Tomoko, wait!"

She heaved the box up into her arms and went to the doorway.

"No time. Move now."

"But you're mistaken," he yelled as she went down the stairs. "You can't come to America with me. I can't take you with me. Do you hear me? I said you can't come to America with me."

She did not reply. Maybe she did not hear him over the loud talking of the movers. Maybe she did not want to hear him. Perhaps she was thinking that if she were already packed and ready to go that he could not refuse to take her along.

At the bottom of the stairs she paused and gazed up at him, shifting the box in her arms.

"*Baka na!*" she cried. He thought the word meant 'fool'—which may have been right. "You silly man! I not go America. Too big place for me. Little girl get lost in America."

"Then where are you going?" he called down.

Again she turned, halting beside the truck.

"I go Nakamori-*san* house," she cried out.

"What . . . ?"

He rushed down the stairs to her.

"What're you talking about? You're moving in with Obâsan? Is that right?"

"*Hai! So desu yo!*"

"Why?"

"We good friend now. She forgive me be friend with Hanako. I go live in her house, take care her, she take care Shun'. We have good family. She kind old woman. We have happy family."

He grabbed her and rolled her into a hug.

"I'm so happy for you, Tomoko!"

It was the perfect arrangement. They could take care of each other.

Otherwise, Obâsan would be alone. Tomoko would not have to work in the coffee shop to take care of her son. She could devote her time to art. He was sure that in time she could earn a good living from her paintings. That must have been what they had been talking about so enthusiastically the past two days.

Then, with a moment to reflect on the situation, sadness swept over him, knowing Tomoko no longer wanted to return with him.

27

THE NEXT NIGHT there was cause to celebrate, but evidently they had the parties crossed. The escorts, having apologized profusely to Ben at the insistence of their employer—Tomoko's uncle—for roughing him up on the wharf, were supposed to make nice with him now. So they directed him into their favorite pub, talking it up in Japanese as they approached the bar. He was less than enthusiastic being in their company, but since Uncle joined them and Tomoko had seen them off, it seemed to have official sanction.

Ben thought they were all celebrating the correction of the earlier misunderstanding. No hard feelings and all. Uncle, wearing a gray suit without necktie, led him down the street. The balding muscular man, maybe fifty or sixty, was a little frightening to Ben. The man waved his lieutenant up to the front of the line, gesturing him to speak some English to Ben.

Out came some remarks about the weather, then on to baseball. Ben politely nodded or responded with short, casual answers. Finally they turned and loudly entered the hole-in-the-wall bar.

The hostess knew Uncle, one of their favorite customers, it seemed to Ben. They got the best table, right in the center of the room. Drinks were served—Kirin beer for the gang members. The hostess knew

Uncle's standard order and took down a bottle of whiskey from the shelf behind the bar and poured some from *his* bottle. Through his lieutenant, Uncle explained that it was always kept there for him.

"You bery good speakingu Englishu," Uncle's lieutenant, dressed in the pink satin suit, told him after the first round of beer.

The man in the pink suit with the flipped hair, the James Dean wannabe, was the one who had addressed him that day on the wharf. His name seemed to be Nobuhide something. Takeda? Takada? He refilled Ben's glass from the huge, three liter bottle, laughing so hard he spilled some of it on the table at Ben's elbow.

"Thanks. I've only been speaking it all my life, you know," Ben replied, not holding back on the sarcasm. He expected none of them would understand him anyway. Still, Ben guessed it was meant as a compliment. Ben doubted it mattered what he said to the guy, as long as he said it with a smile on his face.

Somewhere Ben had read that Japanese get drunk easily compared with Westerners, perhaps because of their typical diet of rice and fish. The alcohol entered the bloodstream quicker. Maybe it was a joke. He was in the midst of his own experiment now and it seemed that these fellows were quite able to hold their liquor, while Ben was failing fast. After all, he never drank much—a beer with his work colleagues once in a while and some wine with Addy, special occasions only.

I wish Addy could see me now!

He was happy, thinking of her, imagining how she would laugh at him in this situation.

Someone grabbed his shoulder. It was Nobuhide. He pointed to the stage at the back of the pub. The lights flickered red and blue as if to get everyone's attention. Ben stared at the stage. The first customer of the night had gotten up there and taken the microphone in his hands.

"It's *karaoke*," Nobuhide explained with a grin and a blast of beer breath. "You know it?"

Ben watched with growing trepidation. He had heard of this kind of musical entertainment even back in Seattle. It was popular in Hawaii, too, yet he had never expected he would be so close to it. The bizarre custom filled him with terror. He was not known for his singing voice. And he was painfully shy when it came to singing in front of others. He did not even sing in the shower, worried that Addy might hear him and tease him.

As a captive listener, Ben cringed at the amateur's poor tone and halting performance. He felt sorry for the man.

Of course, Ben's hosts took great delight in his consternation.

"You singu Englishu song?" his new buddy Nobuhide asked. "We hab many Englishu songzu in dis book."

He tossed the thick book in Ben's lap. It was a catalogue of popular songs available on the pub's library of video disks. The idea was for him to select a song, such as *Yesterday* by the Beatles, then get up on stage, which in this place was little more than one unoccupied corner, and sing the song while a video played behind him. The videos were much like the music videos popular back in America. Unfortunately, the quality of the video was somewhat lacking in every cinematic category, from its grainy images to its lack of relation to the words of the song. He guessed *Yesterday* was popular because the English words were easy for Japanese to sing. Frank Sinatra's *My Way* was also at the top of the list, he guessed, because it fit the salaryman's secret desire for the Westernized, self-centered macho image. The next member of Uncle's entourage was singing it and putting some effort into imitating Ol' Blue Eyes. This guy had some talent.

But it was *Yesterday* that was chosen for Ben by Uncle — a name he used with the same tone as the word 'godfather.'

Ben protested, knowing that ultimately he would have to go up to the stage and sing. There was no way around it. He got up, feigning modesty. His drunken buddies cheered as he took the microphone.

He gripped the microphone, hesitating, but the video for the song started playing. The song started. The background music was right there waiting for his dulcimer tones. He started with barely a mumble then grew more confident. The words were displayed across the video monitor although there was no bouncing ball to tell him which words to sing. Fortunately, he knew the song.

And the video was interesting, too. The main subject was a close-up camera roaming over a nude Japanese woman's body alternating with rather dark, underexposed live shots of an American disco. It was very strange, indeed, but Ben's ring of comrades were literally rolling in the aisles, completely enraptured by his thrilling, if not completely drunk, performance.

The final scene of the video was the woman in an empty room—one with seemingly endless white walls—hugging her bent knees, one breast pointing out from around her knee. His buddies loved it, and they whistled and cried out for her.

"She is good," Nobuhide said when Ben rejoined them at the table. Ben was not sure if it was a question or a statement. He just grinned.

"Okay *desu*, okay *desu*," his buddies cried.

"Not bad," Ben said, sitting down.

As Uncle got up to sing his favorite *enka* song—a genre of Japanese blues music—Nobuhide leaned over to Ben, speaking words he could not understand with the noise in the pub around them.

"Tomoko-*chan* good, *ne*?" Nobuhide continued louder, without a rising inflection on the end to let Ben know whether or not it was a question.

When Ben did not respond immediately, Nobuhide must have thought he was embarrassed. He shouted something at his friends across the table, stretching up from his seat and leaning over the table to slap their shoulders. They all shared a round of uproarious laugh that rocked the small bar like an earthquake.

"What's so funny?" Ben called out above Uncle's loud, warbling rendition of *I'm Using My Old Name Again*, an *enka* standard with half the lyrics in English.

Nobuhide wrapped his arm around Ben's shoulders.

"Kaida-*san* good garu, *ne*? She good wifu for you, *ne*? We—" he waved his arm around the table to indicate all of their friends, "—we want you happy together. Many, uh, *kodomo*—children, *ne*. Long time together, *ne*? She good garu. Bery good garu."

"Bery, bery good garu," one guy added. Another guy laughed.

"Like virgin," the next cried out. Catching Ben's stern expression, the guy snickered.

"So that's what this *enkai*'s all about," Ben asked over Uncle's off-key singing.

They all laughed again. He guessed they knew what the joke was. He did not, however.

By then his head was swimming and he was feeling good in a bad way. Maybe too good. He shook his head, trying to clear it, then wrapped his arm around Nobuhide's shoulders like they were old school chums. Nobuhide seemed somewhat taken aback, but relaxed quickly in his oiled state. It must have been the first time anybody touched him without it being a fight.

"Listen, aaa, Nobu-baby," said Ben. "I think maybe there's been some mistake here. Just a little mistake. I certainly do appreciate you guys taking me around here and showing me a good time and all, but I really think maybe I ought to set you guys straight. Ya know whadda mean, buckaroo?"

Ben had no idea why he slipped into a John Wayne voice.

"*Wakaru?*" Ben added with a cough. Understand?

Nobuhide listened intently but when Ben stopped talking he was still listening, nodding his head in rhythm to the newest *karaoke*, some song by teenage pop singer Miho Nakayama. She must have been his idol. The girl singing on the stage was pretty good, Ben noted.

"*Wakaru?*" Ben asked him again, not acting Japanese but becoming one with his new friends.

He was lost in the world of *karaoke*. There was no harm in a night out, he decided. Then again, perhaps it was better not to tell them the truth. They might take exception to him not wanting to marry their dear "cousin" Tomoko. He definitely could not win them all.

"Never mind, guys."

As Ben sat back in the corner seat, bounded on either side by two of his new friends, all laughing and drinking and singing, he began to sink within himself. A kind of tunnel vision set in, and he seemed to be viewing the club as through a window. A window with blue calico curtains. And a red robin singing on the windowsill. *So desu ne!* He would just let the evening run its course, believing he would be returned to civilization sometime later in almost the same shape in which he departed it.

"Hey!" Nobu-baby was calling him.

"*Hai?*" answered Ben, pulling himself up in the seat.

Nobuhide pointed at the video. A girl with her back turned to the camera was pulling off her blue and white *yukata* and stepping into an *ofuro* to some old *enka* song with a pitiful, quivering woman's voice on the soundtrack. The girl's long, black hair made him think of Hanako and he wanted to turn away, not wishing to share their lustful viewing. His good buddy, Nobuhide, had different plans.

Suddenly, they were all discussing something in serious tones. Then Nobu was duly elected as their spokesman.

"You want go beach?" he asked Ben, slapping his arm as though it was a private joke.

The others laughed.

"Beach? What beach? Why d'you wanna go to the damn beach? And in the middle of the night?"

Ben could tell he was soused. The words he had spoken seemed to come from somebody else, maybe someone across the room.

"You want see beach Nakamori-*san* go swim?" Nobuhide asked.

"She *went* swimming," Ben corrected him. "The beach where she went swimming."

One of the others refilled his glass with beer. He had lost count of the times someone had refilled it.

"She go swim. You know?"

"At night?" asked Ben. Who would want to go swimming in the middle of the night?

"One year—twelve months, last year—Nakamori swim," he tried to explain, his harsh breath threatening to melt the skin off Ben's face. "She swim on za beach. In day—night. Some day sit on za beach—morning, afternoon. All day."

Two of the others had returned their attention to the conversation about Hanako and now chuckled knowingly.

"No clothes," one of them blurted out.

They all laughed.

"Bery beautiful!" Nobuhide exclaimed above the latest singer's crooning. "Bery sexuaru."

"She sexy garu!" another exclaimed.

There in the crazy noise and stifling smoke of the pub, Carmen's words came back to Ben: 'Do you want to know what Obâsan told me about your girlfriend?' He wondered, regarding his buddies around the table. What did she mean?

"You saw her?" he asked Nobuhide.

"Yesu. Bery beautiful."

"I mean, you saw her go swimming at the beach?"

"Yesu. She swim on beach."

"What do you mean? Was she on the beach or did she go into the water?"

"She swim. Za water — *mizu de oyogu. Ii, gomen ne.* Mistake. She no clothes, uh, put on her body some days. She on beach, no clothes. Is bery beautiful."

Ben sat up. "What . . . ?"

Nobuhide's lieutenant, the guardian of Tomoko's stairs, leaned across the table and stared into Ben's face, almost defiantly, as Uncle called for another beer from the bar.

"She swim . . . no come back," said the guardian of the stairs.

It was starting to make sense.

"You're saying she went swimming at the beach? Is that it? Is that what you mean?"

"Bery beautiful!" Nobuhide cried out, making curves in the air with his hands.

"She die in za sea," the stairs guard said. He seemed more sober than the rest. Designated driver? But they had all walked to the pub. His eyes were quite sharp.

Ben stood up as best he could, steadying myself. His buddies stared up at him.

"What are you saying?"

"She go on za beach, no clothes. She bery beautiful!" Nobuhide exclaimed. "Look bery sexuaru."

Two of the others nodded their heads. One drew curves in the air.

"So bery bery beautiful! *Iroppoi!* Bery sexuaru!"

Ben asked the stairs guard again, shouting down the drunken Nobuhide. He had to be sure he understand what they were telling him. "Where did she die?"

"She die in za sea," the man repeated.

Ben dropped into his seat and lay his head on the table, frustrated and angry. Some spilled beer wet his cheek. He did not care.

"You mean she drowned? Out there in the sea?"

The stairs guard nodded and seemed sad to tell Ben.

"Why was she swimming out there?" he asked but the roar of the celebration swept his voice away into nothingness.

That was it. That was what Carmen was trying to tell him. She died in the sea. Some kind of swimming accident. A drowning. Why had nobody told him? Why so secretive? From these punks he had hated immediately upon first meeting them, he had finally learned the answer to the most confusing question.

And yet, it did not make sense.

"An accident?"

They could not understand Ben.

She died in November. On the seventh. Obâsan confirmed those facts. It was far too late in the year for anyone to go swimming in the Sea of Japan. But the date was significant. He did not have to think long, pulling up the calendar in his mind. It was the anniversary of their first date. In Hawaii. They had talked about the sea that day as they walked along Waikiki beach.

Ben tried to climb out from behind the table, pinned as he was against the wall. He stepped over the seats, pushing his friends aside.

"I gotta go now," he shouted at them.

"Where you go?" Nobuhide called to him.

"To get an answer."

"*Nanda*?" To what?

Ben did not reply. Rushing drunkenly out of the pub, he flagged a taxi and headed back to Obâsan's house.

28

IT WAS CLOSE TO MIDNIGHT when Ben got to the house and stormed straight into Tomoko's new room, opposite the room formerly used by Hanako. She awoke immediately, startled, frightened.

"Ben-*chan*," she cried, for the first time using the affectionate suffix with his name, "you are drink!"

"I'm not drink, dammit. I'm *drunk*! But I'm not as drunk as I want to be — not after hearing what all your uncle's guys told me."

She was shielding her eyes from the light.

"Tell me what happened to Hanako!"

"I tell you already."

"No, you didn't. Nobody has. Everyone's been telling me lies — like it's all a big conspiracy, a big secret. Why won't anyone tell me the truth? Now I want to know the whole truth. What happened? How did she die?"

"I don't know," she cried, cringing under the quilt.

He grabbed her wrist, jerked her out of the *futon* and took both her wrists in his hands.

"No, please!" she cried.

"Get up," he shouted.

"Let me go! Please. I tell you everything already."

He pulled her up by the wrists, the quilt falling away from her. She was wearing a blue and white *yukata*, typical sleeping clothes in the summer. She hung her head, acting innocent, yet ashamed, but he knew there was a difference now.

"Tell me how she died."

She settled on her knees, hands stretched above her head where he held them.

"I don't know," she said, weeping. "I can't tell you."

She twisted and tried to pull her hands free, whimpering.

"Let me go! I don't know how she die!"

"Then show me!" He grabbed her shoulder and brought her to her feet. He thrust her toward the doorway. "Show me the beach. I have to know what happened. What could be so bad that everyone wants to keep it from me? I want to know. You've got to tell me, dammit!"

She was crying as he led her from the room. With all the noise, Obâsan poked her head out.

"*Dochira iku*?" Obâsan called after them. Where you going?

They nearly tripped over Tomoko's motor scooter, parked near the front door.

"No," she said when he pointed at it. It was not far, he guessed. "That way."

Across the road and down the opposite slope, they found the trail and followed it. He hurried as if he could prevent a tragedy, dragging Tomoko along by her arm, *yukata* flapping in the night breeze, bare feet dirty against the trail.

When they broke from the trees, the sea lay before them, surging and crashing on the narrow strip of beach. To either side were two towering, jagged cliffs. The sheer precipices discouraged climbing. Out in the surf, he saw, were other spikes of rock, tall waves tearing over them.

"It almost high tide," Tomoko shouted into the wind.

"Where is it?" he shouted back as sea spray hit him. "Where's the pile of stones?"

She pointed to the north cliff.

"There? I don't see it."

"After rock. Can't go there now. Water too high," she yelled.

He pulled her along, more determined.

"No! No, Ben! Can't go there now!"

She was jerking her arm in his tight grasp, frantic to escape.

"I have to know what happened, Tomoko. What happened to her? Why is everybody lying to me? What really happened here?"

"I can't tell you!"

Pulling her along, they crossed the short stretch of beach as the waves grew more savage. The rocky cliffs lay before and above them. The tide had covered the strip of sand that was the passageway, but stepping into it, he found it was only a foot deep.

"Come on!"

Unconcerned with his shoes and pants, he grabbed hold of the rock to steady himself. He pulled Tomoko along with him, the waves soaking her *yukata*. She lost her balance and fell to one knee in the water. Shocked by the chilly surf, she bolted upright. He wrapped an arm around her shoulders and pressed on. After another twenty meters around the rock's eroded face they left the water and reached the next beach.

"Here?" He glanced around the small patch of sand surrounded by a semi-circle of towering rock faces, hidden from the world. Yet open to the sea. "This is it?"

"Yes," she cried, and he could feel her weariness.

"Where? I don't see anything."

He released her arm and she collapsed on the sand.

"It's there!" she tried to exclaim in her exhausted voice, pointing out at the tide.

In the darkness he searched the horizon. Between the waves, he found it: the top-most stone glistening under the moonlight. About a foot and a half stood exposed above the water. It was at least thirty feet out into the surf.

"That's it?"

She nodded, bracing herself on one arm against the sand, holding her stomach with the other.

"What happened here?" he called.

The angry wind seemed to snatch his words and throw them back. "What happened here?" he repeated.

Ben rushed into the surf, trying for a closer look at the stones, then hurried back to where Tomoko was crumpled on the sand, never taking his eyes from the cairn.

"Tell me what happened here, dammit!" he shouted, grabbing her arm once more.

"She died!" Tomoko was crying. "She died here."

"How? How did she die?"

"She swim there—out there—and she die."

He shook his head to clear his mind.

"No, she didn't. That's impossible. Nobody goes swimming in Ishikawa in November! That's crazy. Something else must have happened. Tell me what happened! Tell me!"

"She swim in za sea and she die!"

"Did somebody force her to go out there?"

Tomoko flung her arms at him as he jerked her to her feet. He held her around the waist, ushering her out to the edge of the surf. She resisted as hard as she could, crying out for help and beating her fists against his shoulder.

"Look! That pile of stones out there. What happened out there? Why is it there? Who built it?"

She threw herself into his shoulder, sobbing loudly, her fist weakly punching his chest. He held her in his arms, restraining her. She felt warmth against him and held him tightly. All of her strength left then and she slumped in his arms.

"Obâsan—she did it. And people of Togimachi. They make it to remember her. Everybody build it."

He left her on the sand, ripped off his jacket and covered her.

"You to blame!" she shouted, as though summoning her last ounce of strength. "You love her and go away. She get baby and you not come back. She get sick for you, and she not know what to do. Why you not come back? She tell me always you come back. She believe you come back for her and baby. She tell me and I believe her. Then you send letter, you say you get other girl, get marry. She break heart, very bad. She not know what do, how take care baby."

Holding her tightly, Ben shook his aching head, ears bursting with the painful words.

"Noooo!" he cried out.

He leaped up and threw himself into the surging tide, to his knees in the chilly waters.

Immediately, Tomoko was behind him, ankle-deep in the surf, calling to him.

"She swim here — beside this rock."

He turned to face her, the rugged waves crashing on the shore around them and the salty winds whistled in their ears.

"She swim — far — out there. She go very far but — she not come back. For three day she gone. Then one day — she come to beach — but she dead."

"She drowned?"

"Maybe drown. What 'drown' mean, Ben-*chan*?"

"It means to swallow water or be under the water so you can't breath."

"I think she drown."

"She drowned out there?"

She raised her arm, just as the wind slapped her tangled hair across her face. Her hand pointed to the spot.

"There! Out there — she drown."

"But why? Why did she go swimming out there — in the night — in November?"

Tomoko jumped back out of the rushing waves.

"She not know what do, how take care baby. You never come. She know you come if she die. And you did come. You did come!"

"What?"

He could not hear her clearly in the storm.

"What are you saying? She killed herself?"

Tomoko ran into the water, her *yukata* half-torn and pulled open in front, and wrapped her arms around him from behind, rocking him back and forth.

"You did come."

The wind howled as the cold water stung his legs. Even in May the water was cold. He stared out at the dark, choppy sea, breathing the sea spray. As she had done that night.

"You did come, Ben-*chan*."

Everything was dark before him.

"But too late."

29

OUTSIDE, THE WIND WAS DRIVING A LIGHT SNOW across the peninsula, singing in the woods, whistling through the eaves of the old house.

Hanako turned to the warm fire and held her hands near. The *kotatsu* heater was making her legs toasty. The house was silent, her *obâsan* long ago turning in and her infant daughter even earlier. Now she was alone.

In times past, this was when she would secretly read her lover's letters, free of her grandmother's curious eyes or her daughter's playful tuggings. But those days were long past. No letters came now. How excited she would be when she returned from shopping in town, or walking through the forest, or taking her baby to the marsh where the *tsuru* danced, and find his letter waiting for her! She lived every day for the arrival of the postman, and if two days passed without a letter, she began to worry it might be the last one.

Her grandmother enjoyed seeing her read the letters. Her eyes would light up like the five bright stars of the constellation *Subaru*, and her smile would be fixed to her face for hours. She read each letter several times in one sitting. Her lover must be a kind man, the grandmother mused, and she awaited the day she would finally meet him. Like the *tsuru*, the Japanese snow cranes, they had danced together in Hawaii; they were mated for life. Her granddaughter anxiously awaited the arrival of the man of her dreams.

But no letter had come for six months. She refused to give up hope. After all, he did tell her he would come for her. He told her many times. Maybe the words were not always those words, but there was no mistaking the feelings behind them. Perhaps there was a postal strike in America, she thought. Maybe he was sick and could not write. Or he was just too busy with his new job. She would spend hours conjuring up the various possibilities, and other hours vividly imagining the day he would come for her. There would be a knock on the door, like the postman's only louder, firmer. She would dare not peek out the window, but swing the door right open and take her chances. Usually it was the postman, or some other visitor, never him.

Her daughter was getting bigger now. She could stand and walk short distances. How she wished he could see her! He would be so proud—maybe. But what if he did not like the child? She wanted to make him happy, yet she did not have the chance to tell him of her pregnancy before they parted for the last time. She did not know herself, not until she began to feel sick every morning. Her mother suspected the cause and lectured her sternly. How dare her mother insist on aborting it! It was her baby, and no matter what she had to do, she was going to give it birth. The baby was theirs. She would present it to him some day and it would be the greatest gift he would ever receive. He would be overjoyed. His eyes would sparkle like hers did. His smile would stretch across the whole Pacific Ocean.

But what would she do if he did not like the child? Perhaps he did not like children, she pondered. If he did not, then telling him might cause him to stop writing to her, to never come for her. She could not handle that possibility. In her joyful mind, there was no dark side to her life. If he were not thrilled with the discovery of their baby, then she would be cut to the heart and bleed the rest of her life. Although thoughts of that often came to her, she shooed them away as quickly as she could. She could not let herself think about them.

So she would not tell him. He had promised to come for her some day. He could see their baby then. It would be a fantastic reunion, she was certain, one that would assure their lifetime together. Everything had happened so perfectly thus far, she reasoned, and nothing on the horizon worried her. He might guess about the child, and maybe she would leave clues in her letters, but she would never tell him straight out. That would spoil their reunion.

The *obâsan* agreed with her plan, but secretly she did so only because she wished to see her granddaughter's continued happiness. In her heart, the old woman had had her own experiences which helped her understand her granddaughter's enthusiasm. It had to be tempered, she knew. Believing that this prince would not come for her granddaughter, all she could do was go along with the plan, lest her granddaughter become discouraged. Exiled by her family, sent to far away Ishikawa, the land where people can feel the greatest guilt, it was the next harshest sentence to joining a temple. She had nothing else in her life to make her happy. She had her baby and she had her never-ending hope that he would come.

But how long would that last?

The fire was burning low as she re-read the last letter she had received, postmarked months earlier. It was a terrible letter, difficult to read, with hidden meanings and uncertain ideas. She could not believe the words written there. She did not know how many times she had read it since its arrival, but she read it one more time. Maybe this time, she hoped, the letter would not say that he had found another woman and would write no more. Anxiously, she held each and every word in her mind, analyzing it, until she came to the bottom of the seventh page.

The signature seemed to be fading and she worried that it would completely disappear.

She held it up to the fire in the brazier, to see it more clearly. Yes, it was fading, she saw. She had read it too many times, touched the blue ink of the letters once too often. What would he do if he came for her and saw his signature missing?

She jumped up intending to retrieve a pen from her room to trace over the lines, but in her exuberance the letter dropped from her fingertips and flew into the fire. Half of it was burned before she could pull it out of the smoldering ashes. The first page was turned into a crisp black wafer. The others were destroyed.

Sobbing, she waved them in the air to cool them. In the morning, Obâsan would find them and think she had intended to burn the letter, the last letter. Maybe she had meant to burn it. She was confused.

It was true, she knew. It was time to resign herself to the fact that her life had turned against her. She had fought as hard as she could, resisted every negative thought, prayed every night and dreamed every day. Now she was exhausted. The burned letter was the last mark of defeat. It was time to surrender. She believed in Fate and so succumbed all too willingly to what was expected.

In her room, she opened her box of photos and sorted them, his pictures on the left, pictures of both of them together in the middle, everybody else to the right. She picked up the top photo in the left pile and scanned his face, trying to imagine if he still looked the same. She studied a couple of pictures from the middle pile, remembering how happy she was in them, on that day, at that time, with him. They were beginning to torment her. She could feel it in their touch. They had lost the warmth they had always had. She could not stand for the coolness now. Clearly life had left them. The more she looked, the harder her heart beat.

She quickly scooped them up but most of them were haphazardly knocked off the side of her desk into the trash basket. Not wishing to take time to save them, she took a few chosen photographs to the kitchen and cut them with scissors. Pictures of both of them she cut between the two figures. Pictures of only him she cut crosswise, severing him at the waist. After the first two, she decided to stop. It was foolish, she decided. What if she wanted to look at them again?

At that moment the wind sang in the eaves but she thought she heard her sleeping daughter calling out in her dreams. She went to the *shoji* of her room to listen, leaving the mutilated pictures on the counter beside the scissors where her *obâsan* would find them the next morning and believe that her granddaughter's hatred of Americans had finally blossomed.

Her daughter was safe, and still asleep. With a sigh, she stepped lightly away from the door and went to her room. Staring into her mirror, her breath frosted it. She grasped the cuff of her sweater and wiped it clean. She ran a weary hand through her long black hair, grown down to the small of her back since she was forced to resign from the airline. Wishing she had washed it that morning, she cursed at herself for thinking it mattered how she looked. It was now tangled around the sides of her face. She looked horrible and she made an ugly face at herself.

Kneeling at her low desk, she pulled out a sheet of the lavender writing paper she always used to compose her letters to him and began writing another letter. His letter had hurt her, for weeks and months, so she would make hers as painful to read as possible. He would come, she knew, when he read this letter. Maybe this time he would be impressed enough to make the long journey.

The other letter she had written, when Obâsan finally convinced her that he could not guess about her baby, had landed silently on his eyes. He never wrote a reply, she recalled with a sudden tightening of her throat. She finally wrote and told him in straight and clear words that she had given birth to their child, and he did not reply. And the following letters he wrote showed no acceptance of their child, no acknowledgment of their baby's birth, no words of joy, no words of happiness. How could he write nothing?

She had told her *obâsan* about the letter, saying she had waited long enough. Her grandmother cautioned her that it would not be best if this stranger, this American man, came to see her. Their life had become settled finally after the birth and the scandal and having him visit—or live with them!—that would be too much to accept. It was better to leave him ignorant of the child, her *obâsan* insisted, but Hanako knew better.

One letter was all that was needed, she decided, and when she gave the sealed envelope to her grandmother on her trip into town to mail for her, she began counting the days until his arrival. Months passed before she was compelled to write another letter, identical to the first, and continued to wait. Then the letter came for her, the parting letter, in which he told of the blonde woman in America.

Her weary eyes blinked and she realized she had been staring at the wall, her mind in flight.

Her handwriting was hurried and sloppy, even for writing the strange words of English. How else would he know her thoughts? He did not read Japanese. The words were not slow in coming and she scrawled them as fast as she thought them. Hard, cruel words. Lies that would hurt him. Truths that would make him weep. She pulled another page from the folder, then another. She signed her name on the back of the fifth sheet and sat back in the *zaisu*, stretching her legs and sighing with fatigue.

This letter told him everything she had written before, in the other letters. She told him about the child. The child she named Aiko. She knew he would come when he read the letter. He had to. And she pulled out a favorite photograph from its frame to lay beside the letter, so she would not forget to include it when she mailed it. The photograph showed her in front of Obâsan's house, wearing a *yukata* and *geta*, their beautiful baby in her arms and a sad smile on her face.

A thought struck her as she sat back, staring at the Hawaiian calendar on the wall. Beneath the view of the Na Pali coast of the island of Kauai—which they were never able to visit—she noticed it was November sixth. No, she calculated, since it was past midnight it was now the seventh. She did not need to check the diary she kept during her year and a half in Hawaii to remember the significance of the date. After their meeting on the beach—which she never really counted because they did not know each other—this day was the anniversary of their first official date.

She had not kissed him, though he had tried to kiss her. They had seen a movie, what it was she could not remember, and had Chinese food at the Kahala Mall on the east side of Diamond Head. He had looked very handsome and despite her being tired from the flight that arrived at six in the morning, she was filled with excitement. Discounting their meeting on the beach, this would be when she would know if her feelings for him were true.

She glanced at the clock. It did not feel like one. She had too much energy — or was it leftover anger?

Perhaps a walk in the cool night air before she turned in for the night. After a good sleep, she was sure she could think about her troubles more clearly. Maybe she would decide not to send the letter, after all. Maybe he would come for her next week, or even tomorrow.

She went to her daughter's room, knelt beside the tiny *futon*. The child was dreaming, her eyes darting around beneath her eyelids and her mouth forming words in the darkness. So *kawaii*, so sweet and cute! She bent down and kissed her forehead. She wanted to pick her up and hold her but she did not want her to awaken.

They had climbed up through the forest to the marsh earlier that day to see the *tsuru*. Her child was so tired from the hike, she slept soundly. Her daughter had been so delighted with their long-legged antics. From the brush where they hid to watch them, she wondered if she would miss them every autumn after they moved to America. And her daughter? Would she remember their beauty, their sensuous dance, their mating for life? No picture could capture their spirit. Even her friend, Tomoko, the painter, had tried and failed.

"Soon your father will come for you," she said, leaning over and whispering in English. She spoke a short prayer for her health and happiness. "I know he will love you. He will do anything for you. You only have to love him. I loved him."

She started to rise, paused.

"I still do."

The fresh night air beckoned her, as did her own personal feelings. It was late at night that she would have the privacy to remember how they had loved each other. Just like the snow cranes, they danced so beautifully together. She would never forget those times, either.

She went to the door, slid the *fusama* open.

"But he has lost his love for me."

The *obâsan* heard her granddaughter speaking in the hallway but thought nothing of it. She often stayed up late and she frequently spoke in English. Once Hanako had told her she wanted the child to be able to speak to her father in his language. Listening to her soft footsteps across the *tatami,* the old woman lay her head back to return to sleep.

No one heard the door open and shut. No one heard the steps across the porch or the slush of slippers through the fallen leaves. The wind had stopped dusting the trees with snow flurries. All was quiet now. She gazed about, a calmness coming over her as she saw the beauty of the snow among the pines. Tomorrow would be a beautiful day to see the *tsuru,* dancing in the snow.

Her head was stuffy from the warmth of the fire. The fresh air rejuvenated her and her heart beat quicker.

She climbed up to the road, crossed it, followed the familiar trail down to the beach.

Passing around the north rock—the tide was not yet high—she came to her private beach. It was hers. Not visible from the road above, it was safe to sunbathe. In fact, it was so safe that in warmer weather she frequently removed her swimsuit and lay nude on the sand, pretending it was a beach in Hawaii. The warm days there had set her soul free and she soared on endless flights of fantasy.

Regarding the pine covered hillside, too steep to hold a trail and too rough to climb, she recalled the few times she had seen someone watching her. Sometimes, she sensed eyes examining her body as she lay on her towel. Only once did she actually see a man. She had already been nude and was nearly dressed again when he slipped on the edge of the cliff, grasping at the bushes to keep from falling. She never knew who it was but it had to be one of the young men from town, either the fishermen, the cannery workers, or one of Tomoko's cousins, possibly Nobuhide.

Now the forest was deserted, the trees and the moss dusted with snow. A few flurries danced in the air as she sat on the small rock she used as a chair. The air was not too cold, the sky bright with the moonlight reflecting on the low blanket of clouds. She pulled off her coat and did not shiver.

She stared across the waters.

The sea lay black as obsidian, smooth as a sheet of glass, endless as the universe. She could see no white caps. She noticed no ship lights.

She was alone. In the brilliant night, she was in another world where magic moved life and dreams came true with just a kind thought. This was where she wanted to be. This was her destiny, her life. Here she could feel the greatest guilt.

Standing with hushed breath and nervous fingers, she slowly unbuttoned her green sweater and slipped it from her arms. The breeze made her shiver as she tugged at her Hawaiian Yacht Club T-shirt, but she managed to pull it over her head. She stepped out of her slippers and stood barefoot on the moist, cool sand. She watched the palpitating sea as she released the snap on her trousers, unzipped them with careful precision. It was a ceremony and everything had to be correct.

She turned and laid her folded trousers on the rock, placed her folded sweater and shirt on top of them. The air around her did not seem cold now, she decided as tears filled her eyes. She was feeling the greatest guilt.

She fell on her outstretched coat, gazing up at the clouds, watching a few flurries floating aimlessly above her. As the soft breeze touched her flesh, her hand slid between her legs. At first it was the same as any other time she had run away from the house to be alone in her passion, free from the eyes and ears of the old woman, free of the interrupting cries of her daughter. Soon the feelings coming to life within her took on their own energy. She felt no cold, knew no sorrows, concentrating on the magical sensations coursing through her body. She wanted to cry out in her pleasure, instead bit her lip. Finally, she collapsed on her coat, chest heaving, her arms wrapped around herself.

The air buzzed around her like she was in a stadium with cheering crowds. More snow flurries rained down on her. The moon swelled, burning with its own fire. The audience seemed to applaud, urging her to dance further.

When she had caught her breath, she lay on her coat counting the stars shining through the thinning clouds. Then she sat up, locked her elbows, relished the chilly air against her warm skin. She felt dirty, unworthy of his or anybody's love.

This is my curse, she whispered. And she spoke a *haiku* of her own invention, something solemn and deeply heartfelt.

> *Death drinks me,*
> *Under the dark sea,*
> *Will you save me?*

Would he come to her funeral? If that were a significant enough event to call him, she would gladly sacrifice herself. If seeing their baby was incentive enough for him, she would have sent him the picture long ago. But she was certain it was not enough. A man would not give up his wife to come to the funeral of his *koibito*. Maybe he would. He had to see the child. He had to come for her — and the child.

> *Snowy funeral,*
> *No guests except you,*
> *Weeping too softly*

she composed.

Little *akachan*, she whispered, he will come for you soon. And he will love you more than he loved me. When I am gone, he will come. He will come.

She rose from her coat, her head spinning, intending only to wash herself as she usually did. The lingering touch of her lover stayed on her mind. Some day he would come for her, she repeated as though she believed her words. Then they would make love for weeks and weeks without stopping.

She lost her smile when she began to sense that he might really not be coming for her. Or if he did, it would be too late. She would be an old woman, weathered and broken, gray as old fallen snow, ugly. He would not want her.

Tears came to her eyes as she stepped down the beach toward the lapping surf. She cupped her hand and poured the water over herself. She wrapped her arms around herself for a silent moment, her eyes closed, imagining he was holding her. A breeze stroked her flesh. Her bottom pressed against the coarse sand. Cold waters gurgled between her toes.

Shivering, she sat up and regarded the sea.

The waters lay black, clean, cold, sterile, the sea vast and empty. In its welcoming depths was a world of painless oblivion. The waters were smooth like a sheet of glass, and she could walk on it. She could walk across the sea. She could float over it.

Raising her arms from her sides, she balanced herself as the waters parted for her feet. She shook as she lowered herself into the water. Waves formed and rolled toward her, small waves, then larger ones. They flowed over her body as her feet left the sandy, rocky bottom and floated freely. Her body was directed out into the sea, sliding across the glass. No longer did she feel the cold. No longer did she notice her legs growing numb; they were already without feeling. No longer was her mind filled with his voice. No longer did her icy flesh remember his touch. Now, there was nothing but the sea, with its deep, dark call and its endless, painless serenity.

She raised her arm, brought it down into the water. She stroked the water with her other arm. She pointed her toes, kicked her legs. The water was warm and her lover was cheering for her. Look! There is the golden tower of the Peter and Paul Mission on the hill to her right. There was Waimea Bay's Rock on her left. Somewhere on the beach her lover was calling to her. *No*, she cried, *you come to me.*

Ahead lay the open sea. Behind her was Waimea Beach, its fine yellow sand her heaven, her utopia, her paradise. Beyond that was her worries and her troubles, her ruined life, and her endless sorrow. Further in her wake buoyed her child and the child's father. She was certain he would come to save her. After all, he was not an unkind man. She knew he would come when she was dead.

She swam further and further, the waves lapping at her face and shoulders as she slid through the water.

I'm killing myself, she suddenly realized. *I'm really trying to kill myself, aren't I?*

Her arms swung automatically through the waves, and her legs would not cease kicking. It was not cold at all, she thought, her mind too numb to reason. Perhaps she did not want to die. Maybe she should not have tried to swim this time. In the morning someone would find her body washed up on the beach, dead. They would all stare at her body, at her naked body, exposed to the world. She never meant to kill herself. She never intended that at all, she insisted, though the sea refused to believe her.

She would turn back. Surprisingly, her arms and legs would not respond. They were too cold, too numb, she realized. She cried out in the night that she never meant to die. The wind chuckled and the sea laughed. She did not want to die, she insisted, sinking lower and lower into the deep, cold blackness of the sea.

30

DAWN ROSE OVER THEM bleak and gray. Sitting cross-legged on the sand, his back against the rock Tomoko had used for a seat, Ben regarded the hypnotically pulsing sea. At the farthest reach of his vision, the underbellies of the clouds were tinged with a dark orange. The new day reminded him that he needed to return to life.

She killed herself.

The words could not be spoken. His soul would not be soothed and his heart would not stop aching. She had killed herself, and for no reason. If there were a reason, it was that she thought he could guess her unspoken, unwritten thoughts from far across the Pacific, thoughts she refused to set in print or send over telephone lines.

As Tomoko explained to him, Hanako feared he would not like the child and therefore would not come for her. Although it did not make any sense to Ben, he realized it was perfectly logical to her Japanese mind, especially *her* mind—after being exiled by her family, bearing the baby alone, living an uncertain life at the rim of society. From what Tomoko had told him, what he knew from Obâsan, and his own experiences in Japan, and knowing Hanako, he could fill in the rest. It was all too easy to understand.

If only she had told me . . . .

He detected Tomoko behind him. She had been there all night, but he had been too consumed by his own thoughts to order her back to the house.

"Ben-*chan*?" she called in a low voice. How many times during the night had she called and he not heard?

He rested his head back against the rock. "Yes?"

At his response, she rushed to him, kneeling behind him.

"*Gomen nasai*," she muttered, bowing her head to the sand.

He released a sigh, like he had been holding his breath all night.

She sat up, placed her hand gently on his shoulder and brushed his wind-blown hair.

"*Mo shiwake gozaimasen*," she whispered, her voice shaking. She did not know what words to say.

"*Wakarimashita*," he replied after a moment, understanding.

Her cheek brushed his and her head rested on his shoulder, her hand crossing his chest to his other shoulder, a wary hug. She stroked his head as he let the tears roll down his face.

"One day I come," Tomoko spoke. "Obâsan say she go away. She show me burn letter—and pictures cut—and letter she write. Obâsan say she cry all night, then go away. We call police, they come ask questions to Obâsan. I look for her. Everyone look. I go this beach, find her clothes. She not here. I see foot steps. Go in sea. I know she swim here, so I say to Obâsan she go swim at night. Fishermen go look, no find. Two days, she not found. Obâsan cry, but *akachan* no cry—she think of her in peace."

With his head pressed against her chest, Ben could hear her heart beating faster as she talked.

"Four days after, someone see body on beach, so we go see. It is her body. She dead. No clothes. Doctor look on her, see no hurt, no cut, only bruise from hitting sea rocks. Obâsan say she kill herself. She say kill herself about you, but I say wrong. She tell doctor about you. Doctor say he think so, write on paper."

Ben just wanted to hold her, to feel safe.

"We have funeral, like she want. Christian style. And she lay in long hole and big stone sit there, too. Aiko-*chan* only look at her, no cry — she no understand what happen. Maybe she not know where mama go. I cry for Aiko-*chan*."

He raised his head, wanting to see her face.

"Why did you stay out here," he asked, "in the cold and the wind of the storm? You should have gone back to the house. You could've caught pneumonia out here. Why did you stay here?"

"I protect you." Her voice was choked with emotion. "Maybe you go after her, so I stay with you. I keep you away from swim after her. You was so crazy in the night."

She hugged his head, pressing his face into her bosom. He rolled over in the sand until she was on top of him.

"I love you!" she cried suddenly, cranking her embrace tighter.

They kissed for a long time.

"If I get back to America," he told her when their lips parted, "and I find myself alone, I'll send for you and we'll be together."

"I will be happy," she said. "I will be Hanako for you."

"No, you be Tomoko."

The *ofuro* bubbled and boiled until it was ready for Tomoko to step into it and settle her shoulders below the surface of the water.

Inside the house, Obâsan solemnly presented to Ben the old shoe box in which she kept the ugly mementos of that night. Her eyes were wet but she would not allow any teardrop to fall. He bowed humbly, accepting the gift of memories. She waited as he opened it and examined its contents: the crisp, blackened letter he had written; the lavender letter she wrote; the pieces of cut photographs. He could feel Hanako's touch when he held them.

Later, Obâsan brought more mementos in boxes, bags, sacks, on hangers, and gathered up with her hands. He took the suitcase she had given him previously — the one with Hanako's Hawaiian clothes inside — and tried to fit in some of the items. She gave him an older suitcase she used only for annual trips to Nagoya to visit her son's family. As the only suitcase she had ever owned, she did not think she would be using it again. So she gave it to him. And he collected the clothing, pictures, and personal items of Hanako in it to bring back to America. Some day, Aiko would want to see them.

Obâsan returned later holding a large clear plastic bag containing clothing. He recognized them from Tomoko's story: the green sweater, the white T-shirt, the trousers, and slippers. The bag was sealed with an official tag clamped over the sealed opening. She told him it had been kept as evidence — until the cause of death had been determined. He shuddered, holding the bag, studying its contents, imagining seeing her wearing them that night. The seal would not be broken for several years, he decided, not until Aiko was an adult.

Now he had two suitcases filled with everything Hanako had owned. He locked them, fastened the buckles on the straps, tied rope around them for added security. Then he set the keys on the low desk next to his wallet, knowing exactly where he would put them for safe keeping.

By the time Tomoko rejoined them, Ben had decided to have a memorial service at the shrine.

They knelt before the shrine, Obâsan to his right, Tomoko to his left with Shunichi and Aiko in front of them. Prayers were spoken in Japanese, hands clapped to cause them to come true. Incense was lit and quickly filled the little pine grove.

After the Buddhist funeral in the town's big temple, her body was brought back to Obâsan's house. Hanako had wanted a Christian burial and Obâsan wanted her granddaughter to remain close. The pine grove was chosen. Friends in town built the tiny house that held the stone statue of Amida Buddha, the kindly saint to which Hanako had prayed in life. Every Tuesday, Obâsan had climbed up the hill to the grove, placed an offering at the shrine, and spoke a prayer for her granddaughter's soul.

In turn, they each bowed before the shrine. Aiko bowed last of all. When she rose, she turned and looked at Ben as if asking if she did it correctly. He smiled and she went to him.

They moved over to the gray headstone.

"Hanako-*chan*," he whispered, "dear, sweet, Hanako. You know I will care for our daughter with the same love and kindness as if you were beside me to guide me. As you wished, I did come. I came to care for Aiko—and remember you—and cry for you. We can't come back, so I hope my prayer will last forever."

Aiko listened intently. He gave her a smile and turned to the grave once more. Then, speaking so she could hear him, he said in a soft, gentle voice, "I love you."

With his spirit cleansed, Ben took Aiko back to the house along with Obâsan. Then he hiked down to the beach and sat on the rock, staring out at the sea for a long time, alone. It was low tide and the wide beach lay before him. He reached into his pocket, pulled out the keys to the two suitcases. He had no need of them; when the time came, years from now, he would simply pry them open. They would not need to be resealed after that.

He stood beside the pyramid of stones the townsfolk had made to remember Hanako and heaved the handful of keys out over the waves, far into the sea.

When he returned to the house, he found Obâsan in tears beside Tomoko, both bowing their heads to the *tatami*. Before he could ask why, Tomoko translated the old woman's wavering words. She was apologizing in the most humble way possible, Ben saw, but for what?

Tomoko explained. Hanako had given Obâsan a letter to mail which told him about the baby.

"But I never got any letter like that," said Ben.

However, Obâsan did not mail the letter but threw it away, she tearfully confessed through Tomoko's rough translation. Obâsan told her granddaughter that she had sent it. And Hanako had waited and waited, not understanding why he never sent a reply.

A flood of tears spilled from Obâsan's eyes as she cried out her apologies, begging Ben for forgiveness.

31

THEY SAT IN SILENCE as the train swayed back and forth, Obâsan across from Ben, Aiko in the seat next to him, staring out the window. Tomoko sat across from her, leaving Shunichi with her cousin for this trip. The morning sun was warm shining through the windows and Ben felt a headache coming on.

He regarded Obâsan. Wearing her best *kimono*, she was dressed up not only for the interview, which meant everything, but to see off her great-granddaughter. She would never see her again, they all knew. And yet, she kept those thoughts to herself. Not even her face showed any of the feelings she must be having, thought Ben. She had initiated all of these events from the time Ben received her first letter. Her guilt prompted her to make up for her mistake. Everything was turning out the way she had planned.

Tomoko was quiet, though she glanced over at Ben from time to time and her bright, happy eyes pleased him. Small, vaporous smiles flickered across her face as she, like Obâsan, kept her thoughts and emotions to herself. He could see himself having a life with her. Maybe he was in love, but *love* was too strong a word to use in Japan. He gave her the address and phone number of his house in Seattle so she could contact him — in case the future was not as kind to her — and to him — as he hoped it might be.

Aiko was entertained by the ever-changing scenery outside her window. This was her first trip away from Togimachi and Obâsan's house. She was on her way to see the world, one tiny step at a time. Obâsan had dressed her in a beautiful orange *kimono* with rich golden trim, the same as she had worn the previous November for the holiday of *shichi-go-san*. On that day, even though her mother had died only a week before, Aiko went to the big shrine in Togimachi with Obâsan and received the official blessing. Obâsan was proud of the exquisite *kimono* she had made, worn a long, long time ago by a three-year old Hanako. With combs and ribbons in her hair, Aiko was the twin of the Hakata doll that Hanako had given to Ben in Hawaii.

They took pictures with Tomoko's camera while waiting at the bus station in Togimachi. Ben promised Obâsan that he would take lots of pictures of Aiko and send them to her. He told her that as soon as Aiko was old enough to be able to write, that he would make sure she sent letters.

Smiling in embarrassment, Obâsan told Ben, through Tomoko, that she doubted she would live long enough for that. But he pledged an endless gallery of Aiko photographs showing her growing up in America.

Bill Sharp, Honorary Consul, shifted papers over his cluttered desk, and studied Ben's statement of income.

"And you'll be continuing in your present line of work after you return?" he asked.

"Yes, of course," Ben replied. He hoped he still had his job with Prime Properties, but this was not the time or place to ponder the question. If he did not have the job, he knew he could find a similar position with another company. "And I expect my income to increase according to my seniority. Aiko with have a comfortable life, you can be assured."

"A comfortable life doesn't have to mean having a lot of money,

Mister Pinkerton."

"I understand what you mean. She'll have all the love I can muster, and more. This child is my life now, I want you to know."

"Oh, I can appreciate what you say."

Carmen scooted to the front of her chair. "I told you how much trouble this man's gone through to try and bring his daughter home."

Sharp waved his hand over his desk. "Relax, Miss Tsuruta. These are only routine questions. I have to ask them."

He looked through other pages, turning back to some documents, flipping ahead to others. Finally, he took the sheaf and shook it against the edge of the desk to straighten the papers.

"It seems all the papers are in order."

Ben grinned. "Great! I really appreciate your time and effort on our behalf. I know we were asking for a lot in such a short time, but Carmen seemed to think that we could do it with your help. Thank you."

"You're very welcome." Sharp glanced over at Aiko and smiled. Her attention was on Obâsan as the child fidgeted in her seat. He returned his attention to Ben. "I understand her mother's death was suicide."

Ben nodded slowly. "Maybe. We'll never know for sure."

"Of course."

"I want to believe it was an accident."

Sharp looked down at the stack of papers.

Carmen, who had met them in front of the consul's office and was surprised to see Tomoko, sat up in her chair. "You have my affidavit there, don't you?"

He dug down six pages and pulled it out.

"I hope it's all properly phrased, how I attest to Mister Pinkerton's good character, his kindness to children, and so forth."

"It's fine. Thank you."

She glanced at Ben with a smile.

"Your name and address will be sent to stateside authorities who will continue to monitor Aiko's place in your family. After two years, she can receive permanent residency. I know it sounds a lot like probation, but the probation is yours, Mister Pinkerton, not for your daughter. Everyone believes she'll be a good girl during this time. They have to keep an eye on you, the parent, however."

"I'm gonna be the best damn father any child's ever had," Ben exclaimed, ready to plead his case once more. "You can bet on that. I love this child. She's my first child, my only child, probably my last. I never want to be apart from her again — I mean until she's grown up and marries, of course. She's all I have now, and I love her so much. She's so beautiful . . . ."

He choked. Carmen patted his shoulder.

The Honorary Consul turned next to Obâsan, addressing her in Japanese with the utmost politeness. He asked questions of her. The old woman hesitated, thinking of her response each time. Ben was concerned. What would Hanako's grandmother say?

"He's asking her opinion of you," whispered Carmen, leaning over to Ben.

Ben nodded, held his breath.

"She says you're normal —"

That's good, thought Ben. *I certainly try to be.*

"No, she means you are a man with normal flaws . . . ." Carmen listened, then translated for Ben. "You have grown strong, wise during your stay . . . . You show care and kindness to the girl, to Aiko . . . . She's watched you fall in love with your daughter. She can understand how Hanako fell for you."

Ben was smiling, but Carmen continued.

"She says you have to keep on being the kind man Hanako fell for . . . . As a man, you fall for temptations — well, you know that right? So you have to be good, Ben."

"I'll certainly try to be," he whispered back, "I've always tried to do the right thing."

"*Shhh.* She says she's too old to raise her own daughter — Hanako's mom, that is. She won't take her, so . . . there is only one person she thought to contact. That's you, Ben. She says she didn't think you'd come . . . but you did . . . ."

Ben glanced at Obâsan, saw her fighting back tears.

"Now she says she gives Aiko to you . . . because it's you alone who deserves her . . . ."

"Thank you," Ben said, then in a stronger voice: "*Domo arigatô*."

"She says you must stand up and fight for her always, for your daughter . . . so she will be as strong as . . . as her mother was . . . ."

Carmen paused.

Ben looked at her, mouthing *What?*

Obâsan continued.

Carmen waved him to be quiet. After several minutes of Obâsan's emotional words, Carmen leaned over to him. "She's just apologizing for . . . what she did . . . mistakes she made . . . not important now."

The room was silent and Ben was afraid to look at anyone. Except Aiko. She seemed concerned by Obâsan's speech and watched the old woman intently. Ben let her down off his lap and she went to Obâsan and hugged her knees. The old woman hugged her with one arm, pulling back the long sleeve of the *kimono*, and nuzzled her cheek against the child's forehead.

"I'll tell you," Sharp spoke up, "I just about made up my mind before this interview, but I wanted to meet you. Miss Tsuruta told me about the situation, and Japanese Immigration filed their report rather quick, so there wasn't any problem. Everyone along the line has been very cooperative. And even some man back in your town — Togimachi — he really wrote a book about the child's mother . . . ."

He pulled out the sheaf of pages, maybe twenty or thirty, single-spaced, tied together with a string run through a punched hole in one corner.

"He wrote that he knew the woman during the past two years and wanted to vouch for her good character, adding his own observations about her death, adding a few comments about you and the child's future."

Ben leaned forward, gazing over the desk.

"Who would that be? I didn't ask anybody to write anything."

He flipped over to the last page.

"It's all in English, too. Except the name at the end. I can't quite make out the *kanji*. Sloppy handwriting. Must be why he typed it."

"Let me see," Carmen insisted, leaning forward.

He showed her the text and the signature.

"Yoshinobu Takahiroyama?"

"No one I know," Ben remarked.

"Professor of English, retired, Kanazawa University," she read.

It was the old man in the bookshop! He and Ben had met briefly. They talked about Hanako, then Ben bought some stationary and books and left. He remembered the man saying he had not known her very well.

"Says he taught her English privately," Sharp explained. "Says she was expecting to go to America, wanted to practice it. He writes that she often told him about you and—let me read it: 'her face would light up with a glow that could only have been from a deep, intense love she held within her heart'—unquote. And he writes that she often had him check her letters, to be sure they said what she wanted them to say, then returned home to rewrite them."

"I guess she wanted the words to be just right," said Carmen.

The Consul looked up but Ben was lost in thought.

"Nice guy," said Sharp.

"Yes, I'll have to write him and thank him."

"I guess that's about it."

The Consul directed his eyes at Obâsan. He repeated his statement in Japanese for her and her face became a smile. And a frown. She held her head high, calm in her repose, firmly clutching the cane between her knees.

"Let me get my stamp and we'll get this young lady all set to go traveling."

He placed the visa stamp on the first, crisp page of Aiko's new passport.

While it was still light, they posed for more pictures in front of the Kanazawa bus station, waiting to catch the shuttle to the Komatsu airport where they would fly to Nagoya and on back to America.

Aiko was giddy, running around the sidewalk in her *kimono*, waving her paper fan at everyone. Tomoko was quiet, reserved. Obâsan was smiling on the outside, but her tired eyes reflected the tears within. Carmen was happier than Ben would have expected, but he had not yet had a chance to talk with her privately.

They posed in every combination of two, three, and four people. They smiled, tried to smile, then cried, until the roll of film came to an end. Tomoko rewound it and gave it to Ben.

"Please," she said, "you make pictures. And please make copy for me and Obâsan."

"I will."

She reached in her travel bag, retrieved a medium-sized envelope and handed it to him.

"What's this?" he asked.

She leaned against him and whispered into his ear that it was an A4 glossy photo she took of Hanako for her paintings. Giggling as she pushed away from him, she said, "And me, too."

"What . . . ?"

"You see. You open later."

Their eyes met, pulling happiness from their hearts.

Before Ben could take her in his arms, she was crying and rushed into his embrace in front of all the others. He hugged her, holding her with one arm. Her tears ran down his cheek and wet his collar.

"I not forget you, Ben-*chan*," she sobbed.

Obâsan carefully bent down to kiss Aiko on the forehead. Seeing her struggle to reach Aiko, Ben picked up his new daughter and held her while Obâsan spoke her final, gentle, cautious words to her little companion. Aiko regarded the woman with serious contemplation. Was she able to understand that she would not see Obâsan again?

When Obâsan finished speaking, Aiko reached out with her short arms for Obâsan's head, hugged her. From that angle, he could see the miniature teardrops on Aiko's chubby, rosy cheeks.

"Obâsan told her to be a good girl," Carmen said, coming up behind him. "She told her the two of you were going on a long trip, and she wouldn't see her for a long time."

"That's a big sacrifice for Obâsan."

"And you, too."

"What's that?"

"You're taking an awfully big gamble. I mean, with your wife 'getting her ticket to fly' and such, you're gonna have to go it alone. Don't blow it, guy."

"Don't worry. I'm in 'daddy' mode." He hugged her. "Thanks, Carmen. For everything."

"*Do itashimashite*, Ben."

He nodded at her belly as they parted. "What are you going to do about that?"

"That? Me? I'm as cynical as always."

"What does that mean?"

"It means I talked with Yoshio—as you, in your infinite wisdom, suggested—and now he wants to marry me. Imagine that. To give the child a name, he said. Sounds like the kind of bullshit an American would say."

"Aren't you interested?"

She pursed her lips, thinking. "He's kind, and he seems to like kids. Baseball, that is. If it's a boy he's gotta be a Hanshin Tigers fan, he said. I think I could live with him, but I'm not sure. Anyway, I'm not getting the abortion. Not this trip, anyway. I'm meeting him here tomorrow. We're going to spend the weekend together. And do a lot of talking."

"That's good, Carmen. You should be less cynical now. You're being moody for two now. Probably you should simply cancel your membership in the Mutual Cynics Society. You know I'm letting my mine expire."

"Well, you've got a beautiful reason to, Ben. I envy you. You've fought the system and beaten it, and I've got to respect you for it."

"Now you've got to fight it and win." He winked at her. "Have your career and the baby, too. It's called the ol' *Showa* Shuffle. You can do it."

"Don't make me laugh."

"I'm not, but—hey, I couldn't have done it without you."

She chuckled, shaking her head.

Aiko took his hand and he squatted down beside her.

"Ready to go?" he asked.

Her face was cheerful, but she said nothing.

The shuttle bus was waiting. As the steward threw the bags in the storage compartment, Ben said goodbye one last time to Carmen Tsuruta, Tomoko Kaida, and Nakamori-*sama* whom he preferred to call Obâsan—grandmother.

Aiko waved at the women as she and her father stood in line to board the bus. She never stopped waving, even after they were seated inside where the tinted glass shielded her final gestures from them. The three ladies waited outside on the curb, their faces blank, their eyes still searching for his and Aiko's as the bus pulled away. Their anxious eyes pursued the bus down the street and Aiko gazed back at them until the bus turned a corner and they were suddenly severed, unmercifully, from their lives.

32

THE SHORT FLIGHT FROM KOMATSU TO NAGOYA was quiet, and both father and daughter slept most of the way. Ben had a dream in which he arrived back at the house to find everything missing: furniture, clothing, wife, everything. Then the walls began to slide in on him, smothering him. He awoke with the SEATBELTS ON buzzer as the plane approached Nagoya.

With just under five hours before the connecting flight to America departed, he put their bags in a locker and decided to take the airport bus across the river and through the city to Nagoya Station. Without a break, they boarded the Kamiyashiro subway train. His destination was the same house he had visited so many weeks before, the house Aiko should have been living in. He wanted her to see it.

Perhaps she thought I left Japan a long time ago. That was probably true, he thought, walking from the station to the house, a little girl carried in his arms.

Nakamori-*san* was surprised to see him when she opened the door. He stood sternly, the *kimono*-clad girl posed beside him. He spoke as best he could to Hanako's mother in practiced *Nihongo*, not caring whether he was polite or not. He did not know if his Japanese words were correct, or even if his sentences made sense, but he was certain his tone was true to his feelings.

He lifted Aiko up into his arms, one *zori* falling off her foot. She did not know where she was or who she was being shown to, but it did not matter. He didn't want her to remember this unkind woman, anyway.

"*Kore wa* Hanako-*chan no kodomo desu,*" stated Ben firmly with no emotion on his face or in his voice. This is her child.

The woman startled, feigning weakness, eyes wide.

"*Ima wa watashi no kodomo desu. Mite! Oboete! Monidoto mienai desu!*" he said. Now she's my child. Look, remember, because you'll never see her again.

He lowered Aiko to the porch and her little eyes were still on the woman.

"This is your grandmother, Aiko-*chan* —not that it matters."

The woman was still in shock, unable to speak.

"*Hanako-chan wa nakunarimashita. Kanojo wa oboremashita. Nihon Kai ni.*" She died. She drowned in the Japan Sea, he said, because you wouldn't give her a home. "*Kanojo wa aishimashita. Wakarimasu ka?*" I loved her. Understand? "*Aishimashita!*"

He gathered the fallen *zori* and picked up Aiko, turning to leave.

"*Sumimasen deshita,*" the woman called after them in a voice that seemed strangled. However, 'I'm so sorry' was not enough. "*Dochira ni sundeimasu ka?*" she cried. Where will you live?

He paused half way down the walk and glanced back over his shoulder.

"*Amerika e iko desu yo.* We're going back to America. I'm taking her home. To her home! Where she will be loved."

Her name is Aiko. He should have told that woman, thought Ben after the plane was airborne. Then she would have something more to remember the rest of her life. And the two *kanji* of her name would have great meaning, one character for 'love' and one for 'child.' Love child. A child born of love. No other name would fit her.

"We might visit again," said Ben, more to himself. "Someday."

"Summ-deh," the child imitated.

He regarded her, dressed now in a one-piece playsuit, the *kimono* folded away in a Duty Free bag.

"Yes, someday you will understand all that has happened these past few months. Someday you'll understand it all, Aiko—cheerful child; quiet, contemplative child; never-cries-when-you-should child; brave little girl."

The sky was growing lighter outside the humming jet, the sun melting over the jumbled row of clouds. Ahead lay their new home together. There, beyond the sunrise.

Ben looked down at his side. Aiko was still asleep and he envied her for her size, able to sleep comfortably in the airplane seat. Her eyes darted under her eyelids, her mouth slightly agape, her breath soft. He wished he had brought his own camera. He planned on buying a new one when they returned home. There would be many good photo opportunities in the wonderful years ahead.

Breakfast was soon served and he awoke Aiko. She was so cute picking sleepily at her food. He wrapped up a roll for later and let her return to sleep.

As the sky grew bright and they neared their destination, Ben's mind recalled Japan as a wild dream. Nothing seemed real. Nothing seemed true. The only proof he had was the child asleep beside him, a few pictures, and two suitcases of precious memorabilia.

He tried to remember how his house looked. He tried to picture it in his head. The route from the airport to downtown was foggy in his mind. And inside the house, would anything still be there? He knew the den was going to be converted into Aiko's bedroom. Or he would use the room Addy used as her home office. Aiko would need to use the den when she started college, a place to study. He would have to start a college fund when they returned. And she would need a car eventually. He would need to enroll her in school for the fall, too. Kindergarten! What would the other children think of her? How soon could she learn English? What kind of American food would she like? Could he prepare any Japanese dishes she would like? What would he do if she started crying?

Ben shook his head to clear the endless questions. It was too late. They were on their way to a new life. Father and daughter.

I like the sound of that. And daughter.

"Aiko," he whispered, "you are my daughter."

Then he remembered the envelope Tomoko had given him at the station and he climbed out of his seat, reached into his carry-on bag in the overhead bin and retrieved it.

It was thick, he noticed, although much of that was the protective cardboard. He carefully slid the photographs from the envelope, one at a time, and gazed at them in the light of dawn from the window. He held his breath. Hanako laying nude on a *futon* with the plum branch vase behind her. Hanako standing calf-deep in the surf holding infant Aiko in her arms. Hanako kneeling in the grass with her hands raised over her head, hands filled with an offering of flowers. Hanako wrapped in a white towel, sitting on the edge of the *ofuro* at Obâsan's house, looking back as if caught by surprise. Hanako in the blue and white *yukata* and *geta* before an old style house. Hanako and Aiko gathering wildflowers in the meadow. Aiko alone in the meadow, sitting in her diaper, flowers grasped in each hand, smiling at the camera as big as the sun.

He pulled out the last one.

It was a close-up shot of Tomoko, bare from the top of her hip. In the background, laying on the *futon* apparently asleep, the crumpled sheets barely covering the body, was Ben himself. At his head was the vase decorated with the plum branch. The *shoji* was open, sunlight streaming in. He remembered that morning and the night before, but he never heard the click of a camera. At the lower right-hand corner, she had signed it in bold style: *For Ben—please remember me?*

He was filled with apprehension as the plane approached Sea-Tac airport. Aiko was nervous, he could tell. He hoped she was simply curious about her new city, her new home. There was nothing to be afraid of, he told her, wanting to believe it himself. She held his hand tightly. Her eyes were full of concern.

The stewardesses stopped by during seat check and, in Japanese, wished her good luck. Aiko was not smiling and he told them she was nervous. They said she was cute.

After landing, one of the stewardesses helped him pull down their bags. Ms. Tanaka held Aiko's hand and lead her down the aisle of the plane while Ben carried the bags. At the exit, the captain gave her a bow and a smile. Instinctively, she dipped her little head.

Carrying Aiko in his arms, he pulled their bags down the long gangway with the crowd of passengers.

After gathering the suitcases and passing through U.S. Customs and Immigration, he would get a taxi to take them home. Previously, when he was returning from business trips, Addy used to pick him up. Leaving for Japan, it was Rich who gave him a ride. However, nothing would be the same now.

He was on his own — he and his daughter. He checked the cash in his wallet. Enough for the taxi ride to the suburbs. First, he would arrange the bedroom for her to sleep in temporarily. There would be a lot else to do after that.

The usual crowd of greeters were calling out for their friends and relatives as Ben and his daughter waited their turn, following the flow of passengers. They were pushed from behind and shoved from each side, everyone rushing to escape the confines of the corridor. He and Aiko were ushered along to the exit gate. He picked her up and carried her to protect her from the crush. He struggled to pull the cart loaded with baggage with his other arm.

The bustle of people ahead of them fell through the crowded gate and suddenly the view in front was clear.

Among the line of welcomers was a face Ben recognized.

"Ben," called a woman in corduroy jacket that matched her khakis and boots. She seemed embarrassed to be noticed in the crowd.

He did not know what to say, surrounded by the other passengers and their happy families and cheering friends. He lowered Aiko to the floor and held her hand.

"Addy . . . ."

She stepped up to him, catching her breath, her auburn hair much shorter than before. Their eyes met awkwardly and for a moment the airport fell away, vanishing into the clouds.

"Welcome home," she said finally.

"Why are you here?" He hadn't meant to sound so gruff, but he was tired and, frankly, surprised. "I thought you were long gone. That we were getting a divorce. I thought you hated me."

"Sure, you do have your faults," she said, showing a smirk, "but underneath that stupid exterior is a badly tarnished heart of gold."

He grinned. "Heart of gold, huh?"

"Yes, it's corny, I know," she said, ready to laugh, "but I learned something—learned a whole lot, in fact—while you were away. I really didn't know if you'd ever come back."

"How'd you know I'd be on this flight?"

"Well, Ben, I had a few weeks to think it over, you know. And I—" She glanced around, then faced him confidently. "I admit I was hurt. I talked with some people, and . . . . Well, I decided we could make a pretty good family, after all. At least, I want to try."

He regarded her a moment, a little suspicious.

"I'm so sorry I got you in trouble with Rich," said Addy suddenly. "Everything was crazy here, too. The project wherever it was, it's all a mess now. He needs you back, to take over before it's ruined. He says he's saving your job for you, if you still want it. And . . . ."

Ben took a deep breath, unsure what he was hearing. "And what?"

"He told me how it is raising adopted kids. I met his son. So I want to try. I think I can do it. I want to be in your family." She laughed. "You know, I just bought a child car seat this morning. It's in the car, still in the box. But I knew you'd need it—we'd need it. I hope you can figure out how the straps work."

Ben's heart warmed. "I think we can figure it out. It's always better when we work together."

"And as for your flight, I got a phone call late last night from a woman—Tomoko Kaida? Is that it? I didn't hear her name clearly, but she was very friendly. She said she knew you, worked with you when you were in Japan. She said you'd be on this flight."

"Is that right?" He couldn't help but smile, tried to hide it.

"She said to wish you good luck."

"Good luck . . . ." He smiled at Addy. "I sure will need it."

"*We* will need it." She reached for him, her hands on his hips. "May I kiss you? I know you're all yucky from the long flight but I want to. After all, I am your wife."

He leaned in and their lips touched.

"Yes, you are," he said on parting.

Addy looked down. "Hi, there!"

The little girl, even black bangs framing her sad, chubby face and beautiful, dark eyes, studied the woman and grabbed his pant leg.

"Welcome to America, sweetie," said the woman with a big smile.

The tugging on his pant leg quickened and Ben bent down and scooped his daughter up into his arms.

"This is my daughter," he said proudly. "Her name is Aiko."

Acknowledgements

No story starts from nothing, so the author wishes to say thanks to Hiroko Nakamura for inspiring the character of Hanako in Hawaii.

Thanks to Ellie Fong, evening DJ at radio station KZOO in Honolulu, for introducing the author to Japanese pop music.

Thanks to Akiko Kobayashi for her song *"Koi ni Ochite"* which began everything one spring evening.

A special thanks also to Eiko Nakayama for checking and sometimes correcting all of the Japanese words and phrases used in the novel.

About the Author

Stephen Swartz grew up in Kansas City where he was an avid reader of science-fiction and quickly began emulating his favorite authors. Since then, Swartz studied music in college and, like many writers, worked at a wide range of jobs before heading to Japan for several years of teaching English. *Aiko* was written while living in Japan, with additional references drawn from his time living in Hawaii. Returning from Japan, Swartz has taught writing in Texas, Kansas, Pennsylvania, and New York. He now teaches in Oklahoma. He can be found always writing his latest manuscript, usually late at night.

A Note about the Soundtrack

The conception and writing of the novel *Aiko* were greatly aided by a selection of evocative music.

The author is indebted to the music collected into the program "Winter Waltz/Winter White" (#120) on the *Hearts of Space* program featured on National Public Radio, produced by Stephen Hill. Although unrelated to the novel's story by track titles, the music provided the first soundscape for evoking the mood of key scenes. Selections include Windham Hill composer and pianist Wim Merton, Mark Isham's score for the film *Mrs. Soffel*, the electronic music of Richard Souther, and the cello/organ duo of Eugene Friesen and Paul Halley.

Selected Japanese music was also significant in the writing of the novel:

Koi ni Ochite by Akiko Kobayashi (song)
Kokoro by Sojiro (ocarina; album)
Wind & Reflections by Yuriko Nakamura (piano; album)
Lumiere by Fumie Nishimura (piano; album)
Karelia by Shizuka Kudo (album)
Kinoo Kirisame no Gallery de by Megumi Shiina (song)
Le Port wa Sayonara no Minato by Megumi Shiina (song)